PRAISE FOR *WINTER COTTAGE*

"Offering a look into bygone days of the gentrified from the early 1900s up until the present time, mystery and romance are included along with a multifaceted tale that is sure to please."

—New York Journal of Books

"There is mystery and intrigue as the author weaves a tale that pulls you in . . . this is a story of strong women, who persevere . . . it's a love story, the truest, deepest kind . . . and it's the story of a woman who years later was able to right a wrong and give a home to the people who really needed it. It's layered brilliantly, hints are revealed subtly, allowing the reader to form conclusions and fall in love."

—*Smexy Books*

PRAISE FOR MARY ELLEN TAYLOR

"Mary Ellen Taylor writes comfort reads packed with depth . . . If you're looking for a fantastic vacation read, this is the book for you!"

—*Steph and Chris's Book Review*

"[A] complex tale . . . grounded in fascinating history and emotional turmoil that is intense yet subtle. An intelligent, heartwarming exploration of the powers of forgiveness, compassion, and new beginnings."

—*Kirkus Reviews*

"Absorbing characters, a hint of mystery, an̶ ̶ scovery elevate this novel above many views

"Taylor serves up a great mix of vivid setting, history, drama, and everyday life."

—*Herald Sun*

"[A] charming and very engaging story about the nature of family and the meaning of love."

—*Seattle Post-Intelligencer*

honeysuckle
season

honeysuckle season

season

MARY ELLEN
TAYLOR

Fountaindale Public Library District
300 W. Briarcliff Rd.
Bolingbrook, IL 60440

 Montlake

This is a work of fiction. Names, characters, organizations, places, events, and incidents are either products of the author's imagination or are used fictitiously.

Text copyright © 2020 by Mary Burton
All rights reserved.

No part of this book may be reproduced, or stored in a retrieval system, or transmitted in any form or by any means, electronic, mechanical, photocopying, recording, or otherwise, without express written permission of the publisher.

Published by Montlake, Seattle

www.apub.com

Amazon, the Amazon logo, and Montlake are trademarks of Amazon.com, Inc., or its affiliates.

ISBN-13: 9781542017886
ISBN-10: 1542017882

Cover photography and design by Laura Klynstra

Printed in the United States of America

A garden is always a series of losses set against a few triumphs, like life itself.
May Sarton, poet

PROLOGUE

The unraveling of Olivia's youth had begun in the fall of 1940. The war in Europe was raging, and the Pacific was sowing the seeds of another great explosion. As world events burrowed their roots deeper into her innocence, she desperately tried to replenish the soil, believing she could still sow the seeds of new dreams and hopes. But the earth had continued to shift and erode until finally she had stumbled, and her rose-colored glasses had fallen away forever.

She now sat by the hospital bed, holding the pale hand of her dying friend. Blue veins, so pricked and prodded by doctors and nurses, lined small hands that for the first time were not coiled and poised for a fight. Her old friend appeared at peace, as if she now welcomed death.

That was what age did for the lucky. As life stripped away youth and vitality, it also softened some of the regrets and perhaps exchanged a few devils for angels.

Her friend's face was narrow and deeply lined and her once-wiry body whittled down to bone and skin. Thick auburn hair had thinned and grown as white as her paper-thin skin. IVs dripped sedatives and painkillers while monitors beeped softly. The window shades were pulled closed so that the light did not hurt her eyes. Of all the places she could imagine her old friend dying, it was not here in this dark, sterile room so far from her home in the lush Blue Ridge Mountains.

Olivia almost regretted being here now and perhaps losing the image of the vibrant, strong girl who had dared life at each curve in the road. As much as Olivia wanted to cling to the old images she treasured of her friend and ignore the ravages of this cancer, to abandon her friend now would be a regret her old shoulders could not bear.

Closing her eyes, Olivia stood silent until she felt a gentle stirring in the woman's body. She opened her eyes to see watering blue eyes staring at her.

"You came?" Her voice sounded strained and weak.

Olivia smiled, refusing to give sadness any ground. "Of course I did."

"Is my child here?"

"Yes. She drove me. My eyesight won't allow me to drive beyond my little town."

As if Olivia had not spoken—"How is my daughter?"

"She's grown into a fine woman."

"Good." For a long moment there was silence broken only by the beep of the monitor. "Thank you for looking out for her."

"You did the same for me, didn't you? Looked after my grand-daughter when she needed it most."

"How is she?"

"She just had her second baby."

She thought back to that one single act of courage a half century ago that had bonded the two women. They had risked life and limb for each other and kept so many secrets.

Fragile brows gathered in a frown. "Don't go to your grave with your secret, Miss Olivia. You and I both know it's the kind that binds the soul to the earth," she said.

Olivia had locked away so many memories over the years that they had tangled together. She feared a tug on one would unravel the entire lot. Confession might be good for the soul, but by her way of thinking, it did little else. Her secret had served a purpose, and if keeping it meant her soul was bound to this earth forever, then so be it.

CHAPTER ONE
SADIE

Tuesday, March 15, 1943
Bluestone, Virginia
Blue Ridge Mountains

There were three tricks to hiding. First, it was important to breathe as shallow as possible. If you were doing it right, your nostrils barely flared, and your breathing was as shallow as the James River in drought-hot summer heat. Next, a good rabbit tamed its racing heart and did not allow it to pound and drum against the ribs. Sounds had a tendency to echo beyond the confines of the body.

And the third trick, and not the least by far, was keeping your eyes cast downward. You never looked at whoever was hunting you. A fox might not be able to see a rabbit, but it could feel its stare as surely as if it were being tapped on the shoulder.

Sadie Thompson crouched behind the thick tangle of a honeysuckle bush twisting around the large stump of a fallen oak. Her heart beat fast in her chest, rapping against her ribs so hard she struggled to catch her breath. She was out of shape, and the mile-long run through the woods from her old truck had taken a surprising toll. A year ago, she would have done the run like a deer, twice as fast without breaking a sweat.

Darkness had descended on the Blue Ridge Mountains, tossing an inky blackness over the land. What little moonlight trickled through the thick rain-ripe clouds was caught in the canopy of trees. An owl hooted. Deer, disturbed by her unwelcome intrusion, bolted through the woods.

The poor visibility suited Sadie. She was accustomed to traveling at night and was intimately acquainted with the hills and the valleys of Nelson County. Her father had taught Sadie and her brothers how to negotiate the narrow back roads barely wide enough for a car. It could be rough going, but they were the best routes moonshiners had when avoiding the law. Her pa had made them memorize the sharpest curves in the road, walk the old Indian paths that cut up the side of the mountains, and he'd shown them the secluded caves best suited for cooking mash into moonshine. She and her family knew all the ins and outs of this part of Virginia, and they could stay lost forever. If that was what they wanted.

Sadie pressed her face against the damp leaves and took a moment to shake off the lingering panic that had sent her bolting into the night. Crickets whirred nearby, and a spider crawled over her hand, but she gave neither a second thought. She had a bigger problem facing her now.

Sheriff Kurt Boyd had arrived at her mother's house an hour ago, most likely bent on arresting Sadie for attempted murder—maybe even murder, if the man did not pull through. Sadie was not a bit sorry for what she had done but now wished she had been smarter about exacting her revenge.

She had run from her mother's house with not even enough time to pack a bag or kiss her sleeping baby before sprinting to her truck. She put the car in neutral and coasted down the backside of the hill, careful not to make a sound. Only at the bottom did she start the engine. But the sheriff must have heard the commotion of the rumbling engine and taken off after her. She drove as far as her old truck's radiator would take her until it boiled over, leaving her no way to quickly repair it.

Arms pumping, and her work boots rubbing against her swollen feet, she dashed into the brush as the rumble of Boyd's Dodge grew closer. She thought maybe she could cut across the mountain on an old Indian trail, but Boyd had seen that trick before and would simply circle around. That left her with no choice but to hunker down.

She would wait Boyd out and maybe later circle back to her truck and see if it had cooled enough to run again. Her aim was to get to Charlottesville and then ride a train as far away from Bluestone as she could manage.

As she lay on the ground behind the shrubs, the rumble of a car engine echoed. She recognized the sound of the sheriff's grumbling Dodge engine moving slowly down the road. He knew she was close. He might not have been the smartest man, but he knew Indian paths, mining trails, and hiding spots almost as well as she did.

Seconds later headlights appeared. She pressed her belly closer into the damp soil, her tender breasts still filled with milk, straining against her roughly hewed shirt. Too curious for her own good, she stole a peek in time to see Sheriff Boyd's thick frame pass in front of his headlights. He stopped and stood with his feet braced and a meaty right hand resting on his belt. She could not see his face but guessed he was frowning. Boyd had always reckoned a thoughtful man did not need to smile or say much. That was just as well, because when he opened his mouth, he never had anything worth saying. A flashlight's beam cut deep into the darkness, passing just a few feet above her body.

"Dumb as a box of rocks," her brother Johnny used to joke about the sheriff.

Her brother Danny had laughed. *"Can outsmart him on my worst day."*

Thinking about Johnny and Danny made her throat tighten with a bone-deep sadness she doubted would ever leave her. God, how she missed those two.

"Don't be thinking about me," Johnny's voice echoed in her head. *"Be worried about Boyd."*

"Yeah," Danny echoed. *"He might be stupid, but he's mean, and even a broken clock is right twice a day."*

The advice was sound. She would worry about her brothers and daughter once she was safe. Now she had to deal with Boyd.

What the lawman lacked in intelligence, he made up for in tracking skills. The man was part bloodhound. The state authorities would call Boyd if a prisoner escaped any jail in a twenty-five-mile radius. Even farmers called when they had a coyote killing their livestock. And at election time, he sniffed out enough illegal stills to make the Bible-thumpers happy.

Her father never took it personally when Boyd came after the stills. His job was to find them, and her father's was to hide them. Everyone had to survive. But by Sadie's way of thinking, Boyd had a petty streak in him. Those prisoners he brought back had a black eye or two when they finally made it to their cells. There was always a cow unaccounted for, and when Boyd wielded his bat against a still, he was always whistling a happy tune.

Boyd's boots crunched on the soft dirt and leaves as he walked not more than twenty feet from her. "Sadie, I know you're out there, girl. This is where your brothers used to hide. Make it easy on yourself, and come on out. I won't hurt you."

When she was little, she and the boys had played rabbit and the fox in the hollow. She was always the rabbit because she was the littlest—but also because she was good at burrowing into a small unconsidered place and could stay silent as she listened to her brothers' laughter turn to frustration when they could not find their little rabbit.

Sadie closed her eyes and willed her entire system to slow. She pressed her face hard against the ground.

I'm just a leaf on a twig, she thought.

"Nothing important here," she wanted to say. *"Keep on moving, Sheriff Boyd."*

Booted footsteps moved closer to her hiding spot. Boyd's heavy breathing proved he was not used to running either. He was a good six inches taller than her, but he was not built for speed, especially in the backwoods.

Sadie and her brothers roamed these hills like the Cherokee, Siouan, Iroquois, and the German and Scottish settlers who followed. If she was not hauling water to their house, she was carrying bags of corn and sugar or toting boxes of mason jars filled with shine. Even as a young child she could heft two bucketfuls of water up from the creek in less than five minutes without spilling a drop. No lady was strong like Sadie, but then she had never claimed to be fancy.

"Come on out, Sadie," Sheriff Boyd said. "No one wants to hurt you."

Sheriff Boyd's voice was coated in an extra layer of sugar, but there was nothing sweet about his lies. If he found her, he would put the cuffs on her, just as he had threatened a dozen times before. And this time, he would take her to Lynchburg and see to it that Dr. Carter made sure she never had another child.

She squeezed her eyes tighter and thought about her beautiful baby girl sleeping in the cradle. She willed away her tears and sadness. She was not leaving her girl because she wanted to. Life had taken a hard turn and stripped away her choices. She could only take comfort knowing the child would be fine—maybe even fare better—in her grandmother's care.

Sheriff Boyd's breathing slowed as his big feet snapped twigs. The brush near her shifted and moved. She pictured his big hands pawing through the sticks and leaves and grabbing her by the collar.

I'm a gnat. A bug on a log. Too small to notice.

"Haven't you been enough of a disappointment to your mama? Hasn't she got enough on her shoulders without worrying about your brothers and the bastard she'll surely be raising?"

Tears sprang up behind her closed lids. Maybe she was one of the worst daughters a mother could hope for. But she sure as hell was not going to let this hick sheriff use her own failings to flush her out of the brush like frightened quail.

"You're a sorry girl." Sheriff Boyd's words trickled out on a heavy sigh. "You're trouble." When his berating did not work, he shifted gears. "You'd be so much better off if you let me help you. I'll talk to the judge and tell him to go easy on you. We all know you didn't mean to run that man over with your truck. It was an accident, pure and simple."

His words burrowed under her resolve, and a sob took hold and sprang up in her throat. More tears filled her eyes. She pursed her lips. God help her; it had not been an accident. If given the chance, she would do it again.

Time slowly crawled by as she listened to the sound of his breathing. He took another step closer, and she could smell his cheap aftershave.

She held steady, doing her best not to think about Boyd. Boyd would not find this little rabbit tonight.

"Damn it, Sadie. I will find you." The sheriff muttered a string of curses and ended his tirade with something about her burning in hell. "And I'll see that the judge locks your scrawny ass up for a long damn time."

The leaves rustled under Boyd's boots as he turned back toward the road and the halo of headlights.

His car door slammed with anger, and the engine sputtered like an old man clearing his throat as he shifted into first. The clutch was going bad. She had told him often enough about the worn clutch, but just like everyone in the valley, he did not take her too seriously. Finally, the rubber tires began to roll; the engine ground from first to second gear and rattled off into the night, growling like an old man.

As tempted as she was to move, she stayed pressed against the cool earth. Her right arm, tucked under her body, had gone to sleep and now felt as if a thousand needles prickled under her skin. This was not the first time her arm had been pinned, and she had surely felt worse discomfort than this before.

An owl called out, hunting for its own rabbit, which hopped into a hollowed-out tree near her. Sadie smiled at the irony.

She knew Boyd was a wily son of a bitch, and she would not put it past him to double back on foot.

When she finally lifted her head, the moon had climbed in the night sky, and the clouds had parted, revealing an endless number of beautiful stars.

She tipped her face toward the North Star and then pushed up onto her knees. She paused, listening for Boyd again, before she brushed the dirt from her denim overalls and her brother's old cotton work shirt. It had been his favorite, and normally, he would have been annoyed, but he was overseas fighting a war, and she knew it would be the least of his worries.

Slowly, she pushed through the brush and made her way up to the road. Going left would take her west, back up the mountain. There were plenty of places to hide, but staying hidden from Boyd would mean turning the woods she loved into its own kind of jail. Twenty miles to the south lay Charlottesville and the train station.

She slid her fingers into the big pockets and fingered the money her mother had given her. It was her mother's emergency fund, and it weighed heavily on her soul, but she needed the three dollars. "I'll pay you back, Mama."

Sadie started walking, occasionally stopping to listen for the sound of that Dodge. As she kept walking, she heard only the hum of the crickets and crunch of her boots against the dirt road.

"Good Lord, Johnny and Danny, this is a mess."

"You always did have a talent."

Her brothers' voices echoed in her head. Johnny's letters had arrived regularly until very recently, but Danny had sent only a few since he had gone into the army. She feared the war had swallowed them both up.

As she walked, her breasts ached, and her nipples began to leak milk. Her baby girl must be so hungry by now. There was canned milk at the cabin and Karo syrup. Her mother would know how to prepare the two and see that the baby had been fed. Her mother would not let her down, even if Sadie had shamed her mother with her own foolish choices.

The first hints of sunrise appeared on the horizon, lighting the mountains in rich orange and yellow. As pretty as it was, it was also working against her now.

As she rounded a familiar bend, a set of headlights appeared on the road. The smooth engine did not sound like Boyd's Dodge, but knowing Boyd, he had called on anyone with a car to get out and look for her.

Taking no chances, she ducked into the brush off the side of the road. The aroma of honeysuckle was thick and gave her hope. She would have to find a new way. A new path.

The car slowed, downshifted, and came to a stop. She had not been quick enough. The driver had spotted her.

CHAPTER TWO

LIBBY

Saturday, June 6, 2020
Bluestone, Virginia

They said bad luck came in threes. But that was not really true. Bad luck could come in threes, fours, fives, or any number it chose.

Today's first stroke of bad luck arrived with a hard shove to Libby McKenzie's shoulder and a voice shouting in her ear, "Get up!"

Wrenched from sleep, she sat up quickly, swung her legs over the side of the couch, and knocked over the empty wineglass on the coffee table. Her head spun, and her stomach churned as she pushed back a tumble of dark hair. "What?"

"Libby, get up! You have to be at the wedding venue in one hour." The shouts came from her friend Sierra Mancuso. They had grown up together, her family living next to Libby's, and until Libby had gone to boarding school at age thirteen, they had been inseparable.

Libby's mouth was as dry as cotton. "What about my alarms? I set two."

"The two I just shut off?" Sierra glared down at her best friend. Her blonde hair was slicked back into a bun, and she wore a black shirt and pants along with sensible shoes. All were telltale signs that Sierra was working a catering gig today.

Both thirty-one, they had been through several life-altering losses together. Sierra's major life setback had been her husband's death to cancer last year, and the right cross that had taken Libby down a peg had been three miscarriages and a divorce. They were both the walking wounded and had retreated to their hometown of Bluestone, into their parents' homes, until the dust settled.

Libby looked at her phone and the purple clock that had been hers since seventh grade. The red digital numbers read 8:02 a.m. "Damn."

"I've started the coffee." Sierra clapped her hands. "I'm making eggs. Chop-chop."

"I'm on it."

Libby jumped to her feet and dashed up the stairs toward the small bathroom. After stripping off her oversize T-shirt, she turned on the hot water and waited as the old pipes rumbled and the water heated.

Her dad, Dr. Allen McKenzie, had been the town pediatrician for thirty years. He had never said no to a patient, not even toward the end, when he had been sick. He had died six months ago.

All promises of never returning to her hometown aside, Libby had moved back to care for her widowed father toward the end, and after he passed, she just decided to stay. It made good economic sense versus living in a rented apartment in Richmond. After the divorce, it was hard to afford anything on a photographer's salary. Since January, the plan had been to regroup, save up some money, and then get back to living a real life in a real city by Christmas. She was going on six months of regrouping, and she still was not back up on her feet.

Steam finally rose from the water, and she quickly hopped under the hot spray. Adrenaline had her in and out of the shower in under five minutes, and she toweled off and crossed to her old bedroom.

Her room was as neat as she had left it when leaving for college thirteen years ago. The same SAVE THE EARTH posters hung on the wall along with an Ansel Adams print of the Montana skyline. She had yet to sleep in the twin sleigh bed still made up in the paisley purple coverlet purchased from IKEA when she was sixteen. It was one thing to move home, but it was another level of sad to sleep in her first bed again. It felt equally weird to sleep in her parents' room or the third bedroom, which was her father's office. The upstairs simply held too many memories that hinted at her parents' troubled marriage. That left the couch in the living room.

From the open suitcase on the neatly made bed, she removed a dark pair of slacks and a white blouse. She fished a brush from the side of the suitcase and pulled her hair back into a smooth ponytail. Next came her makeup kit, and she quickly applied mascara and rouge. She replaced all the items in her suitcase and then wiped off the bathroom counter and hung up her towel. By 8:12 a.m. it looked like she had barely been there. Perfect.

Barefoot, she hustled down the steps and grabbed her camera bag and shoes before dashing across the back lawn to the Mancuso house. She pushed open the kitchen door.

"Do you even use the house?"

Libby sat in a kitchen chair and laced up her shoes. "I just took a shower."

Sierra set a cup of coffee in front of Libby, then ladled eggs onto a blue plate and set them in front of Libby, along with a fork. Also on the plate was a strawberry, thinly sliced and fanned.

Libby took a bite of the eggs, discovering the jolt of protein was what she needed. "Bless you."

Sierra filled a large orange mug sporting a Virginia Tech logo. "You're like a ghost. You come and go but leave no traces."

"It's just weird," she said. "I haven't really lived there in years."

"You live there now."

She sipped her own coffee, craving the jolt of energy. "Not really. I'm still visiting."

15

When her father had become ill last year, he had set about cleaning his home and decluttering, tossing away all the unnecessary baggage that came with living. The walls had been repainted a pale gray and the trim a bright white. He had not tackled any of the larger projects like the kitchen and bathrooms, no doubt thinking the new owner would renovate them their way.

He had left her with a stripped-down version of his home that was now ready to go on the real estate market. He had wanted Libby to sell it and take the money to find a new place to live. Libby had told him she would think about it, which she was still doing.

Sierra shook her head. "You're afraid to put down roots."

"I did that, remember? Roots don't always run deep enough."

"They could if you didn't baby them too much."

Libby arched a brow. "You live over your parents' garage, Sierra. It doesn't get any less settled than that."

"At least I'm *living* there. I've unpacked my bags," she said with a grin.

"I like to keep my options open." The sound of a text dinging sent Libby fishing in her bag for her phone. The text was from the bride starring in today's wedding.

Ginger the Bride: Rain on the horizon. Send sunny thoughts.

Libby: I'm on my way.

Ginger the Bride: Mom worried. I say it will be fine.

Libby: Umbrellas always packed. See you in thirty.

Libby grabbed a granola bar from the cabinet that Mrs. Mancuso kept stocked. "Sierra, why are you still here? Shouldn't you be at the venue setting up catering tables or presearing salmon patties?"

"Rick's got me on cleanup crew, not setup." She made a face. "Can I ride with you?"

"Going now."

"And you have your camera equipment?"

"All in the bag."

Libby had been obsessing over worst-case scenarios since the sixth grade. Maybe it had been because of her mother's worsening mental health and suicide, which might have made her mental herself. Regardless, she liked to make lists of all possible disasters.

If she had an event or party that she was excited about, she made lists of all the things that could keep her from going. In college, she could not sleep unless all her homework was done, her coffeepot was set, and her clothes were laid out. Her mother jokingly had called it a "belt and suspenders" approach to life, which she sometimes took too far. So together, she and her mother had both planned for all the minor disasters as major ones swirled around them.

Thankfully for today, she had listed *Sleep through the alarm* and *Hurricane*. There was also *Swerve to miss a deer*, *Road washed out (from the hurricane)*, and *Run out of gas*.

"We're okay on time," Sierra said. She tossed her an extra granola bar. "Better get going."

Libby picked up her camera bag and purse and hurried to her car. She placed it all in the back seat before sliding behind the wheel. As Libby started the engine, Sierra got into the passenger seat and hooked her seat belt. Libby fastened her seat belt and confirmed her gas gauge was full.

She backed out of the driveway, glancing toward the house. "The coffee maker is off?"

Sierra sipped her coffee. "It is. And it's also washed out and unplugged."

"Bless you. I'd hate for your mom's house to burn down."

Sierra pulled down the visor and traced her red lips with fingernails painted to match. "You can mark off *House burning down* from your list."

A smile teased the edge of Libby's lips as she drove down the tree-lined road and onto Main Street, which was the only thoroughfare in town.

Bluestone, population two thousand, was nestled in the foothills of the Blue Ridge Mountains. German, English, and Scottish migrants had settled this part of Virginia's frontier in the mid-eighteenth century, and for a generation, farms around Bluestone had been connected to the outside world by only the Great Wagon Road. The railway had never made it as far as Bluestone, but eventually the interstate had skirted by close enough. In the last decade, the creation of wineries and cideries had brought boomers and millennials to the area looking for a slower pace of life.

"I'm excited to see Woodmont Estate," Sierra said. "I didn't get to go on the walk-through two weeks ago."

"They've done an amazing job of restoring the gardens." Libby drove through the town center, dutifully following the speed limit, and accelerated only as she passed the forty-five-miles-per-hour sign.

Virtually closed to the public since it was built in the eighteenth century, Woodmont sat on two hundred acres that rolled along the James River. Ezra Carter had built the two-story house, made of hand-molded brick, after he had received a land grant from King George II. The Carter farm had begun growing tobacco but had shifted to wheat production as prices soared for wheat during the Seven Years' War. Ezra Carter's savvy ability to read the markets had made the Carters one of the wealthiest families in Virginia for generations. Elaine Grant, the current descendant, had embarked on a massive renovation of the property, but it was rumored the family finances were dwindling.

When Libby was a kid, the estate had opened only once a year for Historic Garden Week, and for several years in a row, she and her mother had visited Woodmont. Even then, the walled gardens had shown signs of age. Many plants, though still pretty, had been overgrown and in need of pruning or replacing. The garden, her mother had said, was due for an overhaul. Libby had never seen the imperfections in the encroaching wildness. For her, the gardens had been a rare magical escape she shared with her mother.

The estate had never been open to weddings or events until today. The bride, Ginger Reese, had grown up on the estate, playing on the grounds her parents had tended. Her father had been the estate's manager while her mother, Margaret, had overseen the inside of the house. These days, her brother, Colton, managed the grounds as their late father had, and her mother still ran the house.

Today's wedding was a kind of trial run for the property. Ginger had reached out to Libby via her wedding photography website, hiring her because she was local to Bluestone and familiar with the venue. Ginger was an ob-gyn in Charlottesville. And her groom, Cameron Walker, was a surgeon at the UVA Medical Center.

Thunder rumbled in the distance. "Did Ginger rent the white tent?" Sierra asked.

"No. She said a tent tempted the law of attraction and would invite rain," Libby said.

"Are you kidding?" Sierra shook her head. "If that's how the law of attraction works, then I have a bone to pick with it. Not once did I manifest this life I have."

Libby could not laugh off Sierra's sarcastic quip stuffed with bitterness. She too had never pictured or imagined any of the lost babies, the divorce papers, or her father's funeral. And yet they had shown up one by one, ready to reiterate that bad luck lived by its own rules.

Clouds hovered over the mountains. "So much for positive thinking."

"As of yesterday, the chance of a downpour was twenty percent." Sierra glanced at her phone, her brow rising. "It's now fifty percent."

"Think we'll beat it?"

Sierra shook her head.

Libby turned down a smaller road and drove past a sprawling vineyard built thirty years ago by a New York investor whom none of the locals had met yet. Beyond that were long stretches of fencing and rolling hills dotted with grazing cows.

Out-of-town folks dependent on GPS often had trouble locating the Woodmont Estate. Two weeks ago, upon her arrival for the walk-through, Libby had overshot the final turn by a few miles. It had taken an extra ten minutes before she had righted her course and finally spotted the brick pillars surrounded by fully blooming yellow-and-purple pansies.

Now, confident in her approach, she spotted the final turn and followed the long gravel driveway flanked by white oaks that dated back to the War of 1812. According to her mother, the planting of the trees had been by design because they consumed so much water that they helped keep the road dry during heavy rains.

Up ahead, she saw the brick home bookended by the gardens on the east and west sides. Many of the April and May blossoms had peaked, but the sunflowers, snapdragons, hydrangeas, and zinnias remained lush, bright, and bursting with color.

She followed parking signs to the closely cut field. There were two catering trucks, Ginger's Volvo, a blue van, and a red pickup truck. Today's bride was dressing inside the main house. At forty-one, Ginger had opted out of having bridesmaids, so the morning shoot should be fairly uncomplicated.

Out of the car, Libby reached across the back seat for her cameras. As she closed the door, the wind picked up, sending a soft breeze through the trees. She glanced toward the river and saw the thick band of gray clouds in the distance.

"You headed up to the house?" Libby asked.

"I am. You'll find me in the kitchen."

Libby hoisted her bags on her shoulders and wondered if she should grab the extra umbrellas from the trunk. "See you around."

"Did the bride and groom bury a bottle of moonshine in the garden?" Sierra slipped a white apron over her head and tied the ends around her narrow waist.

"There was some talk of that at the walk-through, but the groom forgot about it. What's the deal with that?"

Sierra shook her head, as if concerned. "It's the moonshine graveyard, which is a bit of a tradition in these parts. If you want good luck on your wedding day, then you bury a bottle of hooch in the garden."

Maybe Libby and her ex-husband, Jeremy, should have buried a bottle or two on their big day. "So what happens if they don't?"

Sierra nodded toward the clouds. "Rain. Divorce. Locusts. The whole nine yards of bad mojo."

"Terrific."

Sierra waved away Libby's sour expression. "I say screw the law of attraction. And who needs a moonshine graveyard?" Sierra said, smiling. "That storm is at least two hours away, which puts us safely under cover should it hit."

Libby opted to leave the umbrellas behind but hustled up the front steps to shoot the first-look pictures; thunder rumbled on cue in the distance.

CHAPTER THREE

LIBBY

Saturday, June 6, 2020
The Woodmont Estate

The morning pre-wedding shoot had gone longer than she had expected. *Note to self—add to worst-case-scenario list: Grandmother of the groom gets drunk on mimosas.* Now they were fifteen minutes from kickoff, and guests had almost filled the white wooden garden chairs facing the hill that sloped down toward the river.

When the house had been built in the eighteenth century, the main entrance had faced the river, which had been the superhighway of its day. Travelers had come and gone by the river. What was now the main road leading to the Woodmont Estate had been little more than a deer path in the days of Ezra Carter. Modern transportation had moved on, but the house remained steadfastly attached to its origins.

The DJ's speakers emitted the music of a string quartet playing "Are You Gonna Be My Girl." The DJ and his main soundboard were wisely set up inside the main house.

Over the last couple of years, Libby had become accustomed to the songs most couples played at their weddings, and after a while, she had recognized a sameness to the songs. Most couples aspired to be different on their special day, but nearly all fell into predictable patterns.

She looked over her shoulder at the swollen dark clouds moving toward them. At this point the quartet should have been playing the theme to *Jaws*. *"Duunnn, duunnn."* No amount of positive thinking or mason jars of moonshine buried in the dirt was going to stop this beast from rolling over the top of the wedding.

Another clap of thunder had Libby looking toward the parking lot, where her SUV remained stocked with the umbrellas. She checked her watch. If she ran, she could make it to her car and return with the umbrellas with time to spare. She looked again at the angry sky. Decision made—as the quartet's next song, "I Will Always Love You," began—she turned on her heels and took off running toward her car as the thick scent of approaching rain surrounded her.

The first raindrop hit the top of her head as she opened the back of her SUV. She quickly snapped waterproof cases over her cameras and gathered up the umbrellas in her arms. As she nudged the liftgate button with her foot, a loud clap of thunder cracked across the sky.

Juggling umbrellas and her cameras, she saw the storm dumping rain on the other side of the river. She started to run. Heat and thick humidity formed a trickle of sweat between her shoulder blades and on her upper lip.

More water droplets fell on Libby's head as she dashed toward the wedding, hoping to at least get the bride, mother of the bride, and groom under cover.

The wedding march suddenly began, ten minutes ahead of schedule. At most weddings, she had a second shooter on hand to catch the images from a different angle. But Ginger had been certain Libby did not need the extra shooter. Now Libby was not in a position to catch any part of the ceremony. If she delayed another minute, she would miss the entire main event.

A red truck rumbled up behind her and stopped. "Get in," the driver said.

She recognized the man as the estate manager, Colton Reese—the bride's brother. He was dressed in a dark suit and white shirt but wore no tie. Dark hair brushed back behind his ears, drawing attention to a face that was not exactly handsome but somehow very attractive.

Two weeks ago, Colton had had little to say at the walk-through. He had listened to his sister's ideas and patiently agreed to rent the chairs. He had wanted to also secure a tent, but Ginger had told him not to bother.

"Why aren't you at the ceremony?" she asked.

"I saw you take off running. You're either abandoning ship, or you could use the backup. Which is it?"

"Backup." She tossed her umbrellas in the bed of the truck and climbed inside.

"It's going to open up," she said.

"Yes, it is." Colton's trim body leaned over his steering wheel as he stared up at the sky. "It's coming across the river fast."

"They're starting the ceremony early."

"That was Ginger's call. Too bad there's no tent."

"Drive it like you stole it. I've got to get there."

Colton grinned, punched the accelerator, and raced toward the darkening sky. He was in his mid- to late thirties, and she supposed his perpetual frown added a dangerous kind of vibe loved by the ladies. "I warned them this morning to have the ceremony inside."

"Your gardens are the reason Ginger wanted to be outside." Droplets splattered on the windshield, flattening into large watery pancakes.

"What's the plan?" he asked.

"You pass out the umbrellas, and I'll keep shooting," Libby instructed. "Bride first; mother of the bride second. Then go for anyone who looks like a grandmother. The men get served last."

"Just like the *Titanic*." He parked within twenty feet and hustled around the side of the truck just as the sky opened up, pelting down rain. Some guests held their programs over their heads, trying to hold off through the ceremony. Others were already dashing to the estate's narrow front porch, which was quickly filling up.

Colton opened an umbrella and handed it to her. She held it in one hand and raised her camera with the other. She was shooting as the mother of the bride walked her daughter quickly down the aisle. Colton handed his mother an umbrella, but the bride refused hers as she walked to the arch and her waiting groom. They both were laughing as their guests started racing toward the safety of the house's front porch.

Libby gave up on trying to hold an umbrella and shoot. Instead she handed it to a hapless guest hurrying past her and moved up the center aisle, past the emptying seats, toward the bride and groom.

She shifted between cameras as she moved closer. The minister read the vows, his pace quickening with each clap of thunder. The bride and groom held hands, and then the rain really started to pour.

Finally, the minister quickly declared them husband and wife, then took off running toward the house. The bride and groom turned, hand in hand, and ran down the muddy center aisle. Mud splashed up on Ginger's dress and her groom's tux. Ginger's hair and makeup had basically melted, and her gown was now soaked. Libby caught every step and every splash, knowing she had captured the money shot for the day.

She followed the couple toward the main house and onto the porch, where they joined cheering guests. The catering staff and Colton were handing out towels that she would bet he had ordered.

When Libby reached the porch, her pants and shirt were soaked, and her shoes were filled with water.

"Never a dull moment," Sierra said, passing her a towel as she balanced a tray of manhattans.

"They should have buried the moonshine," Libby said.

"Or rented a tent. Cocktail?"

"Thanks, but I better hold off."

"You know where to find me." Sierra drifted away, smiling as she presented her tray to the first soggy guest.

Libby moved inside Woodmont, pausing to shoot pictures of a floral arrangement in an antique porcelain vase. The original house had been built circa 1735 and the newer additions in the 1750s and 1790s. The large rooms to her left were tastefully decorated and restored to their original colonial charm. One was painted in a rich hunter green and the other a deep burgundy. Each fireplace was adorned with a white-veined marble, and the walls were painted an indigo blue. The stone and the plush hues were rarities at that time and had announced to the Virginia Colony that the Carters were indeed well to do.

Drawn to some of the detailed crown molding, marble fireplaces, and handblown glass windows, she snapped several pictures, knowing these were more for herself than the bride.

Libby's wedding photography business was five years old now and growing monthly. She had always had a passion for photography and had collected all kinds of antique cameras when she was a kid. But art, her father had warned, did not pay the light bill, so he had encouraged her to go to nursing school. She had to study hard, but she graduated with honors and became an oncology nurse. To her surprise (and definitely her father's), she had a talent for caring for the sick. Fast-forward a couple of years, and she met Jeremy, fell in love, and got married. Life went on—until it did not.

Libby watched the flow of guests milling about inside the large front level of the house filled with displays of daisies and marigolds. She moved toward a small side room, where she had stashed some of her camera equipment to switch out lenses.

Sierra doubled back, her tray now sporting fewer cocktails. "Do you realize you're shooting the first wedding at Woodmont ever?"

"It's a stunning venue."

"Think it could be an attraction for weddings and events?"

"Definitely. It's a beautiful property, but Mrs. Grant has already turned down several offers. If they jump into the event game, they'll grab top dollar."

Many of the guests had moved toward the two bars flanking the buffet table. The bride and groom had escaped to one of the hidden rooms to collect themselves. Outside, lightning crackled across the sky just as the DJ played "The Devil Went Down to Georgia."

"I need to take pictures of the cake table and the flowers." Libby rummaged in her pocket for the list of *Ginger's guests to be remembered*. The paper was damp, but the ballpoint ink was still intact.

"Off to shoot at the other end of the room."

"Go get 'em."

A young boy and girl with matching raven hair and green eyes—siblings, she supposed—approached her. A thirty-some-year-old woman with the same green eyes coaxed them forward and discreetly reminded them both to smile.

"Ms. McKenzie," the woman said. "I don't suppose you remember me or my children, Robert and Kate. Your father was their pediatrician, and he was mine as well."

"He always had cherry suckers." The boy beamed.

"When he gave a shot, I didn't feel it," the girl said.

"We were so sorry to hear about his passing," the woman said.

Libby fiddled with the aperture on her camera. She knew moving back to Bluestone would mean hearing lots of stories about her father. And hearing those stories would make her miss him all the more. But as much as she wanted to shut herself off from people's memories, she did not. She owed it to her father, who had cared for thousands of area children over the decades.

When he had died in January, the Episcopal church in Bluestone had been packed with mourners spanning generations of families just like this one. There had been people standing five deep in the vaulted sanctuary. Dad would have been proud. He had always thought a poorly attended funeral was a commentary on a man's life.

"Thank you," she said.

The bride and her groom appeared from a side room, and the guests began to cheer. Ginger looked as happy as Libby had on her own wedding day.

"I hear you're back in town for good," the woman said.

"Living in Dad's house." Nothing stayed a secret in small towns. She had spent the better part of the winter hunched over her computer, editing pictures from weddings, setting up new appointments, and traveling to events. The work had allowed her to push aside mourning for her father, her three miscarriages, and her divorce.

"Well, welcome back to Bluestone," she said. "I'm Molly."

"Good to meet you, Molly."

"Did your husband move back too? Someone told me you were expecting."

The baby question still came up. When she and Jeremy had announced to the world that they were trying to get pregnant, the hunt for the emerging baby bump had begun. Each time she took a drink of wine, people noticed. When she did not drink, they noticed. When her first home pregnancy test had come back positive, Jeremy had bought a pint-size Nationals T-shirt. She had found the tiny shirt weeks after the first miscarriage.

"I'm afraid I don't have the husband any longer," Libby said. "No children. I'm going solo these days." Challenge seeped out through the words.

"Good for you." Molly nodded slowly, as if realizing her information on Libby was outdated. "Bless your heart."

In the South, that phrase basically translated into "I pity your ass." Libby kept smiling as she returned to taking pictures of the bridal party.

The next two hours moved quickly. She spotted Colton with his mother and two little boys who looked like mini versions of him. She guessed the kids were his—and about five and six. She was disappointed to think that there was a wife likely lurking among the guests.

She continued shooting, capturing a picture of Ginger feeding cake to her groom and then later snapping images of the groom dancing with his mother as Colton danced with his mother.

As the guests danced to "Y.M.C.A.," Libby checked her list of must-have shots. Confirming they were all filled for now, she made herself a plate and slipped outside to the porch. The rain had stopped, but the air remained thick and hot. In the distance, mist rose up on the river as the sun peeked around the edge of a gray puffed cloud. It was an eerily beautiful sight that reminded her why this area was gaining popularity with out-of-town folks.

She watched as, in the distance, Colton strode into a large barn and seconds later drove out in a burgundy Model T car. Smoothly shifting gears, he pulled up in front of the steps. There was something about a man who could drive a standard. The engine rumbled, and the hood shook a little as he shut off the engine. On the back was a large sign that read JUST MARRIED.

Libby caught Colton's eye as he came around the front of the car. "I haven't had a chance to thank you yet. You were a lifesaver."

"Glad to help."

"Nice getaway car," she said.

He had changed into jeans and a white shirt. His black hair was slicked back and damp from the earlier rain. "The car is part of the estate. There are several more vintage cars in the garage. How much longer before the big send-off?"

"Twenty minutes."

"Great. I'll be right back. Forgot to tie the cans to the back."

"You're going all out."

"Big day for my big sister."

She was smiling as she watched him jog off and did not notice anyone approaching until she heard, "Libby?"

The familiar deep voice had her turning her head toward the set of wide stairs. Her ex-husband, Jeremy, approached her, his smile a little sheepish.

"Jeremy? What are you doing here?" The half-whispered words were tinged with curiosity and dread.

"I went by your house. Your neighbor said you were shooting a wedding here. I took a chance you might have a break."

Jeremy was an inch shorter than her. He had an athletic build that he kept lean by running and lifting weights several times a week. His light hair was starting to thin a little, and the frown lines around his mouth and brown eyes were deeper.

She almost leaned in to kiss him, but she caught herself. Their divorce had been civil enough, but divorce was divorce.

"I wanted to bring you some of your things you left behind in the Dale City house. I'm cleaning out the spare room and painting it and came across these."

The spare room had been earmarked as the nursery. Made sense now to turn it into something more practical. When she had moved out of the trilevel in Dale City, he had bought her out. The cash had sustained her through the temporary move to Richmond and helped her purchase faster computers and more camera lenses.

"Getting that home office you always wanted?" she asked.

He shrugged and dropped his gaze to his hands and his naked ring finger. "I'm getting married again."

"Oh." She waited for the punch of sadness, but it felt more like a soft slap even though she had seen the pictures online. "Good for you."

"Her name is Monica Peterson."

"Right. The paralegal in your office." She compared the image of an athletic woman with short black hair and a keen gaze to her own current state, which could only be described as a drowned rat. Jeremy and Monica had been in an office running group, and Libby had crewed for their team at several races.

"Yeah," he said.

"Good for you." She repeated the words like a scratched record album.

His gaze roamed the large front porch and the lavish arrangement of flowers. "Pretty different than our wedding."

"Yeah."

They had eloped, but a month after the wedding her father had held a dinner for them at the country club along with family and friends.

"I was sorry to hear about your dad," he said.

"I appreciated the flowers and nice note."

"I liked your father. He was a good man. Your father seemed happy for us when he toasted us at our party."

"He was happy for us."

That had been a perfect weekend. They had left the party close to midnight and taken a car to a historic bed-and-breakfast, where they had made love. It had been one of the few times neither was pressed by work or deadlines. Once her father had commented that the divorce had robbed him of a son.

"You didn't have to come all this way," she said. "You could have mailed it to me or even chucked it. If I haven't missed it by now, I doubt I would have."

Jeremy had always been considerate. He had tried not to be disappointed when she had lost the babies. But his kindness had only fueled her rage. How could he not have been furious?

"I wanted to tell you about my marriage in person. Didn't want you to see it on Instagram." He shifted his hands to his pockets and rattled loose change.

She still followed him and from time to time checked in. She had hoped his life was still stuck in neutral like hers. *Guess not.*

"Go on; show me where you're parked," she said with a smile. "I can transfer it to my car."

"Great." As they walked over the gravel pathway dotted with puddles, a silence settled between them. She had never minded the quiet, and neither had Jeremy when they were married. Now, it seemed to bother him. "The Heckmans finally moved."

The Heckmans were their elderly neighbors. They were vegan, and Mrs. Heckman drank so much carrot juice she'd actually turned orange. "How long were they in their house? Thirty, thirty-five years?"

"Forty. They moved to Tennessee to be closer to their children."

"Good for them." Mrs. Heckman was a health nut who had religiously delivered freshly grated carrot juice to Libby each time she had been pregnant.

Jeremy glanced back at the main house as the guests started to spill outside. "Your work looks like it's going well."

"It is. Booming, as a matter of fact."

As soon as she and Jeremy had decided to get pregnant, she had had to stop administering chemo to her patients. After two lost pregnancies, her resolve to deal with the sick or dying had vanished. With Jeremy's blessing, she had then started her photography business.

"You said you hated the weddings and fancy affairs," he said. "Now you'll be at events like this all the time."

That coaxed the first real laugh she'd had in weeks. "They're starting to grow on me. There's something comforting in tradition."

As they reached the Volvo sedan he had purchased after she had become pregnant the first time, she sensed he had something to say and was screwing up the courage.

"Out with it," she said.

He looked up, shaking his head. "With what?"

"Please. You look like you could explode." It was not charitable to take pleasure in his discomfort, but she did.

"You know me too well."

"Three years of marriage. What gives?"

More coins jangled. "Monica is pregnant."

32

And there came the punch to the gut that wiped away any smugness she might have mustered. Memories of lost babies swirled in her brain, and all the old pain, locked so carefully away, hammered to be released. For several seconds, she could not speak, fearful her tone would betray her sadness.

"I know it's a hard subject for you," he rushed to say.

It had been *their* hard subject. *Their* losses. *Their* pain. Now it was all *hers*.

"I should have told you months ago, but I knew you were dealing with the loss of your dad."

"Months ago? When is she due?"

"A few weeks."

She cleared her throat. "Wow. That's really wonderful." Had he saved the pint-size Nationals T-shirt?

"You're upset."

"No. Just surprised." To prove there were no hard feelings and that she was okay, she hugged him. "I know you've wanted this for a long time."

"Are you sure?"

"Of course." Her voice sounded far off, and the tone had an odd vibe to it, like distant thunder before a storm.

"Well, good luck to you both."

He stared at her, his eyes darkening with embarrassment. "I know my timing is lousy."

"I doubt there'd have been a good time."

He retrieved the box out of the Volvo and carried it to her car. She glanced inside. "My running shoes. I've really missed them."

"I thought you'd want them."

"Very thoughtful. Thank you. Got to get back to work."

"Are you going to be okay?" he asked with a genuine kindness that somehow irritated her.

"I'm fine. Don't worry about me." She slammed the car door a little too loudly. "I need to get back to work. My bride will be leaving soon."

He took her hand in his. His heartfelt grip warmed her chilled fingers. "Good luck, Libby. I'll always love you."

She cleared her throat. "Like the song. Same."

She tossed him one last grin and then headed back toward the porch; her legs felt wooden, and tension banded her lower back.

She barely glanced at the Model T as she climbed the front steps and almost bumped into a woman standing at the top of the stairs. "Sorry," she said, and then she looked up and realized the woman was their host, Elaine Grant.

In her fifties, Mrs. Grant was wearing a smartly tailored navy suit and black heels. She had swept brown hair streaked with gray into a french twist. Sierra would have called her classic French chic.

"No trouble," Mrs. Grant said.

"Sorry, I was preoccupied for a minute. Is there a shot you want me to get?" Jeremy's Volvo sped down the long drive.

"Are you okay?" Mrs. Grant asked, eyeing her closely. "You look pale."

"Oh, I'm fine. It's just that my ex-husband decided to show up and return a few of my things. He also told me he's getting remarried and is having a baby soon." She smiled. "But you know what? He returned my favorite running shoes, which was really terrific. You know when you first break in a pair, but they still have good support? It's the sweet spot. I really missed those shoes."

"Oh. Are you all right?"

Her response sounded ridiculous. If her life were a sitcom, she would have grinned as the canned laugh track played. "Sorry, too much information, Mrs. Grant. Your home and gardens are beautiful."

Mrs. Grant smiled. "Shame about the weather. And please call me Elaine."

"Elaine. The weather is always a risk." She cleared her throat, hoping Elaine had already forgotten about her babbling explanation about Jeremy. "It was kind of you to open up your home for Ginger."

"I've known her since she was a little girl, and her mother has always been good to me. She's practically family."

Hoping to move quickly beyond the Jeremy confession, Libby rushed to add, "If you ever decide to open this property for private events, you could charge a small fortune."

"I toyed with the idea a few years ago but didn't think we had much to offer until the gardens were restored."

"They're in peak form now."

"I'm glad to hear you say that, because I'm considering a photographer to catalog the gardens and the house. If we do embark on this venture, we'll also need a website."

"That's a must-have."

"Come by my office Monday at eleven. We'll talk more."

"Sure; that would be great," she said.

There was a loud cheer inside, and she knew the bride had changed into her travel outfit and was ready to depart.

Libby had her camera raised as she stepped away and angled her lens toward the bride and groom. The next few minutes passed in a flurry of laughter, fluttering yellow rose petals, and the couple's exit in the Model T.

Libby kept shooting as she followed the car down the long driveway, watching as the cans, now attached to the car, clanged against the dirt, foretelling better things to come.

CHAPTER FOUR

LIBBY

Monday, June 8, 2020
Bluestone, Virginia

Libby dreamed of the baby girl. Libby had dreamed of her before, and now as then, she kissed the little one on the belly, inhaled the faint scent of sweet milk, and rubbed her nose against the tiny cotton shirt. Small hands fisted her hair, tugging until both mother and child laughed with pure joy.

"Who will you become, little one?" she mused.

Feet kicked, laughter gurgled, and the child said, "I'll be whatever I wish to be. The world is there for the taking."

"You're still too little to take on the world just yet. Stay with me."

"Mothers and children can't always be together." The child's voice held no hint of sadness.

"But that's wrong," Libby said softly.

"That's life."

"No, there's an order to life. It's not time yet. Don't leave me, little one," Libby said.

But the girl was gone, her laughter faded, and the dream vanished, leaving Libby fully awake and staring at the popcorn ceiling of her father's living room.

The rumble of pots in the kitchen had her rising and reaching for her phone. She knocked over another empty wineglass. She couldn't remember the wine or what it had tasted like as she had gulped it down last night and prayed for sleep.

She had spent the better part of yesterday editing the photo files from Ginger and Cameron's wedding while she also compulsively checked Jeremy's and Monica's Instagram accounts. Every ten images she finished for Ginger and Cameron earned her another peek at the expectant couple. She had confirmed that Jeremy and Monica had gone public with their relationship five days after she and Jeremy had signed divorce papers. Their first post was a selfie, and they did not look like a couple. Jeremy was holding the camera high, grinning, and Monica was holding her hands up, as if she was asking a question.

Libby swung her legs over the side of the couch and scrolled through her phone to the couple's latest post, featuring bright smiles, heads tilted close to each other, and clinking coffee cups. Monica's ring finger now sported one hell of a rock, which must have set Jeremy back a pretty penny.

She studied Jeremy's smile as well as Monica's, trying to decide if maybe she looked a little happier than he did. She did not want her Jeremy back. But to think he was not quite whole after their shared losses had been okay. However, she found no signs of a joy imbalance. In fact, he looked positively buoyant after his visit to see her.

The happy couple did not advertise Monica's baby bump, but if Libby scrolled back and looked hard enough, she could see signs of it in March and April under Jeremy's oversize college sweatshirt. Her face was rounder, her breasts fuller. She had all the telltale signs that Libby had missed.

As Libby's hand slid to her flat belly, she remembered when it had been barely rounded at fourteen weeks along. It was getting so hard to remember the soft flutter kicks.

More pots clanged in the kitchen, shaking Libby's thoughts away from her phone. "Sierra, if that's not you, I'm calling the cops."

"What thief would make coffee and scramble eggs for you?"

"Good point." Libby's oversize T-shirt brushed her legs just above her knees as she picked up the wineglass and carried it into the kitchen.

Libby found Sierra standing in front of the stove, which dated back to the 1950s. Her parents had never had cause to replace the appliance, because it worked just fine. That mind-set also explained the refrigerator from the Reagan years and the dishwasher purchased right before Y2K. If her dad had thought she was going to sell the house, he had not gotten the memo stating that kitchens and bathrooms were key to a successful sale.

Sierra's black pencil pants, polka-dot blouse with an exaggerated white collar, and round red earrings created an *I Love Lucy* vibe that meshed with the kitchen.

"Get a lot of work done?" Sierra cracked an egg with one hand as she reached for another.

"I did. It's going to be a crazy week ahead, so I decided to knock out the look book for Ginger and Cameron. I've got to say, there are some pretty magical moments with the two of them laughing in the rain."

"Sounds like a musical."

"Yeah."

"Are you taking any kind of break?" Sierra asked.

"I will as soon as I get through June and the first week of July. Next wedding won't be until September."

"Good. You could use the time off." She poured Libby a cup of coffee and handed it to her.

Libby took a sip and then pressed the warm cup to her temple. "Bless you."

Sierra dug aspirin from the cupboard and put the bottle in front of her. "I won't ask about the two empty wine bottles in the trash."

"They were both half-full and from the wedding. Your boss gave them to me."

Sierra picked up her coffee. "He shouldn't do that, but he does in order to not deal with the bottles."

"Lucky me. What time did you finally get out of there?"

"We finished the cleanup about six. Rick gave me a ride home. I came by but didn't see you."

"I went for a drive." Meandering down the long roads had felt a little less pointless than coming home and staring at the walls.

"At the reception, I was caught up with serving cake and didn't get the chance to ask you, but did I see Jeremy at the wedding?"

"You did." She took another sip. "In a nutshell, he came to tell me he's getting married. Also turns out he and his soon-to-be wife are having a baby. In a few weeks."

"Libby." Sierra dragged out her name, etching sadness and anger into each syllable.

"Don't do that voice. And don't look at me like that. I'm fine."

"You're not fine. Those bottles were more than half-full, and you didn't step outside yesterday. I thought you were tired, so I left you alone. But now I can see you were mourning."

"I was not mourning. I'm a workaholic. You said yourself my energy is totally out of balance and too focused on work."

"Why did he come to the wedding?"

"He was looking for me. He wanted to have this conversation with me in person, but I think he also wanted a public meeting so things didn't go sideways."

"It couldn't have waited until you were finished shooting the wedding?"

"Guess not."

"Well, old Jeremy just dumped a truckload of manure on your head, and I think that stinks."

"I have to respect that he told me in person."

Sierra tapped a red manicured finger against the side of her stoneware mug. "There are days when I rail at the universe for taking Adam from me. If I get really on a roll, I console myself with the idea that at least I'll never have to see him with another woman. Selfish, but knowing we are both alone always does the trick for me. I don't know what I'd do if he had married another woman."

Libby washed down two aspirin with a gulp of coffee. "We got a divorce for a reason. And if your husband found another woman a tad too quickly, you would drink and work too much like me."

"Too much of either is not good for you."

"Like I said, I'm taking a break soon, and I can't blame Jeremy. I left him. He's not a bad guy."

"Then why do I want to punch him in the nose?"

"What would you have him do? Send a text?"

"It's what any self-respecting millennial male would have done."

Libby smiled. "Not him. He's not the bad guy."

The eggs sizzled in the pan, pulling Sierra's attention back to cooking.

"I met Elaine Grant at the wedding," Libby said.

"What did she want?" Sierra lifted the edges of the egg so the uncooked middle could reach the pan.

"She's talking about creating a website for the Woodmont Estate. She's going to need a photographer."

"And you might get the job?"

"Maybe."

"Can you imagine if Woodmont opened for big events? It would drive all kinds of business into Bluestone."

Libby made a mental note to take her laptop so she could show Elaine the shots from the wedding. She'd sent Ginger her link to her look book but was not sure if the honeymooning bride had passed it on. "It would be great for everyone in a fifty-mile radius." She took a long sip of coffee, thinking it serendipitous that Ginger had found her own website. "What's with the 1950s look?"

Her gaze sharpening, Sierra said, "I'm meeting with the bank today."

"Ah, you're going through with the loan to buy the old mercantile store in town." The space had started as a mercantile store in the 1920s, and when the owner had died, the property had been passed through the family, becoming a hardware store at one point and an antique store in recent years until it had closed for good.

Sierra dished out eggs on two plates already decorated with freshly sliced fruit. "I went by the mercantile store yesterday. It has so much potential. Great bones."

"What will it cost to buy and renovate?"

"A lot. Hence the loan. I have enough from Adam's life insurance to pay for most of the building, but I'll need bank money for working capital."

"Reno is always more than you think. Whatever the contractor quotes, add fifty percent."

"I'm trying to be positive here," Sierra said. "I need to make this work."

Libby pushed her scrambled eggs around her plate. She did not need to ask Sierra why she needed this project. Like her, Sierra found it easier to work than mourn. "Call me after your meeting. One way or another, I'll help you figure it out."

Libby arrived at Woodmont at five minutes to eleven. The sky was a vivid blue, and there was not a trace of rain in the forecast.

Libby turned off the paved road onto the long gravel driveway that led to the main house. Slowing as she approached, she took time to enjoy the view unburdened with worry about weather, time, and wedding logistics.

In the field to her left there was no sign of the freshly rolled green hay, which no doubt Colton had transferred to the barn before the rains. Shorn sheep grazed in the north field, and beyond them she could see the gentle bend in the James River.

It really was one of the most beautiful pieces of property in the county. During the Historic Garden Week with her mom, they would sit with the older ladies from the area and sip hibiscus tea while eating biscuits stuffed with Virginia ham. Once or twice her mother had invited her father to join them, but he had always politely begged off.

"Better I let you ladies enjoy it," he would say, grinning as he retreated to his office.

Mother and daughter had shared this adventure until the year Libby turned thirteen and her mother passed away from a drug overdose that her father had always insisted had been an accident. Pain medications did not mix well with wine.

"She left me," Libby had said.

"No, baby, your mother would never have left you."

"My first mother gave me away," Libby had insisted.

"No, she gave you to us to adopt."

"When I'm a mother, I will never leave my baby."

Libby remembered a lush flower arrangement from the Carter family arriving at the funeral home for her mother. It was not the largest by far, but it was stunning, and the blooms looked as if they had been picked from Woodmont's gardens. It simply read CONDOLENCES FROM THE CARTER FAMILY. A similar arrangement had arrived when her father passed in January, though this one came from a florist.

The senior Dr. Carter, Edward, had been an ob-gyn like his father before him. She supposed that her father had crossed paths professionally with Dr. Carter during the years he had practiced medicine, and the family had reached out in their grief as a professional courtesy. It was a small community, and everyone knew each other.

Dust kicked up around her tires as the road hooked to the left and then to the right. A small sign read MAIN HOUSE and pointed left. She went left.

She had been here enough times to know the road fed into a circular driveway that wound around a tall white colonial house.

To the left and right were two large gardens. The one on her left was a floral garden bordered by neatly trimmed boxwoods. Access was made through an archway wrapped in thick strands of honeysuckle. In the center of the floral garden was a copper sundial atop a weathered stone pillar. Etched into the metal were the words from an English poet: "A garden is always a series of losses set against a few triumphs." The floral garden emanated from this center spot, spiraling outward in a circular arrangement of poppies, daylilies, and blue cornflowers.

The garden on the other side of the road was the more practical of the two, though it was no less beautiful. It sported gravel pathways defining square beds bursting with lush fresh herbs, and a trellis displayed vines supporting ripening tomatoes, clusters of cucumbers, and purple and green string beans. Scattered among the vegetables were flowering bushes that added a controlled wildness that kept it from looking too staid.

All traces of Saturday's wedding had been cleaned up, and the place looked as pristine as it had when she had done the walk-through with the bride.

Out of her car, she hefted her backpack on her shoulder. A dog's deep woof followed by the yap of another dog sounded close. Both were moving toward her at top speed. *And this is when the lonely photographer is mauled by the wild animals.*

The deep bark turned out to belong to a black Lab mix who was not more than a year old. The second woof was attached to an old dachshund with short hair, bowed legs, and a big-dog attitude. The Lab scooped up a stick in her mouth, wagging her tail so quickly it was a miracle she made any forward progress. The dachshund remained aloof, though his hackles were not up. The Lab promptly dropped the stick at Libby's feet while the dachshund sniffed the air around her.

"Hey there, guys." She ran her hand over the Lab's collar until she touched the name tag. "Kelce. That's a different name."

The dog barked at the sound of her name.

Libby picked up the stick, tossed it, and watched Kelce bound after it. The dog retrieved the stick and quickly returned. Libby tossed the stick again. Kelce took off running.

The dachshund made no attempt to get in on the game.

"What's your name?" His tag read SARGE. She rubbed him between the ears. "Good to meet you, Sarge."

After walking around the house with her newfound friends, she climbed the hand-hewed stone steps to the porch. At the wedding, the house had been open and welcoming and full of laughter and music. Now, closed up and quiet, it had a standoffish air.

She knocked on the front door as Kelce dropped the stick at her feet. "You can do this all day, can't you?"

Kelce nosed the stick toward her.

"Libby?"

Kelce, Sarge, and Libby turned at the sound of Elaine's familiar voice. "Elaine."

Elaine stood in the circular driveway as the dogs rushed toward her. She wore faded jeans, a T-shirt that read WOODMONT, and boots all covered in dirt. Her hair was pulled into a ponytail on the verge of escaping the rubber band, and she wore no makeup. Her skin was paler than Libby remembered, and there were slight shadows under her eyes.

An odd sense of nervousness slithered up her back. It made no sense that Libby should be so nervous. This was about a job of sorts. She had done hundreds like it.

Elaine walked up to her. "Right on time."

"It's an obsession with me."

"A woman after my own heart," Elaine replied. "I'd shake your hand, but I'm covered in dirt. I've been pulling vines off the old greenhouse, and the job turned messier than I imagined."

"I didn't realize there was a greenhouse on the property."

"Only a few of the old-timers remember it. It was closed down in the mideighties. My grandfather had built it for my grandmother as a wedding gift. After they died, I had it closed up because it wasn't the kind of project my twentysomething self wanted to maintain. Over three decades later, I see its beauty and regret my decision to neglect it for so long."

"You took over this property that long ago?"

Elaine motioned to two white rockers, and they both sat. "My grandparents left the property to me when I was about your age, maybe a little younger. It always goes to the oldest in the next generation, though I was the only Carter left at the time. Ginger's late father, Jeb, managed the place, but as he got sicker, I didn't have the heart to place too many demands on him. He did less and less, and when he passed, I didn't replace him. We stepped back, and nature took over, as it always does."

"The gardens look amazing now."

"I can thank Colton for that. When he called two years ago and asked about the job, it seemed like perfect timing. There was so much work to be done in the main gardens, and Margaret wanted her grandchildren close. I asked Colton to concentrate his efforts on the main gardens and also a major kitchen renovation."

"Colton helped me out at the ceremony. He swooped in and gave me a lift in the rain. But he was scarce for most of the family photos."

"That's Colton."

"So you're gearing up to be an event space? What I saw on Saturday was nicely done."

"That was a favor to Ginger. I've not committed to opening the place up yet. But I want Woodmont photographed and cataloged so that if I do decide to open up, I'll be ready."

"I have pictures to show you from the wedding and some from the walk-through a couple of weeks ago. Neither day was ideal, but if you get a few more days like today, there's no doubt anyone could take a good picture."

"Days like today remind me of why I come back to Woodmont as often as I can."

"You don't live here full-time?"

"I split my time between here and Washington, DC. I've cut back on my law practice schedule so I can spend more time here."

"I don't blame you. I love the early summer here. My mother and I came here for Historic Garden Week when I was a kid. We always had a wonderful time."

Elaine's smile creased lines at the corners of her eyes and around her mouth. "We're thinking about opening up the gardens next year. That's the week when we get to show off all the work done over the winter."

"You have about two hundred acres, right?"

"We're down to one hundred and fifty. Sold off fifty acres a couple of years back to cover the renovations. The new owner has started clearing the land now for his vineyard." She grinned. "Everyone fancies themselves a wine maker."

"Woodmont's been in your family this whole time?"

"Basically. It's passed between various branches of the family until my grandfather inherited the place."

"Would you like to see some of the pictures from Ginger's wedding?"

"I saw some this morning, as a matter of fact. You sent a link to Ginger last night, and she forwarded it to me so I could show Margaret. You made a very rainy day look remarkably cheery. My favorite shot was of Ginger and Cameron running in the rain. Drenched, hands clasped, mud splashing, and both laughing."

Libby had had the same reaction when she had first studied the picture. "Thanks."

"I'd like you to photograph the property as well as the renovation of the greenhouse. My daughter, Lofton, also tells me Woodmont is ripe for social media."

"The gardens and greenhouse renovations will be a sure hit. If you decide to open up the space, it'll get booked quickly. But are you sure you want me to take the pictures? I'm a wedding photographer, and you might want someone with still-life experience."

"I suspect you're up to the task." She brushed away a strand of hair, smiling. "You've been to lots of places like this?"

"Yes. And I'm sincere when I say you have something special here."

Libby reached in her bag for a gray slick folder she used as a presentation package. Affixed on the outside was a round sticker with the LM Photography logo. "I do have a price list if you want to review it first."

Elaine accepted the folder but did not bother to open it. "I was on your website. Your prices fit with our budget."

"I have several packages. Maybe if you show me the greenhouse, I can make a suggestion."

"Sounds lovely." Her gaze dropped to Libby's high heels. "Can you walk in those?"

"Sure."

They both rose and walked down the porch steps. "Then follow me, and I'll give you the ten-cent tour. We'll walk the upper grounds, and then I'll drive us to the greenhouse on the lower property."

Kelce picked up a stick and brought it to Libby, nudging it at her hand. She accepted it and tossed it ahead. The dog took off after it and returned, ready to go again. Sarge trotted behind, woofing every so often.

Behind the main house was a row of white cottages that looked as old as the main house. "In its original form, Woodmont was a working farm," Elaine said. "These structures housed the overseer and laborers who tended the wheat in the fields."

Elaine stopped at the first small white house, which was marked PRIVATE. "This is our newly renovated cottage. I'm planning on spending more time here when I have guests. I want them to have their own space."

Elaine pushed open the door and clicked on the light. The large room was furnished with a four-poster bed made up with a white coverlet. On the opposite side was a kitchenette. While the furniture all looked antique, the kitchenette appeared freshly renovated.

"This is like a B and B."

"If we do become an event space, my daughter tells me we'll need every available corner of the property to maximize income."

"She's been involved in the property?"

"She's a lawyer and very numbers oriented. Every time I have an idea, she crunches the numbers, tells me I can't possibly pay for it, and then finds a way to make it work."

The sound of a Weed Eater had Kelce and Sarge bounding out the door. Elaine leaned out the door and waved, and Libby followed.

Colton's tall, lean frame had looked really good in a dark suit, but in jeans and a slightly sweat-stained T-shirt, he managed to look even better. Under a threadbare camouflage hat, he wore black sunglasses.

"Colton, I think you've met Libby McKenzie," Elaine said.

Libby extended her hand as he tugged off garden gloves and wrapped calloused fingers around hers. Through the dark glasses she felt the intensity of his gaze.

"The hardest-working photographer in Virginia," he said. "Not many people hustle like you do."

"Thanks again for the lift at the wedding on Saturday. We'd have had some very soaked guests."

"Glad I could help."

"I asked Libby to photograph the grounds and the greenhouse," Elaine said.

"Great," he said. "Just let me know what I can do to help." He lowered his voice to a stage whisper. "Elaine's a tough boss," Colton said lightly.

"I'm not the boss," Elaine said, laughing. "That would be Margaret."

"Don't be put off by my mother," Colton said. "Mom's gruff, but she'll do anything in the world for you."

"Nice to know."

"Margaret is not fond of the new kitchen," Elaine said with a smile. "She's missing the old stove with a nonfunctioning burner and the oven that took too long to heat."

"I feel her pain. Change is hard," Libby said.

"That sounds like experience talking," Elaine said.

"I just moved back to the area. Still adjusting. But don't get me wrong; change is also good." She tagged on the last statement for effect. Like Margaret, she was still searching for the payoff for this new life.

"I remember your dad," Colton said. "He was my pediatrician."

"I think he took care of every child in a twenty-five-mile radius."

"When I was six, I went tearing off after Ginger, who had taken my Superman toy. I slipped and fell and split my head wide open. Dad bundled me up, and your dad met us at his office on a Saturday afternoon. Your dad was dressed in golf clothes. Didn't seem to bother him that my antics had ruined his afternoon."

An uninterrupted day off had been a rarity in the McKenzie house. And after Libby's mother died, her father had worked longer hours. Many times, Libby had resented his patients. "He wasn't very good at golf, so he saw the call as a rescue."

Elaine's phone buzzed in her pocket, and when she glanced at the display, she said, "Colton, can you drive Libby to the greenhouse? I'll be right behind you. I've got to take this call."

"Be glad to."

Nodding, Elaine already had her phone pressed to her ear and quickly turned and shifted her focus to the caller.

"She can change gears on a dime," Colton said. "One minute she's here, and the next she's mentally back at the law office. Grab her while you can. She never sticks around long."

CHAPTER FIVE

SADIE

Wednesday, December 24, 1941
Bluestone, Virginia

As her brother Johnny's truck rolled into the town of Bluestone, which was not more than a few scattered wood-framed buildings, fifteen-year-old Sadie scooted to the edge of the worn seat. They rumbled toward Sullivan's mercantile store.

Going into Sullivan's General was always a treat. Although she could not afford a thing in the store, she still liked looking at the fabrics, gadgets, and magazines filled with pictures of beautiful people who lived in far-off, exotic places. Some days when Mr. Sullivan was in a good mood, he held back some of the older magazines for her. She was hoping with the holidays he was feeling generous.

Johnny downshifted into second gear and pulled up alongside the curb by the mercantile store. The town was nowhere as big as Charlottesville. But it had a church, a general store, a feed and seed, Dr. Carter's office staffed two days a week, a small diner that was the only place within thirty miles that served liquor, and, of course, a jail. Since the soapstone factory had closed nine years ago, none of the businesses except the café and jail got much traffic.

The front window of the mercantile store was decorated with a big green Christmas wreath decked out with a crisp red bow. Underneath were several wrapped packages. Two weeks ago when she had been in the store, she had picked up the smallest package because she had been drawn to the bright-red paper. When she had shaken it and realized it was light as a feather, she had shouted across the store to Mr. Sullivan and asked what was inside. He had frowned, mumbled something about them being empty and just for show. She had then jostled all the boxes and sadly discovered they all felt empty.

"Remember, no touching," Johnny warned. "Mr. Sullivan don't like you shaking those boxes and announcing to the store that they're empty."

"Seems a real waste to take the time to put fancy red paper on a box just for show."

"You take the time, Sadie, if you're trying to sell the paper or get folks in the buying mood for Christmas."

She stared at the wrapped packages, deciding to pretend they were full of pretty clothes. "I can't hurt nothing by looking."

"Look all you want. Don't cost a thing." He grinned.

"I bet Mr. Sullivan lets the new Mrs. Carter look and touch all she wants." She had seen the woman only once since she had moved to Bluestone. Tiny and quiet, the new bride reminded Sadie of a mouse.

"You know as well as I do that the folks in Woodmont live by a different set of rules," he said just above a whisper.

"It's not fair."

"Fair has nothing to do with it. It is what it is."

Johnny was just nineteen but looked a decade older. Since their father had died two years ago and their oldest brother, Danny, had joined the army, Johnny had taken to working their farm from sunup to well past sundown. And when he was not growing wheat, he was work-ing the odd shift in the furniture factory in Waynesboro. The weeks he was away were the hardest, as the farmwork and moonshine-making fell to Sadie. She had barely been to school this fall and knew she had fallen far behind the other students.

Prohibition had ended years ago, and the heyday of selling shine had long since passed. But there were folks, including the fancy Carters, who had developed a taste for the Thompson honeysuckle-flavored recipe. And honestly, anything homemade was tastier than store bought.

This time of year, sales generally rose. But this December had been extra brisk after President Roosevelt had told the world over the radio about the Japanese sneak attack on Pearl Harbor. Everyone in town wanted payback, including Johnny. And their mother, who always fretted about Danny, stopped sleeping so well and began pacing the wood floors. She had seen the Great War and wanted no part of it for her two sons.

Sadie hopped out of the truck, burrowing her gloved hands into the pocket of Danny's old gray wool coat. She hurried around to the back, ready to pull out several mason jars filled with moonshine. At Christmas, Mr. Sullivan always accepted three jars and credited their store account.

Across the street, Sheriff Boyd strolled out the front door of his jail. A dark shirt stretched over his rounded belly and tried to stay tucked inside faded jeans but had slipped loose in a spot or two. Pinned on his chest was a star that never shined up well no matter how much he polished it. Boyd recognized Johnny's truck. His dark eyes sharpened with interest.

"Is Sheriff Boyd going to give us trouble?" Sadie asked.

"He and I struck a deal." Johnny removed two of the biggest jars from the milk crate.

"What kind of deal?"

"I give him two jars of the honeysuckle white lightning, and he looks the other way."

Sadie calculated the value. "That's worth two dollars, Johnny."

Johnny tightened his hold on the jars, the frown lines around his mouth deepening. "He threatened to call in the state police and report my illegal still, and I can't have that."

Boyd was not as tall as Johnny but was a few decades older, and he sported at least an extra fifty pounds. Being sheriff did not pay much, but he found ways to skim extra benefits to add to his meager income.

Boyd hoisted his belt over his belly and tucked in the shirt. After looking from left to right, he crossed the street toward the truck.

"Why don't you go inside the store and give Mr. Sullivan his delivery?" Johnny said. "Have a look at the magazines."

"I saw all the covers two weeks ago. They can't have changed. And seeing as I can't touch, I'll have no way of seeing inside the pages."

Johnny clutched the jars close. "Sadie, go inside. No good will come of you mixing with Boyd."

"I can be nice," Sadie countered.

"No, you can't. Go on inside."

Sadie smoothed the folds of her coveralls, which were a castoff from the church bin. Though they were older, age made the fabric soft, and they felt good against her skin. Last year the coveralls had hung on her slim frame, but these days her hips and breasts had filled in the empty spaces nicely. One day she hoped to find a dress in the bin and wear it into Charlottesville or Roanoke to see a picture show.

"I want to stay with you, Johnny," she said.

"Do as I say, Sadie." Johnny's tone was a blend of fatigue and worry. "One thing for us to fight at home, but not now." He was whispering, but his gaze was locked on Sheriff Boyd.

Sheriff Boyd had arrested their brother, Danny, for driving shine and had locked him up. The judge had given Danny a choice. Three years in jail or the army. Seeing as the food was better in the army, Danny had taken that route. Sadie knew deep down Danny was glad for the excuse to leave Bluestone.

"Get!" Johnny ordered. "I'll bring in the crate of jars."

Frowning, she balled her fingers into fists. "I'll be watching from the window."

Johnny was grinning. "Good to see you, Sheriff Boyd."

Sadie glanced back and caught Boyd's gaze darkening as he studied her. Raising her chin to prove she was brave, she then stepped into the store. Bells jingled over her head, obscuring Boyd's comment to Johnny.

She watched out the front window as her brother extended his hand to Boyd, and they shook. Johnny had a practical side that allowed him to smile when he was angry.

"What are you gawking at?" Mr. Sullivan asked.

Sadie turned slowly from the window decorated with the fake presents. Mr. Sullivan was a tall man with broad shoulders, but his frame had softened in his older age, with shoulders now hunched forward. He slicked back his salt-and-pepper hair with oil and parted it in the middle in a way that reminded her of a cartoon character.

"I'm not gawking," she countered.

"You've always got your nose in someone else's business."

"My brother is my business."

Even the store's rich scents of spices and perfumes and the collection of bright labels on the tin cans did not distract her as she turned back toward the window. Boyd lifted a mason jar full of clear liquid and inspected it. He said something to Johnny that deepened that frown. Finally, Johnny nodded and handed over a third jar.

"Bastard," she muttered.

Her brother had barely slept in the last two days, working on this latest batch in the evenings after tending the livestock and working extra hours in the McKenzies' gardens.

Finally, Boyd walked back to his office, carrying his three jars. He glanced back toward the store, as if he was looking for her. When his gaze locked on hers, a smug smile tipped the edge of his lips before he turned and vanished inside.

"Thief," she muttered.

"Does Johnny have my delivery?" Mr. Sullivan asked.

"Yes, sir," Sadie said. "Johnny's bringing in the honeysuckle flavor you like. Johnny made this batch with an extra kick, so be mindful."

Mr. Sullivan glanced out the window as Johnny strode toward the store with the crate. "Remember, Mrs. Sullivan and my daughter, Ruth, don't need to know about this arrangement."

"Yes, sir. They won't hear a word from me. I don't suppose I can have a look inside the November *Life* magazine with Gene Tierney on the cover. It'll keep my mind occupied and my mouth closed."

He regarded her a moment and then pushed the magazine toward her. "Be careful with the pages. I can't sell it if you mangle it."

"I'll be so gentle you won't know I ever looked at it." She tugged off her knit gloves and shoved them in her pocket.

As Gene Tierney stared off into the distance, her dark hair framed her serene face and tumbled over a dark V-necked dress. She wore a two-toned gossamer veil that draped over pale, slim shoulders. The ocean was behind her, and it looked like a gentle breeze was caressing her face.

Sadie had never been to the beach, but she had heard the air tasted like salt, and the water crashed on the shore all day and night. She was saving up her money and as of now had one dollar and ten cents. When she had enough, she was going to go to the beach just like Gene Tierney. That was, after she went to the picture show in Charlottesville.

She turned past the table of contents. She was fixing to go straight to the article on Miss Gene but stopped when she saw the headline *Shooting War*. President Roosevelt said that American ships had been damaged and sunk. More than 2,300 killed. He said America was all but at war with Japan and Germany. She thought about Danny. He had quit school in the fifth grade and did not write well, which was why she supposed he had not written in the last year.

The bells jingled in time to the clink of glass jars knocking against each other. She turned to see Johnny striding through the door. He set the crate of jars on the counter.

"Morning, Mr. Sullivan," he said to the shopkeeper. "How are you doing this morning?"

"Can't complain, Johnny." Mr. Sullivan's gaze lost its sour expression as he stared at the mason jars.

"Thank you for the order, sir."

"Always brightens my holidays when the wife's mother comes to visit. I'll credit your account two dollars."

"I appreciate that."

Mr. Sullivan lifted a jar and let the clear liquid catch the light before placing it back in the crate. "That's mighty nice."

Sadie quickly turned the page, knowing if Johnny saw the war pictures, he would be worried. He was already fired up about the Japanese, and the news in Europe would make it all the worse.

She flipped to a page featuring the actress Rosalind Russell on her wedding day. She was marrying a fellow by the name of Frederick Brisson. Sadie had no idea who the groom was, but she recognized Cary Grant and Loretta Young, who were standing beside the couple. They were all smiling.

"Would you be interested in five more jars?" Johnny asked. "I made extra this year."

"I can't give you any more credit than I already have," Mr. Sullivan said. "The missus will notice if I toy with the books too much."

"I was thinking you might like to sell these. We'll split the profits fifty-fifty."

Mr. Sullivan peered inside the crate. "Taking a bit for myself is one thing, but selling is another. Boyd will have something to say about that."

"I've given him extra, so he'll look the other way for a few days. It's the holidays, so there'll be some looking for a little nip."

Sullivan regarded the jars. He was smart enough to recognize that folks were looking for a little extra nip these days. He held out his hand. "It's a deal, Johnny. Come see me in a few days to collect your half."

Johnny shook his hand. "Yes, sir."

Mr. Sullivan arranged the jars off to the side so that they could not be seen from the street window but would be noticed by his patrons who knew where to look.

Johnny fished a rumpled piece of paper from his pocket and squinted at the dark scrawl that passed for handwriting. "Mama is going to need three bags of flour, a can of lard, and salt."

"That's all?"

"For this time."

The shopkeeper looked over at Sadie. "Go easy on those pages, Sadie Thompson."

"Yes, sir."

"Have you heard any more news about the war?" Johnny asked. "I heard that the National Guard has stepped up their drills. They're likely to get called up any day."

"Don't be in a rush," Mr. Sullivan said. "I was in France in 1918."

"But we won," Johnny said.

Mr. Sullivan slowly stacked the bags on the counter. "Nobody won, Johnny."

"You make it sound like you lost, Mr. Sullivan," Sadie said.

"It was bloody, Sadie. And war's never as easy to win as the politicians want us to believe," Mr. Sullivan said softly.

"Couldn't be hard to shoot a gun," Johnny said. "I been shooting squirrels since I was eight."

"Never easy to shoot a man, Johnny."

As their conversation drifted to the cost of grain and crops, Sadie stared at Gene Tierney's soft curls and her dark eyes and full lashes. The photograph was in black and white, but she would bet her fingernails were painted a pretty shade of red.

"That reminds me," Mr. Sullivan said. "The Carters are having a party tonight, and Dr. Carter said if I saw you for me to ask you to stop by Woodmont. They are celebrating the young Mr. Edward's wedding to his new bride. It's going to be a big shindig."

"And they said they wanted my moonshine?" Johnny asked.

"He asked for you specifically. Might want to take extra. I'm guessing young Dr. Carter will be in a buying mood." He stacked a jar of lard on the flour.

"I'll do that," Johnny said.

Sadie nudged Johnny. "Mama is having a big dinner tonight. She's been curing a ham for weeks."

"Dinner will keep," Johnny said. "We can't afford to turn down the money. Especially now."

"Why now?" Sadie asked.

The worry lines on Johnny's face deepened. "No telling what'll happen."

Sadie closed the magazine. "The war already has Danny. In my book that means the Thompsons have gave enough."

Johnny shook his head. "It don't work that way, Sadie."

CHAPTER SIX
LIBBY

Monday, June 8, 2020
The Woodmont Estate

Colton's truck rumbled and swayed as the tires rolled down a dirt road filled with weeds. The road, like the greenhouse, had been left alone for three decades, and the woods had reclaimed a good bit of it. Though it appeared freshly graded, it would take a few more passes before the road was smooth. The woods around them were thick and mature, just as they likely had been when the first Carters had made their mark on the land.

"I can't believe I didn't know about the greenhouse," Libby said, lifting her camera to shoot the road ahead.

"Family always wanted to keep it private."

The Carters had a reputation for being reserved. The one time they had landed in the public eye had been in the late 1990s, when a reporter in Richmond had done a piece on Edward Carter and his involvement with the Lynchburg Training School and Hospital. According to the article, Dr. Edward Carter had helped sterilize patients considered incompetent. He maintained in the article that he had nothing to be ashamed of and that he had dedicated his life to caring for women. The article had made a small mention of his work with the poor and the thousands of safe deliveries he had made.

Libby remembered her father muttering something about Dr. Carter, but when she had asked him to repeat it, he had told her never mind.

"You grew up in Bluestone, but I don't remember you," Colton said.

"I went to boarding school when I was thirteen. When did you graduate from the high school?"

"In 2003," he said.

"I would have been the class of 2007, so we'd have missed each other either way." As the truck passed over a rut, she grabbed the handle, steadying herself as the nose of the vehicle dipped and then rocked. Colton seemed unconcerned, as if he had done this more times than he could count. "Have you been here all your life?"

"I did eleven years in the navy. I got out two years ago after my wife died. I have two young sons."

Knowing he had lost a wife oddly made her feel more drawn to him. Life had sucker punched him just as it had her. "Were they the two boys at the wedding reception?" she asked.

"They would have been hard to miss," he said, grinning.

"Where are they now?"

"With my mom. She helps out more than I can say."

"And your father was the head gardener at Woodmont before you?"

"That's right."

"I didn't think jobs were passed down from generation to generation in the States. That's a very English *Downton Abbey* kind of thing."

A small smile tugged his lips. "Maybe. I'm glad Elaine decided to keep the property and not parcel it off any more than she had to."

"A lot of old places like this have high overhead and taxes. Unless you have a huge trust to support it, the only viable option is to rent the property out for business events, weddings, and parties. So how do you like being in the event business?"

"I don't think we're quite there yet." He grinned, apparently not put off by the idea. She suspected he was a very pragmatic man, not fazed by taking risks when necessary. "Ginger was our trial run. She decided to get married four weeks ago and was headed to the courthouse when Elaine suggested Woodmont."

"Four weeks is a tight turnaround for a wedding. She's lucky she had access to the place."

"The whole day would have been better if she had listened when I told her to rent a tent."

"Get used to brides, grooms, and mothers of the brides not always listening. Everyone's got their own vision of the event, and practical things like weather don't always get factored in."

"I'll keep that in mind if Elaine decides to go that route. How long have you been taking pictures?"

"Five years. Started my career as an oncology nurse. But there came a point when I needed to step away."

"You stay busy with the photography?"

"Very."

"Good for you."

"Work is always a good thing."

He downshifted and slowed the truck as they rolled down a slight hill. In the distance, the woods cleared, and she caught sight of the James River. The Woodmont land was nestled beside a gentle bend at a narrow part of the river. Spring and early summer rains had left the river high and rolling quickly over its jagged rocks.

"The river is narrower there," she said.

"The waters are normally calm. We get a lot of kayakers this time of year."

"Looks more like white-water rafting today."

"Yeah. There are times when it's lethal."

She noted his hand on the steering wheel and found her gaze drawn to his tanned fingers and neatly trimmed nails. They were sexy hands and reminded her that the last time she'd had sex, she had been trying to get pregnant with Jeremy.

"Where'd you live before coming back here?" he asked.

"Richmond. I rented an apartment in the historic district. Always been a sucker for old buildings and their stories."

The truck nosed down a slight incline, and as soon as he turned the corner, she saw the twenty-by-forty-foot glass structure nestled in the overgrowth. "Is that a greenhouse?"

"I believe the official term is *solarium* or *conservatory*. It's basically a greenhouse but a lot fancier."

Octagonally shaped, the glass sides rose up to form a domed roof. The windows were covered in dirt and moss as well as thick strands of ivy, making it hard to see inside. Thick overgrowth crowded around the walls, making it look like it belonged in a B movie horror show.

"Elaine wants it restored," he said, putting the car in park.

"Not an easy task."

"This entire property has given me a run for my money. But Elaine is determined to bring Woodmont back to life."

"She must really love it."

With his wrist resting on the steering wheel, he stared ahead. "I suppose she does."

"Is she coming down here?"

"She'll be here in just a minute."

"You've not been inside the greenhouse yet?"

"Main door is rusted shut. It's basically a time capsule."

"How long has it been closed?"

"Thirty-plus years," he said. "No one is exactly sure."

They climbed out of the vehicle, and she was glad to have a moment to study the greenhouse more closely. Sunlight cut across the glass, creating stunning shapes and angles. She raised the camera and started shooting. "Her grandfather built it?"

"In 1941. It was a gift to his English bride. Dr. Carter met his wife, Olivia, while he was studying at Oxford."

"Nice gift."

"As the story goes, they married faster than they had planned because of the war. It was during the Blitz, and London was not a safe place to be."

"I'm assuming your grandfather helped her to stock the greenhouse."

"I suppose."

"Any idea about the cost to fix this place?"

"It's not going to be cheap."

She snapped pictures of the dome, which caught the midday sun just right.

The sound of another car engine had her lowering her camera and stiffening a little. Elaine got out of her truck, moving toward them with quick strides that reminded Libby a little of her own gait.

"What do you think?" Elaine asked.

"It's impressive."

Colton walked to the back of his truck and grabbed a crowbar and a small saw. "I was down here yesterday," he said. "The door is rusted shut, so it will take a little work. Will do my best not to break anything, but no guarantees."

"Yes, you've warned me before." Beyond Elaine's smile was an edge of impatience.

Gripping the crowbar, Colton strode toward the arched doorway, where an area had already been cleared. "Ready?"

"I delayed the big reveal until you arrived, Libby," Elaine said. "I thought you might get a kick out of it."

Libby assumed Elaine wanted the entire project documented. "I've already taken a few pictures of it. Mind if I continue?"

"Not at all," she said. "Go ahead, Colton."

Libby raised her camera. She always felt calmer behind the lens, knowing it created a barrier between her and the world. When people looked at the camera lens, they became self-aware and ceased to notice her.

As she took pictures, she allowed her line of sight to follow a beam of sunlight shooting from above the tree canopy. The grime on the domed glass shielded most of the light, but some rays seeped into the interior. It looked a little supernatural, like it was glowing.

"I've been wanting to open this for a couple of years," Elaine said. "But as with everything, it's a matter of priorities. There was so much to fix at the main house and the primary gardens. This was a distant thought at the time."

Colton wedged the edge of his crowbar between the doorframe and the door, moving it gently back and forth. Portions of the fused metal gave a little but still remained stuck. He patiently moved the crowbar upward, working along the entire seam. This went on for twenty minutes as he methodically worked up and down the length of the door until, finally, he wedged it open.

He set the bar aside and with gloved hands pulled the door open. The growing sound of barking dogs drifted down the hill, and Libby turned to see Kelce and Sarge headed their way.

"I'll have to take the entire door assembly off eventually, but for now, we can get inside. Elaine, I'd let you go first, but it might be best if I checked it out for any snakes or other hazards."

"Have at it," Elaine said.

"I'm not fond of snakes either," he said, grinning. "But here goes nothing."

Elaine chuckled. "Woodmont would be in ruins if not for you."

Libby sensed a comradery between the two that came as close to friendship as an employer and employee might have. However, in this part of the world, the line between their places in life would always exist, regardless of respect or love of the land.

Colton stepped into the greenhouse, pulling a small flashlight from his pocket. Libby took pictures, wishing now she had a wide-angle lens to capture more of the eerie beauty of the space.

Libby listened to the steady thud of Colton's footsteps as he stepped deeper inside. Midday light did little to penetrate the darkness or dull the dank smell. She could barely see his shape pass in front of the glass, hazy with moss and mildew.

"Have you ever been inside, Elaine?" Libby asked.

"Yes," Elaine said. "I used to go in with my grandmother when I was a little girl. She and I planted together, and she even gave me my own little garden journal so I could keep notes like she did in hers."

"If she kept gardening journals, then you have a record of what she grew in here."

"I have very detailed records. She created her first journal in 1942 and created a new one each year until the greenhouse was closed in the eighties." Elaine regarded the greenhouse, as if she saw all her regrets reflected back in the murky panes.

Curiosity captured Libby's full attention. "Why did your grandmother stop maintaining this?"

"I'm not sure why she stopped coming down here."

"You must have been really close to her," Libby said, struggling to forge a connection.

Elaine stared at the greenhouse, her thoughts appearing to drift back in time. "She was an amazing woman in so many ways. And she had more influence on my life than anyone. She would have done anything to protect me."

"Is it safe for Colton to be inside?" Libby asked.

"Colton did a preliminary structural examination of the exterior and said the support beams all appeared sound."

"No offense, but he's a gardener," Libby countered. She imagined the entire thing falling in on their heads and made a mental note to add hard hats to her photography equipment.

"He's a gardener with a mechanical engineering degree," Elaine said.

Colton appeared at the door. "It's clear. Just watch your step. There's a lot of muck on the ground." He looked at both dogs. "Stay."

"You want to go first?" Elaine asked Libby.

"No," she said. "This is your project. You should be the first."

Elaine's eyes suddenly filled with nervous energy, and she hesitated at the threshold.

"I'll be right behind you," Libby said. What was she afraid of?

"No, you first," Elaine said. "I don't want to hold you up."

Libby had been born with a natural curiosity and daring. When she was little, she had challenged her parents with endless questions and had often argued with their answers. Her thirst to see and do had compelled her across country to California to attend nursing school. And it had given her the courage to try for the third pregnancy.

In the last few years, her inability to risk anything had grown out of control. She had thought her choice to retreat was strategic, as it had been when she was a kid. However, in the old days, she'd found a way to move forward again. Now, she wondered if she would ever leave her dad's house and get back on the horse.

Here she stood, afraid to go in a damn greenhouse because she was worried about the stupid roof caving in or a snake biting her or whatever. The world was passing her by, as the images of Jeremy and Monica had proved. That realization pushed her over the threshold. After all, what could go wrong? She glanced up at the greenhouse's domed ceiling covered in moss. *Ceiling collapse. Rats and snakes. Broken glass.*

Her first impression of the greenhouse's interior was the smell. The deep, earthy, fetid smell reminded her of vegetables left too long in the crisper. The damp air was musty and nearly suffocating.

Her gaze was drawn to the center of the room, where a fountain stood silent like a sentry watching over its domain. Dirt had filled the three tiers, allowing grass and weeds to take root in all three. Around the fluted base were brick pavers smeared in green moss and arranged in a herringbone pattern that occupied half the floor space.

The rich soil around the edges was filled with overgrown plants that had turned so wild they barely resembled any plant she had ever seen. A honeysuckle vine grew up the side of the greenhouse, searching for more sunlight.

Kelce and Sarge ventured into the room, each enamored by all the new smells. Sarge hiked his leg and definitively marked his territory. Kelce followed suit.

Colton moved to chase the two out, but Elaine stopped him. "That's fine. They're family too."

"I like it." Libby's gaze rose up to the domed ceiling.

"It was pure luxury," Elaine said. "My grandmother loved orchids, and Grandfather built this place so she could enjoy them all year long. She was from London and said this greenhouse matched the one her parents had in London. It was destroyed along with the family house in the Blitz."

Colton walked up to one of the glass panes and inspected a crack that ran the diagonal length of it. "Elaine, you could make a small fortune if you had the place dismantled and sold all the pieces and parts to an architectural salvage company. It's all quality construction."

"We've had this conversation before," Elaine said. "I want to fix it up. Make it what it once was."

"It'll take months," he said.

"And money. I know the drill." Elaine ran her fingertips along the edge of the fountain. "I suspect the plumbing that supplied water to this will need repair."

"Yes," he said. "There's a gravity-fed system that feeds from a well near the main house."

"Quite the engineering," Libby said.

"My grandfather wanted only the best for his bride," Elaine said.

"What was your grandfather Edward like?" Libby asked.

"Very dedicated to his work—that at times was controversial."

"I think I read something about him years ago," Libby said.

"It would have been hard to miss."

Not only was the air thick with humidity, but it was also full of sadness and loss. The greenhouse had been designed to bear fruit, but neglect had left it infertile and a relic, more trouble than it was worth. A chill rolled down Libby's spine, and she wondered if Sierra's curse theory was not far off the mark.

Colton remained silent as he moved toward a far corner and knelt to inspect the foundation. He picked up an empty beer can that was faded and crushed. "When I was in high school, some kids used to sneak in here from time to time."

"Sounds like you were in that group, Colton," Elaine said.

"It was a long time ago," he said.

Everything about Colton appeared to be in place, but Libby wondered if the sixteen-year-old version of him had been so contained.

"Did you sneak in here, Libby?" Elaine asked.

"I went to boarding school, so I missed out on the fun."

An alarm buzzed on Colton's phone. He removed it from his pocket and shut it off. "I've got to go get the boys, who are playing with friends this afternoon," he said. His voice was smooth and mellow, unrushed. "As soon as I get them settled, I'll be back to start on cleaning this place out. Libby, you want a ride back to the house with me or Elaine?"

"She can ride back with me," Elaine said.

"Right," he said.

"Colton, if you need help or extra manpower, get it," Elaine said. "I want this done right, without delay."

"Will do." He strode outside and whistled for the dogs, who happily followed him to the truck.

Libby allowed her gaze to roam over the herringbone brick floor to a small stone table angled in a corner. "I'm glad you're opening the property. From a business standpoint, it will allow you to upkeep all its beauty and history."

"Perhaps," Elaine said. "Or I might keep it private and available exclusively to the family. My husband calls it another one of my rescue missions."

Libby wondered if she too might be one of those rescues, though she would argue she did not need rescuing. "Seems a worthy cause to me."

"I'm glad you feel that way," Elaine said.

Libby pointed her lens toward a small statue of a little angel. It was made of white marble and, like everything else, was covered in a thick coating of moss. She crossed to the opposite side to look back. Libby captured more images, and as she glanced to her right, she caught misshapen letters that had been etched in one of the glass panes. "Sadie."

"What?" Elaine sounded slightly startled.

"Sadie, 1942. The name and date were etched in the glass." Libby took more pictures.

Elaine crossed and gently traced the letters with her fingertips. "I had forgotten all about this."

"Who was Sadie?"

"She was a local girl who worked for my grandmother for a time."

"Is she still in town?"

"She passed away in the 1990s."

Libby wondered if a search in the local archives would reveal much about Sadie. Even as the thought occurred to her, she wondered why it should matter.

Libby followed Elaine to her truck and slid into the passenger seat. Elaine started the engine, put it in reverse, and backed up and turned around as if she had done it a million times.

"It's a beautiful space." Libby clicked back through images of the domed roof—the glass cut the light into a rainbow of colors.

The truck bumped and rocked up the hill toward the road that led to the circular drive in front of the house. Elaine pulled up beside Libby's car.

She wondered again why Elaine's grandmother had turned her back on this incredible space. "I'll put the proposal together and email it by tonight."

"I'm having a little dinner tonight. It'll be Margaret, Colton, and the boys. My daughter, Lofton, might also attend. Bring it in person and join us."

"Are you sure?"

"I am."

"Yeah, sure. That would be great. Thank you. What time?"

"Five. I know it's early, but the boys will be ready for bed by seven. Children have a way of taking over our lives in the best ways."

"So I've been told."

CHAPTER SEVEN

LIBBY

Monday, June 8, 2020
The Woodmont Estate

As Libby was about to drive away from the Woodmont Estate toward Bluestone, her phone chimed with a text from Sierra. Meet me at the general store. S. She texted back a thumbs-up emoji and then put her car in gear and headed for the center of town.

Parked in front of the old store was Sierra's red MINI Cooper. Libby nosed her car behind Sierra's and crossed the sidewalk to the front door. The large picture window was covered in brown paper with a GOING OUT OF BUSINESS sign. The door's worn handle was made of tarnished brass. A spiderweb and a bird's nest sat atop the transom.

She pushed open the door and stepped from the bright summer sunlight into a dingy space filled with shadows and stale air. The floors and the three remaining shelving units were covered in dust. Across the room stood the storekeeper's counter. On top of the counter was a sealed mason jar filled with clear liquid.

Libby picked up the jar and cleaned off its metal lid. She had lived in this area long enough to know that this was moonshine and long past its shelf date for safe consumption. Either way it had to be toxic as hell. "Sierra, please tell me you didn't buy this place."

"I bought it!" Her voice echoed from a darkened back room seconds before she appeared. Sierra had changed into a black T-shirt, fringed jeans that hit midcalf, and red sandals with a thick cork sole.

"You're serious?" Libby asked.

Sierra's grin brightened, as it always did when she was a little panicked. "The good news is that I bargained the seller down considerably."

"What about the bank loan to renovate the building?"

A small shrug lifted her shoulder. "I didn't get the loan."

"Why not? What about the land you inherited from Adam? Wasn't that going to be your collateral?"

"The land is in a trust for the next ten years. His family feared he would marry a gold digger." The bright smile dimmed for a split second and then returned. "Tanner thought I could take out a bank loan against the property, but as it turns out, it requires his father's approval."

Libby kind of sympathized with the man. This was not the soundest investment, and keeping the money in a trust would mean Sierra would have resources down the road. "You can't persuade your father-in-law?"

"He won't budge."

She walked through the dusty room. "And this will be your sandwich shop."

"It's just what the area needs. There are enough pizza places in a twenty-mile radius, which is fine if you're feeding kids or want an easy meal. But if you want a nice picnic lunch to take with you to one of the dozen wineries in the area, then you'll come to me. Anything I sell will nicely complement a picnic basket. In fact, that's what I'm going to call my place. *Picnic.*"

"Picnic." She could kind of see it, but she already knew Sierra would be working long hours for marginal profits at best.

"Simple. Straightforward. How long until you launch?"

"Midfall. Or at least that was the plan. Now that I'll be doing most of the work myself, it will likely be spring."

"Negative cash flow for the next year."

"Give or take." Sierra lifted her shoulders in a slight shrug. "Hard work is not tough. Sitting and thinking is tough. I'll do it all myself if it comes down to it."

"No truer words." She raised her camera and aimed it at Sierra. "Have you ever knocked down a wall?"

"No. But I'll research it on YouTube."

"Seriously?"

"That's how you taught yourself photography."

"Yeah, but there are no structural beams involved in taking pictures. Or electrical wires or plumbing that can kill you."

"I can learn anything on YouTube," she said brightly. "I have utter faith."

"Okay."

"Be happy for me, Libby. I need this."

"I'm happy for you."

It was one hell of a risk, but at least Sierra was not afraid to try.

Libby started clicking pictures. "Might as well start documenting this adventure. When HGTV sees your blog and comes a-calling, you'll have plenty of *before* pictures."

"Ohh, I like how you think." Sierra rested her hands on her hips, angled her body sideways, and smiled broadly. "This is my best side."

Libby snapped several pictures. "You should be on a magazine cover."

Sierra shifted her pose so that she was looking directly at the camera, her arms crossed. "And just so you know I'm not totally crazy, I have a contractor coming by tomorrow. He's going to make sure I don't knock out the wrong wall and bring the entire building down. John Stapleton. We went to high school together."

"Good, you know him."

"We actually dated back in the day."

"Oh, really?"

"Long story."

"I won't ask."

"Better that way, but he's still cute."

Libby pointed to the mason jar. "Is that moonshine on the counter?"

Sierra held up the jar of clear liquid. "I believe so. There was a box of six hidden in a back closet."

"Whatever you do, don't drink it. No telling how old it is. You could go blind, if it doesn't kill you first."

Sierra laughed as she lifted the jar. "I'm not that crazy. I just found it curious. The original owner, Mr. Sullivan, must have had a taste for it. How did it go at Woodmont?"

"Elaine Grant has a fixer-upper project as well. She's restoring a greenhouse that's on her property."

"The greenhouse. I have fond memories."

"How could you know about the greenhouse? I never heard about it."

"You were at boarding school. During high school, it became the place to visit at night when we were seniors."

"Colton said something about that. How did you all manage to get inside?"

"It wasn't easy. We had to hike along the river and then up the hill. It was always done on a dare."

That explained the beer can Colton had found. "Why?"

"Because it's cursed, darling," she said, laughing. "The late Mrs. Carter—"

"Elaine's grandmother."

"I suppose. Anyway, her husband gave it to her as a wedding gift, as the story goes. Rumor has it that somewhere in the mid-1940s, she was complicit in killing a man."

"Who?"

"That detail changes depending on who is telling the story. Family connections saved her from jail or real scandal. It's said the dead man haunts the grounds—especially the greenhouse, because he knows she loved it so much."

"You ever see the ghost?"

"Who needs to see a ghost to be spooked? There's nothing like drinking Fireball while lying under that arched dome and trying to imagine spirits stalking the dark woods around us. Deliciously creepy."

"You ever hear the name Sadie? Her name was scratched in the glass."

"No, I never heard about her."

"She must have been close to the Carters. The date under her name was 1942."

"Very curious."

"I feel deprived," Libby said. "We never had any ghost stories at boarding school."

"Oh, sweetie, I'm so sorry. Maybe when you're at Woodmont again, you'll finally get your wish."

Boarding school had meant a great education, but it had created a disconnect between Libby and her friends, including her father. The summers would have been a chance to keep up, but her father had often sent her to Europe to study.

"Elaine's invited me back for dinner tonight," Libby said.

"My, aren't you getting cozy with the landed gentry?"

"She says it's so we can review my photography proposal."

"That can be done via email and text, dear. I would say you've made an impression on Mrs. Grant."

"Maybe." The scratch of little feet scurrying behind the walls drew her back to the moment. "I'll help you here when I have free time."

"When do you have free time?"

"It rears its ugly head every now and then. Like you said, hard work is easy."

Sierra hooked her arm into Libby's. "Well, aren't we two codependent castoffs looking for a new life?"

Libby laughed. "Put that way, we sound dire."

"Maybe we are."

"I don't want to see us that way."

The shadow in Sierra's gaze brightened. "Then we'll deny it until the end."

Libby spent the afternoon working on the shoot schedule for the coming weekend wedding and trading texts with Joan, the bride. This rehearsal dinner and wedding were going to be held in Richmond's historic Main Street Station. Because it was still an active train station, her lists included not only the names of the wedding party and guests but also the train schedules (6:35 p.m. and 8:30 p.m.). She double-checked her room reservation in town and triple-checked that the second shooter she had hired was on target. Immediately she rattled off another worst-case list. *Hurricane season. An influx of train passengers wandering into my shots. Drunken guests.*

She also wrote up a proposal for Elaine and printed it out on white linen paper and tucked it in a glossy pocket folder embossed with her logo. The time slipped by quickly, and she was proud to report, should anyone care, that she had checked Jeremy's and Monica's Instagram pages only twice. To her disappointment and relief, there were no new pictures of the baby bump or the upcoming wedding.

At four o'clock, she showered and washed and actually blow-dried her hair, something she rarely did on a weekday. She also took time to apply a little makeup and found clean jeans and a white eyelet top that was wrinkle-free. She grabbed a bottle of chardonnay from the wine rack, which was her sole souvenir from the house she had shared with Jeremy.

Now familiar with the twenty-minute drive to Woodmont, she found herself enjoying the rolling countryside more each time. At first she had been frustrated by the area's sparseness, but it had started to grow on her. She pulled into the long driveway, and as the dirt kicked up around her tires, her gaze was drawn to the east field, where two black horses grazed.

Proposal and wine bottle in hand, she parked in the front and walked up to the door. Taped to the door was a precise handwritten note. *Libby, go around to the side family entrance.*

Libby tugged the note off the door and walked around the house, past the boxwood hedges and blooming beds of pansies and irises.

This entrance, recently outfitted with a new door, had no overhang. Before, she had not paid much attention to it. She climbed the newly laid wooden steps and knocked. Seconds later, hard footsteps crossed the kitchen, and the door snapped open.

The woman standing there was heavyset. White hair was cut short and brushed back off her round face, and she appeared to be in her seventies. She wore a loose-fitting navy-blue dress and black sensible sandals.

"Mrs. Reese." As the woman stared at her, Libby gripped the note and the bottle of wine. "I'm Libby. Elaine invited me to dinner. I was the photographer at Ginger's wedding."

"What a soggy wedding that was. I don't think I'll ever get the floors cleaned right again. And call me Margaret. No one calls me Mrs. Reese. Elaine said you were coming. Come on inside."

"Thank you. Am I early?"

"No. Others are always running late."

"What did you think of the pictures I took at Ginger and Cameron's wedding?"

Margaret's face softened. "Elaine showed me how to open the link, and we had a grand time looking at them. They're real pretty. Even in the rain."

"There's no planning the best moments."

"Ginger is a brilliant doctor but would never make a good meteorologist," she said with a laugh.

"She was lucky to get married in such a pretty place."

"Yes, she certainly was."

Libby held up the bottle. "I have wine."

"Isn't that sweet of you. And what's the folder?"

"A proposal for Elaine."

"I'll take it and see she gets it."

Libby hesitated, always liking to deliver her proposals directly. She handed the folder off to Margaret and followed the woman into a fully renovated kitchen that any chef would have envied. The countertops were white marble, the upper and lower cabinets a deep blue, and the large appliances stainless steel.

When she and her mother had toured the house, they had been escorted through the kitchen. Before the renovation, the countertops had been fashioned from wood, the large farmhouse sink had been white porcelain, and the stove, considered cutting edge at the time, had been white enamel with chrome trim, four burners, and two ovens.

"I remember the setup of the old kitchen. Did you cook on that white stove?"

"I learned to cook on it, and it served me well until Mrs. Carter replaced it."

The room smelled of freshly baked bread, hints of cookies, and the savory scent of a roasting chicken. "Smells delicious."

"I miss that old stove." Margaret laid the proposal on the desk tucked in a nook and returned to the stove. Staring at the buttons, she said, "This kitchen has only been in place a week, and I still don't know my way around it. The old kitchen had its quirks, but so do I. We were a team. But this new stove and that refrigerator are strangers to me. Colton turned on the oven for me, but I can't figure out how to operate the burners."

Libby had been in enough professional catering kitchens in the last few years. She pressed the black knob and twisted. A flame appeared. "There you go."

Margaret drew in a deep breath, nodding. "Push and twist. I should have known."

"Would you like me to chill the wine?"

"Swap it for the other chardonnay in the refrigerator. And if you can find the wine opener, that would be great. I have no idea."

"When I moved into Dad's house in January, it took me weeks to figure out what was where."

Margaret opened a box of fresh elbow macaroni. "Elaine said it was a nice funeral."

"I didn't realize she'd gone. The church was so full I didn't get the chance to see everyone."

Libby swapped her bottle for the cold one in the refrigerator and opened and closed three or four drawers before she found one jammed with a collection of odd utensils. She wasn't sure how they'd gone from wine to funerals.

Minutes later the bottle was open and sitting next to two glasses from the cabinet. "Can I pour you a glass?" Libby offered.

"I don't drink as a general rule. But you go on."

Libby poured a glass. "Have you worked at Woodmont long, Margaret?"

"Came here to work a few years before Miss Elaine was born."

"You must have been a child."

"Eighteen years old."

"And you've been here this entire time."

"I have. Helped Miss Olivia raise Elaine when her folks died. Met my husband here and raised my kids on this property." Margaret spoke with pride. She was as much a part of this place, maybe more so, than the Carter family.

The woman's entire life had been spent in such a small area. Was this what the rest of Libby's life was going to look like? "That's amazing."

Margaret peered in the pot. "Good, the water is boiling. I must admit this stove works a good deal faster than my old one."

"What are you making?"

"Noodles for the boys. They'd starve without them. I've roasted a chicken for us along with potatoes and a salad."

"Terrific. Can I help you with anything?"

"You can help me set the table. It would have been done by now if I hadn't had this stove to tangle with."

"Sure."

Sipping her wine, Libby crossed to the long mahogany table and set down her glass. She smoothed her hand over the polished wood, which smelled faintly of lemons. The dishes were Wedgwood china. They were ivory with faint blue flowers ringing a silver edge. The glass was crystal. "Putting out the finest, I see."

From the refrigerator Margaret removed a glass pitcher filled with ice tea and sliced lemons.

"Elaine wanted to use the best. Though I'm giving Sam and Jeff plastic cups no matter what Elaine says."

Libby set the seven plates out carefully and placed the silverware. Glass went just above the knife and spoon. She folded each green linen napkin on several diagonals, creating seven pyramid shapes.

"Well, look at you," Margaret said.

"Hard to work in the wedding business and not know how to fold a napkin."

"I thought you took pictures."

"I've spent plenty of time in the catering kitchens eating a quick meal and helping the staff in a pinch. I not only can fold napkins and turn on stoves, but I also can cut a wedding cake in even slices and sew up torn or ripped wedding dresses," she said with a laugh.

"Torn dresses?"

"Amazing how many grooms and fathers of the bride step on dress trains."

The sound of barking and young boys' laughter had her turning to the window to see Colton and his two sons walking toward the house with Sarge and Kelce. The boys were throwing a ball, but only Kelce chased it. Sarge yawned.

Colton had changed into a light-blue shirt and clean jeans. His hair was brushed off his face, and he had shaved. The boys were also dressed in clean jeans and T-shirts. And like their father, each boy had his damp hair brushed back, showing a few freckles from the sun.

"The world is about to stop turning," Margaret exclaimed while smiling at the boys. "It was hard enough getting those boys cleaned up for the wedding, and now they're cleaned up again! Tonight must be for your benefit, Libby."

"I didn't realize I was such a big deal," Libby said.

"Oh, you're all right. Elaine has been a nervous Nellie since she invited you to the property this morning. Is the house clean enough? What food will she like? What should I wear? What will we do? Endless fretting."

"Why fuss over me?"

Margaret shrugged. "You'll have to ask her."

The side door opened, and Colton, keeping Kelce and Sarge outside, hustled his two young sons into the kitchen. His gaze swept briefly over Libby, and she had the vague sense he liked what he saw.

Desire had once burned in Jeremy's gaze, but the fires had dimmed with each miscarriage. Their sex had become mechanical as they had focused on making a baby, and when that had failed, his desire had turned to something that was less. It was as if he no longer saw her as a person, a woman, and he pitied her on some level. That pity was what drove her out of the house.

There was no sympathy in Colton's gaze, and for a brief moment she remembered that it had been two years since she had been intimate.

"The dinner smells good," he said, striding toward the stove. He kissed Margaret on the cheek. "Hope there's enough to feed an army."

"You and your two privates are the closest thing," Margaret said.

The boys lingered close to their father, both staring up at Libby. The youngest boy was a replica of his father and had dark hair and thoughtful brown eyes. The older one was a shade fairer and had more freckles over the bridge of his nose.

"Libby, I'd like you to meet my boys," Colton said. "Jeff is the older of the two, but Sam is only a year behind him."

"I remember you two from the wedding," she said, smiling. "You boys looked very handsome in your suits." Like their father, they had worn dark-blue suits, white shirts, and no ties.

Colton coaxed Jeff forward with a gentle nudge. The boy extended his hand to Libby. "I'm Jeff. I'm seven."

"He's six," Sam said.

Jeff shot his brother an angry look. "I'll be seven in *two* weeks. Close enough."

"You're *still* six."

She took Jeff's hand, surprised by the strength of his grip. "I'm Libby McKenzie. Pleased to meet you."

The younger boy, not to be ignored, elbowed his way past his brother. He put out his hand, waiting for Libby to shift her focus from his brother to him.

When she did, he grinned. "I'm Sam. I'm really five, and I'm in kindergarten."

"Wow, that's pretty big," Libby said.

Jeff rolled his eyes. "I'm almost in second grade. That's bigger."

"It is not!" Sam said.

"It is too, dummy," Jeff retorted.

"Watch the language," Colton warned.

"Well, kindergarten is not bigger than second grade," Jeff said.

Libby felt her nerves ease. "I think you both are very big for your ages. I would have thought you both were much older. Maybe fourth or fifth grade."

The boys looked at each other. Jeff looked pleased. Sam scrunched his face as if to say, *"There!"*

"Libby brought wine," Margaret said. "And there's beer in the refrigerator."

"I'll grab a beer." Colton moved to the new refrigerator. "Mom, how do you like all the fancy new equipment?"

"We're still getting acquainted. So far, it's giving me fits."

He handed two sodas to the boys, allowing Jeff to open his own and try to open Sam's. The little boy protested, insisting he could do it himself. Colton waited patiently, watching him struggle with the tab. When he tried to help, Sam refused. Colton left the boy to figure out the can and filled a bowl of water, which he set outside for the dogs. As he grabbed a beer from the refrigerator for himself, Sam held out the can to him.

"Dad, it's broken," Sam moaned.

Colton set down his beer and popped the top on the soda and then his beer. "Here, buddy." He turned to Libby. "Mom has been fighting the old kitchen for years. The burners always needed repair, the old freezer was temperamental, and it's a miracle the house didn't burn down. It was a love-hate relationship."

"Well, I'm not ashamed to say I miss what I now don't have. She was a fine kitchen who served this family for years." Margaret set out a plate of crackers and cheese on the table. Both boys grabbed several chunks of cheese.

The boys were rough and tough with each other, and their aggression surprised Libby a little. As an only child, she had never competed with a sibling for her parents' attention.

Jeff made a face at Sam, who quickly pushed him. The last time she had been pregnant, she had secretly searched Pinterest for images of nurseries. And when the ultrasound had confirmed she was having a girl, her focus had shifted from blues and toy trucks to pinks, little dresses, and bows.

Footsteps sounded on the stairs as Libby took a sip of wine. The soft, mellow blend of grapes tasted lovely, and if she were not so worried about carrying on a conversation with Elaine, she would have indulged a bit more.

Elaine appeared with a bright grin on her face. She smiled at Sam, Jeff, Colton, Margaret, and then Libby. "You all do clean up nicely. My apologies for being late. I was on the phone with Lofton. Turns out she can't make it tonight, so it will just be us."

Margaret cast a pointed gaze at Elaine before she said, "You folks need to get out of my kitchen for another fifteen minutes while I finish up supper. Go on outside and enjoy the weather."

Elaine grinned. "Yes, ma'am."

The boys were out the door first, and as they burst outside, the dogs joined them in their hurried scramble across the yard toward an old oak tree. Colton held back as Libby went next and then Elaine.

"Come and see the letters," Sam shouted to Libby.

"Letters?" she asked Elaine.

"It's been a family tradition for generations to carve one's initials into the tree," Elaine said. "It's said that George Washington himself carved his initials in the tree as he was heading west to survey the frontiers of Virginia."

"Are your initials in the tree?" she asked Elaine.

"They are. My husband and I carved ours together the day we got married."

"You were married at Woodmont?"

"Right under that tree. It was a small gathering. My grandfather had passed, so it was just my grandmother Olivia and Ted's parents and siblings. Margaret and her husband were here. So were Colton and Ginger. Neither Ted nor I wanted to make a fuss."

"What about you, Colton? You on the tree?" Libby asked.

"I'm there somewhere, but I've forgotten where my letters are." He took a long pull from his beer.

She guessed he knew exactly where he had left his mark and that they were attached to initials he did not want to remember right now.

Libby crossed the grass to the tree and ran her hand over the rough bark. There were dozens of letters, some carved deep into the wood and others less legible. Many had dates beside them. '19, '41, '00, '05.

"Who was the last to carve into the tree?" Libby asked.

"Ginger and Cameron. They carved their initials on Friday night," Elaine said.

"What a coincidence. I heard they didn't bury a bottle in the moonshine graveyard," Libby said.

"Sadly, they did not." Elaine's tone was serious, but her eyes danced with humor.

"I warned them, but they did not take heed," Colton said with a grin.

"Where did that moonshine tradition come from?" Libby asked.

"Rumor has it that it started a couple of hundred years ago. The Carter men have always loved a good sip of moonshine, and I think it was their way of paying homage. My grandfather was known to prescribe it from time to time to expectant fathers while they waited on the birth of their child."

"Can I put my *S* on the tree?" Sam asked. "I'm big enough now to hold a knife. Right, Dad?"

"He's not big enough, Dad," Jeff said. "He's not six."

"Daaaad!" Sam shouted. "Tell him I'm old enough."

A faint smile tipped the edges of Colton's lips. "I don't see why he can't start working on his *S*," he mused.

"Can I make mine deeper?" Jeff asked.

"Sure." He fished a penknife from his pocket. Jeff rushed to snatch the knife, but Colton held it out of his reach. "Your brother goes first."

Sam stood a little taller and puffed out his chest. Colton flicked the knife open with a quick flip of his wrist.

"I'm going to hold it too," he said.

"I can do it by myself," Sam said.

"My help or nothing," Colton cautioned. "Your choice, pal."

"Okay."

Elaine grinned as she raised her glass to her lips. "He reminds me of Lofton. Always needing to prove herself."

"How old is your daughter?" Libby asked.

"Twenty-seven. She graduated from the University of Virginia law school last year and is now working for a Washington, DC, law firm. Takes after her father and me. Loves to argue. My grandfather wanted me to be a doctor, and he even set up an internship with me in your father's office, but I could never stand the sight of blood."

"So you knew my dad?"

"Our paths crossed for just a few weeks. I remember how gentle he was with the kids, especially the ones that were afraid of needles. He almost had me convinced to make a run for med school, but in the end, my heart just wasn't in it."

Libby sipped her wine. "I'd say small world, but Bluestone is super small. Did you know my mother?"

"I never met her. After college I moved away, but my grandmother and Margaret kept me updated on the goings-on in town. I remember when they told me when your parents adopted you."

It felt a little odd to have someone Libby barely knew be so familiar with her history. "Dad never mentioned that he knew you."

"I lost total touch with him and didn't catch up with your dad until last fall. We ran into each other and ended up having lunch. He talked about you a lot. He was very proud of you."

Libby swallowed a lump of emotion, hoping a smile would keep tears in check.

Just then, Margaret called them all in to dinner, and Libby was grateful to follow the boys inside. Colton refreshed the dogs' water bowl and set out handfuls of kibble for them.

Dinner turned into a little bit of a blur. Maybe that was the second glass of wine. But Libby listened to the boys tell stories about school, Sam establishing himself as the guy who always needed to upstage his brother. Colton was patient as Sam spoke, but when the boy took a breath, he redirected the conversation back to Libby and her work.

"I'm basically a couples' photographer," she said. "Engagements, weddings, anniversaries, you name it."

"And there's a broad market for that?" He sounded genuinely curious.

"Yes. In fact, business is booming. Which is a great problem to have."

"Did you start off wanting to do this work?" Elaine asked.

"No. I wanted to be an artist," she said, nodding to Elaine. "But it doesn't pay, and my dad convinced me to go to nursing school for a steady paycheck. I became an oncology nurse."

"You have children?" Sam asked.

The honest question was so straightforward it did not knock her off balance. "No, I don't have any children."

Her tone had Colton clearing his throat as he set down his fork. "Sam likes to ask questions. Did he just step in sensitive territory?" Colton asked.

"It's no big secret," she said. "I was married; we tried to have children. None of it worked out." She tapped her ring finger against the side of her empty glass, missing the clink of metal. As tempted as she was to reach for the wine bottle, she did not. Experience had taught her a hangover did not make anything better.

"Your father told me a little about what you were going through," Elaine said.

Again, weird they had been talking about her. "We all have something, don't we?"

"I suppose so."

Margaret rose from the table and reached for her plate and Libby's. "I have dessert. A hummingbird cake."

Libby stood. "I'll help."

"You'll do no such thing," Margaret said. "You're our guest."

Still, she stood and reached for the boys' plates. They had each eaten the noodles and had done an expert job of pushing around the chicken and vegetables while consuming little of both. She carried the dishes into the kitchen and scraped the bits of food into the trash can under the sink.

While Margaret sliced the fruity hummingbird cake, Elaine scooped ice cream. As Colton set more dishes on the counter beside her, faint hints of his aftershave mingled with a masculine scent.

As he scraped dishes, she studied his wrists and again felt a pull she had not experienced for so long. What was it about this guy's hands?

Colton did not remind her of Jeremy in any way, shape, or form. And for that, she was glad. She had her hang-ups, but she was certain there was no desire to re-create what she'd had with an ex-husband. Maybe that was why she was so attracted to him. He was truly different.

Sierra would have called it stress sex. Easier to focus on desire than on what was really happening in your life. Whatever stress she was feeling, it would hopefully pass as soon as she left Woodmont and returned to her real life.

"This hummingbird cake recipe has been in Margaret's family for generations," Elaine said. "How far does it go back?"

"My great-grandmother, I think," Margaret said. "My grandmother made it for me when I was growing up, though then she flavored it with honeysuckle syrup." And then turning to Libby, she said, "I was raised by my grandmother."

Margaret offered no other explanation about her mother, and Libby, who had been on the receiving end of too many intrusive questions, did not press.

Libby helped carry the dessert plates to the table and sat down again next to Colton. Coffee gurgled in a dated percolator that hinted at Margaret's attachment to the old kitchen.

More small talk rattled around the table. Most of it centered on the cake, which was delicious. She drank two cups of coffee and, between the caffeine and the sugar, chased away the effects of the wine.

Finally, Colton gathered his sons, wished them all a good night, and escorted his boys, who were not really ready to leave yet, back to their home, located on the Woodmont Estate.

When Colton drove off with the boys, a welcome silence settled over the house. Libby knew children were work, but the boys had consumed all the energy in the room.

"Lofton always made a racket as a kid," Elaine said, smiling. "Were you a busy child?"

The question hung between them. "Always asking questions. I liked to draw and play soccer. But I didn't have any siblings, so there was no competition for attention."

Elaine frowned. "Did you mind being an only child?"

"It's all I knew. And I lived next door to Sierra, and she and I were like sisters. After Mom died, I spent a lot of time at her house. Her mother took me under her wing, and they're still there for me now."

"But they aren't family," Elaine said.

"Just like it."

"Either way, you're not really alone," Elaine said quietly. "You have such a full life."

She drew in a slow breath. "You're right. I have good friends and a great job. I stay on the go." She smiled, but it felt stilted and a little forced. "Don't mind me. Just having a little pity party at the moment."

Elaine's eyes softened. "Everyone is entitled to a short one. I've certainly had my share over the years."

They stood side by side, neither speaking as their own thoughts walled the other off. The silence grew heavier, and as it stretched, Libby grasped for something to bridge the gap widening between them.

Elaine shifted and cleared her throat. As she looked at Libby, her expression suggested she had more to say. However, she simply smiled. "It was nice having dinner with you, Libby. I look forward to working with you."

"Thank you for dinner. Margaret put my proposal on the desk in the nook. Call me if you have any questions about the prices or anything."

"I'm sure it's just fine. Can you be here tomorrow morning? Colton is cleaning out the greenhouse. Currently, it's in a terrific *before* state, and it would be worth photographing for posterity. Everyone loves a comeback story."

"Sure. I can be here. I'm in town until Wednesday afternoon. I'll see you bright and early."

"I look forward to it."

CHAPTER EIGHT
SADIE

Wednesday, December 24, 1941
Bluestone, Virginia

Sadie shifted gears on the truck, wincing when the engine ground and sputtered. "Don't make that face; you know the clutch sticks sometimes. And it's hard for me to reach the pedals."

"You got to push the clutch in the whole way now," Johnny said.

"I know." She scooted up on the seat, not bothering to look at her brother. She guessed he was frowning like always. "My legs are too short. Pa used to put blocks on the pedals for me."

"Well, I don't know where the blocks got to, so you best grow a couple of inches. You need to drive this truck proper so that it lasts," Johnny said.

She shifted in her seat, hating the way the cold air blew up through the floorboards and froze her backside. "I don't like being out on Christmas Eve when there's a ham waiting for us back home," she said. "I'm starving."

"You've told me a few times. And Dr. Carter's daddy always pays me six dollars for moonshine around the holidays."

"Six dollars. I don't think I've seen that much money ever in one place. You think his son will pay the same?"

"I don't see why not. It's a tradition."

The gears strained as she downshifted to turn a corner. When he frowned, she added, "I don't see why it's so important I drive us up to Woodmont."

"Better get used to driving."

"Why?"

He was silent for a long moment. "I'm not going to be around for a while."

Her struggles to get the stick shift in third distracted her from the full weight of his words. Only when the truck was rumbling along the dirt road did she speak. "What do you mean? Are you leaving?"

"I signed up for the army," he said.

"The army? When did you do that?" The headlights showed barely a dozen feet in front of the truck, but she had driven the roads enough to know there was a sharp curve up ahead.

"I signed up a week ago when I was in Waynesboro making a delivery. They are looking for men to fight."

"Why in the world would you do that? You heard Mr. Sullivan say that war ain't all that easy."

"I suspect because it ain't easy, that's why they're going to need men like me."

She twisted toward him, knowing every bit of shock she felt was on her face. "I need you."

"Not as bad as the country does. Watch the road."

She refocused on the headlights barely penetrating the darkness ahead of them. "When do you leave?"

"The second of January."

"What?" she said, glaring at him again.

He pointed ahead. "The road."

The truck's wheels rumbled over a small pothole, drawing her attention back to the narrow band of headlights. "That's less than two weeks!"

"I know." He stared ahead, his gaze not really looking at anything, especially her. It was as if he felt poorly about his decision at this moment. But his jaw was set in a way that signaled he had made up his mind. He could be so stubborn that she often joked he was part mule.

"What are Mama and I going to do?" Her question was selfish. He was heading off to fight in a war that she wanted no part of, and here her first question was for herself.

"You two will be fine. You'll keep making the shine, Mama's got her piecework sewing, and I'll send money home each month like Danny."

"And the farm?"

"It'll be more work for you, but that's just the way it is."

"Danny never sends money or writes."

"Well, I will. The army pays better than the factory in Waynesboro, and I won't be having to pay for the back-and-forth travel."

"That's why you're making me drive tonight?"

"Might as well get used to it." She had first driven when she was twelve, but her first driving lesson had been cut short when she had hit the side of the barn as she had tried to park. Her father and Johnny had been in the car, and neither had let her forget it for years.

"I don't think you should leave." The panic churning in her belly leaked out in her tone. "Your place is here."

"The war is going to need me. Nazis and Japs are killing people right and left, and someone has got to stop them."

"Why does it have to be you? The army's already got Danny."

"And they're going to need me. Besides, someone's got to do it."

She slowed as the truck approached the twin pillars that marked the entrance to the Woodmont Estate. Downshifting, she made the turn and headed down the long driveway flanked by tall bare trees dusted with snow.

She had never been to the Woodmont Estate, but Johnny had worked here several days in October helping a crew from New York put in a house made of glass. She had wanted to see it, but he had never felt comfortable bringing her along.

As they rode in silence down the long driveway, the bare tree limbs draped across the road, reaching for them like clawed hands. As the truck came over the last rise, Woodmont came into view. It was the biggest house she had ever seen, and every window in the front was lit. As they pulled around the side, she heard the faint notes of music.

"Go in that side entrance. That's where the kitchen is," he said.

Sadie kept silent as he shut off the engine and set the parking brake.

"You need to be on your best behavior, Sadie," Johnny said. "No cussing. Speak when you're spoken to. In fact, better you don't talk at all. You can get long winded."

"I do not get long winded. I just say what's on my mind, and you know my brain is full of all kinds of ideas."

Johnny rubbed the back of his neck with his hand. "Like I said, keep quiet."

As she opened the car door, a gust of icy wind caught it. She barely grabbed it before it all but flew off its hinges. "Damn it."

"No cussing like that," he said.

She slammed her car door, determined to show her brother just how angry she was over his leaving.

Johnny carefully closed his door. "You ain't going to see a revenuer at Woodmont." As they met at the back of the truck, he added, "Better to not speak at all. Let me do the talking."

"I'm going to have to talk to them at some point if they want more hooch." Prohibition had ended a decade ago. During the dry years, her pa had said he could not make the shine fast enough, and the money from it had built their house. The sales were not near the same anymore, but they still got enough orders to make the still worth keeping. The

Carters could have afforded any kind of booze, but Dr. Carter considered the honeysuckle blend a holiday tradition.

"It'll be up to you to make all the deliveries now," Johnny said. "And you'll be mixing the mash too."

"I have been doing that for years."

"Yeah, well, most folks don't know that. They think it was Pa, Danny, and me."

"I'll just keep pretending you're doing it magically from wherever you are."

He lowered the tailgate on the truck. "Tell folks I mixed up a good amount before I left."

"Who's going to believe that?"

"You like to make up stories. If that one don't work, find a better one."

Johnny took the heavier of the two milk crates while she lifted the smaller.

Jars rattled as icy wind off the James River cut through her thin coat. "Must be nice to live in a house like this. Did you ever wonder what it would be like?"

"No. I'm too busy to wonder."

"I bet Gene Tierney lives in a house like this. She's like the Carters. They don't worry a bit about putting food on the table or heating the house in the winter. If they got problems, it's only the kind rich folks have."

"More thoughts to keep to yourself."

The Carter family roots went back over two hundred years, and it was said the first Carter was a Scottish nobleman born a second son. He had made a fortune growing wheat, and his son had continued to build the family farm and had also managed to skirt real trouble during the Revolutionary War.

However, the last couple of generations of Carters had turned to medicine. The latest heir, Edward Carter, had done the same. Like his daddy before him, Edward had a general practice and one day a week donated his skills to the Lynchburg hospital and the poor.

Johnny climbed the side porch steps first and knocked on the door. The kitchen door opened to a tall sturdy woman with red hair and a complexion that was as white as a summer cloud. Mrs. Fritz always wore her hair back in a tight bun, and her dresses, stockings, and shoes were black.

Sadie had seen Mrs. Fritz at church often enough and once or twice had been tempted to ask if her underdrawers were black too. But she had held her tongue, fearing, as her mother often said, her questions were *"too well acquainted."*

"Evening, Mrs. Fritz," Johnny said.

Sadie rubbed her fingers together, wishing her gloves were thicker. "We have the Christmas order for the Carters."

A thick red brow rose. "Come on inside. You and Sadie can set your bottles on the counter."

In the original house, the kitchen had been a separate building located a hundred feet from the house. That kept the risk of kitchen fire spreading low, but it also made for a lot of running back and forth for the help. Dr. Edward Carter's daddy had converted the west side of the house into a modern kitchen complete with a white enamel oven that could heat four pots and roast a turkey in the firebox all at the same time. He had also installed large porcelain farmhouse sinks and built enough counter space to make food for two dozen guests.

Johnny nodded for Sadie to go first, and she gratefully stepped into the warm kitchen. The soft scents of freshly baked biscuits and lemon cake enveloped her. Sugar was too expensive for wasting on baked goods and needed to be saved for money-making mash. However, at Christmas her mother often skimmed a little extra sugar off the top and baked a buttermilk pie. Sadie's stomach grumbled as she thought about that warm pie waiting for her. "Where would you like us to put it?"

"Right on the counter," Mrs. Fritz said.

Johnny set his crate beside Sadie's and pulled off his hat. "We appreciate the business, Mrs. Fritz."

"You never let us down. The dearly departed Dr. Carter always thought highly of you and your father." Mrs. Fritz reached in her skirt pocket and pulled out several bills neatly folded over each other. "Mr. Carter said I owe you five dollars."

As she held out the money, Johnny frowned. He was too polite to remind her the price was six dollars.

Sadie, however, was not the least bit shy about pointing out the error. "Mrs. Fritz, we always get six dollars at Christmas."

Color rose in Johnny's cheeks. "My sister is right about that."

"That's not what Edward Carter told me," Mrs. Fritz said.

Johnny's jaw pulsed, and Sadie could see he was swallowing a good bit of anger right now. He was worried more about hanging on to the bird in the hand than going after the one in the bush. He shook his head and reached for the money. "It's okay, Sadie."

"But Dr. Carter Sr. *always* paid us six dollars if we had his delivery by Christmas Eve." Sadie smiled, hoping it took some of the bite out of her tone. "I know the Lord called him home this past spring, but the order was placed last Christmas."

A door down the hallway opened, and music from a phonograph tangled around male and female laughter as it drifted toward the kitchen. Hurried footsteps raced down the tiled hallway seconds before the door opened.

Standing in the doorway was a young woman barely out of her teens. She had dark hair that curled gently around her heart-shaped face and down over her slim shoulders. Full lips painted a bright red looked vibrant against ivory skin. Her dress was an emerald green with a hem that fluttered just below the knee and drew attention to silk-stocking legs and shiny patent leather heels.

For the first time in her life, Sadie was fully aware of her own appearance. She knew her overalls did not fit her right, and her coat was one of Danny's old ones. Her scuffed boots had come from the church poor box.

When she saw the fancy women in the magazines, she did not feel so plain and, well, country poor. But now she felt every bit of both. She brushed a stray curl from her face and then, noticing her coat's threadbare cuff, dropped her hands to her side. She curled her fingers into a fist to hide her dirty nails and calloused palms.

Standing behind the woman were two young men. She recognized one of the two as Edward Carter. He had always been a fixture at the county fair when his mother and father had been alive. Girls in town whispered that he was as handsome as Cary Grant, but she reckoned Carter was better looking. He had been in England studying medicine when his father died last spring. Folks were still talking about him missing his father's funeral, as if he could have crossed an ocean just like that.

The man beside Dr. Carter was a little shorter and his frame softer and rounder. And if she had to say he looked like an actor, it would be along the lines of Mickey Rooney. Not handsome but right pleasant to look at.

Each man had waxed-back short hair and sported fine dark suits, white shirts, and bow ties fit for a movie premiere.

The trio stared at Sadie and Johnny, but it was Edward who thrust out his hand first. "Johnny, you made it. I was worried you'd not be here by the holidays. Father always loved the honeysuckle moonshine, and we were all hoping to raise a toast to him in his memory tonight."

"Thank you, sir," Johnny said.

Sadie smiled, speaking quickly before Johnny could shush her. "Mr. Carter, sir, that seems like a real fitting tribute. I will say, sir, that your dearly departed daddy always paid Johnny six dollars for a Christmas delivery." She thought the addition of *sir* was a deferential touch. "Mrs. Fritz isn't sure of the price."

Mrs. Fritz squared her shoulders. "You gave me five dollars, Dr. Carter."

"That's the going rate in the summer," Dr. Carter said.

"It is, sir," Johnny said. "But your daddy always paid six dollars at Christmas."

"An extra dollar?" Dr. Carter said.

"Yes, sir." Johnny had a way of speaking that did not stoke tempers. Sadie, on the other hand, had a tone that riled up folks no matter how much she smiled or how many *sirs* she sprinkled around.

"Well, if that is what my father agreed to, then, Mrs. Fritz, please give them an extra dollar," Dr. Carter exclaimed.

Mrs. Fritz turned toward a cookie jar shaped like an apple and, after lifting the lid, rooted around inside until she had a crisp dollar bill. She handed it to Johnny.

Her brother's face was a shade or two redder, and Sadie could not tell if he was embarrassed or relieved. "Appreciate it."

Dr. Carter pressed his hand to the woman's back. "This is my wife, Olivia."

Johnny nodded. "We heard you had married. Our best wishes."

"Thank you, Johnny," Dr. Carter said. "We've been married a full three months now."

Miss Olivia smiled sweetly but did not extend her hand. "It's a pleasure."

Her voice was soft and had a different kind of sound that Sadie supposed was the way it was back in England.

"This is my cousin, Malcolm Carter," Dr. Carter said. "He's spending the holidays with us and celebrating our nuptials."

When Malcolm grinned, it made him all the more like Mickey Rooney. "Pleasure."

"Again, our congratulations to you, Dr. and Mrs. Carter," Johnny said. "We're happy for you both; isn't that right, Sadie?"

"Yes, sir. Real happy." Sadie noted the woman was looking at her. The polite thing to do was to drop her gaze, but Sadie was not feeling so polite right now. They had almost been shortchanged on Christmas Eve of all days.

"Johnny's family has lived in the area for as long as the Carters," Dr. Carter said to Malcolm and Olivia. "What is it you do, Johnny, now that the soapstone plant closed?"

Sadie wanted to point out that the plant had closed nine years ago and that Johnny had never worked there. But her brother's warnings of staying silent kept the words bottled up.

"Working in the machine shop in Waynesboro when I can get the work. But I'll be leaving in a couple of weeks. I've enlisted in the army."

"Army?" Dr. Carter said. "My wife, Olivia, and I experienced the war firsthand when we were in London. The Blitz was a terrible thing."

"What's a blitz?" Sadie asked.

"They are bombing raids," Dr. Carter explained. "The city endured nightly bombing raids for eleven straight weeks. My wife was nearly killed in one of the explosions last summer." He rubbed his hand over his leg. "I would be signing up for military service if I hadn't also been injured in one of those raids. My leg will never be the same."

Miss Olivia did not speak, but her brow knotted, as if the dark memory was not far away. "You be very careful, Johnny," she said. "We will pray for you."

"Thank you, ma'am," Johnny said.

"If I had my way," Sadie said, "I would follow my two brothers into the army and maybe find me a job driving trucks. Heck, I'd be willing to work in a mess hall peeling potatoes if it meant I could go."

Johnny shot her a glance that told her to stay silent. "My sister will be staying put in Bluestone."

"Sadie, can you really drive?" Dr. Carter asked.

"Yes, sir," she said with pride. "Been driving since I was twelve."

"How old are you?" he asked.

"Almost sixteen." She was five months from her sixteenth birthday but close enough.

"Is she a safe driver, Johnny?" Dr. Carter asked.

Her brother did not spare her a glance. "Yes, sir. She knows the roads in the county as well as I do."

"Hey there, I have an idea," Dr. Carter said. "Olivia is going to be on her own much of the days while I work in my office. I often have long hours, and I know she is going to need help getting around. Perhaps your Sadie could assist us, Johnny."

Sadie straightened her back, trying to look a little taller. Her own smile felt as tense as Miss Olivia's hoity-toity face looked.

"She's been driving a good three years," Johnny said. "No one knows these roads better other than my brother and me."

"You still drive that jalopy of a truck?" Dr. Carter asked.

"Yes, sir," Johnny said. "It runs well enough. Never left me on the side of the road, and I'll be leaving it behind with Sadie."

"I can't have Sadie driving Olivia around in your truck," Dr. Carter said. "No offense, Johnny, but it's too rough for her."

"Perhaps not the vehicle for a lady," Johnny said.

"I can drive any kind of car," Sadie said. "Give me a minute or two to figure it out, and I'll have the wheels rolling."

Miss Olivia laid her hand on her husband's forearm. "I don't want to impose on Sadie."

"It won't be an imposition if I'm paying her," Dr. Carter said. "And we both know you can't drive yourself. Without Sadie, your trips into town will be limited to my rare visits."

Sadie knew the cost of ingredients for mash and how much the final product was worth, but she had no idea what the pay for driving would be. "How much would you be willing to pay?"

Dr. Carter smiled at her as if she were a young child. "How does a dollar a day sound?"

Johnny nodded and, before she could toss out a reply, said, "That sounds fair. When would you like her to start?"

"The first of February?" Dr. Carter said.

"That sounds just fine, sir," Johnny said.

"Sadie, can you find your way back up here?" Dr. Carter asked.

"Of course," she said, doing her best not to laugh.

The money Sadie could earn as a driver would go to her mother, but she figured she could shave off a nickel or two and add it to her savings stashed under the floorboards of her room.

Miss Olivia's grip on her husband's arm was barely perceptible but Sadie saw it. It felt like a subtle slight, and that annoyed her. She never cared what rich folks thought about her, but having this woman look down her nose at her stung.

"That's okay," Sadie said. "If Miss Olivia's afraid, it's best not to push her." She tried to sound as sweet as she could, but when Johnny shifted his stance and tossed her a sideways glance, she knew he had seen right through her.

Malcolm's lips twitched with a small smile, and Dr. Carter was nodding as if he agreed with Sadie. "I say, Olivia, I think Miss Sadie has thrown down the gauntlet." Dr. Carter glanced over at his wife. "Darling, if this arrangement doesn't suit, then of course, you don't have to accept."

Miss Olivia's red bow lips pursed. There was a flash of challenge in her blue eyes as she stared at Sadie, suggesting she was not as cotton candy soft as she first seemed. She had more going for her than just a pretty face.

"On the contrary," Miss Olivia said, "I'm not the least bit concerned. I simply did not want to trouble the young lady."

"I doubt Sadie would be bothered by a job," Dr. Carter said. "The Thompson clan is known for being hardworking."

"In that case, I would be more than grateful if Sadie is available to drive me." Miss Olivia still did not extend her hand, but that might have been the way in England.

Sadie was already wondering how fast a dollar a day would add up. Hell, she might earn enough to buy herself a magazine or, better yet, a nice dress.

CHAPTER NINE

MARGARET

Monday, June 8, 2020
Outside of Bluestone

As Margaret drove off, she waved to Elaine, who was standing on Woodmont's porch, a thick shawl wrapped around her thinning shoulders. The evening air was not cool enough for a shawl, and Margaret worried that Elaine was again feeling poorly.

The dinner had gone as well as could be expected, though Margaret found it awkward to have Libby seated at the table. Everyone was on their best behavior, and the boys' antics had actually helped ease the tension and worry Elaine was carrying.

She drove down the long driveway and then made a left at the road. Seven miles down the road, she turned into the much-shorter driveway of her home. It was a white clapboard house with a front porch big enough for a couple of rockers. The yard was neatly cut, and the azaleas planted by Colton and the boys always made her smile.

Her knees ached as she stepped out of the car. Carefully, she rolled her head from side to side before she crossed the lawn.

Her grandmother had raised her in this house, and after GeeMom had passed, Margaret had stayed on here. Miss Olivia had hired her when she had turned eighteen, so there had always been money to be earned. She had been thirty-one when she had married Woodmont's new gardener. He had moved in with her, and together they had raised Ginger and Colton here.

Ginger had tried to get Margaret to move to Charlottesville and into a one-level house close to her, but the city was too bustling for her taste and too far for a twenty-five-mile daily commute to Woodmont. She did not know what she would do if she could not see her boys every day.

This old house was barely twelve hundred square feet and had only three tiny bedrooms. Over the years, there must have been several coats of off-white paint added to the walls, but in the evening light, it looked faded and a little tired. She had been meaning to change the color to something brighter. Yellow, maybe. She had told herself there was too much work at Woodmont, and now that Elaine was getting over her sickness, taking time to change a paint color seemed silly.

She walked over to the dining room table, piled high with magazines and china she had still not put away from her own Easter supper with Colton, Ginger, and the boys.

After flipping on the lights in the kitchen, she walked past an unfinished one-thousand-piece puzzle she had been working on for five years. She crossed the small room to the electric teakettle that Elaine had given her last Christmas and filled it with water. A push of the button, and it was heating.

As she waited, she looked at the puzzle, disappointed by her limited progress. She had finished the border but had done little to finish the image featuring an enormous basket of sleepy golden retriever puppies. She should just give up and dismantle it, but her grandmother had always complained that no one saw anything through. Margaret's own mother had not stayed around to raise her, so she had decided years ago she would style herself like her grandmother and never quit anything. So the puzzle stayed.

When the kettle whistled, she fished a tea bag from the cabinet and dropped it into a favorite mug covered in honeysuckle flowers. It had belonged to her grandmother, and though the rim was slightly chipped, she was willing to avoid the rough edge for the sake of the memories.

She poured hot water over the bag, swirling it gently and watching as the water darkened.

Her old phone rang, and she crossed to the wall and picked up the receiver. "Hello."

"It's me, Mom," Colton said. "Just making sure you got home."

"Alive and well."

"Dinner was fun."

"It was nice."

"What did you think of Libby?" he asked.

"I like her. She's a strong young woman."

"What's her deal with Elaine?"

"I don't know," she lied. "Best ask Elaine."

He chuckled. "Fine, don't tell me. I'll see you in the morning."

"Sure thing, son."

"See ya."

She hung up the phone and picked up her cup, running her finger over the chipped edge. She sipped tea and walked over to the puzzle, fingering a few pieces before she lost interest and walked out onto the back porch.

Margaret sat on the vinyl-covered cushions nestled in the porch rocker seat. Gently, she swayed back and forth, sipping her tea and staring up into the cloudless night sky at the bright pinpoints of starlight.

The stalemate she had with her house and her inability to move on toward a new future did not have anything to do with caring for Elaine or Woodmont. It had to do with Libby.

Margaret had been waiting for the girl to return. And now that her father had passed, she hoped the young woman would sink her roots deep in this valley. Libby being here would be good for everyone.

The tea tasted too bitter. She considered adding more honeysuckle syrup but decided it was not worth the bother.

She tipped her head back, tracing her finger over the chipped edge of her mug as she stared at the stars. "I don't know where you are right now, Dr. Carter. But if there's any justice, you're burning in hell."

CHAPTER TEN

LIBBY

Tuesday, June 9, 2020
Bluestone, Virginia

Hours before the sun rose, Libby's eyes popped open, and she was fully awake. She was back in her father's home and sleeping on the couch in the living room. Glancing at her phone, she confirmed it was 3:24 a.m. Willing herself to enjoy the remaining hours of sleep, she closed her eyes and breathed deeply several times. The harder she tried to sleep, the more awake she felt.

She stared at the tiny luminescent stars that she had glued on the living room ceiling when she was in sixth grade. The stars had annoyed her father, but her mother, who had watched her affix them all, had declared them delightful. By then, he never went against his wife's wishes, knowing it always led to an argument. So the stars remained. She was surprised now—and a little pleased—they had survived last year's renovation.

Libby did not have to be at Woodmont until eight. But the longer she stared at the stars, the more worries nibbled at her. Another worst-case list materialized. *Elaine forgets she's hired me. More rain. Overcast skies. All my shots are boring and expose me as the newbie photographer that I really am.*

More aggravated with each passing wakeful moment, she finally tossed back her covers and got up. Carefully, she folded the quilt and draped it over the couch.

Grabbing her pillow, she climbed the stairs and carefully placed the pillow on her bed. In the adjoining bathroom, she turned on the shower. As steam rose, she glanced in the mirror at her hollow cheeks and pale skin. On her return home last night, she'd had a few more glasses of wine, making the grand total too much.

No amount of hydration or coffee was going to soften the dark circles or hollow cheeks. "Damn it, Libby."

She stripped off her oversize T-shirt and stepped under the hot spray, willing it to pummel the stiffness and fatigue from her body. She lathered her hair in rose-scented shampoo and washed with fragrant bodywash. If she did not feel great, she could at least smell good. Twenty minutes later makeup was applied, and she was dressed in black jeans, a loose white T-shirt, and sneakers.

She brewed a pot of coffee and, after filling her cup, moved out to the front porch, where she checked her email on her phone. The tree-lined street was quiet as the nearly full moon hovered just above the horizon.

The emails in her in-box were standard. One client wanted a retouch, complaining her pictures had made her look too heavy. One bride thought she did not look tanned enough and wanted to be photoshopped. There were three new inquiries from potential brides-to-be. And a local real estate group that wanted headshots for the newest members of their million-dollar club. All good for the company, but still boring.

Her mind drifted to the greenhouse covered in moss and dead foliage, concealing a broken fountain and a pack of small animals that had likely lived for generations in the shadows of silence.

She checked the time. Over two hours to go before her appointment. Still, Woodmont was a working farm, and everyone would be up early.

After pouring her morning coffee into her travel mug, she grabbed her cameras and put them all in the back seat of her car. As she started the drive out of town, she tried to script what to say to Elaine and Colton when she arrived two hours early.

Pulling into the long driveway past the twin pillars, she determined her early arrival was attributed to the morning light. For a photographer, it was the purest, and she would capture the best of the greenhouse's domed roof.

Libby parked in the circular driveway and then climbed out of the car, grabbing her cameras and flashlight from the back seat. She strung two cameras around her neck and, after clicking on the flashlight, retraced the path she had driven with Colton and Elaine yesterday. Trees ripe with foliage blocked most of the remaining moonlight, making it tougher to track.

As she eased down the dark road, she calculated how long it would take for someone to find her if she fell. If her body was on the road, less than a few hours, she thought. If she rolled into a gully, it could be considerably longer. After doing the calculations, she moved closer to the middle of the road, knowing rescue crews would have a better chance of finding her and getting an ambulance to the scene so she could be carted to the trauma center in Charlottesville.

Too curious about the greenhouse, she pushed aside fear and followed the glow of the flashlight. The dark road narrowed as it sloped toward the river. The dirt, now mud from last night's rain, stuck to her shoes, staining the sides as she left impressions of her footsteps.

"Damn it."

The morning air was already warm, and by the time she saw the structure, her shirt was damp. The sun was nearing the horizon and bringing with it streaks of gold and orange light.

She angled her body through the open door and moved to the center of the greenhouse. Enveloped by the thick, moist air, she shut off her flashlight and tucked it in her back pocket. She snapped a few pictures of the dome but knew with one glance into her viewfinder the light was not right yet. Good photographers understood the right moment could not be rushed, and if captured, patience and speed were essential.

Seconds grew into minutes as the sun shyly nudged up over the sloping eastern horizon. The hints of light were brilliant.

She moved to the fountain and raised her camera to the dome. She clicked once or twice and glanced at the image. The right time was close. Water dripped, an animal scurried, and somewhere a glass pane rattled slightly in the breeze.

The air thickening, she sensed someone was standing behind her. She turned, expecting to see Colton or Elaine, ready with a babbling explanation about timing and light.

But no one was there. There was only the whisper of wind in the trees that stirred an odd sensation within her.

"Don't be silly," she whispered to herself.

And then, as if a curtain on a magnificent stage had opened, the sun tipped above the horizon and made its entrance. Orange and yellow light kissed the glass dome and expanded into a rainbow of colors. Her mind calmed as she raised her camera, knowing she would get the shot.

She rapidly snapped images, quickly checking the position in her viewfinder before shooting until the sun's first light was spent. When she finally lowered the camera, she was slightly breathless with excitement. Satisfied that she had something special, she was glad she had pushed beyond the day's rough start.

The sunlight illuminated the pane of glass etched with Sadie's name. She crossed to it and ran her fingers over the rough edges.

"Sadie, are you the one haunting this place?" Of course, she did not expect an answer, but when a tree limb outside cracked and fell to the ground, she took that as a yes and hurried outside.

The morning sun made for an easy return journey up the hill toward her car. Ahead, light glowed from the last and largest of the cabins. She knew Colton and his sons lived on the property, and unless there was another family here, it had to be his house. Curious, she kept walking toward his cabin, uncaring that it might look off if Colton saw her.

As she approached his house, the front door opened, and Colton stepped out onto the porch. He scanned the dawn, his face tight with suspicion, as if he had sensed that something in his sphere did not belong. His gaze settled on her.

"Good morning," she said quickly. Her voice, still rusty with sleep, sounded graveled. She cleared her throat.

"Libby, you're early."

"I wanted to see the greenhouse at dawn."

"Why?"

"The light. It's always a little magical this time of day."

Rising early for the sake of magic seemed to amuse him. "Magical?"

"Yeah. It was special. It's a stunning structure. I can see why Elaine wants to save it."

"This is my favorite time of day," he said. "I'm drawn by the soli-tude. The calm before the storm."

"I'm convinced the two are intertwined," Libby replied.

He grinned. "I've fresh coffee brewed if you'd like a cup. The boys are still asleep for another half hour. No chaos, I promise."

She stepped toward him, feeling another tremor of excitement. "The boys aren't so chaotic."

He held the door open as she climbed the steps to the wide front porch. "Then you must be hard of hearing or a saint."

This close she could see his hair was still damp from the shower, and the scent of soap clung to his skin. A tingle warmed her belly.

The cabin was large and spacious but simply decorated with a worn overstuffed couch, a recliner, and a wide-screen television. Kids' shoes lined up neatly on the hearth, hats dangled from hooks on a rack by the door, and wall space was filled with pictures of the boys. There were no pictures of Colton and the boys' mother.

"How long have you lived here?" She followed him toward the small kitchen.

"Two years now." He filled a cup and held it up. "I have milk and sugar."

"Black is fine." She accepted the warm earthenware mug. "And you like living in the country?"

"I was afraid I'd hate it," he said. "But it made sense for the boys having my mom close. Now I love it as much as she does."

She sipped her coffee. She was happy for him and the boys. Always best to enjoy the smooth waters while you could, because choppy ones lurked over the horizon. The seas in her life had been so full of gale-force winds the last few years she welcomed even a small respite.

Her gaze rested on Colton's forearm and the T-shirt snug over a full bicep.

"Crews arrive at eight. They're removing the contents and stripping away all the vines on the outside."

"Shame to see the honeysuckle go."

"It's tangled up in the ivy that's eating into the stone foundation. I'm betting there'll be plenty of repointing with fresh mortar. Once all that is done, we'll shift to the glass."

"You're moving fast."

"That's Elaine. Once she sets her mind to something, it's full steam ahead."

"I'm very intrigued about what story it'll tell."

"That's almost exactly how Elaine put it. She can't wait to figure out why her grandparents suddenly closed it up."

"It would have cost a fortune to build it. So whatever reason they had for walking away must have been powerful."

"Hopefully, we'll figure it out."

"Is Elaine like this with all the projects?" She was intensely curious about Elaine.

He regarded her over the rim of his cup. "I've only worked with her here for a couple of years. She's owned Woodmont for at least twenty-five years, and Mom said she had little interest in the place until recently. I'm glad she's tackling the renovations. Old places like this deserve full attention."

"Does she spend a lot of time here?"

"Since January, a few days a week."

"Do you think she'll make this an event space?"

"I hope she does. It'll ease the money situation, and Woodmont deserves to be admired."

She swirled her cup as more questions churned. "I'm curious," she said. "Nosy, as my mother used to say."

A slight smile tipped the edges of his lips. She noticed a tiny remnant of shaving cream below his sideburns and was so tempted to reach up and brush it away. She would have done exactly that with Jeremy.

Instead, she drank coffee, wondering if she should drive home and take a cold shower.

Small footsteps hit the floor in one of the bedrooms, and then came the steady stream in the toilet. There was a flush and a turning on of the tap. Seconds later, Sam appeared. His hair was sticking up, and a black Batman T-shirt skimmed his knees.

"Dad," he said, yawning.

Colton set down his cup. "Hey, buddy."

Sam yawned again and then rubbed his eyes, his gaze now locking on Libby. "What are you doing here?"

"Having coffee," she said matter-of-factly.

"Oh." The boy padded across the floor and scrambled up on the barstool beside hers. "That's Jeff's chair."

"I'll be sure to move when he gets up," she said.

"He never lets me sit in that chair." Sam scratched his belly.

Colton filled one of the bowls with oat cereal and then milk before setting it in front of Sam. "Eat up, pal. Is your brother awake?"

Sam scooped out a large spoonful of cereal. Milk dripped on the countertop. "I don't know."

Colton shifted his attention to Libby. "Be right back."

"Take your time."

Colton vanished around the corner, and she could hear the low rumble of his voice mingling with the crunch of Sam's cereal.

"Did you have a sleepover?" Sam asked.

Libby looked at the child, realizing quickly the meaning of his words. "I didn't sleep here last night. I slept at my house."

Sam sniffed and rubbed his nose. "Are you Dad's girlfriend?"

She sipped her coffee, feeling her cheeks flush a little. "We just met."

"Oh." He took a second bite and regarded her closely. "Do you know Elaine well?"

"I just met her too," she said. "But I like her."

"Oh."

"I like you, Sam."

"But we just met last night," he said with a puzzled expression.

"Sometimes it works that way."

The toilet flushed, and seconds later Colton appeared with a fully dressed Jeff. His hair had been dampened and combed, but a thick black cowlick stuck up in the back.

"She's in your chair, Jeff," Sam announced.

"It's okay," Colton said.

Jeff looked up at his dad, as if the boy would argue. And then, catching a slight look of warning, he said, "It's okay."

Libby rose up out of the seat, sensing that she was intruding on their morning routine. "That's very nice of you, Jeff, but I'm tired of sitting. Take your seat." And then to Colton, she said, "I didn't mean to intrude on your breakfast."

"You're not. Nothing exciting happening here this time of day." Colton inspected Sam's empty bowl. "Wrap it up, pal. And then put on the clothes I laid out on your bed."

Sam took another bite, chewing slowly as he regarded Libby. "Dad, is she your girlfriend?"

"No, pal."

"Sam and I just had this discussion," Libby said. "He isn't taking my word for it."

"He doesn't take anybody's word for anything," Colton said, amused. "I'm convinced he's going to be a lawyer or a policeman when he grows up."

Sam grinned at Libby. "I could carry a badge."

"Yes, you could," Colton said.

"Do you have a boyfriend?" Sam asked.

"Sam," Colton warned. "Enough with the third degree."

Jeff scooted into his chair. His body relaxed a fraction as Colton set a cereal bowl in front of him and then pulled two brown-bag lunches out of the refrigerator. Each boy's name was written in neat block letters.

When Libby was a kid, her mother had often overslept, and her father had always been working. Being the best pediatrician in the area had left little time for his own family. Breakfast had generally been a banana or a piece of fruit as they had hustled out the door. Lunch had been from whatever money her mother could scrounge from her wallet or sometimes the bottom of her purse. She had never gone without, but there had been no routine.

"You're very organized," Libby said.

"Blame it on the navy."

"It's good," she said. "Chaos can be draining when you're a kid."

"Sounds like experience talking."

"Most of my life has been a little unorganized. Hoping small-town living will tamp it down a notch or two. Once I get past the next two weddings, the plan is to set up my old photography equipment stored in Dad's shed." How many months had she been making that promise to herself?

Outside, the dogs barked. The sounds grew louder and louder until she heard the thud of footsteps on the porch and then a knock on the door.

"I thought Kelce and Sarge were your dogs."

"They are. But when Elaine's at the big house alone, she likes to have them sleep in her room."

The barking grew louder.

"The day has arrived," Colton said. He crossed the small living room and opened the door to Elaine.

She wore jeans, a dark-blue sleeveless shirt, and work boots. Her hair was pulled up into a ponytail, and a splash of rouge added much-needed color.

"Good morning," Colton said. "Looks like everyone is ready to get to work on the greenhouse."

Libby stood. "Morning."

"Libby?" Elaine asked, clearly puzzled.

"I decided to come early this morning," she added a little too quickly as she set her coffee cup down. "I thought the light might be better at dawn."

"You should have called me. I would have gone with you," Elaine said.

"It was so early."

"I'm a terrible sleeper," Elaine said. "Knock on the front door anytime, and there's a ninety-nine percent chance that I'm awake."

"Sure. Okay."

"Ladies," Colton said. "I've got to get the boys ready for school."

"Which means we need to get out of his hair," Elaine said, smiling. "Libby, come up to the main house, and I'll give you a tour while Colton wrangles the boys."

"Sounds great."

"See you soon," Colton said.

A few feet separated them, and again a strong sexual urge rumbled through her body. Sam leaned over and said something to Jeff, and the two giggled.

"I'll leave you to the boys," Libby said.

"Right."

The morning sun had risen well above the horizon, burning off the morning mist. The day stretched out before her.

Kelce and Sarge ran up to Libby, their tails wagging. Kelce dropped a stick at her feet. Libby tossed it, this time putting some heft into the toss. The dog took off running as she leaned down to scratch Sarge, who was now eager for attention, between the ears.

They climbed the back steps and moved into the kitchen, already filled with the aroma of cinnamon and apples. There was no sign of Margaret, but the oven had several items baking.

"Would you like to see some of the pictures I've taken?" Libby asked.

"I would." Elaine reached for a pair of light-blue readers and slipped them on.

They sat at the table while Libby scrolled through the pictures. Several had caught the sun at a stunning angle that split the light into a rainbow of colors.

"These are magnificent," Elaine said.

"Hard to go wrong with a subject matter like this."

"You do any photography for art's sake?"

"Not since high school. I fancied myself a wet plate photographer back in those days. Collected lots of old cameras. The plan was to start up again this summer, but it hasn't happened just yet."

"Why not?"

"Time, I guess. And dealing with Dad's death, and the rest has taken longer than I thought."

"Ah, the rest. It can fill up a great deal of time."

She spoke as if she understood the term amounted to an emotional quagmire that sapped creativity and brainpower.

Libby paused at one shot of the fountain. A bright light swept across the stone, as if she had snapped something fluttering quickly by. She moved to the next image, but there was no light.

When she clicked on the last image, the engraving of Sadie's name in the glass, her attention was drawn to the light. "That's odd."

"It doesn't look from this world."

"It's the kind of place that looks like it could be haunted," Libby joked.

Elaine's expression remained serious. "I believe it is. I think this entire property is filled with restless spirits."

"Why here?"

"Old places often have difficult pasts."

"You said your grandfather built it for your grandmother."

"It was built in the summer of 1941. My grandfather wrote to his estate manager and included the sketch of a solarium he had seen in London while he was practicing medicine there. He ordered construction to begin immediately. When he returned home in November 1941 with his new bride, he presented it to her as a gift."

"That's love."

"I suppose it was."

"How long were they married?"

"Forty-seven years. My grandfather died in 1989."

The oven timer chimed, and Elaine rose and, using mitts, removed the two steaming dishes. One appeared to be bread, and the other cinnamon rolls. "Margaret left these for me last night with instructions to put them in the oven at seven. I thought you or the crews would be hungry. There's also coffee here. Help yourself."

Libby rose and filled a cup, hoping she had not maxed out her morning caffeine quota. As she stood beside Elaine, she noticed the dark, full veins on the back of her hand and the faint mark that indicated a recent IV.

Elaine served up a plate for Libby and then grabbed a ginger ale from the refrigerator for herself.

"You're not eating?" Libby said.

"I'm not much of a breakfast person."

Libby cut into the moist, gooey cinnamon roll, stabbed it with her fork, and took a bite. She almost sighed with pleasure. "Amazing."

"That's Margaret. Never a minute of formal training but can cook with the best of them."

Libby noted that in the morning light, she could see that Elaine's hair was thinning in some spots. She took another bite, wanting to ask but thinking better.

"You can ask," Elaine said, as if reading her mind.

Libby covered her surprise with a sip of coffee. "Excuse me?"

"I've caught you eyeing my arms." Likely subconsciously, Elaine smoothed her sleeves down over her arms.

"I'm sorry. I didn't mean to be rude."

"I never sensed any rudeness. Only curiosity and concern."

"That's the nurse's training," Libby offered. "I'm always diagnosing. It's a tough habit to break."

"It was breast cancer," Elaine said. "Stage three. I was diagnosed two years ago. I've had surgery and finished two rounds of chemo. So far it seems to be working."

"When will you know?"

"By the end of June."

"I'm sorry."

Elaine tapped her finger against the cold ginger ale can. "Don't be. Cancer has a way of stripping away whatever doesn't matter. I wouldn't be here now if it weren't for the treatment."

"Colton said you hired him and started work on Woodmont two years ago."

"I decided the craziness of Washington, DC, was too much. Lofton was immersed in law school, and suddenly the idea of spending the rest of my life living in a congested city didn't make sense. I'm still only here part time, and I'm not sure Ted will ever be able to live in the country. But I spend as much time as I can here."

"I didn't see him on Saturday."

"He's preparing for a trial. He's making this coming weekend longer and arriving tomorrow."

"How long have you two been married?"

"Thirty years in August. We're planning on a big party here at Woodmont. Consider yourself invited."

"That's very kind of you."

"I mean it. I like you, and it would be an honor to have you here. It's going to be a real celebration."

"Thanks. I'll take pictures as my gift to you."

Elaine sipped her ginger ale. "I shouldn't have been surprised by it. The cancer. My mother had it but recovered. She'd still be alive if not for the car accident. And my grandmother also died from it."

Libby paused and then said, "My mother never had a physically sick day in her life. She struggled with mental illness. Of course, neither of those things really mean much to me in terms of genetics. I'm adopted."

"Have you always known about your adoption?" she asked.

"No. I found out when I was twelve. A cousin told me at a family reunion. Looking back, I always wondered how my parents could have thought they could keep it a secret in a small town."

"Do you know anything about your birth family?"

"I know I was born in New Jersey and that my mother was single. My original birth certificate is sealed, so I don't have much beyond some nonidentifying information provided to me by the state." She swirled her coffee cup. "If I can work up the courage to go through Dad's desk, I might find something about my past."

"You haven't looked yet?"

"Lots of changes in the last year. I'm not quite ready for another one."

"You might be one day."

"I'm sure I will."

"Discovering your roots is important."

"I want medical information more than anything. I've had three miscarriages. It would be nice to know if that kind of thing runs in the family. Peace of mind, I guess. A heads-up would be welcome."

"I'm sorry about your miscarriages."

Her words carried a deep empathy that was touching. Personal suffering had a way of helping to bond with another's misery. "Thanks."

"When did they happen?"

"The last was nearly two years ago. I made it to fourteen weeks." She resisted the urge to skim her hand across her belly and search for the faint flutters.

"I had no trouble carrying Lofton. My grandmother Olivia had several miscarriages in the 1940s."

"The greenhouse was built for her, right?"

"Yes."

"What can you tell me about her?"

"She met my grandfather, who had been studying at Oxford. Apparently one of their first dates was in her parents' solarium. They fell in love. Her parents wanted her away from the bombings in London, so they encouraged the two to marry quickly in London so Olivia could come to the United States."

"She must have led an interesting life."

"She did. Very independent woman. She was an artist and an avid gardener. She kept detailed notes and made lovely drawings of the flowers she planted."

"She was your paternal grandmother?"

"Yes, my dad was born in 1943."

"And the miscarriages?"

"They came before he was born. She only had my dad."

"Only?" An unexpected bitterness had seeped out.

"I didn't mean that the way it sounded."

"I understand," Libby said.

"My parents were killed in a car accident. My grandparents raised me. They were both very kind to me. It was important to my grandmother that I get a good education and be able to support myself. She often said if not for the war, she would have continued her schooling. I'm a lawyer because of her."

A large truck rattled down the driveway, carrying a large construction dumpster.

Colton drove his truck toward the driver and stopped. Each talked, and she could see the truck driver laugh. He seemed to know Colton and was comfortable with him. The driver nodded, and the vehicle headed for the dirt road that led toward the greenhouse.

Elaine's phone rang. "Colton. Yes, I see it. Okay, I'll walk down and make sure the dumpster is placed in the spot you designated." She slid her phone into her pocket. "Colton will be back in twenty minutes. He's left instructions for the driver explaining where to place the dumpster. He just wants me to double-check. Walk with me?"

"Sure."

The two followed the truck down the hill, and as they grew closer, they heard the beeping of the vehicle as it backed up.

Libby surveyed a spot boldly marked with a handwritten sign. Colton's directions were simple and crystal clear. PUT THE DUMPSTER HERE.

"I didn't see it in the dark, but now it's hard to miss," Libby said.

"Colton doesn't like to leave anything to chance."

As the driver backed up, Elaine hurried to the driver's side and motioned him back several more feet. The driver complied and then lowered the dumpster.

Elaine returned to Libby's side. "Colton has this entire project mapped out. He needs the dumpster accessible but clear of the road so his subcontractors can get in."

"Who else is coming?"

"I've lost count," Elaine said, smiling.

With the dumpster in place, they exchanged waves, and he drove off.

"Mind if I have another look inside?"

"By all means," Elaine said.

As Libby stepped through the front door, she was amazed how the extra hour of light had transformed the space. It reminded her of an old bear, stretching and yawning after a long hibernation. She could feel the potential for life, and whatever spirits she had imagined had vanished.

She walked to the fountain, running her fingers along its marbled edge. She tried to picture Olivia here, standing in this spot. They had both wanted children and lost them. Olivia eventually had gotten her wish.

"The greenhouse in its day was full of orchids," Elaine said.

Her gaze skimmed the bed filled with weeds and dirt. "How do you know?"

"Olivia's detailed gardening journals. Each journal began in the spring and went through to Christmas."

"How many years did she keep it?"

"Until Olivia closed it in the mideighties."

"Did you ever ask her about why she closed the greenhouse and stopped journaling?"

"A couple of times. She never answered me." Elaine smiled. "But I suppose she was just getting older."

"Could I see the journals?" Libby asked.

"Sure. Anytime."

Libby picked up a smooth stone from the fountain. She rubbed her thumb against its dark-gray surface, now very curious about Olivia Carter.

A horn beeped three times in the distance, drawing Elaine's attention toward the main house. "Three beeps. Sounds like my husband is here."

"I thought he wasn't due until tomorrow," Libby said, setting the stone back in the fountain.

"He worries about me." The words were wrapped in affection.

"That's sweet."

"Come on. I'd like you to meet him."

"Sure."

Libby followed Elaine toward the main house. In the circular driveway stood a man beside a black Mercedes. He was in his early sixties, tall, with a build that looked as if he had been athletic in his younger days but had grown soft sitting too many years behind a desk. He wore jeans, a white shirt, and brown shoes that looked too polished for farm life.

"Ted, this is a nice surprise." Elaine hugged him and kissed him on the lips.

His gaze studied his wife's face as his hand came up to the small of her back. "How's it going?"

"Great. We're cleaning out the greenhouse today." Elaine turned toward Libby. "I'd like you to meet Libby McKenzie. She's going to be photographing this project."

Ted stretched out his hand to Libby and wrapped long fingers around hers. His grip was firm and his gaze direct. "Pleasure to meet you, Libby. I hear good things about your photography work."

"Thank you."

"Elaine said you handled yourself very well during Saturday's wedding with the downpour."

"If you don't count the monsoon, the day went off without a hitch." Libby grinned.

Ted chuckled. "What's a wedding without a little drama?" Ted's face sobered with his next sentence. "Libby, we were sorry to hear about your father's passing."

"Thank you."

"I met him once when our daughter was about two. Lofton had a terrible ear infection while we were visiting Woodmont. Your dad was on call that night. He fixed Lofton right up."

"Dad was always great with kids. I'm still getting letters from former patients sharing lovely stories about him."

"I know I was glad he was here for me that night," Ted said.

Colton's truck crested the hill. He parked and, when he got out of his truck, offered his hand to Ted. "Ted, this is a nice surprise."

"Checking on my girl," he said as they shook.

"Your girl is doing fine," Elaine said. "She had dinner with Libby, Colton, the boys, and Margaret last night."

"Sounds like it was a party."

"We'll do it again when Lofton arrives." Elaine turned to Libby. "Can you make it this Friday?"

"I can't, Elaine. I'll be in Richmond shooting a wedding."

"That's right. I forgot. Maybe Sunday when you return?"

"I won't be good company for anyone," Libby said. "I'll be knee deep in edits for a few days afterward. That's when the real work begins."

"We'll find another time," Ted said.

"I'll set a place at the table if you finish early," Elaine said.

"If you're going to the trouble, I'll make my best effort but may be running late."

Elaine grinned. "Great."

"I don't know about you all, but I'm starving," Ted said. "I hope that's Margaret's baking."

Elaine chuckled. "Yes, rest assured it's not my cooking. Libby, I'm the worst. I could burn water."

Libby held up her hand. "It's an elite club."

Elaine high-fived her. "But a noble one."

"Best you all clear out," Colton said. "The crew I hired is ten minutes out, and it's going to get pretty busy down there."

"How long will it take to clean out the greenhouse?" Ted asked.

"Two days, if there are no surprises. Once we have the overgrowth stripped away and debris cleared out, we'll check the structure and repair the glass. By Sunday, there should be some solid progress."

"We leave it to you," Ted said.

Libby glanced back in the direction of the greenhouse, feeling a pull she couldn't describe. "There are no secrets that time doesn't ultimately reveal," she said, more to herself.

Elaine stilled. "Where did that come from?"

"A seventeenth-century French playwright, I think. Must have seen it on a plaque or a Pinterest page," Libby mused.

"The greenhouse had its secrets, I'll wager," Colton said.

Libby felt a lift in her spirits she had not felt in a long time. "I can't wait."

CHAPTER ELEVEN

SADIE

Monday, February 2, 1942
Bluestone, Virginia

Sadie was nervous as she drove onto Carter land without her brother. For all her talk just before Christmas about being the best driver, she was scared of the Carters. They were rich, and even though her mother said rich folks put their pants on just like the poor, Sadie knew different. They lived by their own set of rules.

The old engine groaned as Sadie downshifted and drove along the winding road toward the big house. Last week's snow had melted, but her mother had said to expect a good bit more. Winter was not nearly finished with anyone yet.

Woodmont came into view. The brick exterior without the green wreaths wrapped in red bows looked bleak and unwelcoming. The trees were bare, and the only splash of green came from the boxwoods that filled the front beds.

Sadie hated this time of year. It was like the world was asleep, and they were all just waiting for spring.

She hated Bluestone even more now that Johnny was gone. She and her mother had driven him the twenty-five miles to the train station in

Charlottesville. None of them had said a word in the truck, and when Sadie had hugged Johnny on the train platform, she and her mother had both cried like small children.

She downshifted and drove to the side of the house and parked next to the kitchen. She shut off the engine, waiting as the motor sputtered and coughed itself still before setting the parking brake.

Her mother had tried to get her to wear her Sunday dress. "Important to make a good impression," she had said.

But Sadie had insisted it was too hard to shift the old truck's gears when she was wearing a dress. Plus, there was no telling when the engine would up and stop on her, and she would be forced to climb up on the front bumper and fix whatever was broken. Engine grease was a sure way to ruin Sunday best.

Still, she had let her mother put a comb to her auburn hair and smooth the curls down as best she could before fastening it back with a ribbon. She was wearing the best overalls she owned and a clean shirt and had brushed all the dirt off her scuffed brown shoes.

Sadie hugged the frayed folds of her coat close, conscious that the buttons did not match. She hurried up the steps and knocked on the kitchen door.

She turned her back to the door, staring at the land that rolled down toward the river. Without the leaves on the trees, the porch offered an unobstructed view of the James. The waters were meandering slowly today, as if they too did not care much for the cold.

The door snapped open behind her, and she turned, expecting to see the cook. Standing in the threshold was Edward Carter, a frown creasing the lines of his face. He was dressed in gray suit pants, a white shirt with the sleeves rolled up to his elbows, and a vest cut from the same fabric as his pants.

"You're late," he said, glancing at his wristwatch.

"It's eleven a.m., just as we agreed." Sadie had gone to the general store and used Mr. Sullivan's phone to call the Carter house last week.

She had asked Mrs. Fritz the time twice and had scribbled it on a piece of butcher paper.

Her rebuttal appeared to irritate him more. "The time was ten."

She slid her hands into her pockets, ready to pull out the note, when her mother's warning rang in her ears. *No sass, girl, even if you're right.*

"Sorry about that, sir," she said. "Does Miss Olivia still want me to drive her into Charlottesville?"

"As luck would have it, she is just finishing up breakfast and should be ready any minute. You're lucky she runs so late."

"Yes, sir."

"Come on inside. As soon as she arrives, I'll show you both to the garage and familiarize you with the car. Then I'm afraid I won't be able to stay. I've patients to see this afternoon in Lynchburg."

"Yes, sir."

"Which means if you two girls get into trouble, I won't be able to help. We do have a telephone at the house and one at the hospital. Do you know how to use one?"

"Sure I do. But we won't get into trouble. We'll take it slow and steady."

"Your brother wrote me a letter, telling me again what a good worker you are. Don't prove him wrong, young lady."

She would have liked to see the letter, just to have another piece of her brother. "Johnny's never wrong about anything."

Dr. Carter nodded, satisfied with the answer.

Sadie stepped into the kitchen, savoring the warmth as it soaked into her bones. She wished she could store some of that heat somehow for the ride home later.

"I'll let Olivia know you're here. There's a plate of biscuits on the table if you're hungry. Your brother says you always have an appetite."

That surely was true. "Thank you."

Unrolling his sleeves, he pushed through the swinging doors and vanished inside the house. She lifted a red-and-white-checkered cloth. Underneath was a plate of beautiful warm biscuits staring up at her. She took a bite out of the first and then gobbled the rest of it in seconds. It would have been better to eat it slowly like a lady, but there had been little extra at breakfast this morning at home. She had told her mother to eat the extra herself because she had been ailing from a cold for a couple of weeks.

Sadie removed a handkerchief and wrapped two biscuits and stuffed them in her pocket. Heeled footsteps sounded in the outer hallway as she pushed a second biscuit whole in her mouth.

Miss Olivia pushed through the swinging door, hurriedly brushing back a dark curl from her milk-white skin. She was dressed in a brown dress with embroidered flowers along the hem, which hit her slender legs midcalf. Her shoes were polished and looked made of soft calfskin, matching the purse dangling from her forearm.

"Good morning, Miss Thompson," Olivia said.

Sadie swallowed and smiled. "Morning to you, ma'am." Biscuit crumbs gathered on her cuff, which she quickly brushed away. "You can call me Sadie. Everyone does."

"Sadie it is, then."

Edward arrived, and Olivia smiled up at him and kissed him meekly on the cheek.

Some of the frown on Dr. Carter's face softened. "I want you to be careful today."

Olivia grinned. "I will." She opened her purse and removed gloves. "I don't see how a ride in the country can be all that dangerous."

"The roads are still icy in spots."

"I've survived far worse." Olivia sniffed.

Ignoring the comment, Dr. Carter shrugged on his own wool coat. "If you ladies will follow me, I'll show you the car."

Unhurried, Olivia carefully tugged on a soft kid glove. "Have you really been driving since you were twelve, Sadie?"

"Yes, ma'am."

"I'm from London, and many of us don't drive at all."

"Driving is the way to get around these parts unless you're willing to walk or hitch."

"How far is it to Charlottesville?"

"Twenty-plus miles, give or take."

"Ah."

Edward opened the kitchen door, allowing in a blast of cold air. He waited for Olivia and Sadie to pass before he followed, pulling the door closed behind him. "Ladies, let's get you to the garage and see if Sadie is as good a driver as her brother says."

Sadie was better, especially if she could reach the pedals, but she chose not to point that out. Her driving would put an end to Dr. Carter's doubts.

As a cold wind careened over the hill from the river, the trio walked toward what looked like a barn. Dr. Carter's quick steps set a fast pace, and though Sadie could keep up well enough, she expected to look back and see Miss Olivia lagging. She was surprised to see the woman a few steps behind, matching her step for step.

Edward pushed open the barn doors, but instead of horses inside, there was a row of three cars. On the right, a farm truck, and it was the plainest of the three but far nicer than her truck. Next to it was a blue Ford Deluxe coupe with a sleek polished body. Beside it was a green Pontiac station wagon with a big back seat and wood paneling on the side.

A thrill of excitement raced through Sadie as she thought about driving one of the Carter family's fancy cars. Her brother had told her a car was a car, and if she could shift gears in one, she could in another. The main difference, he had mused, was that the fancier models did what they were told, whereas Old Blue had to be sweet-talked into starting sometimes.

These were the kinds of cars she had seen starlets driving on magazine covers. In Charlottesville, there were a few folks with nicer cars, but none were as new as any of these. She wiped the toes of her boots against her pant legs, wishing now she had been more careful to avoid the muddy spots as she walked around this morning. Good Lord, if Johnny could see her now driving such a fancy car, he would be tongue-tied.

"You ladies will take the Pontiac." Edward fished a set of keys from his pocket. "Today, it might be wise to stay on the property and get used to the automobile."

"I thought we were going into Charlottesville?" Olivia said. "I hoped to do some shopping."

"Safety is more important. I don't feel right about turning you two loose on these roads unless I'm certain you'll be safe. Driving can be very dangerous."

"Depends on how fast you go," Sadie said. "Or the roads. If we take it slow and easy, it won't be dangerous at all, especially in a fancy car like this."

A hint of disappointment flickered in Olivia's gaze. "See, Edward, there's nothing to worry about. Sadie is going to treat me like I'm a fragile egg. We won't take any unnecessary chances."

Edward opened the car door and got behind the wheel. "I don't have time to argue. I almost lost you once, and I won't risk it again."

She squeezed his hand. "We're far from London and the bombs here in Virginia."

A smile flicked the edge of his lips as he seemed to realize his beautiful wife was right, though he wouldn't admit it. "I'll show Sadie the basics of driving, and then I'll leave you two to drive up and down the driveway. Don't leave the property."

"We shall observe all safety protocols," Olivia said.

Sadie tugged off her glove and ran her hand over the cold metal. "Can I get inside?"

"I don't see how you're going to drive it if you don't." Edward got out of the car.

Sadie slid behind the wheel, amazed how polished leather smelled so good. Johnny kept his truck clean, but once a hound dog or chickens rode inside, there was no getting the smell out of it.

She smoothed her fingertips over the white wheel, wondering how far she could drive in a car like this. She bet she could make it all the way to New York City or maybe California.

Sadie pulled out the choke button to her right and turned the ignition key. The engine roared to life. It did not cough, sputter, or complain but hummed.

She climbed out and opened the back door. "Miss Olivia, why don't you have a seat, and I can take us for a spin."

Miss Olivia looked at the empty back seat. "I would rather ride up front. I shall be able to see better."

"Sadie, you won't drive too fast," Edward warned.

"No, sir," she said as she closed the back door. "I'll drive her like I would my mama."

"Very well; then I'll observe for a moment and then leave you to it."

Sadie was back behind the wheel and closing her door as Edward crossed around the front of the car and held Olivia's door for her. He closed it carefully and then stepped back a safe distance.

Olivia settled in her seat. "I've ridden in dozens of cars. None ever felt too fast for me."

Sadie released the brake, pushed in the clutch, and shifted into first gear. "Then you weren't driving with the right person."

Olivia laughed. "Try to be restrained around Edward, or he'll never leave."

"Yes, ma'am."

Sadie pressed the accelerator as she eased up on the clutch until the gear engaged, and they inched their way out of the barn. She kept on driving, shifting gears so smoothly she nearly giggled.

She drove around the house and past her old truck, which now seemed a little sad to be left behind. After going around the circular driveway, they made their way to the end of the long driveway.

After ten minutes of them navigating the driveway, Edward backed the coupe out of the barn. He pulled up beside them, and he and Sadie rolled down their windows. "You ladies look like you have it under control."

"No need to worry about us. We're fine. Don't work too hard, dear."

Edward's gaze bore into Sadie. "Be careful."

"Yes, sir."

They waited as he drove past, the muddy earth spitting off his back tires.

"Give it a few more minutes," Olivia warned. "Edward might double back."

"Why?"

"To make sure we're being safe."

"We are."

"I want to go to Charlottesville," Olivia said.

Sadie downshifted, rolling around the circular driveway, back toward the long driveway. "We said we would stay."

"I promised to be safe. I didn't promise to stay on the property."

"To the end of the driveway for starters," Sadie said.

Annoyance pursed Miss Olivia's heart-shaped lips. "We can at least go out on the main road. I want to see the open fields and the mountains in the distance." She adjusted the folds of her skirt and folded her hands in her lap. "I've barely left the property in weeks."

"I don't know. Dr. Carter said to stay put."

"We won't go far." And when Sadie hesitated again, Olivia added, "You aren't afraid, are you?"

Sadie recognized what Miss Olivia was trying to do, but it wouldn't work. "I am. I don't want to lose this job."

"You won't. Now let's go for a short ride."

Sadie paused at the end of the driveway.

"I won't tell," Olivia whispered.

Muttering under her breath, Sadie made the turn and nosed the car down the road. She scooted her bottom closer to the edge and gripped the steering wheel as she searched for any signs of Edward.

"Why did you learn to drive at such a young age?" Olivia asked.

"Daddy needed help with moving supplies, and Mama never learned."

"You must have been terrified."

"First time or two. Then I took a liking to it."

That first day behind the wheel, Sadie had been scared to death. Her daddy had never had much patience, and she'd had a devil of a time learning when to press on the gas so as to let up on the clutch. Once she had done it so quickly the car had bucked, and her daddy had hit his head on the dashboard. He had been madder than hell. Later he had said he was sorry for losing his temper, but Sadie had known not to try his patience.

"Where do you live, Sadie?" Olivia asked.

"On my mama's farm. Not far from here."

"Is that where you make your moonshine?" she asked.

A grin tugged Sadie's lips. "No, ma'am. Making shine on your property is a sure way to get caught. We have a little spot by the river. There are a few little hollows that you can't see from the road."

"Can you show me?"

"That would be too far to drive," Sadie said. "Besides, this time of year, the driving is tougher."

"How well do you think you know this car?"

"Well enough. There's not much to it. The engine is smooth."

Olivia watched as Sadie slowed and downshifted the gears. "You make it look easy."

"It is."

"I rode in several ambulances in London, but I never drove one."

"What's an ambulance?"

"A car that carries injured people to the hospital. London's been under attack for a while now. Bombs from planes catch buildings on fire if they don't tumble first. It leaves a lot of wounded civilians."

"What's a bomb like?"

"Have you ever heard an explosion?"

"No, but my brothers knew a fellow who lost a leg when there was a gas explosion in the mines near West Virginia. What are they like?"

"It's a lot like that, only much bigger and louder. Except the explosion is coming from bombs dropped by planes that can level a city block."

"Are those loud?"

"So loud that the sounds leave your ears ringing for days." Olivia's voice took on a faraway tone as she stared out over the open fields.

"How do you get away from them?"

"There are shelters underground to hide. But no place is completely safe."

"The war is pretty far from here, right?"

"Yes. For now, we're safe."

The road ended at a T intersection, and Sadie, half expecting Dr. Carter to be waiting for them, turned the car around and headed back to Woodmont.

"I would like to learn how to drive," Miss Olivia said with a mischievous grin.

"Why do you want to know how to drive? You have me to drive you everywhere."

"But you might not always be here. It's better that one knows how to take care of oneself."

"I'm pretty sure Dr. Carter will fire me if I teach you how to drive."

"He doesn't need to know. He is rarely here, and this place feels rather small, especially in winter."

"You have that greenhouse to plant and won't have time to learn."

"There's time for both. Teach me. I'll pay handsomely."

"But I'm already getting paid."

"Think of this as a bonus."

Sadie knew at the rate she was earning money in her new job, she might never save enough money to move off the mountain. A bonus from Miss Olivia would speed that process up mightily.

"You won't lose your job, Sadie. I will forbid Dr. Carter from firing you."

"No disrespect, ma'am, but he doesn't look like a guy that takes orders from anyone, even you."

"Don't worry about my husband. I'll handle him."

That was easy for her to say. The engine rumbled, and a look over her shoulder showed no sign of Mr. Carter. "We will just drive back to the house," Sadie said. "We went on the hard roads, and if I push it much more today, I'm going to get in trouble."

There were times when Sadie pushed the edge of her mother's and brothers' patience, but disobeying a man like Dr. Carter just tempted trouble.

CHAPTER TWELVE

LIBBY

Sunday, June 14, 2020
Bluestone, Virginia

There was always a good reason not to fill in the blank. Libby had gotten home from the wedding around one o'clock on Sunday afternoon. Blissfully exhausted, she had fallen onto the couch and slept until three. Energized, she showered and changed into a relaxed-fit top and black linen pants.

She had plenty of time before she was supposed to leave for Woodmont, so she contemplated checking out the shed stocked with her old photography equipment. If that did not suit, she could get a jump on some of the photo editing or even go through the trove of papers in her father's desk.

Instead, Libby made herself a cup of coffee and then settled back on the living room couch. Reaching for her phone, she scrolled through her Instagram account, reviewing the pictures she had posted from the wedding and smiling as she read the comments from several of the wedding guests.

Libby could have stopped there and left well enough alone. But she pulled up Jeremy's page and found herself staring at the couple's smiling faces as they posed in front of the courthouse, holding up their marriage license. Their megawatt smiles beamed on the screen. The license blocked Monica's tummy, but Libby could see that Monica's face was nicely rounded and her breasts fuller. If only Jeremy had been a little fatter or less pulled together.

"Happy. Fat. Happy. Fatter."

The words rolled over and over in her head like a mantra as she scrolled back in time. In April, the two were standing at a country estate that looked a great deal like Woodmont. He had his arm around her, and both were holding up cans of soda.

Jeremy had given up wine and beer all three times she had been pregnant. It had been a solidarity move, showing more than telling that they were in this parenting thing together. He had held her hair back during her bouts of morning sickness. He had never complained when she had asked him to buy mint chocolate chip ice cream at eleven o'clock at night. He had been there for her. Her rock.

And now he was there for Monica. And their soon-to-be baby.

Libby had done everything she could think of to make her pregnancy work. There had been dozens of lists of what to do and not do, and she had dutifully followed each every day. She had resisted the urge to list potential disasters detailing all that could go wrong with her baby. She had been determined to stay positive.

Sitting up straighter, she tossed the phone aside. It was almost five o'clock, and she had promised Elaine she would stop by her place. She still was not sure why Elaine was looping her into this gathering, but the idea of mingling with strangers had far greater appeal than cyberstalking Jeremy.

She climbed the stairs. She always kept the doors to her parents' old room and her father's office closed. It made it easier to pretend she was just here for the weekend and that any second now she would have to get in her car and drive back to her real life.

Since she had moved back in early January, she had not gone in her father's study. Her father had prepaid his housekeeper, Lou Ann, to clean the house every two weeks, and she could tell by the sharp scent of lemon polish that Lou Ann dutifully cleaned without exception.

So when she opened the door to her father's office, she was not surprised to see the polished, clean surface of her father's desk.

Stepping into the room, she could not miss the freshly painted walls.

"Dad, why are you having the inside of the house painted?" It had been one of a dozen visits she had made to his hospital bedside during the last eight weeks of his life. If she was not shooting or editing, she was with her dad.

"I promised myself I wouldn't leave you a mess. The house is going to be in tip-top shape and ready to sell whenever you're ready."

"Dad, we shouldn't talk about selling." This was Libby's denial stage regarding her father's illness. She and denial had met up a few times before, so when it strolled in, it sadly felt like an old friend.

"I want you to take the money and do something nice for yourself."

"Like what, a cruise?" Mention of a cruise sent her mind gathering fresh concerns such as rogue waves, pirates, and shipboard illnesses that debilitated passengers and crew with nausea.

"You could set up a studio."

"I don't need a studio."

"Don't just sit on that house, Libby." His pale hand gripped hers with surprising strength. *"I want you to move on with your life and be happy."*

"I'm happy."

He shook his head and said nothing.

"Don't worry, Dad. I always figure out a way to make things right."

He had stared at her a long moment with clear, bright eyes glistening with unshed tears. *"I've never worried about you, kiddo. You are the strongest McKenzie there ever was."*

Libby hurried down the stairs, grabbed her phone off the couch, and dialed Sierra's number.

She picked up on the third ring. "Yes."

"What are you doing?"

Water from the tap ran in the background. "I'm washing out my mixing bowl so I can bake a lemon cake."

Knowing her friend, she asked, "How many have you already made?"

"Five."

She headed back up the stairs to her father's office. "And why do you need six? Do you have an order?"

"Law of attraction. I'm willing my business to come to me."

Libby glanced up at the fresh pale-gray walls and the white trim. "What say we use my dad's house as collateral for your loan?"

The water shut off. "What? No way. That's your house."

"It's not my house," Libby said. "It was Dad's."

"You can sell it and make good money."

"Yeah, and then I guess I could loan you the money for the sandwich shop renovation, but why not just use it as collateral? It'll save me from having to get a real estate agent."

Silence vibrated over the line.

"Still there?" Libby asked.

"Yes."

"And?"

"If we do this, and I mean *if*, I'll pay you back every cent."

"Technically, you won't owe me any money. You'll owe the bank. As long as you don't default, we're golden." She could have scribbled down several worst-case scenarios. *Sandwich shop doesn't earn a dime, and Sierra defaults on the loan. The sandwich shop burns. Sierra runs off with the money and moves to Mexico with a guy named Manny.*

But Libby did not feel like jotting that list down.

"Is this a yes or a no?"

"It's a yes," Sierra said softly.

"Say it like you mean it," Libby said.

"Are you sure?"

"Yes."

"Seriously?"

"Set up a meeting with the bank. Knowing my dad, the title to the house is in his desk. I'll go through it tonight."

"Okay. Then yes!"

"Good." She looked around the room and for the first time was glad her father had left it to her.

"You've got that thing at Elaine's tonight. I forgot, what kind of party is it again?"

"I'm not really sure."

"Hey, you want to take a lemon cake?"

It was nearly six o'clock as Libby drove up Woodmont's long driveway toward the house. Sitting on the seat beside her was a large cake box filled with lemon cake number three, which Sierra believed was the best of the six.

She spotted Colton's truck parked beside a Mercedes and a Land Rover and was grateful he would be here among the landed gentry. The ping of anticipation was unexpected but kind of nice. It was what she had felt once for Jeremy, what she had seen in Ginger's eyes, and what she had heard in Sierra's voice as she had screamed, "This is going to be so great!"

She gathered up the lemon cake and followed the sound of laughter and music to the east garden. As she stepped through the gate, she was transported back to an issue of *Martha Stewart Living*. It was all that anyone would expect in a slick, glossy lifestyle magazine. A long rustic farmhouse table dressed with white earthenware plates, cobalt-blue

Depression-era glasses, white linen napkins, mismatched chairs that should not go together but somehow did, and a long garland table runner festooned with small vases filled with white roses.

Elaine stood at the head of the table. Her coloring was better today, and she was laughing, surrounded by her husband and daughter, who was a carbon copy of her mother.

Libby did not look like her adoptive parents, and it had always sparked questions about whom she did resemble. She had asked her mother a few times about her birth mother, but the question had always put her mother in such a dark mood she had stopped asking.

As she approached Elaine, her stomach tightened with nerves. As if sensing her, Elaine looked up and smiled. "Libby, you made it."

Libby held up the cake. "Thank you for having me."

Elaine took the cake. "That's very sweet of you."

"My neighbor Sierra Mancuso is opening a sandwich shop soon. She's very good, and she wanted us to enjoy it."

"It smells amazing."

"It is."

Ted came up beside Elaine. "Welcome back. I know I'll be having at least two pieces. I know Margaret won't mind an unplanned dessert."

"Ted is grilling, and Margaret is just finishing up a couple of side dishes in the kitchen. I did set the table," Elaine said, laughing. "It's the extent of my culinary talents." She turned toward her daughter. "I would like you to meet Lofton."

Ted took the cake from Elaine, and as he set it in the center of the farmhouse table, Elaine clasped her daughter's hand and tugged her forward. "This is Lofton. I think I told you she just graduated from the University of Virginia law school."

Libby shook her hand. "Nice to meet you, Lofton. And congratulations on the law degree."

"Thank you," Lofton said. "Mom tells me you took some amazing pictures at Ginger's wedding."

"I think I got a couple of great shots." For some reason, she felt the need to toot her own horn.

Ted handed Libby and Lofton glasses of red wine. "I opened a bottle Elaine and I bought in Naples last year while in Europe. Seemed the perfect night to try it."

The warm fruity flavor tasted good, and the alcohol would soon take the edge off. "I saw Colton's truck out front." She wasn't going to ask a forward question about whether he was coming or not, even though she hoped the extra place setting was for him. "How is the greenhouse coming?"

"It looks fantastic," Elaine said. "The vines are all stripped away, and the inside is all cleaned out. We'll have to walk down after dinner."

"I'd like that."

"Next up is to remove the stone flooring and excavate down so he can install a new gravity-fed water system. That starts in a day or two. I have a few of Olivia's early gardening journals. You said you were interested."

"That would be great. I'll have them back to you shortly."

"There's no rush," Elaine said.

"Are you giving Libby my great-grandmother's journals?" Lofton asked.

"Sure," Elaine said. "Libby is photographing the estate for me. If we go into this wedding venue business as you have been suggesting, then we'll need photographs with background history."

Lofton's polished finger tapped against the side of her glass. "Yes, but she doesn't need the journals."

"Lofton, help me with the grill," Ted said. "I don't want to burn the steaks."

As if sensing a warning in her father's tone, Lofton grinned. "Sure, Daddy."

Lofton and Ted retreated to the grill. Libby took another sip of wine.

"You know what?" Libby said. "I'll take a raincheck on the journals. I don't have time to read them anyway."

"You strike me as the kind of woman who finds the time, and Lofton has just become a little overprotective since I got sick. Don't worry about it. I'll send them to you."

"Did I miss much?" Colton's deep voice mingled with Sam and Jeff's chatter. Margaret walked beside him carrying a bowl of potato salad. Colton had a platter filled with steamed corn on the cob.

The boys ran past Libby and straight up to Lofton, who promptly grabbed Jeff by the midsection and turned him upside down. Jeff laughed and flailed his arms as Sam jumped up and down, begging, "Pick me up!"

Margaret set her bowl of salad on the table, glancing up at Elaine. The two exchanged glances, but Libby couldn't decipher their silent communication.

"Last summer the boys spent a lot of time with Lofton," Elaine explained.

"They ask about her all the time," Colton said.

"I wish she were staying longer this summer. She and Ted have such fun together," Elaine said. "But she's clerking in DC. Very big step for her."

Libby sipped her wine, remembering the last time she and her father had had real fun together. She had to go back a few years and sort through the days before she'd met Jeremy.

They had been cleaning out the family attic. He had found a box of Libby's baby clothes. Tiny pink, yellow, and white outfits adorned with ruffles. The fancier frocks looked almost pristine, but it was a faded pink New York Jets T-shirt covered with washed-out milk and juice stains that almost brought her father to tears. "You just about lived in this the year you turned two."

"Who bought me a Jets T-shirt?"

"I'm not sure," he'd said. "You spent most of that summer digging in the dirt."

She thought back to that little T-shirt and wondered if it had been one of the few things her father had saved in the boxes stacked neatly in his office. For the first time since she had moved back to Bluestone, she wanted to open those boxes.

CHAPTER THIRTEEN

SADIE

Tuesday, March 3, 1942
Bluestone, Virginia

> *The war is gearing up. Towns as small as Bluestone have sent boys down to Fort Benning. We hear the daily reports about what's happening in Europe and the Pacific, and we're all itching to jump in the fight. From what the brass is saying, once we get to Europe, it won't take long for us to end it. Can't beat an American fighting boy.*

Sadie stared at Johnny's sure-and-steady handwriting, and she pushed the letter across the kitchen table to her mother. "He sounds full of fire."

The letter went on to say that some of the boys had already been in air raids throughout Britain. He was openly worried about Danny. The war was much different than he had imagined.

But she did not read this part to her mother. Johnny knew their mother could not read and trusted Sadie to use her discretion.

Her mother took the letter and smoothed her hands over the page, as if touching the ink was her way of hugging her son. "Are you sure he didn't say anything about Danny?"

"No, Ma, no mention of Danny." Unlike Johnny, who wrote almost weekly, Danny had written only one letter since he had joined the army in 1938.

"I sure do miss those boys. When do you think they'll be home?" Her mother carefully folded the envelope and tucked it in her pocket. Later it would go in the cigar box with the others for safekeeping.

"I don't know. But I sure hope it's soon." The ground was still hard from the winter and would not thaw for another few weeks. That was when she and her mother would begin tilling the soil for the kitchen garden.

Sadie smoothed her hands. "You heard what I read. I wish he wouldn't worry about how I mix the mash for the moonshine."

"He worries because you always add too much sugar." Smiling as if she and Johnny had shared a private moment, her mother picked up one of Johnny's socks she had been darning. The sock was at least ten years old and now too small for Johnny, but that did not stop her mother from sewing up the hole and then carefully removing the threads over and over. The stitches never seemed to be perfect enough for her boy.

"What does Miss Olivia say about England?" her mother asked. "She should know."

"She talks about the gardens mostly. Her parents had a greenhouse by their home in the country." The greenhouse was no longer filled with flowers but with vegetable plants. Two days ago, they had driven into Charlottesville, and Miss Olivia had mailed a package to her parents. It had been stuffed with canned milk, tea, potted meat, and tinned biscuits.

"I heard Mr. Sullivan saying the Germans are still bombing England," her mother said.

"There seems to be no end in sight."

A frown furrowed her mother's brow. "It's a dangerous place to be."

"Johnny won't be near London."

"How do you know?"

"Because I asked Miss Olivia," she lied. "Miss Olivia said he'd be staying in a safe place. Besides, he's tough. He's outrun enough revenuers and the sheriff. No German is going to catch him."

Her mother's scowl softened a little. "He is the quickest boy I ever met. Remember when Mr. Brown was kicked in the head by his horse? Johnny ran five miles for the doctor. Saved Mr. Brown's life."

"I remember." Her mother had told the story a dozen times since Johnny left.

The clock on the wall ticked, and when Sadie glanced up at it, she said, "I've got to go. Driving Miss Olivia today."

"You girls sure do get around. You've been to Charlottesville and Lynchburg more in the last couple of months than I've been in my entire life."

"She gets restless. Finds it hard to sit in the big house alone. Dr. Carter is always away at the hospital, working."

Her mother opened the small wooden cigar box and carefully placed Johnny's letter on top of the dozen others.

"What are you doing today?" her mother asked.

She was not exactly sure what was planned for the day but, for her mother's sake, said, "Ordering more flowers and orange trees. Miss Olivia wants orange trees in her greenhouse. Says it will be good for the baby."

"Baby? She in the family way again?"

"I'm not sure," Sadie said. "But she's always hoping." She shrugged on a jacket. The garment was a hand-me-down from Olivia. Nicer than anything she had ever owned, the jacket was the color of a new penny.

It fit her body as if it had been made for her, and the fabric was soft and fine. It was nothing like the coarse, worn shirts and socks passed down to Sadie from Johnny and Danny.

Sadie kissed her mother on the cheek. "I'll see you this evening."

"Take care of yourself, girl."

"Always, Mama."

Sadie drove the old truck down the very familiar road to Woodmont. As she turned onto the property's main driveway, she now felt like she belonged. She was not worried that the sheriff would arrest her for trespassing or the gardener would chase her off with a pitchfork. Scooting forward in the seat, she downshifted and slowed as she rounded the main house and parked around the side by the kitchen entrance. She straightened her shoulders, stood a little taller, and opened the kitchen door. She had stopped knocking almost a month ago.

Greeted by the scent of rich, buttery biscuits fresh out of the oven, she crossed to the kitchen table and the pile of fluffy biscuits stacked on a blue-and-white plate. She had eaten only half of her mother's biscuits and brown gravy this morning, knowing if she saved room, there would be better waiting. "Mrs. Fritz," she called out.

"In the back, baby. Go on and have yourself a bite. I know you're hungry."

"Appreciate it."

Mrs. Fritz showed in the doorway, drying her large hands with a red-and-white-checkered towel. "You're about the only one in this house that enjoys my cooking. The doctor is always gone, and Miss Olivia eats like an itty-bitty bird. I might start to feel down about my cooking if it weren't for you."

Sadie bit into a biscuit. "Don't ever fret about your cooking, Mrs. Fritz."

The older woman laughed. "I hear you two girls are going to Lynchburg today?"

"I never quite know where we're going until we start out."

"You two seem to be getting along well enough. You're even wearing her clothes."

"She said they didn't fit her anymore."

"Well, they look nice on you. Just you remember not to get too well acquainted. You might clean up nice, but you're help, just like me."

"Yes, ma'am."

Mrs. Fritz set a wicker picnic basket on the table and carefully began wrapping up most of the biscuits and placing them gently inside. "She's taking lunch to Dr. Carter today."

"To the hospital where he works?"

"That's right. It's a surprise." Mrs. Fritz shook her head. "That poor boy works so hard they never see each other."

Sadie had not seen Dr. Carter since the first day he had warned her to be careful, and that suited her just fine.

Footsteps sounded in the hallway, and Sadie quickly finished her biscuit as Miss Olivia appeared. Her naturally pale skin had a pink glow to it, and her dark hair, loose around her shoulders, looked vibrant. She wore a royal-blue jacket that matched a fitted skirt that brushed below her knees.

She tugged on pale-gray leather gloves. "Good morning, Sadie."

"Morning, Miss Olivia."

Miss Olivia's eyes sparked with excitement. "We better get going. By the time we arrive, Edward will be starving. He performed surgery today, so he left before breakfast."

Sadie grabbed the basket. "Yes, ma'am. I'll bring the car around."

"Excellent."

Sadie hurried out to the barn, opened the door, and grabbed the key from the hook on the wall. In the car, she always noticed the softness of the leather seats first thing in the morning. But by afternoon and after hours of driving, she found herself irritated by the way the seat hit her lower back due to her small size.

She backed out of the barn and pulled the car around to the back entrance. Miss Olivia hurried down the stairs and let herself into the back seat. There had been no more discussion about Miss Olivia learning to drive. Sometimes she still sat in the front seat, but that was only when they were sure no one would see.

"You look mighty happy. Excited about visiting the big city?" Sadie asked.

Miss Olivia smiled. "Lynchburg is more like a charming small town."

"Pretty big to me." Sadie shifted gears, and the car rumbled down the driveway.

"There are cities that are a hundred times bigger."

Sadie tried to picture a bigger city. The idea of a place packed full of people, buildings, and things scared her.

"Like London?"

"That's right."

She adjusted her grip on the wheel. It troubled her she had lied to her mother about Johnny being safe. She wanted to believe it was true but knew he would never worry her. "Johnny is headed to England."

Olivia looked up and caught her gaze in the rearview mirror. "Where in England?"

"He doesn't know yet."

"Be sure to let me know when you do. Perhaps I can suggest a few places for him to visit if he gets a pass."

"The bombs are still dropping over there?"

Olivia nodded slowly. "They haven't stopped, and I've not received word from my family."

"Was it pretty bad?" Sadie wasn't asking in a nosy kind of way, but she wanted to be able to picture where Johnny was staying.

"It was quite bad when I left," she said softly.

"How did you meet Dr. Carter?"

She was silent for a moment. "I was volunteering in the hospital. It was taking every man or woman on deck to take care of the wounded. A bomb hit the hospital, and I ended up trapped in the rubble. Edward was finishing up his fellowship at Oxford and working that same night. He dug me out."

"You were buried alive?" Her chest tightened at the thought, and she drew in a deep breath, trying to process the terror Olivia must have felt. "How long were you trapped?"

"They tell me it was close to nine hours. Edward visited me at my bedside, and several days later when I was up and about, he invited me to tea. The rest moved along fairly swiftly."

"Is that the way love is supposed to be? I mean that quick."

"It was for us. One look at him, and I knew. So did he. We were married within a month."

"Does it still bother you? I mean being trapped like that."

Miss Olivia raised her chin. "No, of course not. Many others had it far worse."

Sadie felt trapped by the confines of the county and her life. But as bad as it got sometimes, it could not have been nearly as bad as having bricks and stones pinning you in the darkness.

The two rode in silence for the remainder of the trip, and when Sadie drove into Lynchburg, she stopped to ask directions several times. Quizzical looks aside, the folks she spoke to seemed friendly and helpful.

The hospital was not what she had expected at all. It was a gray, stark place, with not a tree or blade of grass on its grounds. Only two stories high, it had no shutters on its dozen windows, and the curtains were drawn closed. Not very inviting. Sadie parked and came around to meet Miss Olivia as she stepped out.

"You want me to stay with the car?" Sadie said.

Miss Olivia looked up at the heavy front door. "You can carry the basket for me."

Sadie followed, but she had trepidation about the building. It had a presence about it that made her stomach knot and her palms sweat. Olivia rang the bell, and both waited. Finally, footsteps approached, and the door opened to an older woman wearing a dark dress. Her hair was pulled back, and her face had a sour expression.

"May I help you?" she asked.

"I'm Dr. Carter's wife," Miss Olivia said. "I've come to pay him a visit."

"He's in surgery and won't be out for a half hour, but you're welcome to wait."

Olivia raised her chin. "Yes, that would be nice. Thank you."

The two moved to a pair of wooden chairs aligned against the wall. From somewhere deep in the building, they heard what sounded like wailing.

Miss Olivia shifted in her seat and settled her purse on her lap. "Edward volunteers here one day a week. He's very civic minded."

"Yes, ma'am."

The wailing eased, but Sadie's sense of fear did not. They sat in silence watching doctors scurry about. On the upper floor, another woman's scream echoed in the building.

She was not sure how long they sat before Dr. Carter appeared. He looked rushed and slightly annoyed as he approached the pair.

"Darling, what are you doing here?"

Olivia stood and allowed him to kiss her on the cheek. "I thought I would bring you lunch, and we could share it. I don't see much of you these days."

"I know, and I'm very sorry. Building a practice is harder than I ever imagined."

Sadie rose and was somewhat confused about the place. "What do you do here?"

"We take care of the poor women who don't have the means to pay for a doctor."

"You deliver babies," she said.

"Sometimes," he said. "Sometimes we do other surgeries to help them."

Sadie wanted to ask about the other times but did not dare.

"Why don't we go outside?" he said to Olivia.

"Yes, that would be nice," Miss Olivia said. "Sadie, would you wait for me in the car?"

"Is there a blanket in the trunk?" Dr. Carter asked.

"Yes, sir."

"Fetch it for us," he said, smiling at his wife. "We will make a picnic of this fine lunch."

"Yes, sir." She retrieved the plaid wool blanket with thick fringe and handed it to Miss Olivia. As they walked along the sidewalk, Sadie was glad to retreat to the car.

Inside the car, she pulled the folds of her jacket closed and watched the Carters stroll hand in hand toward a single bench stationed at almost the edge of the property.

Dr. Carter fluffed out the picnic blanket over the bench and then held out his hand for his wife. She accepted it and sat.

Sunshine warmed the car, and Sadie found some of the tension had faded from her body. Her eyelids grew heavy and soon drifted shut. She glided just below consciousness, thinking she was aware of her surroundings but not realizing they were meandering further away like a log on a slow-moving river.

A hard smack against the glass snapped her back to consciousness, and when she looked at the driver's-side window, she saw the face of a young woman. She appeared young, but her features looked drawn and weathered, as if she had already lived a lifetime. Her eyes were bright blue and filled with terror and tears.

Two men came up beside the girl and wrapped their arms around her. She recognized one of them as Sheriff Boyd right off, but the other was a stranger to her.

It took both men to pry the girl's fingers from the car's side mirror. She screamed and tried to bite their hands, but the men were too strong. Finally, her frantic fingers slipped from the mirror.

The woman dug her heels into the hard dirt as she tried to twist her body and flee. But she was no match for the strong arms that pushed and shoved her up the steps to the door. The sheriff smacked his palm against the bell, and seconds later it snapped open, with the sourpuss nurse on the other side. The trio dragged the girl inside the building.

Sadie's mouth was so dry, and her heart was beating so fast she thought it would break through her ribs.

"Dr. Carter," she shouted as she ran toward the couple. "Is that girl all right?"

Dr. Carter helped his wife stand. "She's fine."

"But she looked so afraid," Sadie said. "Like she thinks they are going to do something terrible to her."

"The girl is feebleminded like her mother was," he said, more to his wife. "She's confused and easily terrified. I promise you that we're only going to help her."

"That scream," Olivia said. "It was pure terror."

"We get girls in from the country who've never seen a doctor. They don't understand that we're here to help."

"What's wrong with her?" Sadie asked.

"Nothing that I can't fix." His gaze remained on Olivia. "You trust me, don't you?"

Olivia stared into his eyes. "Yes, of course I do."

They kissed on the lips, and Sadie, feeling like she wasn't supposed to see, dropped her gaze to Dr. Carter's polished brown shoes. As she studied the tied leather laces, she noticed several dull-red spots that looked like dried blood.

Two days later neither Sadie nor Miss Olivia mentioned their visit to the hospital when they drove into Charlottesville to pick up an order of plants. Dr. Carter had ordered them special and had warned Sadie not to let the plants sit out long at the railroad loading dock before she loaded them in Woodmont's farm truck.

Sadie had not been to the rail station in Charlottesville since she took Danny there, and she was excited to see the trains. There was something thrilling about seeing people coming and going to different places in the world. One day, she would be on one of those trains.

She loaded the plants quickly into the truck bed while Miss Olivia signed for the delivery, and when Olivia smiled at the railroad man, he seemed to melt at the sight of her. She was dressed in a soft brown dress that skimmed her calves and was cinched with a slim polka-dot brown belt. Her brown shoes were polished and had just enough of a heel to make them pretty but useless for work.

As much as Sadie wanted to linger in the city, she feared the plants would be damaged by the cooler weather, and Dr. Carter would be annoyed.

Sadie drove them back to Woodmont and then backed the truck down to the greenhouse. It took Sadie a good half hour to unload and carry all the plants inside the warm, moist air of the greenhouse.

As she carried the last spiky green plant into the greenhouse and set it in the corner, she was grateful to be out of the cold. She looked up at the greenhouse's domed roof, marveling at the way it caught the afternoon light. As pretty as this place was, it felt confining.

Miss Olivia regarded her plants as if they were precious children. "Can you move that last one a little to the right?"

Sadie dragged the pot five inches toward her and stood back. It was going to take more than a few inches to help this plant.

"It's really very stunning," Miss Olivia said.

"Yes, ma'am, if you say so."

Miss Olivia frowned. "You don't like the plants?"

"No offense, Miss Olivia, but I don't see the point of these plants. They don't look like you'd eat them."

"No, of course not. They're all Leucospermums."

"What?"

"Shrubs that remain green all year, and then for a brief time they flower."

"These things are going to make a flower?"

"They will indeed. They're designed to be lovely and interesting." Miss Olivia walked up and inspected a flat spiny leaf. "Edward had them brought in from Richmond. A friend of his has an English garden. He's not one to sell his plants, and Edward said he had to be very persuasive to convince him to sell him these."

"If you say so, miss."

"The plant comes with its own story, you know," Miss Olivia said. "Do you want to hear it?"

Sadie shrugged, doubting a story would help the look of this plant. "Sure, I could use a good story."

Miss Olivia walked around the plant. "The man who gifted them to Edward is of British descent. He had a great-great-great-grandfather who sailed the seas as a young man for the British navy. In the 1780s his ship came upon a Dutch vessel that was sailing out of Cape Town, South Africa. They of course boarded the ship and took the cargo from the crew."

The idea of traveling far caught her attention. "Why would they do something like that?"

"Britain was at war with the Dutch."

"Why?"

"Because the Dutch were helping the American colonists with their little war of independence."

Sadie placed her hand on her hip, feeling like she needed to stick up for her country. "Couldn't have been so little. We won, and now we're back in Europe helping you out of a scrap."

Miss Olivia's lips curled into a slight smile. "You are right about that."

Sadie studied the plants again, trying to find something pretty about them but still unable to see much beyond spikes and hard angles. "Was this plant on the ship?"

"No. One of the Dutch crewmen had collected seeds near Cape Town. And when the British took control of the ship, they took all the Dutch sailors' belongings, including these seeds. When one of the Brits returned home, he planted them. This plant is a descendant of those seeds."

"Figures a handful of seeds would have traveled farther than me."

"You are young; you will travel one day, Sadie."

"That is my plan. I want to see California and New York City."

"You are a bright girl. I have no doubt you will see both."

Sadie squared back her shoulders a fraction. "Seems to me if you are going to go to all the trouble of growing an old seed, then you should at least be able to eat it. What's the good of a plant that doesn't do anything of real importance?"

"It has a role. It's lovely."

Sadie shook her head as she looked outside at the still-bare trees. "Yes, ma'am, if you say so."

"You don't approve," Miss Olivia said.

"Not my place, ma'am. I do love looking at the starlets in the magazines, because they are pretty. But I wouldn't go so far as to think I could ever wear anything so beautiful. Just isn't practical."

"Does something always have to be practical?"

"For me, it does. Everything in our life, including the plants in Mama's garden, are of use. All we have are carrots, potatoes, snap peas, and squash. It's all got to fill our belly."

"Don't you have any flowers?"

"Well, we do have the honeysuckle bushes around the house, and they do smell nice. But as soon as they bloom, I pick the flowers so I can make them into the syrup to flavor the moonshine. The honeysuckle flavor is our most popular."

"Edward enjoys it, but I've never tried it."

"Well then, I'll caution you to be careful. It's mighty strong."

Miss Olivia raised her chin. "You don't think I can handle it?"

"I'm sure you could. I'm just saying it'll take getting used to. Don't go guzzling it like one of those fancy lady drinks."

"You've drunk it?"

"Well, no. I taste the honeysuckle syrup, and then when it's mixed, Ma does the final tasting. But it's a matter of time before I'll be doing the final tasting."

"Aren't you worried about the law?"

"I suppose. But I know all the back roads and old Indian trails, so I'll be fine as long as I stay out of the sheriff's way."

"Why do you take the risk?"

"Money's got to come from somewhere. Kind of like when you were trapped in that building. The only choice you had was to figure a way out. That's what I'm doing with the moonshine. Figuring a way out of a tight spot."

Miss Olivia stared at her a long moment. "I do admire you, Sadie."

Color warmed her cheeks. "Why? I'm just a poor girl from the country."

"You are brave. And I respect that."

"I'd say you were pretty brave."

"I had no choice, and now I have fled my country when it needs me most, and I am hiding out in a glasshouse filled with pretty plants that serve little purpose. That's hardly brave."

"I thought you liked this greenhouse?"

"Edward built it for me. He says it's where I belong. And it's a good place for me to hide." Clearing her throat, she turned toward a pot filled with another green fern. "I can't imagine being all alone and driving your truck at night, running from the law. I'm scared enough as it is."

Sadie came around and picked up the pot, filled with lavender. "What do you have to be afraid of?"

"Everything," she said softly. "This new life. Losing another baby. Disappointing Edward."

Sadie was silent for a moment. "Mama always said if you aren't a little afraid, then you aren't living."

"What are you afraid of?" Miss Olivia challenged.

"Never getting out of Bluestone. Living and dying here, and never getting a chance to see the world."

"As I said, I predict great adventures for you."

Sadie liked hearing the words, and she wanted to believe them even as her thoughts turned back to the girl at the hospital. For her, there was no getting out of Bluestone.

CHAPTER FOURTEEN
OLIVIA

Thursday, March 5, 1942
The Woodmont Estate

"I want to learn how to drive," Olivia said from the back seat.

It had been two days since Olivia and Sadie had visited the hospital, and Olivia could still not shake the memory of the wailing woman being dragged inside. Edward had asked her to trust him, and of course she did, but as they now approached Woodmont she realized she needed more independence from him at this place.

"We've been through this. I could lose my job," Sadie said.

"I know. And I appreciate your concern, but I'll not tell Edward. I know he wouldn't approve. He's quite protective. I would hope in the last few weeks that I have gained your trust."

"I trust you just fine," she said. "But if someone sees us, then it will get back to Dr. Carter."

"I feel helpless," she said. "I'm as trapped in my house as I was in that rubble."

"What are you talking about? It's the biggest house I've ever seen."

Olivia smoothed out a wrinkle in her skirt. "It can feel very small. So can this county."

Sadie could not argue with her on that score. "I don't know."

Olivia scooted to the middle of the seat and leaned forward. "My mother says that it's good for marriages if they have a few tiny secrets. She, for instance, used to go to the movies every Friday with her friend. She never told Father about it because she said details like that bored him. She said the movies made her a better wife."

"You think driving will make you a better wife?"

"Yes." She would not feel so trapped or lost or useless. When she had worked at the hospital in London, she had felt alive and excited about each day.

"Don't you have all those plants and trees coming to the greenhouse soon? Won't that make you feel better?"

The greenhouse was Edward's idea of what she needed. And though she was touched by the gesture, she realized now that plants in a greenhouse were more of an excuse to keep her on the property.

"There are times when I feel like that girl we saw at the hospital," she said.

Sadie frowned. "You aren't like her."

"I'm trapped in my life. *Please.* I'll never tell Edward."

Sadie slowed the car and turned into the estate's driveway, and as Olivia stared down the long dirt entryway, she thought she might cry.

Instead of pressing forward, Sadie stopped the car. As the car idled, she twisted around in her seat. "This is our secret from Dr. Carter?"

"Of course. I won't breathe a word."

"What about Mrs. Fritz? She might see."

"I'll speak to her."

"I'm going to be sorry I did this."

Olivia clapped her hands. "Then you'll do it!"

"I suppose." Sadie slowly shook her head and shut off the engine. "It ain't as easy as it looks. There's a trick to working the clutch and the accelerator. You don't get do-overs."

"Nothing I can't master."

"All right, then; get out of the car, and come around."

Olivia bounded out the back seat as Sadie climbed out from behind the wheel and waited for her to sit. She closed the door and came around to the passenger side and got in.

Olivia smoothed her gloved hands over the steering wheel and felt her heart beating fast, as it had when she had been on the merry-go-round in Piccadilly.

"You'll find that I'm the best student you'll ever have met. The doctors at Holy Cross in London said as much. I was on the floor less than two days before I was bandaging wounds."

"Good. Those three pedals on the floor all have a job." Sadie explained the purpose of the accelerator, the brake, and then the clutch. Next, she talked about the key, the choke, and the starter. By the time she was finished, Olivia's brain was spinning.

"Best way to learn is by doing," Sadie said. "Turn the key, and let's get this car moving."

Olivia turned the key, and when the engine roared to life, a tiny nervous giggle bubbled out. She pressed the pedal on the right, and the engine roared. She immediately let off it. "What have I done?"

"Nothing yet. Now for the tricky part," Sadie said.

Olivia scooted forward in her seat, gripped the steering wheel, and pushed the clutch against the floor. She struggled to move the gear into the first position. Sadie finally laid her hand over Olivia's and guided it into place.

"Was that the tricky part?" Olivia asked.

"No, ma'am. That would be now. Lift that clutch up slowly, and press on the gas *slowly*."

Olivia let the clutch up quickly and pressed on the gas slowly. The car lurched forward and shut off. "What did I do? Did I break it?"

"No, ma'am. It takes practice; that's all. Let's go ahead and try it again."

The second, third, and fourth results were not much better, and with each new failed attempt, Olivia's face burned hotter and hotter. Edward would call her silly and foolish for having tried.

"You're doing real well, Miss Olivia."

"How can I be? We haven't moved ten feet!"

"The first time I tried to learn on that old truck, it just about hopped all the way to Charlottesville."

"You were twelve. I'm a grown woman."

"First time is hard no matter what. You'll get the hang of it."

"I don't know. Maybe I'm not cut out for country living. My mother feared I wouldn't last."

"Why would she say such a thing?"

"Because I love the city. I like the theater, the shopping, the restaurants, and all the sounds that come with it."

"Then why are you here?"

"Because I love Edward. I'm his wife. Besides, London was not safe."

"You ready to quit, then?" Sadie asked.

There was the challenge in that girl's voice again. She'd dared her once before right in front of Edward. "I'm not quitting."

"Looks like it to me."

She had survived almost nine hours in the rubble, her body pressed so tightly between the debris that she could barely breathe. Water and filth had dripped on her face as more bombs had dropped nearby, shaking the very rubble that trapped her.

Olivia tightened her grip on the wheel and raised her chin. She pulled out the choke and pressed the starter button.

Drawing in a breath, she gently pressed on the accelerator and very slowly let up on the clutch. The gear caught, hopping only a little before the front wheels moved forward.

Olivia looked in shock at Sadie before she grinned broadly. "I did it."

"You sure did."

"Why won't the car go any faster?"

"Because we're only in slowest gear. We need to shift again."

"Can't we stay in first?"

"You can walk faster than you can drive in first gear."

Olivia put her hand on the gearshift. "I'm ready."

Sadie laughed. "You ain't facing down a mountain lion. It'll be okay."

Again, the clutch went in, the gear shifted with just a little bit of choppiness, and soon the two were picking up speed. By the time they had reached the main house, they had been through the first three gears.

Mrs. Fritz came out on the porch, smiling and nodding as Olivia drove around the circular driveway and brought the car around to the barn. She shut off the engine and climbed out, her chest puffed out as if she had slain a beast.

Sadie glanced toward Mrs. Fritz, who offered a slight nod of approval before she vanished back into the house. "That was really good, Miss Olivia."

"Can we do it again?" Olivia asked. "Next time I'd like to drive on the roads."

"Dr. Carter is sure to find out if you go out on the roads."

"Maybe, but better to ask for forgiveness than get permission."

"Did your mother tell you that too?"

"Yes she did."

Olivia lay curled next to Edward, drawing comfort from his warmth, as she had since the first night they had slept together.

That night had been a scandalous three weeks after he had pulled her from the carnage. She had been home, alone in the dark, listening to the distant rumble of heavy bombers flying over the city. The room had suddenly felt painfully small, and she had risen and dressed in the dark.

Since the war and its bombing had begun, London residents had grown accustomed to living and moving in the dark. She'd made her way to his tiny apartment and knocked on his door. When he opened it and saw her bathed in shadows, he did not say a word or move a muscle. She was the one who stepped toward him and wrapped her arms around his neck. Their kisses were never tentative when they were in London. They had always held pent-up passion that had come from the stress of war.

Olivia thought she knew Edward. She had followed this brave man to America, knowing she was driven by her love and fear. Love for him and their unborn child but also fear of the bombs in the darkness. And when she had lost the child she was carrying on the voyage to America, he had cared for her with such tenderness. "There will be more babies," he had whispered.

But in the last week since Olivia had seen how he had dismissed the suffering of that woman, she'd wondered.

She quietly slipped out from under the covers and put on her slippers. Moving carefully to avoid the floorboards that creaked, she left the bedroom and made her way down the stairs. She put on her coat and walked down the cobblestone pathway toward the greenhouse. The plants had begun to arrive; she, with Sadie's help, would soon arrange them in the glistening space, filling the greenhouse with green, white, purple, and red blossoms.

She opened the door, greeted by the fragrant scents and the warmer air. Carefully she closed the door and crossed to the small sofa in the center. She curled up on the soft cushions and, hugging the folds of her coat close, stared up through the glass ceiling toward the clear night sky. When she was younger, she had known the constellations so well, and when the bombings had begun, plunging the city into darkness, she had become reacquainted with the stars.

Tonight, her guides were a waxing moon near the constellation Lynx and, to the east, Cassiopeia. Her hands slid to her belly, and she sat as still as she could, trying to calm her fear so that the baby growing inside her would flutter and move, reminding her he was going to be all right. "Just a small kick, my boy," she whispered. "And then you can get back to sleep."

Olivia had realized she was expecting again the day she and Sadie had driven to Lynchburg to see Edward. That had been part of her reason for going. She had wanted to share herself with him in the bright sunshine and share the exciting news with him. She was always calmest and happiest throughout the day.

The news had been on the tip of her tongue until the girl had captured their attention. Her screams had been so loud and agonizing. The sounds had transported Olivia back to London and the nights when similar screams were often heard in the rubble.

Edward's response to the girl's plight had taken Olivia aback. She sensed her husband did not see the girl for who she was but instead as a clinical problem to be dealt with.

The door to the solarium opened, and she turned toward it to see the shadow of her husband. "I can hear your thoughts all the way back at the house," he said drowsily.

She moved over on the sofa, making room for him, and when he stretched out beside her, she nestled close to him. "It's the night. You know I don't sleep well any longer."

"Do the stars help?"

"Yes, they're peaceful."

He smelled of clean soap from the bath he always took when he came home from the hospital. His hand slid softly to her slightly rounded belly. "Are you pregnant?"

She looked up at him, remembering his face had been the first she had seen while trapped. "Yes."

His face broke into a wide grin as he hugged her closely. "When?"

"Christmas, I would say."

He buried his face in the loose curls of her hair. "God, I'm so happy."

"Me too," she said.

As much as she wanted to surrender to the joy of this moment, her mind kept returning to that woman she had seen in Lynchburg.

"I can't get that woman's face out of my mind."

"What woman?" He seemed genuinely confused.

"The day I brought you lunch at the hospital."

"Ah, yes. What about her?"

"She was so upset."

"Many of the women we treat are easily upset. Many aren't right in the mind, and they need our help. It's unsettling. I'm sorry you had to see that."

"I was buried alive for nine hours, but it paled to her terror."

He was silent for a moment. "I've no doubt her life is never going to be easy."

"What did you do for her?" Olivia asked.

"I did what was right for her. I saw to it that her suffering wouldn't be passed on to the next generation."

She felt his steady heartbeat under her fingertips. "What does that mean?"

"The girl's mother is as troubled as she is. It's hereditary. The father did not want his daughter to have children that were bound to suffer."

"What did you do?"

"A very quick and easy procedure that ensures she won't have children. She'll live a happy life that will be as normal as she can manage, but there won't be children."

"How do you know they would suffer?"

"Her father was certain that she should have no children."

"Why was he so certain?"

"He knows his child."

"Are there others like her?"

"Too many sometimes." Edward pulled Olivia closer to him and tightened his hold around her slim waist. "I don't want you to worry about her or that place. Focus on the baby and how you can make the plants in here grow. I was down here earlier, and I'm impressed at their beauty."

Some of her worries drifted away at the sound of his soothing voice.

"I haven't asked, but has Sadie worked out?"

"Yes, she is a great help."

"I like and respect her brother. Johnny is a hardworking young man. The other brother, Danny, not so much. And Sadie is strong willed and spirited."

"Is that why you hired her as my driver?" she asked.

"I thought she would bring you out of yourself. Not someone who would always try to ingratiate themselves to you. I also know how you like to help others. Maybe you could raise her up a bit."

"You were right about that." She drew her finger over his chest, drawing a heart. "She has been a breath of fresh air."

"Should you slow down on your driving adventures now that the baby is on the way?"

"It's good for me to get out. I think the ship was too confining, and the stress of crossing the Atlantic took its toll. I feel different this time. Hopeful."

He kissed her on the forehead. "I want the three of you to be careful," he said with a grin.

"Absolutely."

SADIE

Six days later, Sadie drove Miss Olivia into Bluestone and parked in front of the general store. She was aware that the folks standing about noticed the car's beauty. Sadie puffed up her chest, stepping out with her used new coat on. She was used to being noticed but never for good reason. She was Johnny and Danny's wild little sister who wore dirty coveralls and ran barefoot most summers. She was the girl who did not do so well in school and struggled to read passages in books assigned by teachers. She was the girl who ran shine and was rumored to be drinking the brew as young as twelve. A backwoods hellion.

But today, she was the girl who worked for Mrs. Olivia Carter and got to wear a fancy coat.

She watched as Miss Olivia walked inside the store, her head held high and her gaze just a little cool as it swept over the interior. Mr. Sullivan stood a little straighter and welcomed her as she tugged off her gloves and then took a piece of gingham fabric between her fingers and felt it for softness.

"What can I do for you today?" Mr. Sullivan asked.

"Miss Sadie has a list for you," she said with her proper English accent. "Supplies the cook needs for supper."

Sadie removed the carefully folded note from her pocket and handed it to Mr. Sullivan. A slight smile curled the edges of his mouth as he looked at the long list. Knowing Mr. Sullivan, he was already calculating the profit he would make today.

"It'll take me a few minutes to fill the order," he said with an air of deference to the pair.

"Take your time," Miss Olivia said, moving to a bolt of soft yellow fabric. "Sadie, is there anything you need?"

"Ma'am? No, I'm fine."

Sadie moved to a collection of soaps packaged in pretty white paper. She hesitated to touch the soaps until Mr. Sullivan turned to grab a box of salt. She lifted the soap to her nose, inhaling the soft scent of honeysuckle. She considered spending some of the money she would earn this week on it, but a glance at the twenty-five-cent price tag made her almost drop it.

As she looked around, her gaze settled on a green dress draped from a hanger near several other articles of clothing. She took the fabric in her hands, amazed at how soft it felt. She glanced down at her coveralls, wondering if folks would see her differently if she were wearing a dress like this.

"I have the bill ready," Mr. Sullivan said, smiling. "Including that gardening journal that you ordered from Richmond."

Miss Olivia opened her purse and handed him a crisp five-dollar bill. Sadie could only stare at the tremendous amount of money.

"Ruth," he said, calling into the back. "I'll need your help."

Ruth was his daughter, with whom Sadie had gone to school up until Sadie had dropped out last year. Blonde with a pretty enough face, Ruth dressed the best of any girl in school and had the pick of the handsome boys.

"Yes, sir."

Ruth pushed through the curtain separating the back and front of the store and smiled at Miss Olivia. When her gaze shifted to Sadie, her expression dimmed, as if she might have bitten into a sour apple but did not want anyone to know it.

Ruth went about finding the small items on the list, including cinnamon sticks, baking soda, and rose water. She carefully placed all the items in a box her father had already loaded with flour, sugar, and lard.

Aware Ruth was eyeing her, Sadie dropped her gaze to a hand-drawn sign featuring two dancers. She was not an especially good reader but knew enough to realize there was a party in March.

"Sadie, you sure do look lovely today," Ruth said.

"Thank you," she said, stepping away from the dress.

"You thinking about buying that and wearing it to that party?"

Ruth knew darn well Sadie could not afford the dress, and the chances of her going to any party were slim to none. Maybe if her mother could have mended a dress from the church box for her, and maybe if one of her brothers could have taken her to a dance. But neither brother was in town, and her mother was not going to mend a dress and send Sadie alone to a dance.

"I'm chewing on it," Sadie said.

"I'm going with my beau," Ruth bragged.

"Really?" Sadie shifted her attention away from the sign to the new *Life* magazine, featuring four young women dressed in sparkling dresses.

"I wish I'd have known you were coming; I would have saved my old magazines." Ruth's voice was so sweet it was a miracle the words were not drawing honeybees. "I know how you like to look through them."

"No trouble," Sadie said.

"Mr. Sullivan." Miss Olivia held up a brown box-shaped camera. "Could you show me this?"

Mr. Sullivan came around the counter with a pep in his step, as he always did when he sold something expensive. But these days, times were hard on most, and money was tight. "Sure. It's a Kodak camera. Supposed to be easy."

As the two discussed the contraption, Ruth said in a softer voice, "Remember that time you tried to fix your hair like Carole Lombard— or was it Gene Tierney? I don't know which, but you tied your hair up in rags the night before, expecting a soft wave. But in the morning, it was a mass of curls that looked more like a German helmet."

She remembered rushing home and dunking her head under the pump outside the house, soaking her head until the curls were gone. "I don't remember."

"You don't? Good heavens, I still get a little chuckle out of it. You were so cute."

"How do you like driving Dr. Carter's Pontiac?" Mr. Sullivan asked as he returned.

"It's real fine, sir."

"Not driving like you do when you carry the shine, are you?" Mr. Sullivan said with a grin.

"No, sir. Slow and steady."

"Attagirl. Don't want the sheriff coming after you."

"No, sir."

"Mr. Sullivan," Miss Olivia said. "Do you have any new magazines in stock?"

"Just got the most recent *Life* yesterday. Not even Ruthie has read it."

"It looks real good," Ruth said.

"Would you also add that to my order?" Miss Olivia said. "Along with that green dress."

He glanced toward Sadie. "Sure."

Mr. Sullivan scanned Miss Olivia's list and then the contents of the box before declaring the order filled. He hefted the box. "Ruth, get the door for me."

"Sadie's right there," Ruth said. "She can get it."

Sadie grabbed the handle, knowing Ruth's father would scold her afterward for her poor manners.

After Mr. Sullivan and Miss Olivia walked through, Sadie waited until Ruth approached before she released the door. It closed in Ruth's face.

Ruth's outrage tickled Sadie as she opened the trunk for Mr. Sullivan, who placed the box in the rear compartment.

"Mr. Sullivan, would you be so kind?" Miss Olivia asked. "I'd like you to take a picture of Sadie and me. She's my first friend in America, and I think that should be documented."

Mr. Sullivan did not hesitate, but Sadie saw the tension rippling through his body. Miss Olivia stood in front of the Pontiac and waved Sadie to her side.

Sadie came closer, eyeing the camera like it was trouble. She had had her picture taken when she was little, along with her mother and brothers. Her daddy had declined to be included. Sitting there had been no good reason for him to have a picture taken. The picture still sat on the mantel over the fire, but she did not remember who took it or where.

Miss Olivia straightened her shoulders and angled her body sideways. Sadie, too nervous to pose, stared at the lens. "Sadie, you look as if you're facing a firing squad."

"Feels odd to me, I suppose. My pa never saw a good reason to have his picture taken."

"Smile," Ruth coaxed.

The two women stared at the camera. Miss Olivia's smile was wide, whereas Sadie's reflected her unease. Mr. Sullivan gently handed the camera back to Miss Olivia.

As Miss Olivia took her place in the back seat, Ruth hurried up to the car. "Thank you for coming, Mrs. Carter. You let me know if there's anything I can ever do for you."

"Thank you, Ruth," Miss Olivia said.

"Sadie, hope to see you again soon," Ruth said with a wave.

Sadie slid behind the wheel, ignoring the hollow farewell. She started the car, revving the engine a little to impress the Sullivans.

She pulled away, and neither she nor Miss Olivia said a word. They drove back to Woodmont in silence, and after Sadie pulled around by the kitchen, she hefted the heavy box.

"Can you get that?" Miss Olivia said.

"Yes, ma'am. My mother says I'm part plow horse."

"Does she?" Miss Olivia opened the kitchen door for her and watched as Sadie carried the box to the kitchen table. "Mrs. Fritz can unload it."

"Yes, ma'am."

Miss Olivia reached for the copy of *Life* magazine and the bundled dress. She handed both to Sadie. "This is for you."

"Me?" She held the slick, glossy paper and the wrapped dress. "Why?"

"I think you might enjoy both."

The pages were smooth and the edges sharp, and the four ladies on the front, dressed in sparkly dresses with hair tumbling gently down to their shoulders, looked like starlets.

"Ruth seemed a bit disappointed she wouldn't get a chance to read the issue," Miss Olivia said. "And if you decide to go to that dance, you'll need a dress."

"Yes, ma'am." Her voice sounded tight like a drum. "Thank you."

Miss Olivia smiled. "Enjoy."

OLIVIA

It had been raining for three days, and now on this fourth day, the downpour stopped. The clouds remained dark and foreboding.

Olivia had found she could not stand to be cooped up in the main house. She needed to be moving about and breathing fresh air blowing in the open windows of the car.

When the back-right tire hit a slick spot on the road, the Pontiac skidded and jerked to the right. If Sadie had been driving, she would have easily corrected it. This kind of thing happened all the time, especially on back roads.

But Olivia had been driving. And when the wheels jerked and slid, she did not know what to do. Sadie reached over and grabbed the wheel. She avoided some of the looming disaster, but the car skidded off the road with a hard jolt.

Sadie insisted immediately that they switch seats. When Olivia's nerves had calmed, Sadie had left her in the passenger car and hiked the two miles back to Woodmont for help. Several of the men had come and pushed the car out of the ditch. No one had been hurt. The car had suffered minimal damage.

But that night Olivia had lost her baby.

CHAPTER FIFTEEN

LIBBY

Sunday, June 14, 2020
Woodmont Estate

Libby had enjoyed the dinner and smiled as she wiped lemon cake from Sam's mouth. The boy sat to her right during the meal and Jeff to her left. She had enjoyed their company and found their rough-and-tough banter very charming. Several times, she and Colton had shared a laugh over something one of the two had said.

"So, Libby, how do you know my mom?" Lofton asked.

Elaine's daughter, the newly minted lawyer, had been studying Libby from the far end of the long table. She sat to her mother's left, directly across from her dad.

"Like she said, I was shooting Ginger's wedding here at Woodmont."

Colton laid his napkin beside his plate. Though he remained silent, something in Lofton's demeanor seemed to catch him by surprise.

"And you two must have hit it off?" Lofton asked.

Elaine's smile dimmed, and she shifted her gaze to her daughter, as if she were waiting for a storm cloud to dump its rain. "Lofton, would you like another glass of wine?"

The young woman smiled at her mother. "No thanks, Mom. I guess I'm curious because it's not like Mom to invite outsiders to family dinners."

Colton, sitting to Libby's right, shifted forward in his seat. He said nothing but did not take his eyes off Lofton.

"I grew up in Bluestone," Libby said. "In fact, your dad took you to see my dad when you were a sick baby. My father was Dr. McKenzie."

"He fixed you right up," Ted offered. "You had a raging ear infection that could have cost you your hearing if gone unchecked."

"What were we doing in town?" Lofton asked.

"Your great-grandmother Olivia had passed," Elaine said. "We were here for the funeral."

"But you and my mother had never met before the wedding?" Lofton continued.

"Correct." Libby had attended a female boarding school and knew when she was being sized up. "Is there a point to these questions, Lofton?"

"I worry about my mom," she said.

"I'm capable of taking care of myself," Elaine said.

Lofton smiled, swirling her half-full glass of wine. This was her third, and the wine was beginning to talk.

Ted sat glaring at his daughter.

"That's okay, Ted. I don't mind Lofton's questions. I'm an open book. Lofton, is there something you want to get off your chest before I leave?" Libby asked.

"Maybe," Lofton quipped.

"Lofton," Elaine warned. "She is our guest."

"I'm sorry if you felt offended," Lofton said.

The backhanded apology stoked Libby's temper. She was not sure what bur was under Lofton's saddle, but she was not going along for the ride. Did she have feelings for Colton that Libby did not see?

"I like having her," Sam said. "She's fun."

"Me too," Jeff said.

Libby pushed aside her wine and reached for her coffee cup, sitting next to the dessert plate dotted with lemon cake crumbs. She took several sips, knowing it would take the edge off the wine. The trade-off, however, would be that she would not fall asleep before one o'clock the next morning.

Aware that Colton was watching her, she gulped down the last of the coffee, savoring the hint of sweet from the settled sugar in the bottom of the cup. "This has been a lovely evening, but I really have to get back to town."

"Do you have to go so early?" Elaine asked.

"I really do. It's going to be a crazy week of edits, and I have several new business meetings. Always have to be hustling when you work for yourself."

"I admire that," Elaine said.

When Libby rose, so did Ted and Colton. She shook hands with them all and extended her hand to a seated Lofton, who did not make eye contact.

"Thank you for having me."

Elaine halted her quick getaway. "Let me wrap up some food for you. We have so much extra."

"That's really not necessary," Libby said.

"I insist."

To refuse would be rude, and Elaine had been nothing but hospitable. "Thank you."

Ten minutes later, armed with a bagful of plastic storage bowls stuffed with food, Libby said one last goodbye as she went out the door.

"The boys and I will walk you to your car," Colton offered.

"You don't have to do that," Libby said.

"It's all they can do to sit still," he said. "It's a minor miracle nothing was broken or spilled yet."

The boys and the dogs raced ahead out of the garden and across the lawn to her car as the sun dipped below the horizon. The farther she got away from Lofton and her pretentious attitude, the more settled she felt. She had not belonged at the dinner.

As if reading her thoughts, Colton said, "Lofton already has a lawyer's mind. She's always asking questions and searching for arguments."

"I have no doubt she'll be a huge success."

She pressed the button on her fob, and the door locks opened. Jeff and Sam raced to the door handle and fought for who could be the one to open it.

"Jeff, let Sam," Colton said.

"But I want to open it," Jeff said.

"Maybe you could open the back liftgate for me," Libby said. "I need to load this food."

Jeff let go of the handle, and Libby pointed to the button that made the liftgate rise. His expression was so serious as he pressed it and then stepped back as it opened.

"Well done," Libby said.

Colton placed her bags in the back. "You shouldn't go hungry for a few days."

"Or weeks," she laughed. The boys ran up beside their dad. She extended her hand to each. "Thank you, gentlemen, for a lovely evening. It's been a real pleasure." They shook her hand and giggled.

When her gaze rose to Colton's, her smile dimmed a little as she felt that twinge of desire rise up in her. Again, her timing was off. "It was fun."

"See you soon," he said.

Colton, making sure all little fingers were away from the door, closed it for her. She started the engine and rolled down the window.

"When should I come back to photograph the greenhouse? Anything exciting happening this week?"

"Glazing windows. Removing stones. Nothing exciting."

"If that changes, let me know. I want to capture the images."

"Will do."

As she drove off, she glanced in the rearview mirror and saw the boys waving at her and jumping up and down. She honked the horn and waved back.

On the way to town, she was still unsure if the evening had been a success or an awkward mess.

Fifteen minutes later, she pulled into her driveway and then carried her leftovers into the kitchen, where she dutifully stocked them in a near-empty refrigerator. Restless, thanks to the caffeine, she walked out back, suddenly curious to see if her old camera equipment was still in the shed.

She crossed the backyard, stepping from flagstone to flagstone until she reached the shed. Though near the center of town, the lot was almost an acre in size. Her father had had the large toolshed erected when she was five, and his plan had been to create a woodworking shop. When he had installed a television and easy chair before the first saw was purchased, her mother had declared it a man cave.

Her father never took up woodworking. His eighty-to-ninety-hours-a-week medical practice made that impossible. But when Libby found her first bellows camera at a flea market and dragged it home, he placed it in the shed. She found more photographic equipment, including a developer, a workbench, and chemical trays. After a year of her stocking and laboring on her photos while home for the summers and holidays, the man cave had been no more. It had become her studio.

She switched on the light and was pleased to see that her father had not removed one item. Instead, he had covered all the equipment with white sheets to protect against dust.

With a tug, she removed a sheet from a developing machine that dated back to the 1970s. It had been her favorite during the summer her mother died. She had spent many hours in the darkroom, creating pictures that she now would consider not particularly artistic. But then, art had not been the goal that summer. It had been to take her mind off her mother.

She crossed to a file cabinet and opened the top drawer. It was filled with black-and-white images. The top ones were of her dad's dog, Buddy. He had been a German shepherd–mutt mix who had ridden into town each day with her father when he had gone to work. The dog had had a keen sense of time, always knowing on Fridays the two went through the drive-through on the way home, and he would get a hamburger.

She sifted through the images of her backyard, the town, trees, clouds, and lots of nothing that had been of such great interest to her that summer.

At the very bottom was her collection of pictures she had taken of her mother with an old Canon One Shot her dad had given her for her twelfth birthday. It had been spring break, and to cheer her mother up, Libby had taken her to Woodmont for Historic Garden Week.

She had almost forgotten about that last visit to Woodmont when she was thirteen. There were pictures of her mother in front of the main house, wearing dark slacks and a white shirt, her salt-and-pepper hair pinned up into a neat twist. She was wearing bright lipstick that Libby remembered had been a vibrant red.

The next series of pictures featured her mother in the very side garden where Libby had just had dinner this evening. She stood next to a vibrant bush of white roses, and there was a bright grin on her face.

Two weeks later, her mother had taken a handful of pills. Her father had come home from work and found her lying on her bed.

She smoothed her fingers over her mother's face. Carefully closing the drawer, she held on to the image and carried it back into the house with her. She attached it to the side of the refrigerator with a magnet, knowing tomorrow she would find a frame. "It's good to be home, Mom."

She filled a glass with water from the tap and stood over the sink as she drank it. Catching her breath, Libby carefully set the glass down and tightly closed her eyes. "I miss you, Mom."

She had said the words often during her years at boarding school. And as she had done then, she stood in complete silence, listening for a response that never came.

Tonight, it was just the hum of the air-conditioning. Just as she had as a kid, she felt alone and lost.

She walked upstairs and opened the door to her father's office. Her mother may not have answers, but her father would.

"Okay, Daddy, let's see what else you left behind for me."

CHAPTER SIXTEEN

LIBBY

Sunday, June 14, 2020
Bluestone, Virginia

Libby sat at her father's desk, smoothing her palms over the polished wood surface. The overhead fixture did not emit enough light to fully illuminate the room, so she switched on the floor lamp she had bought for her father a couple of years ago. The extra light boosted visibility and chased away the shadows.

She tapped her finger against the neat desktop. Finally, she opened the file drawer and saw only two files. She knew immediately they were there for a reason. The first file read *Important Papers* in her father's customary Sharpie scrawl on the tab. The second folder was not marked.

She removed both and carried them into the kitchen, where she set a pot of coffee to brew. Already resigned to insomnia, she pried off the lid of the plastic tub containing the lemon cake. Fork in hand, she took several bites as she stared at the two folders. A wall clock ticked in the house in chorus with the sound of the coffeepot gurgling.

She poured herself a cup and opened the *Important Papers* file first. As advertised, it held a list of items that needed to happen after his death. Her father had given a duplicate to his attorney, and so far, his attorney had dutifully ticked off the items on the list. Taxes. Utilities paid. Stock sales. Lou Ann. Even lawn care was covered.

Dad had planned well, but this she already knew.

She took several more bites of cake and drank coffee as she went through the papers. There were her parents' marriage certificate, unused passports, the deed to this house, and finally her birth certificate.

She inspected her birth certificate. It was not her original from New Jersey but one issued by the Commonwealth of Virginia that listed her adopted parents' names. It was an amended birth certificate—a.k.a. an ABC to those in adoption circles. It did not tell her full story but was the official document that had gotten her registered for school and allowed her to apply for a driver's license and passport. It was her official identity, but it really was not totally her.

She smoothed her fingertips over the official watermark and the state seal embossed on the ivory paper trimmed with a blue border design. She replaced the papers in the file folder, closed it, and shifted her attention to the second folder.

She centered it in front of her, held her breath, and opened it. Inside was a letter in an envelope. It was not postmarked, but inscribed in neat handwriting was *My Dear Girl*. Carefully, she opened the envelope and removed the single sheet of paper.

My Dear Girl,

You are but hours old, but already you're proving to have a strong set of lungs and a bit of a temper. I like that about you. Better to come into this world knowing what you want than spend decades pretending that another's dream is your own. As I stare at you in the nursery, I can already see that you will rise above the others of your generation and achieve great things. You're a little marvel, and I still can't believe you are a part of me.

In the years to come, you will learn that your mother could not keep you. Like you, she was not really grown up. She can barely take care of herself, and though I know she loves you, she doesn't yet have the thoughtfulness a good mother lavishes on her child.

Like you, I believe she is destined to do great things. It is my prayer that you both will realize your dreams and that one day you will meet again and compare your wonderful lives.

I want you to know, neither she nor I made this decision lightly. Giving you away has broken my heart, and I will never forget you. Ever.

Always know, my perfect little angel, that your mother and I love you a great deal.

Yours always,
Olivia

Libby sat back, her head spinning. She did not know whether to faint or throw up. Tension rippled through her body until finally she reminded herself to breathe.

Olivia. As in Olivia Carter?

She was Elaine's grandmother. Hers was the greenhouse that Elaine was restoring.

Jesus.

If Olivia had written this to her . . .

I still can't believe you are a part of me.

From what Libby had pieced together about Olivia, she knew Olivia had had only one child. A boy. And that boy had had one daughter. Elaine.

Libby's father would not have saved Olivia's letter unless it was vitally important. He had created a sole file for the letter because he was worried it might get lost in the shuffle of the other documents.

Absently, Libby held the letter to her nose, inhaling the very faint perfumed scent of Olivia Carter. The woman had been dead twenty years, but if she closed her eyes, she could feel her presence in the room.

Her father had not had the guts to give her this when he was alive. He needed death to stand between them before he could reveal the truth.

Elaine was her birth mother.

CHAPTER SEVENTEEN
SADIE

Friday, March 6, 1942
Bluestone, Virginia

"Sadie, you're damn lucky," the sheriff said as he sat at her kitchen table. Sadie's mother sat beside her with her hands folded in a white ball. "Mrs. Carter has refused to press charges or lay any liability or property claim against you. She refuses to blame you for the accident."

"It wasn't my fault," Sadie said. But she stopped short of saying that Miss Olivia had been driving or that she had been teaching her how to drive for months.

"Of course, Dr. Carter doesn't want you to return to Woodmont or to drive his wife ever again," the sheriff said with a slight smile. "And if he sees you on his land, he'll swear out a warrant for your arrest."

"It was no one's fault. The road was slick," Sadie argued.

Her mother laid her hand over Sadie's. "We hear what you're saying. Sadie won't be a trouble to the Carters no more."

The last few days, Olivia had spent her time digging in the cold soil, chopping through the fine layer of frost. Sadie tried to imagine the lush green vegetables that would spring from the earth by summer. It all looked so bleak now, but in time it would be lush and full again.

Sadie had hoped that time would ease the anger of Dr. Carter. She had hoped the wounds would mend and bear fruit like the winter soil. Come summer, when the honeysuckles bloomed, she hoped all would be fine.

"And I don't want to see you making any more mash," the sheriff said. "I'll be paying frequent visits here to make sure of that."

"But you had an agreement with my brother," she said. "Johnny said we could cook and sell as long as we gave you a cut."

The sheriff cleared his throat. "There'll be no more of that. The last thing I want to do is get on the wrong side of Dr. Carter."

There still was no word from Danny, but Johnny was sending some money home from the army. Her mother had her piecework, but all of it together was not enough to settle the rent due at the end of the month.

"I got to make a living," she said. "There's no work for me here in Bluestone. Making the shine is all we have."

"You two would be wise to pack up your belongings and leave Bluestone. What you did to poor Mrs. Carter was damn foolish, and you have made an enemy of her husband."

"I didn't mean any of it."

"You never mean harm," her mother said. "Never mean to hurt anyone."

"But you did," he said. "Troublemakers like you end up on the wrong side of the law and find themselves at the Lynchburg hospital. You don't want that, do you?" His pointed look was intended to trigger Sadie's memory of the girl who had begged for help as she had been hauled away into the gray, dark building filled with screams.

"No, sir," she whispered.

The sheriff nodded. "Seeing as Sadie can't stay out of trouble, it's best you two leave town."

"Where are we going to go?" Sadie demanded. "This is our home. Johnny and Danny won't know where to find us if we leave."

Her mother drew in a breath and rose. "Sheriff, I appreciate your words, but I'll have to ask you to leave now. I won't have my boys coming back to town with no home to welcome them. I'll see to it that Sadie doesn't get into trouble."

Sadie curled her fingers into tight fists, digging her nails into her palms. She should never have taught Miss Olivia to drive. No matter how much she had begged, she should have just done as told by Dr. Carter.

The sheriff rose, lifting his wide-brimmed hat. "Sadie, don't mess this up for your mother. It wouldn't be right for you to get sent away and leave her here alone."

"I'll never leave my mama," she said.

"That's up to you." He settled his hat on his head. "Mrs. Thompson, don't make me come back here for Sadie."

Sadie closed her bedroom door and put a chair in front of the handle before she slipped on the green dress that Miss Olivia had given her weeks ago. It was softer than anything Sadie had worn in her whole life. It reminded her a different life was possible. She did not know how she would make her way, but she would.

She carefully skimmed her calloused palms over the material, feeling a little like Vivien Leigh or Carole Lombard. Of course, they wore these kinds of clothes all the time. It was just another day for them. But for Sadie, it was the best thing she could remember in a long time.

She slid on her old coat over her dress and wrapped a scarf around her neck before she slipped out of her bedroom. Her mother was sitting by the radio in her rocker, holding one of Johnny's socks while Jack Benny played on the radio. Her mother had slipped into a deep sleep.

"Mama, I'm going out for a bit." She did not speak too loudly but was testing.

Her mother's eyes remained closed as Jack Benny's voice mingled with laughter.

She twisted open the front door and closed it softly behind her. She climbed in the truck, released the parking brake, and let the car roll down the hill to the road before she pulled out the choke and pressed the starter. The car engine sputtered to life. She shifted quickly into first gear and was gone.

Ruth had teased her about the party. She had made Sadie feel as if she was not good enough. Her taunts had festered for the last week, and maybe before the accident she would not have gone to the party, fearing what the Carters would say. But now with no job, Sadie did not see the harm in having a little fun.

She drove down into town and parked by the Elks club. There were dozens of cars parked out front, and the inside was lit up and filled with music and laughter. She felt her spirits rise as she climbed out of the truck. Shrugging off her jacket, she left it in the truck and smoothed the folds of her dress.

As Sadie walked toward the door, her nerves jangled with fear and excitement. As she passed a parked car, she could see there was a couple in the back seat. She couldn't make out who was who, but she could see through the steamed glass that they were kissing.

The very thought of a man kissing her made her heart race a little faster. Maybe tonight she would find herself a boy and kiss him right on the lips. Just like in the magazines.

According to Ruth, the band playing tonight had come all the way from Charlottesville and was playing swing music.

She did not know what swing was exactly but dared not ask. Ruth would only roll her eyes as she liked to do and remind Sadie that she just did not know that much.

The girl in the back seat wiggled closer to the boy and slid her hand over his thigh like she had done it many times before. Sadie glanced at her own fingers, trying to imagine doing the same. Color warmed her cheeks, and she tore her gaze from the couple. She imagined it was the dress that was making her feel different. Tomorrow she would be back to her old self, dressed in overalls and a long-sleeve shirt. She imagined then all these crazy thoughts would leave her.

But the idea of going back to who she was made her depressed. She had only just slipped into this new role as Miss Olivia's driver, which had allowed her to dream of a better future. Now that was gone, and all she had left was the magazine and this dress.

Laughing couples were walking inside to a festive interior, and she wished she was not alone. It would have been nice to have a friend.

Ruth and a boy Sadie did not recognize approached the party entrance. Both were laughing, and neither seemed to notice her.

"Hello, Ruth," Sadie said.

Ruth turned and studied Sadie a beat, as if she did not recognize her. "Sadie. Look at you. You're looking mighty spiffy tonight."

Even the way she gave a compliment made Sadie feel lesser. "Thank you."

"Who are you here with?" Ruth tucked her hand into the crook of her gentleman's arm.

"I'm alone." She tried to say it like it did not matter and was her choice.

"That's very bold of you," she said. "Do be careful in the party."

"It's just music and dancing. What's there to be afraid of?"

Ruth shrugged, smiling like a barn cat that had cornered a mouse. "Nothing, I suppose."

The couple hurried past her, and as Ruth shimmied her shoulders, she said, "Ooh, can you hear the music? It makes me crazy."

Bright lights bathed the dance floor filled with couples moving in a quick style that was hard for Sadie to keep up with. This had to be the swing that everyone was talking about.

In the far corner, a four-piece band gave their all to the tune. There was a fella on banjo, another on trumpet, and two on guitar. She tapped her foot, anxious to figure out the dance.

A couple brushed past her, hand in hand, as they hurried to get started. She tapped her foot and lost herself in the music. "My word, this is just about the most thrilling time of my life," she whispered.

"Can I get you some punch, Miss Sadie?"

Sadie turned at the sound of the deep masculine voice. She recognized him right away. It was Malcolm Carter. His dark hair was slicked back, and he wore a dark suit, a collared shirt, and a tie wound into a crisp knot. The tips of his shirt collar were held in place by a fancy gold pin.

"Mr. Carter, what are you doing here?" Sadie asked.

He extended his hand, smiling. "I came to visit my cousin and his wife, but both are not their regular sort these days. Very understandable, but I needed some air."

"How did you hear about this party?"

"The grocer's daughter is very forthcoming."

"Oh."

His gaze flittered over the lines of Sadie's body, and she could see the appreciation in his eyes. She felt a bit shy about the open stare, but there was also pride that she could make a man look at her twice. *It must be the dress,* she thought.

"How is Miss Olivia doing?"

"She's up and about. Though steer clear of my cousin. He's still angry about the accident."

Sadie grew silent and suddenly questioned if she should be here. She had promised her mother she would be good but was not sure about this place.

"I can hear your thoughts even with the music," Malcolm said with a grin.

"You can't hear anything."

"Don't worry about Edward. He'll cool off, and Olivia will give him a baby. The world will get back into its axis."

Maybe for them it would, but Sadie did not have a clue how she was going to right her course.

"This is your first party, isn't it?" He reached for a punch glass, filled it with lemonade, and handed it to her.

"How can you tell?" She took a sip, loving the sweet citrus flavor of the cool drink that somehow did little to cool off her flushed cheeks.

"It's the excitement in your eyes," he said. "I can always tell when a girl attends her first dance."

"You go to a lot of these dances?" she asked.

"Almost every weekend in Richmond."

"I can't imagine doing this every week. It must be so much fun." The music was chasing away her worries, and she was not feeling so out of place.

"It can be work," he said, laughing. "But I always get a second wind when I meet a pretty girl like you, Sadie. It's worth every bit of trouble it took to get out of that stuffy old house." He fixed himself a cup of punch and stared at her over the rim of the glass like she was the only girl in the world.

Sadie sipped and looked past him to see Ruth and her beau moving in time to the tune. They were laughing, and when Ruth missed a step, she was not worried at all but just laughed all the harder.

"Do you want to dance?" Malcolm asked.

"I don't know how," Sadie said.

"I can teach you."

"I'm not sure my body knows how to move that way."

"Everybody's body moves that way. It's easy."

Nerves fluttered in her stomach. "I don't know."

Malcolm took her glass from her and set it on the table beside him. He took her hand in his and pulled her toward the dance floor. She hesitated but then smiled.

Challenge sparked in his gaze. "Don't be scared."

"I'm not scared."

"You look worried."

"I don't want to make a fool of myself, is all."

Malcolm looked toward the band and signaled them with a wave. One of the guitarists nodded, and he said something to the band. They wrapped up the song several notes later, and the music turned to a much slower pace.

"How does that work for you?" Malcolm said. "It'll be easier to learn now."

Some of her trepidation eased, and she figured everyone had to learn at some point. "All right."

The smile grew wider. The color burned in her cheeks, and before she knew it, she was in the middle of a dozen couples. Malcolm put a hand on her hip, and her first reaction was to push it away. He stood still, waiting for her body to relax, and when she drew in a breath and ordered the worry to go away, he placed his other hand on the small of her back and coaxed her body toward his.

She stiffened, resisting the urge to touch him any more than she already was right now. He chuckled. "Put your hands on my shoulders, and I'll guide us around."

Sadie laid her hands on his wide shoulders. His gaze was filled with amusement as he started to move their bodies in time with the music. Several times she stepped on his feet, and her gaze dropped from his to her feet.

It took all her concentration to figure out the moves of the dance, but finally after several minutes she began to relax into the steps.

"You're a natural," he said.

"I don't know how I could be. My feet have no idea where they really are going."

"You're doing just fine, Sadie."

They continued to move through this slow song, right into another just like it. Somewhere along the way, her body moved closer and closer to his until her breasts were pressed against his chest.

She thought about her mother. Good Lord, the hell she would pay if her mother saw this. She should pull away. Take a break. Where the devil was Ruth? But each time she either looked around or tried to put distance between them, Malcolm held her tight.

When the song ended, the crowd called for another quick dance, and Sadie saw that as her opportunity to take a break. "I believe I'll have that lemonade right now," she said.

"Sure. I'll refresh our glasses." Malcolm took her hand in his and guided her off the floor. As he refilled their cups, she looked out on the floor, watching the quick steps of the couples. She tapped her foot.

Malcolm returned and handed her a brimming glass of punch. "Drink up, Sadie."

She took a sip. It was sweeter than she remembered, and the tang of citrus had more bite to it. "You put something in this."

"A little bit."

The shine she had sipped before had had a bite to it, and it had burned on the way down. This was sweet and smooth and did not taste strong at all. Before she knew it, she had finished the glass, and he had pressed a second into her hand.

When he was refilling her glass for the third time, Ruth and her beau broke away from the group and came toward her. "Looks like you're having a good time."

"I am." Her muscles had relaxed, and she was fairly sure she could dance as fast as any of the other couples.

Ruth raised a brow and smiled at her beau, as if they shared a private joke. "Yes, some girls always have a good time, don't they?"

"What's that mean?" Sadie asked.

"Nothing. Have a good evening."

When Ruth and her date vanished out the front door, Malcolm returned. "Would you like to step outside? You look a little flushed."

She sipped her punch. The idea of stepping into the cool air did appeal to her. Not only did she feel a little flushed, but she realized if she was going to kiss Malcolm, then she better do it outside, where there were no prying eyes.

"Sure, I'd like that."

His grin returned. He watched as she drank the last of her punch and then set their glasses aside. A hand on the small of her back, he guided her outside. She was aware of some of the people staring at her. They were judging her again, but like Ruth, they always were judging her. That was the way in Bluestone. No matter how fancy her dress, she would always be Sadie Thompson.

She followed Malcolm into the darkness broken up only by the stars in the clear night sky. The moon was just a sliver. It would have been a good night to make a run of shine. Just enough light so that the driver did not need headlights, but dark enough to hide you from the law.

Malcolm walked her over the dirt patch of land toward a polished Pontiac coupe parked off by itself. The paint was faded, and she could see that it was an older car. "This your car?"

"Yes." He reached in his pocket and pulled out a cigarette and lit it with the strike of a match against his heel. Smoke rose up around his face, and he reminded her of Clark Gable.

A slight wave of dizziness rolled over her, and she leaned against the shiny black roadster to steady herself. Malcolm was beside her, staring at her as if she was the only person in the world for him.

"You're very beautiful," he said.

She raised her fingertips to her warm cheeks. "No one has ever said that to me."

"That's because the boys in this town are blind fools," he said.

She pulled her shoulders back a fraction. "That's nice of you to say."

"It's true." He inhaled and then dropped the remainder of his cigarette into the dirt. He exhaled as he ground the glowing tip into the soil. "I'd like to kiss you, Sadie."

The music and the lights of the party faded, and she felt as if she were a million miles away, and it was only just Malcolm and her.

"Why do you want to kiss me?" She wanted him to tell her she was pretty again.

He moved in front of her and tipped her chin up with his fingers. He smelled of tobacco and a faint aftershave. She stared into his dark eyes and moistened her lips. She'd said she wanted a kiss.

"You want just a kiss?" she asked.

"That's all." His voice was smooth, and he was staring at her lips.

"And then we go back to the dance?" Her voice sounded distant and far away.

"That's right."

Before she could answer, he lowered his lips to hers and pressed slowly against hers. A heady rush washed over her, trailing down from her lips all the way to her toes. She knew now why Ruth liked kissing her boyfriend.

"Was that nice?" His lips were close, and she could feel his warm breath on her face.

"Yes," she said honestly.

"Want to do it again?"

The temptation was strong—but not enough to override her mother's words about staying out of trouble.

"Afraid of what your mama would say?" His tone was light, as if he was teasing an old friend. "You must be her baby girl."

"I'm not a baby."

Boyish dimples appeared when he grinned. "I know you're not."

Just to prove it, she kissed him on the lips. It was a quick peck designed more to prove she was grown up.

He pressed his hand into the small of her back and this time covered her body with the full length of his own. He felt hard all over, and she could sense an urgency in him that was as thrilling as it was unsettling.

"I want to show you something," he said.

"What?"

He took her hand in his and tugged gently. She resisted at first, but the challenge returned to his dark gaze, so she followed just to prove she was her own woman. Malcolm opened the door to the back seat of his car and nodded for her to get inside. When she hesitated, he pushed her gently.

"You're so beautiful," he said.

She angled her body forward and sat on the smooth leather seats. They were nicer than her truck but not as fine as the leather seats of the Carters' Pontiac. She scooted toward the other side as he sat and closed the door.

Inside the car, his midsize frame seemed to grow larger. He laid his hand on her thigh. She pushed it away.

"You want me to kiss you again?" Malcolm asked.

"No." But she did not really mean it. She liked kissing. It was just that the car made her feel trapped, which made her nervous.

"I think you do want me to kiss you, Sadie Thompson." Without waiting this time, he leaned forward and pressed her back against the seat. He kissed her lips and slammed his tongue into her mouth.

This time her head spun, and she was certain this was far more kissing than she had bargained for. She tried to sit up, but his weight kept her back pressed against the seat.

His hand trailed over her thigh, down to the hem of her dress. He tugged so quickly it was halfway up her thigh before she could protest.

"I don't like that," she said as she pressed her hands against his chest.

"Sure you do. Or you wouldn't be here," he said.

"I want to go back to the dance."

"I'll take you back in a few minutes. Don't you like being here?"

His fingers slid up under her skirt, and he fumbled with her drawers. She tried to push his hand away. "Stop. I don't like it."

"That's because you've never tried it." He rose up slightly, reached for the center button on his pants, and was on top of her again.

Her head swirled. The music outside was so far away she wondered if it had stopped. "I don't want to try anything else."

He covered her mouth with his. "You asked me to kiss you. And that's what I'm doing."

What happened in the next few minutes stunned her entire body and soul. He tugged down her underwear and reached for the most intimate part of her. Desire had abandoned her completely, and all she felt was shame. "I don't want this."

In her struggles, her skirt twisted up by her waist, and she could see her bare legs glowing in the moonlight.

He pushed her left leg to the side, and for a brief flash she saw his most private parts. He shoved inside her with a hard push, and she cried out. Pain seared her body as tears pooled in her eyes and rolled down her cheeks.

He moved inside of her, back and forth, tearing at her insides. The tempo quickened, and all she could do was draw within herself and try to convince herself that she was not going to die. He went rigid and then collapsed against her.

She stared over his shoulder out the car window at the stars. For some reason, they all looked different now. They had been pretty before, but now she found their sparkle annoying.

"Ready for another dance." He sat up and fixed his pants.

She scrambled to a sitting position and tugged her skirt down. "What?"

"It's only nine o'clock. The night is young. Let's dance."

He opened the car door and stepped out. He lit a cigarette. "Better hurry. The longer we're gone, the more questions you'll face later."

Her insides ached as she scooted across the seat and stumbled to her feet. When she found her voice, it sounded far off and foreign to her. "I'm going to tell Miss Olivia."

Malcolm grinned as he straightened his tie. "You'll not tell a soul. No one will believe you. And if someone did believe I would sleep with you, there would be plenty of people who would tell the sheriff about the green dress you wore. No girl dresses like that without wanting a man's attention."

"I didn't want that!" she shouted.

"Shh. Of course you did. Otherwise you would not have gotten in the car. And I'd be careful whom you tell. It'll make you look like a whore, and you're already in trouble with Edward. The Carters will run you out of town without a second thought."

Outrage burned inside her as she stared at his smug face. "This was your fault."

"No, darling. This is the kind of thing that happens to troublemakers."

CHAPTER EIGHTEEN

LIBBY

Sunday, June 14, 2020
Bluestone, Virginia

So how did Libby handle the news that Elaine Carter Grant was her birth mother?

She walked out her back door and toward the shed, where she had left her newly rediscovered photography equipment. With thoughts of storming Woodmont Estate chewing on her, she pulled all the remaining covers off the equipment and tossed them in the trash. The dustcovers had not exactly done their job, so she grabbed a rag and started wiping down the black bellows camera that sat on a tripod. Next, she hauled out the glass negative-development box and set it at the end of a slightly shorter workstation that she and her father had built when she was fifteen. Neither had carpentry skills, so the bench had always been a little lopsided and required shims under the back-right leg.

Testing the table for sturdiness, she was pleased it did not wobble. Her father had gone out of his way not to leave her any problems, except the birth-mother-identity issue. "No biggie, right, Dad? Just a minor damn detail."

Until she bought developing chemicals, the best she could do now was wipe down the enlarger that she used to develop thirty-five-millimeter film. Again, no chemicals to actually develop the negatives and prints, but that problem was easily fixed with a couple of online orders.

"Jesus, Dad," she muttered as she settled a box of old cameras on her workbench. "All the things you could have told me while you were sick!"

It was all she could do not to slam down the box of old cameras, coughing as dust plumed around her. "I could have done with less talk about where the water shutoff valve to the house was and more talk about genetics."

Libby quickly did the math and realized that Elaine would have been about twenty-two when she'd had Libby. Young, but certainly not a teen mother. And her family were hardly paupers.

"And what the hell was Elaine doing in New Jersey?" she shouted to the empty room.

Had Elaine been shacking up with her birth daddy or taking summer school or hiding out in a group home for unwed mothers? The last theory would have held true if Libby had been born in the 1960s or even the 1970s. But in 1989 people were pretty cool about an unwed pregnancy, right?

It was clear her great-grandmother Olivia had known about her. But what about her great-granddaddy? Was he some kind of throwback judgmental ass? Was that why she was such a big secret? She rubbed the back of her neck. Nothing like finding out that she had not been wanted by a family with the means to care for her.

And what about her birth daddy? Did he figure into the equation at all, or was he just an afterthought?

When her phone rang at one o'clock in the morning, Libby fished it out of her back pocket. "Sierra."

"Why are the shed lights on?" She yawned. "My mother is concerned that you're doing something dangerous."

Libby drew in a deep breath. "Setting up my photography equipment."

"Again, why this time of night?"

"Haven't you been after me for months about this?" Libby asked.

"Not in the middle of the night, dear. Did something happen at Woodmont?"

She rolled her head from side to side. "Nothing happened at Woodmont. Elaine's daughter was a little rude, but it was no big deal."

"What did she say?"

Olivia's letter explained a lot about Lofton's behavior at dinner. Libby would bet that Lofton, her baby sister, knew about the adoption. (God, had she really strung those words together?) Which led to the next question: Who else knew? Ted? What about Colton or Margaret?

Libby swatted away the buzzing thoughts. Too much to process. "I found my dad's deed to the house." She took the coward's way, but she simply was not ready to talk about this. It had taken her months to speak about her miscarriages, and though finding a birth mother certainly was a different kind of gut strike, it hurt so bad she could not begin to voice her feelings.

"Set up an appointment with the bank," Libby said. "The sooner the better."

"Are you sure about this? I mean we're talking about putting your father's house up for collateral."

She lifted a Brownie camera out of the box. It was small and compact. She had never found film to test it out. Turning away from the equipment, she shut off the light and shut the shed door on her way out. "It's my house now, Sierra. And you're right. I can't just let it collect dust."

"Yeah, but this is not what I was aiming for."

"I know. And I'm glad it can come to some good use. Set up the meeting. The sooner you can start your business, the better."

"Do you want me to come over? You sound a little weird."

She started back to the house she had grown up in, wondering if it had all been a lie. "What do you know about Elaine Grant?"

"What brought her up? Wait. Something did happen at dinner."

"No. Dinner was fine. I'm just curious about Elaine."

Sierra sighed, as if sensing now was not the time to press. "I know she moved away after college. After her grandfather died, she inherited the property but really didn't start visiting regularly until after her grandmother died. My mother always thought Elaine must have had a falling-out with her grandmother."

"Like what?" Libby asked.

"Not privy to the workings of the Carter family. I know Elaine didn't show any interest in Woodmont until a year or two ago."

"Why did she come back?"

"I don't know. Maybe older and wiser, and the old wounds had healed. Shame your dad isn't still around. I think she and your dad were friends."

She climbed the back steps and into her kitchen. "Why do you say that?"

"I had taken Mom to the Hotel Roanoke's brunch. She loves their french toast and the mimosas. Anyway, I saw Elaine and your dad at a table. Mom being Mom went over and said hello, and I went along for the ride."

"And?"

"They both looked a little tense."

"Tense how?"

"Like a big conversation. Neither one looked well, and they didn't look happy to see anyone from Bluestone," Sierra said.

"You never told me."

"I guess I forgot about it. Didn't seem that important. I mean, it was a public place. And they said they were looking to do a fundraiser for the pediatric cancer unit at UVA. It never happened, but then your dad passed away."

The fundraiser excuse did not smell right. They had to have been talking about Libby. "Okay. Well, unlike the fundraiser, your bank meeting will take place, and you'll get the loan," Libby said.

"You going to stay up all night?" Sierra asked.

"Most likely."

"Are you sure you don't want me to come over?"

"Sierra, sometimes grief rears its ugly head and won't let me sleep. You know what I mean?"

"I do. Have you been on Jeremy's Instagram page again?"

"Guilty," she lied.

"Just unfollow him, Libby."

"I know. And I will."

"You need to stop looking back."

A spontaneous, tense laugh burst out. "Don't I know it. But tell that to the past. It keeps biting me in the ass."

"I could bake you cookies," Sierra offered.

"Then I would be sad, sleep deprived, and fat."

"How can you be sad if you're eating a cookie?" Sierra asked.

Libby laughed. "I appreciate you; I really do. I'm just having one of those nights. You know how it goes; you think you're finished with an emotion, and then it doubles back on you."

"You're right about that."

"Really, I'm fine."

"You can sleep on the couch here. Mom said this morning she already missed you."

"Thanks. But it's time I graduate to my big-girl bed."

"You can get a new, real bed. The feng shui of abundance."

"Saying goodbye now, Sierra."

"Have breakfast with Mom and me," she added quickly. "I bet she has something on Elaine."

And there was the carrot Libby could not resist. "What time?"

"Seeing as you're pulling an all-nighter, how about seven?"

"I'll be there."

The all-nighter ended at three o'clock, when Libby—finally too tired to clean, polish, or worry—retreated to the couch in her living room. She lay back on the sofa, hoping she would not stare at the popcorn ceiling until dawn as caffeine, memories, and what-the-hells raged in her system. Fortunately, the next thing she knew, the sun had risen, and her phone was ringing.

She cleared her throat and raised the phone to her ear. "Sierra. What time is it?"

"Seven fifteen."

She sat up and swung her legs over the side. Her head pounded, and her mouth was dry. "On my way."

"Sounds like you slept."

"No questions before coffee."

"Understood."

Libby rose, pulled the ponytail holder from her hair, and combed her fingers through her hair before refastening. She made a quick stop in the bathroom, then dashed out the back door and slipped through the small gap in the fence into Sierra's yard just as she had done a million times as a kid.

She climbed the back steps and entered the kitchen as if it were still 2000, sans the dental braces and a plaid jumper. The smell of bacon and coffee reminded her that life was full of good things, and somehow the latest mess would sort itself out.

Mrs. Mancuso stood at the small stove, pushing a wooden spoon through her cast-iron skillet filled with scrambled eggs. She was several inches shorter than Sierra, and her once-dark hair was now peppered with gray, but she and her daughter both had the same high cheek-bones, full lips, and expressive eyes. Mrs. Mancuso was wearing jeans, a blousy light-blue peasant top, and Birkenstocks.

"Morning, Mrs. M." She kissed her on the cheek and reached for a coffee mug. "Thank you again for saving me."

"Always, honey. Get a cup and sit. I want you two girls well fed. You two never sit."

Libby poured, sipped several times, and began to feel a little more human as she sat at the kitchen table. "Where is Sierra?"

"If she can get out of the shower and stop fussing over what she's going to wear, she'll be right here," Mrs. Mancuso said, frowning.

In an odd way, Libby was glad Sierra's fashion obsession had remained intact. Any more change, and she would go nuts.

"Sierra said you were asking about Elaine Grant," Mrs. Mancuso said.

"Yeah." The hypercommunication between Sierra and her mother always amazed her, although it was not surprising.

"Elaine and I went to elementary school together, and then her grandmother Olivia sent her to boarding school. The same one you attended, as a matter of fact."

"Small world. She was raised by her grandparents?" Libby asked.

"Yes. Her mom and dad died when she was in the third grade. It was a horrific car accident. Dr. and Mrs. Carter took her in without a second thought. She seemed to get on with things, but you know how that goes. Nothing's the same afterward."

"No truer words." She swirled the coffee in her cup. "Did you see much of her after she enrolled in boarding school?"

"Sure. Summers—when she wasn't working in her grandfather's medical practice. She answered phones and filed. He was hoping she would end up becoming a doctor."

"She became a lawyer."

"A very successful one. And I would like to think that Dr. Carter would have been proud of that accomplishment. He and his wife built their entire world around Elaine."

"Elaine said Olivia suffered miscarriages."

"That would have been before my time. Elaine did say once her grandmother thought the family might be cursed. Mrs. Carter was always dressed to the nines, and she always had a big smile on her face. But when Elaine moved away after college, I think she lost her sense of purpose."

"Where did Elaine go to college?"

"Princeton."

"In New Jersey."

"Yes."

"After Mrs. Carter died, no one really lived at Woodmont?"

"There was the caretaker and his wife but no real life to speak of on the property."

"And now Elaine is back," Libby said.

"You know she's sick, right?" Mrs. Mancuso said.

"I did." She let the words dangle, hoping Mrs. Mancuso would fill in the pieces.

"Breast cancer. The surgeons think they got it all but advised on the chemo just to be sure."

"And Elaine's daughter. What's her deal?"

"I barely know Lofton. She didn't grow up around here."

"I met her yesterday. She clearly loves her mother." Lofton's underlying irritation with Libby had to stem from fear. Libby was an unknown entity, and it made sense Lofton would be overprotective of a mother who was sick and perhaps vulnerable.

"Did Elaine have a boyfriend in college?" Libby asked.

"She dated Scott Waters during her freshman year, but he transferred to a school out west, and that ended that."

"What year was that?"

"Umm, 1987-ish."

Unless Scott had doubled back and reconnected with Elaine around the time of her conception, he was not the daddy. And she'd said she had not met Ted until she was twenty-three, which would have been after she was born.

"Why all the questions about Elaine?"

"Just curious. They had me to dinner last night, and I can't really figure out why."

"Have you thought about asking her?" Mrs. Mancuso said. "I have always thought the direct approach was the best."

Libby called Elaine, knowing if she hesitated it would be like pulling a bandage off slowly. Better to just do it.

She dialed the number several times but each time put the phone aside and found a reason to watch the news, do a load of laundry, or edit the pictures from Saturday's wedding.

Sierra then called at ten to say they had a loan officer appointment in two days, and that gave her something else to think about for around thirty minutes.

Finally, at noon, despite her best efforts, Libby had run out of delay tactics.

She dialed Elaine's number and hit call. As she counted each ring, her heart thumped louder in her chest. After four rings, the call went to voice mail. *"This is Elaine Grant. I can't take your call right now, but if you leave me your number, I will return your call promptly."*

Libby pulled back her shoulders, feeling the ache of tension that refused to leave. She had practiced her response to this scenario countless times over her life. *Birth mother ignores me. Birth mother denies our past. Birth mother rejects me.* How many times had she played out those scenarios in her head? Now faced with leaving a message for her birth mother, she wondered what tone would best fit her well-rehearsed words. Should she summon outrage, a cheerful ring, or a "no big deal; I am fine" tone?

"This is Libby McKenzie." Her voice sounded rough, and she was not sure where she fell on the tone spectrum. "Elaine, if you could call me at your earliest convenience, I would appreciate it."

She hung up and spent the next five minutes staring at the display, half expecting, hoping, and dreading it would ring. But it remained silent.

CHAPTER NINETEEN

ELAINE

Monday, June 15, 2020
The Woodmont Estate

Elaine stared into the bathroom mirror. Her cheeks were flushed, and her hands were trembling slightly. For thirty-one years she had dreamed about the day she could spend with her daughter. She had gone over and over in her head what she would say to her but still did not have the words that felt right.

And when Libby's name had appeared on her phone, she had panicked and had not picked up. Last night had not gone as smoothly as she had hoped. Lofton had been difficult, and as much as she had wanted to rail against her before she left this morning, she did not have it in her. Lofton was a smart young woman and very good at seeing what others did not. Elaine had known from the moment Lofton had taken a hard look at Libby she had recognized a family connection.

For most of her life, Elaine had pictured Libby as a little girl. The McKenzies had sent Elaine pictures on each of Libby's birthdays. The one taken on her first birthday was always the one she looked at when she needed a lift. Libby's little face was covered in cake as she grinned up at the camera, displaying her three teeth. At age two, she was standing on a field of green with a black Lab puppy. At six, her grin was gap toothed.

Elaine had always waited with excitement for the pictures to arrive and would spend hours staring at Libby's face, searching for traces of her own features. Whose nose did she have? Did they share the exact same shade of green eyes? The comparisons were endless.

The pictures of the smiling girl confirmed Elaine had made the right decision. But it also drove home the ache that never healed, even when Lofton was born. She had two children, and not having her first-born with her was a forever kind of wound that would never fully heal.

"Libby is here now," she whispered. "That's what matters."

She wanted this to work, to build a bridge to her daughter. But she had been warned by the experts to go slow. It could not be rushed.

And then there was the matter of Lofton. Her youngest daughter had been unusually antagonistic last night, as if she understood exactly who she had met, even though Elaine had been careful to guard her secret.

Her phone rang, and when she saw the name, she smiled. "Ted, are you safely back in Washington?"

"Made it ahead of the traffic and sitting at my office desk. Sorry again I had to leave."

"It was nice having you here."

"How are you feeling? Yesterday was a big day."

Her husband had known about Libby since their third date. She had known then she was in love with him but needed him to accept her child. He had never faltered, smiling when she had shown him the three birthday pictures the McKenzies had sent her.

"I'm doing fine," she said. "It was so lovely to have Libby here again."

"She has your nose." It had been his first response when she had shown him her precious collection of Libby pictures. The sincerity

behind his words had deepened her love for him, and she had known then she would marry him.

"What was going on with Lofton last night?" he asked. "It's not like her to be rude."

"It's as if she knew the truth."

"How?"

"She's not only smart but also perceptive, Ted," Elaine said. "Did she ask you about Libby?"

"No, but she does suspect something. It would be like Lofton to pretend she knows more than she does, hoping you'll spill the beans. I stopped falling for that trick when she was in the seventh grade."

Elaine smiled, remembering how the freckles had stretched over the bridge of Lofton's nose at that age.

"Are you worried about telling Lofton the truth?" Ted asked.

"She has to be told at some point. And this kind of truth rarely stays hidden forever."

In the background a car beeped. "Why do you sound worried?" he asked.

She rubbed the side of her neck. "Libby just called me this morning."

"And that's a bad thing?"

"After last night, judging by the tone of her voice in the message, I think she must know."

"How?"

"I gave Olivia's letter to her father last November. She may have found it."

Silence crackled over the line, and she knew Ted was holding back his thoughts on Dr. McKenzie. He had never been happy about keeping the secret but always respected Elaine's wish. "She seems like a fine woman, Elaine."

Elaine knotted her brow. "She is. I can't claim her, but I'm proud."

"Why can't you claim her?"

"I didn't raise her."

"But she has your DNA in her. That's a big part of who she is."

"The McKenzies did a great job with her."

"And yet they couldn't have done anything without you."

She raised her chin. "I know. I just have so much regret."

"You need to call her back."

"What if I tell Libby the truth, and she ends up hating me?"

"Either way, you'll have done right by her, Elaine."

"She's had such a terrible few years with the miscarriages and the divorce. What if I'm simply a bridge too far?"

"Libby has a right to know."

"Ted, I gave her away. How can she forgive that?"

"You didn't give her away."

As many times as he said it, Elaine still did not believe it. "I feel like I've betrayed her."

"Do you think twenty-two-year-old Elaine could have raised her?"

She pressed her hand to her forehead. She had asked the same question so many times she had worn down the finish of the words. "Grandmother Olivia didn't think so."

"You know how I feel about your grandparents' lack of support," Ted said.

"They were very old world. Girls who got pregnant in their day were shunned. She was fearful for me. And especially considering what my grandfather did to girls like me back in the day."

When Elaine had told her grandmother about the pregnancy, Olivia had told her all about the hospital in Lynchburg where her grandfather had worked. Then she sent Elaine to a small New Jersey town to live with an old friend of hers whom Elaine did not know. The woman was kind and helped Elaine through the last months of her pregnancy. Elaine had felt so isolated.

Her grandmother made it very clear that Elaine had a bright future, but it did not include a baby. Olivia also forbade Elaine to mention the baby to her grandfather. When Libby was eight days old, Elaine had been moved into the apartment she would inhabit during law school.

Elaine looked in the mirror, wondering how Libby would accept the truth. When her own parents had died and her world had turned upside down, she had been so angry. It had taken her years to let go. Libby too had that fire in her eyes.

"You need to tell her everything," Ted said.

"I want her to get to know us a little bit before I tell her the entire unvarnished truth. One bombshell at a time."

There was a long pause. "Don't wait too long, Elaine."

"I won't." Her stomach twisted in knots, and she wondered how she would find the right words under these circumstances.

"I love you."

"I love you," she said warmly.

"It will be okay."

"I hope so."

She hung up and stared into her mirror for a long time. Ted was optimistic by nature, and she loved that about him. But sometimes life simply did not work out as planned.

CHAPTER TWENTY

SADIE

Saturday, October 3, 1942
Bluestone, Virginia

Sadie tried to pretend that night months ago in Malcolm's car never happened. It was easy enough during the days when she was busy doing piecework involving sewing dresses and mending torn sleeves. Or even pulling weeds in the garden and then canning. She always kept busy to quiet her mind.

In the evenings, she and her mother listened to the radio, paying close attention to the news on the war. Johnny had left Norfolk, Virginia, on a transport ship in early September, and it had taken two weeks to cross the Atlantic. He said he had never heard about seasickness but sure was an expert now.

He was in southern England and was living in a camp full of soldiers. He said he'd been lucky to get a tent that he split with three other men. They shared a small heater, which came in handy, as England was normally wet and chilly.

Johnny had worked on the heavy bombers, repairing the damage inflicted by German Luftwaffe and flak from antiaircraft guns. He counted planes each morning as they took off with a crew of ten men and flew south. They were bombing enemy targets mostly within occupied France. He always made it a point to count them as they returned. Most days, half the planes did not return.

More and more boys from the valley had signed up for the army and had left town. The war brought more piecework, as boys preparing to ship overseas needed uniforms hemmed, waistbands taken in, and rank sewn on. Each time Sadie got a uniform to work on, she thought about Johnny.

Sadie read Johnny's letters over and over to her mother, and as she did, her mother's needle would stop sliding in and out of the fabric while she listened. Her mother hoarded each word as if it were gold and never tired of hearing what Johnny had said. There was still no word from Danny, but there had also been no telegram from the army saying he was dead or missing.

There had been no contact from Olivia Carter and, more importantly, no word from the sheriff. She thought about Olivia a lot, knowing she was hurting over the loss of her child. Sadie understood that dropping by Woodmont was not an option, but she had hoped to see her when in town buying supplies.

Sadie was nurturing that hope as she parked the old truck in front of the mercantile store and carried in a crate of tomatoes. This was the last of the season and the best she had to offer. The last of the bruised and overripe tomatoes, cucumbers, and squash would all be canned in the coming days.

She passed by a truck and noticed a young woman was sitting inside. As Sadie hefted her crate and shifted the weight off a splinter digging into her palm, she looked at the woman. Bright, wild green eyes that all but overtook the small pale face stared at her. Sadie paused and returned the woman's gaze, realizing suddenly she was the girl from the hospital in Lynchburg.

Sadie's heart beat faster as she took a step closer to the truck. She had thought a lot about this girl over the last few months, wondering if she had survived whatever had happened in that place.

As she drew closer, the woman folded her arms over her chest. She made no attempt to roll up the window, and when Sadie was within a couple of feet, the woman looked down. She was shaking her head and fidgeting, like the underside of her skin was crawling with ants.

Sadie stopped and took a step back, hoping the woman would realize she was no threat. But the woman never looked back at her. "My name's Sadie," she said. "What's your name?"

Gaze still anchored on her lap, the woman did not speak.

"Can I offer you some ripe tomatoes? I got a few extras I'd be glad to share."

The woman looked up at her with a sadness that felt as deep as the caves that burrowed into the mountains. She slowly shook her head and then looked away.

Finally, Sadie turned toward the store and, balancing her crate on her knee, opened the door. Bells rang overhead as she stepped inside the store. Mr. Sullivan was behind the counter, boxing up an order for a tall, broad-shouldered man. Thankfully, there was no sign of Ruth.

She settled her crate on the end of the counter and glanced around the countertop for an old magazine. There was a *Harper's Bazaar* that dated back two years, but that did not dampen her excitement.

"That will be two dollars, Mr. Black," Mr. Sullivan said.

The man fished change and a crumpled bill from his pocket and carefully counted it out. She recognized him from the hospital. He had been dragging that girl toward the front entrance.

"Mr. Black, my name is Sadie. Is that your daughter in the truck?" Sadie asked.

Black did not spare her a glance. "What of it?"

"I just said hello to her. She seems nice." That was not exactly what she meant, but she did not think she would win any points with a stranger by saying his daughter looked lost and sad.

"Stay away from my Sally." He scooped up his purchases. "The last thing she needs is a friend like you."

Sadie waffled between retreating and fighting. "You don't know me."

"I know your type."

As Mr. Black turned around, he regarded Sadie. His gaze hesitated, as if he might know her. He shook his head and strode out of the store.

"I'm trying to recall where Mr. Black lives in the valley," Sadie said to Mr. Sullivan.

"About ten miles from here. He doesn't come into town that often."

"I've never seen his daughter before." She glanced at a page in the magazine, as if she were just making conversation.

"I don't think I've seen her since she was a little girl. Pretty little thing but simpleminded."

Did that explain the odd look in the girl's eyes? "She doesn't look much older than me, but I never saw her in school."

"She never went to school. No point, I suppose."

Sadie was smart enough to realize that whatever was happening in the hospital was not good. "She looked smart enough to me."

Mr. Sullivan shook his head. "Did you come in here to gossip about the Black family or sell me tomatoes?"

"I came to sell tomatoes."

Mr. Sullivan reached under the counter and set a stack of older magazines on the counter. "These are for you."

"Me? When did you start giving me magazines?"

"They are from Olivia Carter. She was in the other day and left them for you."

Sadie smoothed her hand over the magazines, catching a hint of Miss Olivia's perfume. "She left these for me?"

"Said they would go in the trash otherwise."

"How's she looking?" Sadie asked.

"Seems well enough. Her husband was with her. He frets over her."

The old truck outside rumbled to life and pulled away from the curb. She turned and watched through the window as it drove off. "He loves her."

"I haven't seen much of you the last couple of weeks. Where have you been?"

She faced him, gathering her magazines. "Had a touch of the flu. Mama said it was best not to drive into town. But I'm right as rain now."

"You look different," he said. "Getting fat."

"With Johnny and Danny gone, Mama's been lavishing all her cooking on me. She makes the best biscuits."

"How are your brothers faring?"

"Doing well."

"Six more boys from the county have left for the army. There won't be anyone left." He carefully inspected the tomatoes.

"When do you think it'll be over?" she asked.

"I hear now that we're in the fight, it's a matter of time before the war turns. But that's what they said last time. Everyone thought we'd be done by Christmas."

"I wish so, but I know it ain't likely."

Mr. Sullivan counted out one dollar and fifteen cents for the produce. She glanced at the grocery list, knowing she could afford only the flour and lard. She had hoped there would be some extra for sugar so her mother could make her a cake.

She left the store with fresh supplies in her crate and the little bit of money in her pocket. She put her parcel on the passenger seat and got behind the wheel. The engine did not start right away, forcing her to wait before she tried to coax it to life again. As she waited for some of the gas to settle out of the carburetor, the Carters' Pontiac rushed past.

She searched for Miss Olivia but saw only Dr. Carter. He had a sour look on his face, and judging by the direction, he was headed to Charlottesville to see patients. He would be gone for hours, likely all day.

If Sadie had a lick of sense, she would go home and mind her own business. But she found herself thinking about the greenhouse and Miss Olivia. It seemed only right to thank her for the magazines. Before she knew it, she was driving out toward Woodmont.

Fifteen minutes later, she paused at the twin pillars. But before she could talk herself out of driving on down the road, she pulled into the driveway. She drove around the side as she always did and parked at the kitchen entrance. She rubbed damp palms against her pant legs and then got out of the truck. She climbed the back steps and knocked on the kitchen door.

Mrs. Fritz's gaze narrowed, as if she did not trust her eyes. She hurried to the door, drying her hands on her white apron.

"Morning, Mrs. Fritz," Sadie said with as much cheer as she could muster. "I come to thank Miss Olivia for the magazines."

"I don't know what you're talking about. And if the doctor were to find you here, he would call the sheriff. It took all Miss Olivia had in her to keep him from having you carted off to jail."

"I didn't mean to hurt anyone," she said, her voice tight with emotion. "It was an accident."

Mrs. Fritz shoved out a sigh and pulled her inside. "I know it was. Miss Olivia is just real delicate when it comes to having babies."

"Is she doing all right?"

"Thankfully, she's off that laudanum. It helped with the pain, but she slept all the time. I was glad to see her quit it. She now spends a lot of time in her greenhouse. In fact, she's there now."

"So all the plants have arrived?"

"They have indeed. She planted most of them by herself. The doctor didn't want her to work so hard, but she said she would go crazy if she didn't have something to do. The more that greenhouse thrives, the better she seems to get."

"A bit like magic."

"Well, I don't know about magic, but something good happens to her when she's in there with her plants." Mrs. Fritz looked over her shoulder to make sure they were alone. "Run on down there quick, and give her your thanks personally. I know she would appreciate the kind words. The doctor ain't supposed to be back until after supper."

"Thank you, Mrs. Fritz."

Her sour expression softened. "Go on now."

Sadie ran out the back and down the path toward the greenhouse. When she rounded the corner and saw it, her breath caught in her throat. The leaves on the trees had turned orange, yellow, and brown. They had thinned, allowing more sunlight on the glass dome. It sparkled like the diamonds in the magazines.

It was now filled with pots bursting with plants. Miss Olivia would know the proper names, but Sadie had no idea. Most had an odd look that did not resemble anything close to an apple tree or a tomato plant, and the delicate blossoms were shades of rich purples, yellows, and reds.

She opened the door and was struck by the humid air, which was at least twenty degrees warmer than the outside. There was no sign of Miss Olivia as she walked down the row of plants, letting her fingertips brush against the lush leaves. At the back of the greenhouse, she stared out into the woods. This space was another world, so separate from the life she lived.

She reached in her pocket and removed the truck key. And before she really thought, she carved her name into the glass. She might have lived in this world for only a little while, but she wanted to leave some kind of mark on it.

"Sadie."

She turned at the sound of Miss Olivia's voice. She stood behind her, a light-brown gardening jacket covering a navy-blue dress and gardening gloves protecting her slim hands.

Sadie slid the key in her pocket. "Miss Olivia."

"I thought I heard your truck. It has a very distinctive sound."

"You're looking just fine," Sadie said.

"I'm feeling more like myself."

"I came to thank you for the magazines."

"I was wondering when you would pick them up. They've been sitting at the store for two weeks."

"I was slow getting into town." No need to whine about feeling poorly. "It will give me something to read for weeks."

"Good."

Sadie tugged at a brown button dangling from her jacket cuff. "I'm so sorry about the baby. If I hadn't let you drive—" The words had barely passed over her lips, and she teared up.

"It wasn't your fault."

"I never told anyone you were driving."

"I know, and I appreciate that. I should have cleared up the confusion with my husband, but he was beside himself with grief over the baby. I did convince him to leave you be."

"I appreciate that."

Miss Olivia regarded her a moment as she approached. "You look different."

"Mr. Sullivan said I look fat. Which I suppose I am, for all the biscuits and gravy I eat. Can't seem to get enough of them."

Miss Olivia's eyes drew together in a frown. "Did you wear the green dress to the dance?"

Sadie straightened. She had burned that dress in the barrel out by the barn. "Thank you again for it."

Miss Olivia closed her eyes for a moment as she allowed a sigh. "Did you meet a man at the dance, Sadie?"

"No one to speak of, and if I did, I don't remember."

"But you did meet a man."

"Why are you asking all these questions?" Sadie asked. "I was just here to give you my apologies and thanks."

Miss Olivia closed the gap between the two of them in a blink, and her hand slid to Sadie's belly. The instant fingers touched, Miss Olivia recoiled.

Sadie quickly stepped back, covering herself with the folds of her jacket. "Why did you go and do that?"

"You do realize what's happening?"

"What are you talking about?"

"Sadie, you're with child."

CHAPTER TWENTY-ONE

LIBBY

Monday, June 15, 2020
The Woodmont Estate

Libby parked in front of Woodmont and shut off the engine. Without the hum of the air-conditioning, the sun quickly warmed up the car. For a moment, the heat felt good, but as soon as it chased away the chill, her skin flushed with the growing heat. Out of the car, she heard the rumble of a truck and the beep-beep of another large vehicle as it backed up. Work on the greenhouse continued, and though on a normal day she might photograph the work, today she had other plans.

She rang the bell and then stepped back, bracing to see Ted or Lofton ready to ask more questions. There was no plausible reason to explain why she was there other than the truth. *"Hey, folks, guess what? Your little girl is home! I'm Elaine's daughter. Surprise!"*

Inside the house, she heard steady footsteps that she now recognized as Elaine's. Libby fidgeted with the letter in her back pocket like a process server with a subpoena. *"You've been served!"*

Instead, she curled her fingers into fists and then quickly released them, fearing she looked angry. Which she was, but that was beside the point. She was mad at Elaine and her father. Why the hell was it so hard to tell the truth?

The door opened to Elaine. She was dressed in a simple pair of slim-fitting khakis and a white shirt. Her brown hair was brushed off her face, and she wore only a little makeup but managed to look totally pulled together. *Why did I not get that gene?* Libby thought.

"Libby?"

"Did you get my message?" Libby's voice sounded tight and tense.

"I did."

Libby did not need to ask why Elaine had not called her back. She would bet money that Elaine had heard the bottled tension in her voice and guessed that the cat was out of the bag. "We need to talk."

"Sure." She came outside and guided Libby to a twin pair of rockers under a slow-moving ceiling fan. "Would you like something to drink?"

Vodka, bourbon, or wine might have hit the spot and taken the edge off. "No, thank you."

Elaine lowered into a chair and watched as Libby removed the letter from her back pocket. "You've finally gone through your father's papers."

"I was looking for the deed to the house."

"Are you planning on selling?" Elaine asked.

"Using it as collateral. It's a long story and not the reason I'm here. I found the letter Olivia wrote to me. Dad had it in its own folder."

Elaine stilled, staring at her. Tension rippled through her body.

"When were you going to tell me?"

Elaine's eyes glistened with tears. "Are you angry?"

Libby's heart raced quickly, pounding loudly in her ears. Even with the letter in hand, a small part of her had hoped maybe it was not true and that her father had not lied by omission. "I'm not sure what I feel, Elaine. I've made it to age thirty-one, and no one has been honest."

"That was a condition of the adoption. I was never to contact you. But your father sent me pictures of you each year around your birthday."

"I'm not a child. Don't you think we could have had a conversation, I don't know, in the last dozen years?"

"I always thought I would wait and let you come to me. I thought your father would tell you. When I finished my second round of chemo, I called your dad to meet for lunch. I gave him Olivia's letter, and he promised me he would give it to you. He wanted to be the one to tell you, so I respected that."

"He did not breathe a word."

Elaine folded her hands in her lap. "Your father said he would give you the letter. He said he owed you the truth."

"Did he tell you this while you two were having lunch in Roanoke?" When Elaine looked surprised, Libby added, "Roanoke isn't so far away from Bluestone. My friend Sierra saw you two."

Absently, Elaine rubbed a callus on her palm. "He swore to me he would tell you the truth. But then I saw you at his funeral, and you politely shook my hand like a stranger."

"You're a stranger."

"I know. I would like to change that."

Elaine appeared more fragile now, and Libby could see this was a strain on her. "He never liked to deliver bad news." She stopped herself. "I didn't mean bad as in *bad*. I should have said difficult news. It was all he could do to talk to me when my mother died. And when I say my mother . . ."

"I know what you mean. Kathy was your mother. She raised you, and I won't take anything away from her. I know she loved you very much."

"Did she know about you? I think about all the times she brought me here for the Garden Week open houses. Maybe it was just the plants."

"She knew about me."

"So the story about me being abandoned in the New Jersey hospital wasn't true."

The first flash of anger sparkled in her eyes. "No, it was not. Your father knew I was expecting and living in New Jersey."

"How did my father find out?"

"My grandmother told him a couple of weeks before you were born. And as soon as she did, he contacted me and asked what I planned to do. I had met with an agency but had made no final choices."

"Why did Olivia tell him?" Libby asked.

"He was the local pediatrician. Her husband was a doctor. She also knew she would be able to see you from time to time if the McKenzies adopted you."

"And you said yes, just like that?"

Elaine picked at a loose thread. "I didn't say yes, just like that. I thought long and hard about it. When I finally called him, I was in labor and absolutely terrified."

"Mom said she and Dad got the call that there was an abandoned baby ready to adopt. They hopped in the car and drove up to New Jersey."

Elaine frowned. "You were not abandoned. I called your father when I was in labor. Your parents appeared about two hours after you were born."

"Mom said you didn't want to see them."

"I did not. I was afraid I would lose my nerve."

"Did you ever think to keep me?"

"A million times."

"Why didn't you?"

"I've asked myself that very question every day since."

"Money couldn't have been an issue. You come from money."

"Remember, I had no mother or father to help me with this, and my grandmother came from a different generation. When she was young, a girl who became pregnant out of wedlock was shunned. She was afraid for me."

"But that was the late eighties."

"It made no difference to her. She was a strong-willed woman. She made me swear I wouldn't tell my grandfather."

"Why not?"

"My grandfather was a kind and loving man. He was a second father to me. But he too had very steadfast beliefs about women getting pregnant out of marriage."

"Kind of Stone Age."

"He was born in 1920. If you're curious, he's mentioned in several articles about eugenics in Virginia."

"What about it?"

"Perhaps it will help explain him better. My grandfather, like other medical professionals of the time, believed they were doing a service to women by sterilizing them."

"Sterilizing them?"

"Mentally challenged, disabled, and sometimes just poor women. I'm not defending what he did. It was terrible. But in his mind, he was performing a necessary service."

"Jesus."

"I was very angry with Olivia for a long time. But over the years, I gained some perspective. I read her journals, and I got a glimpse into her early days in Virginia. You'll learn a lot about her."

"Through her plants?" Libby struggled to keep a civil tone.

"She talks a lot about the people she knew then. There was one girl in particular, Sadie Thompson. My grandmother befriended her and tried to help her."

"The name etched in the greenhouse glass?" Libby asked.

"Yes."

A car pulled up, and Libby pushed back a jolt of annoyance as she saw Lofton striding up the front steps. She wore a dark-blue long-sleeve shirt that she had rolled up, jeans, and wedge sandals.

Libby ran her hands through her hair. Of all the times.

"I forgot my phone," Lofton said as she kissed Elaine on the cheek. "I had to come back."

Libby rose. "Lofton."

Tension drew Lofton's full lips into a tight line. "Hello, Libby. What brings you back? More photography?"

"I was having a talk with Elaine."

Lofton's lips thinned. "Really?"

Elaine sighed. "Libby found a letter Olivia wrote to her when she was born."

"Why would Olivia write a letter to Libby?" And even before her sentence was finished, she shook her head. "I see."

"You see what?" Elaine asked.

Lofton clenched her hands. "I don't want to have this conversation in front of her."

"You might as well." Libby wanted to spare Elaine any more tension, but her baby sister was pressing too many nerves. "You clearly have a problem with me."

"I don't know you," Lofton said. "None of us really know you."

"What's that mean?" Libby asked.

"It doesn't matter," Lofton said. "And I don't want to upset Mom."

"You've figured it out," Libby said. "You know who I am."

"I didn't know for sure. But then I saw Mom interact with you. She was nervous, and she is never nervous. Dad was being super polite to you. I'd never felt those vibes from them before. Finally, you look like Olivia, for God's sake."

"Why would you even suspect?" Elaine asked, clearly shocked and surprised.

"When I got my passport, I had a good look at my birth certificate. It stated I was your second child."

Elaine closed her eyes. "I should have told you."

"Yeah, you should have," Lofton said.

"Other than you three, who else knows?" Libby asked.

"Margaret and Ted know," Elaine said. "But beyond them, no one else knows."

It didn't surprise Libby that Margaret might have known. Margaret likely knew everything that went on in this house. "So I'm basically still a secret," Libby said.

"I kept that secret to protect myself and you," Elaine said. "Giving you to the McKenzies was something I didn't like to talk about because I was ashamed. I didn't think it fair for me to show up and present myself. I wasn't turning your life into a reality television show."

"She's a great mom," Lofton interjected.

"Easy for you to say." The unexpected bitterness surprised her. "She didn't pretend you didn't exist."

"I never did any such thing," Elaine said.

"You never told me the truth," Libby said.

"I agreed a long time ago to let your parents handle every aspect of disclosure. Your father promised he would tell, and I believed that. I only approached you when I realized he had not."

"It always struck me as a little odd that Ginger called me out of the blue to take pictures at her wedding."

"Margaret told me Ginger wanted to get married, and I offered up Woodmont if she would use you as her photographer."

"Very clever."

"I wanted to get to know you under more normal circumstances."

Elaine leaned slightly toward Lofton, as if she needed her support. Lofton wrapped an arm around her mother's slim shoulder, and Libby felt more an outsider than she ever had. "I appreciate you taking the time to speak to me today."

"You'll come back, right?" Elaine asked quickly.

"I don't know," Libby said.

Lofton's features hardened with anger and suspicion.

"My door is always open," Elaine said. "I want you to know you're not alone, and you do have family."

"Elaine, I'm not even sure what that means anymore."

CHAPTER TWENTY-TWO
LIBBY

Wednesday, June 17, 2020
Bluestone, Virginia

The sun peeked through the drapes, slicing across Libby's closed eyes. She rolled away, pulling the pillow with her. Her head pounded while she felt unsettled, with no hint of an appetite.

After shoving the hair from her eyes, she reached for her phone and checked the time. She could not remember when she had been sleeping late in the morning unless Jeremy was with her and they were purposefully whiling away the hours together. In those days, sex had been for the sake of pleasure. There had been no agenda, no sense of angst, and no feeling of failure. There were times when she missed those days.

As soon as she had left Elaine's, her knee-jerk reaction had been to call Jeremy. He had been her best friend and had listened to her worries about not having a genetic history. In fact, it had been her wild card genetics that had prompted them both to get genetic counseling before they had even tried to get pregnant. And as she'd miscarried, she had wondered if that hidden history had been the cause.

On reflex she pulled up Jeremy's Instagram page. There was a picture of an overnight bag that said, ONE WEEK TO GO!

She stared at the image a long time. When she had been pregnant the first time, she had dared to think ahead to her delivery and what she would pack in her bag. By the third pregnancy, no such thoughts had been allowed until she had hit the twelve-week mark. For two beautiful weeks, she had allowed herself to dream.

Had Elaine prepared a bag like that when she had been pear shaped and on the verge of delivery? Had Olivia been in New Jersey when she was born, or had the grandmother left her granddaughter to deal with the delivery on her own? The more she was learning about Olivia, the more she disliked her.

Swallowing tightness in her throat, she rose and moved into the kitchen. She set up a pot of coffee. Twenty minutes later she was showered and dressed in a black pantsuit, white shirt, and kitten heels.

The instant she smelled the coffee, her spirits lifted. It was nowhere near euphoric, but she knew if she kept putting one foot in front of the other, she would find her way through this. That was the black magic of a strong cup of coffee. It restored souls and mended all wounds.

She filled a travel mug and was out the front door, where she found Sierra waiting for her. She was dressed in a sleeveless black sheath dress accented by a large gold necklace and chunky red heels. Her hair was swept up into a neat ponytail, and her makeup was subtle. She carried a brown retro briefcase that looked like it dated back to the sixties.

"So what's the look you're going for today?" Libby asked. "I'm rocking the prison matron look."

That coaxed a small smile. "I'm the kind of woman who borrows money but doesn't really need to because she has secret stores of cash."

"Then why do you need a bank at all?"

"Because banks like to lend money to people who really don't need it."

"Ah, well then, you've hit the nail on the head."

In Sierra's car, Libby hooked her seat belt as Sierra started the engine and pulled onto the tree-lined street. "Did you get any sleep last night? When I fell asleep at one, your lights were still on."

"I got a little," Libby said.

"I saw Jeremy's post. Is that what's bothering you?"

"I'd be lying if I said it didn't. But I really do wish him the best. He'll be a good father."

"Then what's going on with you?"

"Let's get this loan taken care of, and then I'll tell you all about it."

Sierra shot her a glance and seemed to grasp that it really was better to wait on the news. "As soon as we have the deal, you spill."

"Done."

They arrived at the bank in Charlottesville. After circling the block twice to find parking, Sierra eased into a spot a block away. Fifteen minutes later they were sitting in front of Harold S. Mason's desk.

In his midthirties, Harold had thinning blond hair and a round face that expanded even wider when he grinned at Sierra. His attire was a charcoal-gray suit and a crisp white shirt accented with a bold red tie.

"Welcome back, Ms. Mancuso," Harold said.

"Thank you for working us in today." Sierra aimed her electric smile at Harold, who was already falling under her spell.

Clearing his throat, he adjusted his tie. "What can I do for you?"

"Mr. Mason, you said to return if I have sufficient collateral. And I do." Sierra quickly introduced Libby and explained the new development. "May I introduce my friend, Libby McKenzie."

Harold's expression changed. "McKenzie. When I was a kid growing up in Bluestone, my doctor's name was McKenzie."

"That was my father," she said. "He had a thriving practice for thirty years."

"He was my doctor until I was eighteen. I took a bad fall when I was ten, and he was at the hospital when I arrived. Nicest guy. I think my mother had a crush on him."

Libby remembered how her mother had complained half-heartedly that the mothers of her father's patients were always flirting with her father. He had never paid them any mind, as her mother had always been quick to say, but they had never stopped trying, even up to his retirement.

"Dad loved his patients," she said.

Harold smiled and nodded slightly in agreement. A few clicks on his keyboard, and Harold was looking at Sierra's file. "The collateral securing the loan is a house on First Street?" he asked.

"That's the one," Libby said.

"It's a great piece of property and well maintained. And you're sure you want to use it to fully secure the loan? Restaurants have a low success rate."

"I have faith in Sierra," Libby said.

Harold smiled at Sierra. "She has a clear and concise business plan."

"Like I said, I have faith."

An hour later, the papers were signed, and Sierra's loan was in the works. If you had money, the banks did not mind lending.

"Welcome to the club," Sierra said, tipping her face to the sun.

"I hear the air is sweeter there," Libby joked.

"It is."

Back in the car, they had traveled only a few blocks when Sierra said, "First, thank you for backing me up. It means a lot. Second, what the hell is going on with you?"

"You're welcome. And Elaine Grant is my birth mother."

Sierra shot a glance at her but said nothing for several seconds, her gaze locked on the road ahead. "Say that again?"

"Elaine Grant is my biological mother." Libby said the words slowly, as if she still did not believe them herself.

"How the hell did you find that out?" Sierra asked.

"I was looking for the deed to the house, and I found a letter Olivia Carter wrote to me when I was born."

"Are you sure you have this right?"

"Two days ago, I visited with Elaine and asked her point blank. She unconditionally confirmed it on the spot."

"Damn."

Libby stared out at the rolling countryside as it buzzed past. "That's some news, isn't it?"

"But you asked your parents about all this when you were in middle school. I remember you were bummed that they had no answers."

Libby remembered. She had been upset, and despite their denials, she had sensed they were holding back information. And when her mother had died, all thoughts of a birth mother had been washed away in grief. Maybe on some level, Libby had associated the grilling she had given her parents with her mother's death. Her mother had died weeks later, and her father's devastated expression still haunted her. She had blamed herself, but he had assured her she had done nothing wrong. However, she had never asked her father again.

"Damn," Sierra said.

"Yep."

"So what are you going to do?"

"There's not much I can do right now. She had to head back to DC today. I'm sure when Elaine returns, we'll talk more."

"Ah, yeah. She has some explaining to do."

"Right now, I don't want to think about it. I want to see your new building again," Libby said.

"It wouldn't be much to look at without your help. I don't know how I can thank you."

"Don't default on the loan, and toss in free coffee. That'll make us square."

"Deal."

When they parked in front of the old mercantile store, Libby tipped back her sunglasses, pulling her long hair with it. Stepping out of the car, she studied the mercantile store. Days ago, when she had walked through it, she had regarded it with a sense of nostalgia. She had seen charm, character, and possibilities. Now that she had skin in the game, she noticed the aging roof, the peeling paint on the exterior, and the broken windowpane.

"And you did have this place inspected?" Libby asked.

"Yeah. A friend from high school is a contractor now. He walked the place with me."

"And he knows his stuff?"

"Yeah. He gave me a detailed list of the repairs so I could factor it into my loan." She reached under the mat, grabbed a key, and opened the front door.

"You might want to hang on to that key," Libby said.

"The contractor wanted to come through again last night. I told him to let himself in."

The sound of a barking dog had her turning to see Colton's truck pull up behind Sierra's car. Kelce and Sarge were in the front seat, a ball in Kelce's mouth and their tails wagging. Out of the car, he paused at the open window to remind the dogs to stay before walking toward Libby.

As his long legs chewed up the distance quickly, she decided she liked his walk. It was not rushed but confident.

"Sierra, don't tell me you bought this place?" he asked.

"Lock, stock, and barrel," she said, grinning.

His head cocked slightly. "It's going to cost a fortune to fix."

Sierra grinned. "It sure will. And by the way, Libby is my new business partner."

"Really?"

"Absolutely," Libby said. "This town needs a decent sandwich shop."

"And light meals, sandwiches, cookies, all the good stuff that makes life worth living," Sierra added.

"Looking forward to it," he said. "Who's doing the work?"

"John Stapleton," she said.

"He's a good man," Colton said.

"I know," Sierra said.

"Libby," Colton said, shifting to her. "I thought you might like to know that we're sealing the greenhouse windows. It should be ready for planting in about a week."

"That project is moving fast."

"Elaine is on a mission."

"I guess when her mind is made up, there's no turning back." Libby tasted the bitterness souring her words, so she quickly smiled, as if that would help. "Did she leave for DC?"

"She's leaving after lunch today."

Hearing that Elaine would soon be gone released enough tension. Distance gave her the chance to process and breathe. "Okay."

"Stop by anytime to take more pictures," he said.

"I will."

He got back in his truck, where Kelce and Sarge were now asleep in the front seat. The three drove off.

Libby stared after them. "I hear his wife died. What happened?"

Sierra grinned. "Ah, curious?"

"Maybe."

"She died two years ago. In fact, he and I ran into each other a couple of times at the grief group."

"Wow."

"Yeah." She was silent for a moment, as if reliving a piece of the past. And then finally snapping back to the present, she said, "He knew staying in the navy and raising the boys wasn't going to work. He left the military and moved home to take a job at Woodmont."

"I met the boys. Nice kids."

"They're fun."

"So was his late wife the love of his life?"

"Pretty much," she said.

"How did she die?"

Sierra was briefly silent again. "Brain aneurysm. It was sudden. No one saw it coming. She never regained consciousness."

"It's the shit you don't see coming that gets you."

"Now you're quoting me?" Sierra asked.

"You're a wise woman."

"Colton has kept to himself since he got back. It's either the boys or work. This is the first time I've seen him look at a woman the way he just looked at you."

"What?"

Sierra rolled her eyes. "Oh, please, *you*. 'We're sealing the windows,'" she said in a throaty voice. "Might as well get invited to his room to see his etchings."

Libby wondered if the universe could have had any worse timing. "He was just being nice."

"Yeah, to me. He was flirting with you!"

"He asked me to photograph the greenhouse project."

Sierra's wink was exaggerated and almost comical. "You keep telling yourself that."

Libby's hormones did act up when he was around, and honestly the idea that Colton had suffered a loss was oddly appealing to her. She had no use for a man who did not have a few of life's battle scars.

Sierra laughed. "What's the line from the movie? 'Chicks dig scars'?"

"Pain heals."

"And glory lasts forever."

Libby laughed. And for just a moment, she allowed herself to savor the feelings of joy and optimism.

Sierra stepped inside the building and flipped on the light. "This was the last place on the planet I thought I'd end up."

It was not where either of them had intended to be. In fact, given a choice five years ago, they would have both passed on this version of life. But here they were.

"I'm having a party late Sunday," Sierra said. "Nothing fancy. Barbecue and beer. You'll be back from the wedding then?"

"Yes. I should be back by early afternoon."

"Good, you can come."

"What's the occasion?" Libby asked.

"New business venture. Blue skies. Friend of a friend is having a birthday. I don't need much of an excuse for a party."

Her first reaction was to retreat on the excuse of work. Instead, she said, "Okay. I'll come."

"Good." She smiled. "And this thing with Elaine can be a good thing in the long run."

"It hurts like hell now."

"We both have a high tolerance for pain."

"Lucky us."

Sierra hugged Libby tightly. She did not believe in quick hugs or "drive-bys," as she called them. When she gave a hug, she held the person close, as if she were infusing all her goodwill and well-wishes into the recipient. "I'm glad you're back in Bluestone."

"Technically, I'm still sleeping on the couch, so I'm not really back."

"You're back. You just don't know it yet."

CHAPTER TWENTY-THREE

COLTON

Wednesday, June 17, 2020
The Woodmont Estate

Colton had seen Libby on the property on Monday and had noticed the intensity in her expression as she had left the house. He had almost called out to her, but she had been moving fast and had looked like she wanted to get the hell out of there. Next, Lofton had left, and she had not looked any happier.

Lofton was smart as a whip, but she was spoiled, and Elaine indulged her daughter too much, which had always seemed out of character for her. He knew something had gone down between Lofton and Libby, and he would bet Lofton was the spark that started the fire. There were a lot of undercurrents, but his main priority was to steer clear and focus on work and especially the boys.

And still his thoughts kept returning to Libby and the morning she had been walking toward his cabin. The morning light had shone behind her, illuminating her in a way that had taken his breath away.

Over coffee, he had seen the desire in her eyes and had known she wanted him. Given a little more privacy, they could have shared more than a cup of brew.

"Damn," he muttered.

He reached for a thick stalk of vines and tugged them away from the brush circling the greenhouse. Untangling the honeysuckle vines had been slow going. Not only were the vines intrusive, but also snakes and mice had set up shop in the lush foliage and were not excited about his destruction of their homes. There was also poison ivy and the inevitable itchiness. Nature was doing its damnedest to wrestle the greenhouse from him.

"You're making progress," Elaine said.

He turned. She looked thinner, tired. Whatever had happened with Libby was taking its toll on her as well. "Slow and steady."

"This has been one tough project," Elaine said. "Was I foolish? Should I have just torn the place down?"

It was a little late to be asking a question like that. "Why do you say that?" Colton thought about the construction dumpster he had filled with vines and rotted plants.

"If we ever do rent this property for events, a greenhouse won't make us much money. And there are other projects on the property that need your attention."

"That's always the case with old properties like this, Elaine. It's always going to want more."

"But I'm asking you what you think."

"Why do you care so much about the greenhouse?" he asked.

"It's a legacy."

"For Lofton?"

"Lofton has no interest in Woodmont. She never has and never will."

"Then why sink so much energy into the place?" he asked. Colton had never known Elaine to be so indecisive.

"It's complicated."

"Only if you want it to be."

She stared at him, her brow narrowing. "I'm sounding foolish, aren't I? I should know what I want."

"I think you do."

"But *wanting* and *getting* are two different things."

Colton wanted to tug off his gloves, walk up to her, and ask what the hell had gone on in her kitchen on Monday. But that was crossing the line. As much as he respected Elaine, he could not forget that she was his boss. And he needed this job.

"I asked Libby to come back and take more pictures next week as we seal the panes of glass. The place is shaping up." He cast the statement out like he would a baited hook into a pond rich with trout. If he was patient, the answers would come to him.

"When did you see Libby?" she asked.

"Today in town, looking over the property she and her business partner bought."

"Normally, I'd say a new restaurant would be a long shot. But in this area, they might do well enough."

He gripped a thick vine and pulled hard, listening with a bit of satisfaction as the leaves and stems tore.

"I feel like I should apologize for Lofton at Sunday dinner," Elaine said.

"You don't owe me an apology." Lofton was great with his boys, and she had a wicked sense of humor. But he also recognized that she was used to getting exactly what she wanted.

"Lofton is going through a few things, and she took it out on Libby," Elaine offered.

"Libby doesn't strike me as soft. She's taken a lot of blows in the last year or two and is still standing. Libby can handle herself." It wasn't like him to meddle in Grant family business, but he needed to champion Libby. "In Libby's world, Lofton's remarks were child's play."

A faint light flickered in her gaze. "I hope you're right."

"I'm a good judge of character."

"Thanks for the advice."

"Always free and available," he said with a grin.

LIBBY

"Don't Stop Believing" blasted in Libby's earbuds as she uploaded the wedding albums. She was a huge fan of *Journey*, even though her idol Steve Perry left the band when she was only seven.

As Perry's final note reverberated, she emailed the link to this bride's look book and switched off the computer.

The sound of a delivery truck stopping in front of her house coaxed her onto the front porch. Sitting in the afternoon sun was a neatly wrapped box. Picking it up, she tipped her face upward to absorb the sun's warmth after hours of working on the digital files.

She pulled off her reading glasses and pinched the bridge of her nose. Without the distraction of work, her mind turned to Elaine.

More hard conversations to be had, but until she soldiered through this latest patch of work, she did not need the distraction.

Drawing her shoulders back, Libby straightened her spine, trying to bend it out of the perpetual slump that came with leaning into a shot or toward a computer screen. She sat on the rocker and carefully unwrapped the package. Inside was a neatly written note in handwriting very similar to hers. It was from Elaine.

> *There's plenty of family history to share, but I thought you might like to start with Olivia's first gardening journal. She was just a decade younger than you are now,*

and it might help you understand her decisions later in life. When we've both had time to process our meeting, I would love to talk. Best, Elaine.

Libby ran her hands over smooth leather binding now worn and faded by a half century. Wrapped around it was a faded blue ribbon that held the edges closed. She carefully undid the ribbon. As she opened the notebook, the spine crackled and groaned. On the front page, written in precise handwriting, was *Gardening Journal 1942. Olivia Wellington Carter*.

Olivia's handwriting was meticulous and measured. Libby took comfort that both Elaine's and Olivia's penmanship were very similar to her own.

When she turned the first page, a few black-and-white pictures stuck out from the crease. The first square image featured two women standing in front of a huge Pontiac parked in front of the mercantile store.

The older of the two appeared to be in her early twenties, and she wore a lovely tailored suit and had painted on bright lipstick that even the black-and-white photography could not dull. The second woman was in her midteens. She wore overalls and was not grinning. In fact, she looked a little impatient as she stared at the lens. The car was parked in front of the very mercantile store Libby had just partnered with Sierra to renovate.

She turned the image over and read, *Olivia Carter (with Sadie Thompson)*.

Sadie. She was the girl who had scratched her name in the greenhouse glass. Libby studied the girl's face closely, knowing that by now she would be in her nineties if still alive.

The next few pictures featured Olivia standing by her greenhouse, but there were no more images of Sadie.

Olivia was always smartly dressed, her outfits including hats and gloves and stockings that would not have been easy to come by during the war.

The last image in the stack featured Olivia holding an infant. Her smile was slightly stiff and her eyes sad. It struck Libby as odd. A woman who had suffered miscarriages had finally had her baby. But she did not appear happy. She flipped the image over. It was simply dated *Spring, 1943*.

She carefully tucked the pictures back into the journal's fold, then turned the page to the first entry. There was a hand-painted bundle of peonies. Their pink, delicate petals were so detailed they looked almost lifelike. Rich thick green stems wound down the side of the page and were bound at their base by a wide strand of blue ribbon tied into a bow. Beside the picture was a quote from Elizabeth Barrett Browning: *Beloved, thou hast brought me many flowers.*

"Hey, what's that?" Sierra climbed the steps to the porch.

"Elaine sent me Olivia's first gardening journal."

"Why?"

"Family history. Olivia was Elaine's grandmother. She suffered several miscarriages and was a key player in my adoption."

"Oh."

"I suppose, in a way, we are kindred spirits," Libby said. "Though if my granddaughter had a baby, I would like to believe I would do anything to help her keep it."

Sierra leaned over Libby's shoulder and studied the page. "She was a fantastic artist."

"She was." Libby retrieved the black-and-white pictures. "Check out the first one. They're standing in front of your mercantile store."

Sierra studied the image closely. "Wow. Time goes so fast." She flipped the picture over and read the caption. "Wow. Olivia knew Sadie Thompson."

"Who was Sadie Thompson?"

"Supposedly a real wild child," Sierra said. "She ran moonshine with her father and brothers and at one point ran a man down right in front of the store with her truck. I think there are folk songs written about her."

"Who did she hit?"

"That I don't remember, but I can ask Mom."

Libby looked at Sadie's solemn face, drawn to her moody gaze, which felt vaguely familiar. "What happened to her?"

"She vanished," Sierra said. "Sheriff came to arrest her but couldn't find her anywhere. There was a big manhunt, but she never was found. Legend has it that her ghost still haunts the woods near Mrs. Carter's."

"Her ghost? Seriously? Why didn't you tell me this before?"

"Because it's not true. It's just a story."

"What's the story?"

Sierra shrugged. "They say if you drink corn liquor on a moonless night on the Woodmont property, you'll see her."

A ghost would have explained the odd sensations she had felt in the greenhouse the other morning. But so would her imagination and nerves. "Oh, I bet your mind can conjure up all kinds of things if you drink corn liquor in the woods. All late at night."

Sierra laughed. "No comment."

She studied Sadie's small bow-shaped face. "I hope your mom can shed more light on this girl."

"We'll see. Have you and Elaine spoken since Monday?"

"No. I guess this is her way of keeping in touch without irritating Lofton."

"The infamous Lofton. Spoiled and drives too fast in town. Let me guess, she's not happy about having a big sister."

"No. She looks at me as if she thinks I'm going to take all her mother's money or love or both."

"Twit."

Libby smiled. "I guess I can't blame her. I came out of nowhere, and it has to be a shock."

"You didn't ask for any of this."

"Agreed. But neither did she."

"I see the journal as a great sign. Elaine wants to stay connected despite Lofton's reservations."

"I suppose," Libby said.

"Did Elaine answer all your questions? I remember you always had a list of questions for your birth mother."

"I didn't get a chance to ask very many. I was just a little overwhelmed."

Sierra traced the shape of a purple iris drawn on the corner of a page. "She sent you this for a reason, Libby."

"Why not just tell me what I need to know? Why hide behind letters and journals?"

"Are we talking about Elaine or your father now?" Sierra asked softly.

"Right now? My dad tops my shit list. Why couldn't he just tell me?"

"He was afraid he would lose you. He already lost a wife."

Libby released an exasperated sigh. "Why would I turn away from him over something like this?"

Sierra knitted her fingers together and then pulled them apart. "Logic and emotion rarely speak the same language."

"He knew I loved him."

Sierra tipped her head back against the rocker and stared toward the blue sky. "Once you've been hurt badly, it's hard to open yourself again. Although not well, your mother essentially left him."

"How did you get so smart?"

Sierra rubbed her finger along the edge of her jaw. "Sadly, the hard way."

"But you've done a good job of moving on."

"That's the thing; I'm staying busy, but I haven't moved on. I'm stuck in this whirlpool of activity, treading water as fast as I can to keep from being pulled under. Your dad might have been that way after your mother's death."

"I thought you were thriving."

"I'm surviving." Sierra drew in a breath and rolled her shoulders, as if shrugging off a weight she knew would reappear within seconds. "Don't let grief and anger weigh you down or hold you back. Do a better job than I am."

CHAPTER
TWENTY-FOUR
LIBBY

Wednesday, June 17, 2020
Bluestone, Virginia

Olivia's journal sat untouched as Libby responded to several brides-to-be with proposals, tips, and notes for each. Of the three, she guessed she might get a callback on one, and then there was no guarantee it would result in a contract. Making it in this business—at least in this stage of her career—meant being available all the time.

After scanning email and wading through the 50 percent–off summer-sale ads and current events, she glanced back at the journal. The clock chimed five times, and her stomach grumbled on cue. "I don't want to deal with you, Olivia. Not right now."

After rising, she walked to the kitchen. The leftovers from Elaine had yet to be opened. Since she was a little kid, she had always been picky about leftovers. Her mother had loved them, swearing the food's flavors improved overnight. Not Libby. When a meal was done, it was done.

Her fallback was a pizza place in town. She had swung by a few times last fall when she had visited Dad. The carbs were off the charts, and just thinking about the fat grams made her want to cry. God, it was good. And so it would be tonight as well. And maybe for a little while, she could forget about Elaine. There was always a bright side, she reminded herself.

More than ready to leave the silent house, she grabbed her purse and decided to walk. The center of town was less than a mile away, and the weather was pleasantly warm, with no humidity. That would not last much longer, as summer was ready to kick in.

As she passed the mercantile store, she saw Sierra inside with a guy dressed in jeans, a blue T-shirt that read LANE CONSTRUCTION, and work boots. Not a stretch to assume he was the contractor.

She knocked on the window, and Sierra waved her inside. Sierra was smiling, but the contractor was not. He had that "time is money" look that she appreciated. "Not staying long. Getting pizza. Can I bring you anything?"

"No, thanks. Mom is cooking tonight. Libby, I'd like you to meet John Stapleton. My contractor." Libby picked up on the underlying excitement in Sierra's voice, which she knew was attributed to the project more than John.

Libby crossed the room and shook John's hand. "Pleasure to meet you. You going to have your hands full with this building?"

"Not as bad as I first thought. There's some foundation work that needs to be done, but overall it's in good shape."

"We like the idea of that. Can you stick to the sixty-day renovation schedule?"

"It'll be ready by late summer or early fall," he said.

"I like the sound of that," Sierra said.

"Good. I'll leave you two to get back to work," Libby said. "I'm starving. Sierra, call if you need anything."

"Will do."

As Libby left the mercantile store, she realized she was good at starting things. So far, nothing she had undertaken had lasted more than five years, including her marriage, her nursing career, and her attempts at motherhood. How long would her interest in the mercantile store or Bluestone last?

Libby arrived at the pizza shop, ready to push aside all worries and chow down on a pepperoni pizza. She pushed through the front door, savoring the scents of roasted tomato, oregano, and cheese. Bluestone Pizza was the hangout for local high school kids who wanted to impress their dates by trying to score beer. As in all small towns, everyone knew everyone, including their birthdays.

A girl about nineteen stood behind the counter. She wore her dusty-blonde hair streaked with purple in a ponytail. She smiled brightly as she reached for two menus and looked past Libby for the other members of her party.

"Just me," Libby said. "Table for one." She felt proud that the words no longer stuck when she spoke them. Yeah, there were a few sinkholes in her life, but she was navigating around them well enough.

The girl stepped out from behind the counter, and Libby noticed her rounded, pregnant belly, which looked to be in the final trimester.

"I know you," the girl said. "You're Dr. McKenzie's daughter."

"That's right."

"He was my pediatrician. I was kind of thinking—when I first found out about my peanut—Dr. McKenzie would be my baby's doctor as well. I didn't realize he had been sick."

"He kept it to himself."

"I heard he kept office hours into last fall, when he retired."

"He loved his job."

"I could tell. I don't think I ever saw him upset or flustered."

"It didn't happen often."

Libby thought about Elaine, who had not been much older than this girl when she was pregnant. Had Elaine's family cut her off completely when she was pregnant? Had she had to work in a place like this until she gave birth? When Libby had been expecting, she had not lifted anything higher than a mug filled with herbal tea. And here this young woman was on her feet, moving around without a care in the world.

She seated Libby at a table in the back, away from the main dining room. The dinner crowd had not arrived, which was just as well. She could eat in peace and quiet. Without looking at the menu, she ordered the extra large cheese-and-pepperoni pizza and a medium Diet Coke. It was her perfect pizza-to-drink ratio.

Her diet soda arrived, and she had just dropped the straw in the fizzing caramel liquid when a small hand smacked her table. "Libby!"

She looked up to the curious, direct gaze of Jeff Reese. "Jeff!"

"Did I scare you?" Hope wove around the question.

"You did! When did you learn how to drive?" she teased.

He laughed. "I didn't drive. My dad brought me."

She looked past the boy to see Colton striding in with Sam at his side. "Good to know you aren't wandering around alone." When Colton stepped to the table, she rose. "Great minds think alike."

"Hi, Libby!" Sam said, giggling.

"Hey, big guy!"

"Sorry for the sneak attack," Colton said. "Believe it or not, it means he likes you. Jeff, enough with the giving people heart attacks."

Jeff frowned, studying Libby closely. "I didn't give her a heart attack."

"Still debatable, Jeff," Libby said.

The boy shrugged. "Shake it off."

That sounded more like an echo of Colton's advice. "You're right." She pretended to shake. "My worries are all gone."

Colton grinned. "If you would like more mayhem with your meal, you can join us. And *no* is a perfectly acceptable answer."

A *yes* translated into a chaotic dinner. And *no* meant she would likely end up wondering which mother loved her less while she scrolled

Jeremy's Instagram page. "Mayhem and pizza sound pretty good." She rose and picked up her purse and drink. "Let me tell the waitress to bring my pizza to your table."

"Pizza!" Jeff said.

"Pizza!" Sam echoed.

"Boys, we'll order our own."

"No need," Libby said. "I have ordered enough to feed a small country."

"We're a small country when it comes to pizza," Colton said.

"Then you can consider mine an appetizer."

"Thanks. The twenty-minute wait for a pie with these two boys can be very long."

She quickly told the girl where she had moved, and just as she approached the new booth, an extra large pizza arrived with four plates. Jeff sat closest to the wall, and when Libby took the seat next to him, he grinned at Sam, as if to say he had won.

Sam glanced up at his father, clearly hoping for justice, but Colton told him to sit. They could swap seats later if it still mattered to him.

As Colton unrolled his napkin from around the knife and fork, he raised a brow. "You weren't kidding about feeding a small country."

"Go big, or go home," she said. While Jeff wrestled with silverware, she reached for a plate and slid a piece onto it, setting it in front of Jeff. "Don't eat it yet. Too hot."

Colton did the same just as Sam stuck his finger in hot cheese. He patiently wiped it off and then stuck his finger in his own ice water.

"Never a dull moment," she said with a grin.

"Never."

Milk with straws arrived for the boys and an ice-cold beer for Colton. "Did you come here when you were a kid?" Jeff asked.

"I did," she said and then cut his pizza into a couple of smaller bites. "I think it's cooled down enough."

He stabbed his fork in the pizza and jammed it into his mouth. If her daughter had gone to term, she would be about two years old now. She wondered what it would be like to have her in a high chair with her own cut-up pizza to gnaw on. Would she be more delicate than the boys or dig right in like her mom?

Libby grabbed a big slice and took a bite. It was hot, gooey, garlicky, and tomatoey and just tasty enough to distract her. The four ate in silence for several minutes, though Colton caught a cup of milk from spilling and cut up more pieces for Sam before he took his first sip of beer.

"You live right down the street, right?" he asked.

"Seven blocks," she said.

"You walked?"

"I did."

"You should come back to Woodmont with the boys and me. We can give you the first look at the greenhouse all cleaned out."

"You've finished the sealing?"

"Not quite, but the interior has been scrubbed clean. Elaine has a good eye for projects like this."

Mention of Elaine had her coiling a piece of cheese around her finger. "What do you think you'll do with the space once it's restocked?"

"She's warming to the idea of holding events at Woodmont and talked about hosting smaller weddings inside the greenhouse."

"I thought the Carters were well off."

"Maybe at one time. Dr. Edward Carter was not good with money. It's either sell to developers or generate income with the property to maintain it properly and cover the taxes."

"Did you ever see yourself overseeing weddings?"

"I did not. But I love the property. It deserves to be enjoyed. Like I said, come and see it."

She took a long sip of her soda. "Sure, I'll come back."

"Great," he said with a genuine grin.

The kids finished, and when the check came, Colton insisted on paying. He also insisted the boys visit the bathroom, explaining the drive home could be long if someone had to go. The four piled into his truck, the boys in their booster seats and her in the front seat next to Colton.

The drive back to Woodmont took less than twenty minutes, but by the time Colton turned down the long driveway, the boys had both fallen asleep. Colton parked in front of his cottage.

"Carb overload works every time," she said, though she did not feel the least bit tired. She felt energized and glad she was not at home alone.

She unhooked Sam from his booster and hefted him up. He did not wake and wrapped his arms around her neck, nestling his nose against her chest. He was a solid kid and heavier than she had imagined, so she was not moving as quickly as Colton, who bounded up the steps with Jeff into the house. The boys' room was outfitted with twin beds already turned down for the night.

"Just take off his shoes and pants," Colton said.

"I've done this before," she said, tugging off a pint-size Spider-Man shoe as well as a blue sock.

"Not your first rodeo," he said, grinning.

She removed the second shoe and sock and placed the sneaker beside the other at the foot of the bed. After unsnapping his jeans, she tugged off the oversize pants and then slid him to scoot under the covers. He rolled on his side and popped his thumb into his mouth.

"Is that okay?" she asked.

"It's one of those habits we'll have to break, but not tonight."

He dimmed the lights, switched on an overhead fan, and turned on a green night-light.

In the hallway, she glanced at a collection of pictures that had been taken of the boys when they were babies. "They're cute."

"I fell hard for both of them." He paused to study a picture of the boys. "I'll call Mom and see if she can come sit with them so we can go see the greenhouse."

"I don't want to trouble her."

"She's still at Woodmont. She always works late at the house when the family isn't there. Says she's getting it back under control."

"As long as she doesn't mind."

His cell phone was already to his ear. He quickly asked Margaret if she would come up for a little while, and she agreed. He grabbed two longneck beers from the refrigerator, twisted off the tops, and handed her one.

"We can sit outside," he said.

"Too pretty an evening to waste."

He opened the front door for her, and she took a seat in one of the rockers. As she passed by him, she caught the scent of him. It was not really cologne but a man's scent. It vaguely reminded her of Jeremy. Colton's scent was rougher around the edges—in a good way, like handmade paper or frayed jeans.

"Do you get a chance to sit out here often?" she asked.

"Some nights when the boys are asleep. Lately I've used the time to catch up with vendors and contractors."

She took a long sip. "Never a dull moment."

Footsteps crunched on the path, and a security light clicked on, lighting the pathway.

Margaret rounded the corner, her head bowed as if she was concentrating on the ground. When she looked up and saw Libby, there was no missing the surprise.

"Libby, what brings you back out here?" she asked.

"Colton is showing me the greenhouse."

Margaret shifted her gaze to Colton for only a split second, but it conveyed the kind of warning a mother sent to a son, even if he was grown, was widowed, and had two kids. "Well, you two go on and get down the path. I'll sit with the boys."

"We won't be gone long," Colton said.

"You take your time. I'm going to watch *Wheel of Fortune*."

She followed Colton down the path. As they rounded the last corner, she looked up at the greenhouse. Its dome caught the evening light and reflected it back like a diamond. No longer covered by vines, each pane had been cleared and cleaned. There was also a three-foot perimeter around the structure now. He opened the door for her, which now slid easily, and held out his hand. "After you. You get the first look."

She passed by him and stepped inside. Without all the clutter and stacked pots filled with dirt and dead plants, the space felt larger. The heaviness in the air she had felt the first time was gone. "A-plus job, Colton."

"It turned out better than I thought."

"This space will get Woodmont noticed. No venue I know of has anything like it."

He sipped his beer as she crossed the space. When he turned to look at her, his gaze rested on her. A heat rose up, warming her cheeks. She knew the look. God, she had missed the thrill of a man looking at her with desire.

"Margaret must think we're up to something." Her voice sounded huskier than normal.

"I came to show you the greenhouse."

The bland, noncommittal tone had her moving closer to make sure she was not getting her signals crossed. "And I see that it's a lovely space. I suppose now that we've seen it, we can head back to your house and watch *Wheel of Fortune* with Margaret."

He regarded her as if he was considering her suggestion. And for a moment, she thought she had terribly misread his vibe. Maybe he really was showing off the work he had done in the greenhouse. *Oh shit.* Was she that out of touch?

A tiny smile tugged the edges of his mouth as he set his beer down and then hers beside it. He took her hand in his and pulled her up to him. Her breasts grazed his chest. Her heart, she swore, was about to explode out of her chest.

He rubbed his calloused thumb over her palm in a slow, seductive way that sent chills over her skin. Her thighs brushed against his, and she could feel a taut energy radiating off him like a tonic. "I've wanted to kiss you from the moment you hopped in my truck."

"Me too." She angled a little closer to him. She wanted him to kiss her first. She wanted to be wanted.

He cupped her face in his hands and tilted it slightly before he pressed his lips to hers. His lips were soft and tasted like beer and pent-up energy. Despite her best plans to let him pursue her, she wrapped her arms around his neck and pulled him toward her. Desire surged in her, and she did not care that they were likely on display in this snow globe for all to see.

As if sensing her thoughts, he broke the kiss and crossed to the switch and turned off the lights. The bright light vanished, allowing the setting sun and the rising stars to light the room.

She turned to him and kissed him. Hard. And before she thought much about it, she was reaching for the snap on his jeans.

"I don't have protection," he muttered.

"After my last miscarriage, my doctor told me I'd likely never get pregnant again," she said.

He drew back and studied her.

"It's a long story. And I haven't slept with anyone since my ex two years ago. I'm about as safe as they come."

"There's nothing safe about you," he muttered, cupping her face.

She unsnapped his button. "I'm assuming this is breaking a dry spell for you?"

"It is."

"Then if we can trust each other, this could be fun."

That seemed to catch him up. He studied her in the moonlight, smoothing the hair from her face, as if he could somehow peer into her soul.

"Jump or dive. Not forever, but now," she whispered. "We've got to take the plunge sometime."

His eyes darkened and, after finally nodding, he kissed her again. Once the decision was made, the rest came very quickly. They undressed each other in a fevered pitch. Her hands were trembling; several times she reminded herself that this was sex. They both were deprived and starved, and a quick trip to erotica land would do the trick for them both.

When he lowered her onto their pile of clothes on the floor, she had no sense of time or place. This. This was what she wanted.

Their joining was hurried and full of repressed emotions, and when their desires boiled over and they plummeted into the abyss together, she was fairly sure her heart had burst.

After, she curled next to him, absorbing the heat from his body. She had never done the one-night-stand thing, and she wondered what the walk (actually drive) of shame back to her house would feel like. She tried to locate an ounce of remorse but could not find anything. For the first time in a couple of years, she felt alive.

CHAPTER TWENTY-FIVE
OLIVIA

Saturday, October 3, 1942
The Woodmont Estate

Sadie's child had kicked Olivia's hand, and she had immediately withdrawn it, as if she had been burned.

"Sadie, does your mother know?" Olivia asked.

Sadie drew the folds of her coat closed and turned away from Olivia, as if unconscious fears had roared to life. "There's nothing to tell Mama. Whatever is going on with me will pass. What you felt was indigestion."

Olivia stared at the girl now, noticing her face was rounder and her breasts fuller. "That was a kick. A baby's kick. You have a baby growing inside of you."

Sadie kicked the stone floor with the heel of her boot. "I'm getting fat, is all. That's all it is."

"No, Sadie, you're pregnant. Who is the father? You never told me about any young man."

"I don't have a boyfriend."

"But you were with a man. Maybe in the spring."

Sadie buried her face in her hands. "I just went to the dance."

"You did more than dance."

"I didn't want to do what he did. I thought we were just sitting in the back of his car. And then he started messing with my dress and was on top of me." Tears welled in her eyes and spilled down her cheeks. "I can't have a baby inside of me. My mama will be heartbroken, and then she's going to call the sheriff, and they're going to take me away."

Olivia took Sadie's hands in hers. "No one is doing that."

"They will," she shouted as she snatched her hands away. "I don't have a husband, and the sheriff already warned me after the accident that I'd go to jail if he had any more trouble with me."

"He did what?"

"The sheriff came to my house after the accident and told me I was in big trouble."

"You didn't do anything. I was driving the car, and even that wasn't enough to lose the baby. The doctor said it is more to do with me than anything that happened."

"It doesn't seem right, you losing babies and me with one I don't want. I wish I could give you this baby right now; then you could carry it in your belly and love it like your own." Tears now ran down flushed cheeks. "Then I could leave town, and you could have the child you been wanting so bad."

Olivia wished the same. She would like nothing better than to take this child and make it her own. But her husband would not accept it. She loved him but understood he would not raise a child that was not of his flesh.

"When did this back seat event happen?" Olivia asked.

"In March."

"Which means you're nearly seven months pregnant and due in December."

Sadie's face tightened with worry, as if the mere mention of the child terrified her. "December's so close. I can't have a baby in a couple months. What do I do?"

"Do you have the father's name, Sadie?"

"He told me not to tell." Her voice hitched with desperation. "He said no one would believe me."

"Who was it?"

Sadie dropped her gaze to her calloused palm. "It was Malcolm. Your husband's cousin."

"Malcolm Carter?" He had a reputation as a ladies' man, and he had visited them in March to cheer up Edward after the loss of the baby. He had invited them both out to hear the band, but she had been feeling poorly. Edward, too, had declined his offer. If she had gone, she wondered if her presence would have spared Sadie.

"Please don't tell your husband." Her voice sounded desperate.

"Why not? He should know what kind of man Malcolm is."

"Malcolm said if I told, it would get me in more trouble. I don't want to get sent away."

Olivia wasn't naive. If it came down to Sadie's word against Malcolm's, everyone would take Malcolm's version of events over Sadie's. For girls like Sadie in this kind of situation, the reality was unjust and bleak. "Go home, Sadie, and tell your mother what is happening. You need her help."

"She'll throw me out."

"Is your mother a kind woman?"

"Of course she is. She's my mother."

"Then trust that she'll help you. You need her."

"I don't want this baby."

"That doesn't matter now. Unfair as this may sound, you also need to stay away from town until after the baby is born. If you weren't so small, I'm sure someone would have noticed by now."

"I've been wearing my brothers' pants because mine don't fit."

"You have the advantage of the winter as well," she said. "People tend to stay at home and not socialize as much."

"What about supplies? I got to go into town to get those."

"I'll bring you your supplies."

"How are you going to do that?"

"I can drive."

"I thought you didn't want your husband to know."

"Don't worry about him. I'll handle it."

"What about Malcolm?" Sadie's face was pale and stricken with fear.

"Leave him to me."

"What are you going to do to him?"

Olivia shook her head. "I haven't decided yet."

Sadie and her baby were not far from Olivia's mind as she drove the car into Lynchburg. Driving alone, she found herself second-guessing each twist in the road. Several times she took a wrong turn and was forced to turn around. Once she found herself on a hill and had a devil of a time. But she kept driving until—at around two o'clock in the afternoon—she pulled up in front of the hospital in Lynchburg.

As she sat in the car and stared at the place, she sensed a darkness emanating from the bricks and mortar. Her husband was a good man. She had seen pure kindness in his eyes.

After Sadie's visit to the house, Olivia had quizzed Edward more about this place and why he had chosen this line of work. He had sidestepped her questions and, in the end, had only said, *"If not me, then who?"* Then as now, she sensed in her bones that terrible things happened within the brick walls.

She set the parking brake and shut off the car. After reaching for her purse, she opened the compact and checked her hair and makeup. She reapplied the red lipstick, taking care to contour the lines. After adjusting the collar of her dress, she opened the door and rose. She carefully smoothed out the wrinkles in her skirt before reaching into the back seat for a picnic lunch.

Drawing in a breath, she stared at the bleak building. It reminded her of an attic—full of unwanted items that could not be tossed away.

She walked up to the front door and rang. Footsteps echoed inside before the door opened to a stern man with a thin face. She gripped the handle of the basket and, forcing a smile, walked up to the front desk, where an older man dressed in a frayed dark suit sat. "I'm Olivia Carter. I've come to see my husband, Dr. Edward Carter."

"Yes, ma'am." The man appeared both curious and hesitant. "Does Dr. Carter know that you're coming?"

As with the first time, she was hit by the smell of unclean bedding and the musty scent reminiscent of the London hospital during the bombing raids. As much as she had scrubbed and cleaned herself after her shifts on the ward, there had been no getting rid of the bleak smell.

"He does not," she said. "It's a surprise. And before you tell me that he is busy, I must tell you that I know he finishes his surgery by two each day."

The old man raised the black telephone receiver to his ear and stuck a bent finger in the zero on the rotary dial. Next came the nine. Then the two.

Olivia's burst of bravery waned as she heard the ringing of a phone on the other end. Edward would be glad to see her, of course. Then he would wonder how she had gotten here. And then she would tell him she could drive and had been driving and was responsible for the accident with Sadie.

The old man nodded and then hung up the phone. "He'll be right down. You may have a seat."

She moved to a small wooden chair and sat, resting the picnic basket on her lap. The lobby was quiet, and there was not the fast-paced comings and goings of people that would be expected in a regular hospital. It was an eerie stillness, as in the moments after the air-raid-shelter doors had closed in London while everyone sat in silence, awaiting the rain of bombs.

She had hated those quiet, in-between moments the most. In those gaps, the past, present, and future would be irrevocably changed for so many.

"Olivia, darling," Edward said as he pushed back a lock of his dark hair. "What are you doing here?"

She raised her gaze to her husband's bemused expression as she stood, allowing him to kiss her on the cheek. "I have brought you lunch. Roast beef and fresh bread."

"That's marvelous. I'm starving." He wrapped his arm around her shoulder and guided her toward the door. "But how did you get here?"

"I drove."

His eyes brightened, as if she had told him a joke. But when she did not deliver a punch line, he grew serious. "Darling, how could you have driven here? You don't drive."

"I do, as a matter of fact. And I'm fairly good at it. Though getting into first gear on a hill still vexes me somewhat."

He took her elbow in his hand and guided her out the front door to the porch. "Who taught you how to drive?"

The crisp fall air did little to cool her warming cheeks. "Sadie."

"Sadie." The softness hardened into disapproval. "When?"

"Over the spring." Though tempted to take a step back, she held her ground. "I was the one driving the car when we crashed. Not her."

He held her hands in his grip, tightening slightly. "Don't do that."

"Do what?"

"Cover for that girl. I know you had a fondness for her. You have always worried about the less fortunate. It's one of the things I love most about you. But she's not the kind of person worth your time."

"I do have a soft spot for the girl, but I'm not covering for her. I was driving when we crashed. The front tire hit a slick spot and then seemed to have a mind of its own. Once in the ditch, I took the coward's way out and asked her to switch places. She agreed."

He pressed his long fingers to his temple. "Why are you telling me this now?"

"I don't want you to blame her for anything. She's a good girl."

He drew in a slow and steady breath, as if he was trying to control his annoyance. "I'll not be rehiring her, if that is what you're asking."

"I understand that is not possible, but I would like to visit her from time to time." She nodded toward the Pontiac.

"I don't like this or the effect she is having on you."

"The only consequence of my knowing Sadie is that I have a friend, and I can drive. I could have visited her without consulting you. However, I would rather have your blessing."

"Why do you want to visit the girl?" he demanded.

"Her mother is ill, and her brothers are away at war, fighting for my country. I don't see why it would be so terrible for me to try and help out the family."

"The girl is trouble. Malcolm has warned me a couple of times, but I didn't listen."

"Malcolm." Anger rose up in her, chasing away any uncertainty. "I wasn't aware you had seen him lately."

"He's my cousin and calls me from time to time."

She tugged at the pearl button on the cuff of her sleeve. "And what did he say about Sadie?"

"That she is a wild girl. He saw her at the spring dance unescorted, which is exactly the kind of thing I would expect from a girl like her. Johnny would be mortified. This was after I had fired her, so I didn't give it much thought. She was out of our lives, so it all worked out for the better."

"It seems Malcolm knows quite a bit about Sadie."

"All I know is that he has sound judgment, and I take him at his word."

"So he was at this dance alone and drinking as well, I presume." She tugged at the edge of her white glove, flexing her fingers against the soft cotton.

"You and I both know it is different for men than women."

That Olivia knew all too well. "Where is Malcolm these days? I haven't seen him since that March weekend."

"He's in Richmond finishing up his law degree. He's smart as a whip and already has several job offers."

"He is an accomplished man." She did not confuse intelligence with honor.

"So you understand why I would trust his assessment of a girl like Sadie."

When words poised on the tip of her tongue were too harsh to vocalize, her mother had always cautioned her to count to ten and then smile. She barely finished the count before she said, "Why do you trust him more than me?"

He shook his head, as if he were unraveling a puzzle. "That's not what I said."

"Of course it is," she snapped.

"Don't challenge me on this, Olivia," he warned. "I'm willing to forgive, even allow the driving, but my opinion takes precedence in our home."

"I'm sorry that my differing opinions and driving trouble you so, but I won't be backing down from either."

His frown deepened, and his jaw tightened.

"Edward, you're talking to a woman who worked in a London hospital that was bombed. I survived under the rubble for nine hours. I'm sure if I could survive in the rubble, I can drive a motor vehicle on a regular basis and have a difference of opinion with you. Besides, my driving will free you up from those tedious trips into Charlottesville for shopping."

"I don't mind taking you," he quickly offered.

"That's sweet of you, but it will lift my mood. Get me out of this slump I've been in." She took him by the hand and guided him off the porch toward the car. Glancing back at the hospital to make sure no one was looking, she leaned in and kissed him on the lips. She wanted him to feel the promise of a new and stronger wife and friend.

He raised his hand to her waist and tugged her very gently toward him. His fingers curled into a loose fist, as if he was fighting the urge to take what he really wanted right now.

She drew back, pleased with herself. "Let's have lunch. And then when you get home tonight, I'll arrange a special dessert for you."

A slow grin curled his lips. "It's nice to have you back."

This was the first time since the rubble had buried her that she truly felt like herself. It was as if she had just tossed off the last rock pinning her down. "Good to be back."

She handed him a picnic blanket, which he spread out on their bench. She sat, curling her legs beside his as she unpacked the basket.

"I feel as if you have somehow played me," he said.

"I have, darling. And I suspect you're okay with it." She served him a plate of fried chicken with corn bread, along with a red-and-white-checkered napkin.

He took a bite, frowning a little as he regarded her. "I don't like the idea of you driving on the roads alone."

"What if I promise only to drive in the daylight? No night driving."

"Good Lord, I had never even considered night driving."

"I'll also never drive more than, say, twenty miles."

"In the daytime. When it's not inclement weather?"

"Yes, if that will make you feel better. My driving days will be picture perfect like today."

"It still makes me nervous."

She grinned and leaned toward him, ensuring him an ample view of her bosom. "That sounds like a yes to me."

"It is a reluctant yes."

"And I shall always take a slow yes over a fast no." She plucked a piece of chicken out of the basket and raised it to her lips. "Do remember to invite Malcolm."

"Why?" Suspicion darkened his tone.

"I know how you have missed him, and I would dearly love to catch up."

"What are you planning?"

"Nothing."

"Malcom is family, Olivia. Don't ever embarrass me in front of him—or publicly, for that matter." His gaze hardened as he glanced up toward the brick building and then back at her.

Her breathing slowed. "What are you saying? That you would lock me up in a place like that?"

"I spend my days dealing with troublesome women, and I refuse to do it in my home."

"You didn't answer my question."

A heavy silence lingered between them. He smiled finally and kissed her softly on the cheek. "Don't ever force me to make that kind of choice."

She met his gaze, absorbing the full meaning of his threat.

CHAPTER TWENTY-SIX

LIBBY

Wednesday, June 17, 2020
The Woodmont Estate

They did not have the luxury of cuddling or spending the night together. After they made love, they dressed, each tossing the other sheepish grins, and he drove her home.

"That was nice," she said.

"Just nice?" he teased.

"It was great. Just what the doctor ordered. But I don't want things to get weird between us."

"Nothing about this feels weird to me. I'd like to do it again. Maybe a proper meal that doesn't involve elementary school boy talk and does include a proper bed."

That felt a little like a commitment. Maybe not a huge lifetime thing, but it was a start. She could not even begin to think about anything beyond next week, but more sex with Colton was totally acceptable.

"I have a bed." She reached for her door handle. "And I can cook for us. Unless being here is a little too close to home. I know how small towns can be."

"Here is fine." He leaned over and kissed her on the lips.

"Weekends don't work for me for the next few weeks, but week-nights do."

"Next Wednesday?" he offered.

"Done."

She kissed him one last time and got out of the car, climbing her front steps as if a weight had been lifted from her shoulders. Of course, the weight would return, but for tonight that was good enough. She opened the front door and glanced back to see him waiting. She switched on the light in the front entryway, and when she closed the door behind her, he drove off.

She sat on the couch, grabbed a pillow, and hugged it to her mid-section. Her phone rang. It was Sierra.

"What have you been doing?" she asked.

"I had a date, sort of."

"With Colton?"

She all but sang the words. "Yes."

"I hope mad passionate sex was involved." Her grin echoed in her tone.

"Maybe a little."

Sierra laughed. "Good for you. Very life affirming. I won't force you yet to give me all the details, but I want you to know I'm happy for you."

"It was just one date. It may not be a long-term thing."

"There's no such thing as long term. All you got is now. Sweet dreams." Sierra hung up.

Libby lay back against the couch pillows, feeling a genuine peace. As she stared at the popcorn ceiling, it was not even the least bit annoying. Well, not that much.

Her phone rang. She did not recognize the number, but thinking it might be a stressed-out bride, she answered it.

"Libby McKenzie."

"This is Lofton Grant."

She sat up and swung her legs over the side of the couch, as if ready to spring into action. "Lofton. Is Elaine all right?"

"I want you to stay away from my mother."

Lofton's voice sounded as if she had been doused in too much wine. "Excuse me?"

"You know as well as I do that she has not been well. I want you to stay away from her. She doesn't need this kind of turmoil in her life."

"I'm her daughter, Lofton," Libby said carefully.

"An accident by birth doesn't make you her legitimate daughter."

"I'm pretty sure she would take exception. She's the one that set these wheels in motion, not me."

Her tone shifted up an octave. "Like I said, she's sick, and I don't want her being taken advantage of."

Libby rose and started to pace the floor. "She's always been sharp and clearheaded whenever I've spoken to her."

"I'm warning you."

"Oh, wait a minute. You're warning me to not see Elaine? You don't get to do that, you spoiled piece of . . ." She caught herself and drew in a breath. "You don't get to do this."

"Are you the one that encouraged her to change her will?" Her voice grew quieter, as if she was ducking her head and leaning into the phone.

"A will? Hold on a minute. Is this about money or your mother's health?"

"Her health, of course."

"Bullshit. It's about money. And for the record, I don't want anything from Elaine other than some family history and maybe one day a friendship. And if you ever call me again, you and I will be having our next conversation in front of *our* mother."

"She's not your mother," she screamed. "She is *my* mother!"

"You're drunk, aren't you, Lofton?"

"I've had a few drinks."

"You've had more than a few. Cut your losses and hang up."

"She wants to give *you* Woodmont!" Lofton shouted.

At first, Libby did not say anything. She could not have heard correctly. "Woodmont? She has not said a word to me about that."

"I don't believe that. I heard the way you were going on about the gardens and the house at dinner."

"She told you this?" Libby asked.

"I heard her talking to my father!"

A muscle pulsed in the side of her neck, and she rolled her head from side to side, trying to release the building tension.

"I don't know anything about this," Libby said.

"I don't believe you."

"Goodbye, Lofton."

She ended the call and tossed the phone on the couch. A string of unflattering words rolled off her tongue as she paced. She had always wondered what it would be like to have a younger sister. What a little brat.

Libby grabbed her phone and searched out Elaine's number. She dialed, and her thumb was poised to hit send when she caught herself.

She was thirty-one, and she needed to act like it.

If Lofton thought she was going to stand between Libby and Elaine, she was wrong.

CHAPTER
TWENTY-SEVEN
LIBBY

Thursday, June 18, 2020
Northern Virginia

Take the bull by the horns. That was the motto of Libby's day as she drove into Northern Virginia.

Guided by the directions on her phone, she wound her way up I-66 and then around the beltway into Old Town Alexandria via the George Washington Memorial Parkway as it meandered along the Potomac River. She had come up here in third grade on a field trip to Mount Vernon, never realizing that she was less than five miles from her birth mother. On that day, she had been so excited about the cupcakes her mother had packed in her lunch box that she had eaten them all before they had reached Fredericksburg.

Thinking about that trip and the lunch her mother had packed for her triggered a pang of guilt. Her mother had done her best, despite her struggles. She had been there.

She turned into a lovely tree-lined neighborhood featuring a collection of older brick homes with large green neatly edged lawns, towering magnolias, and mulched beds of azaleas that had shed their pink-and-white spring blossoms recently.

She parked, shouldered her bag, and walked up the freshly black-topped driveway. Her stomach churned, chewing into her resolve to have a very frank discussion with Elaine. It was all fine and good to give Libby a journal that detailed Olivia's first year at Woodmont. She appreciated knowing that, like her great-grandmother Olivia, Libby had trouble carrying a baby to term. And the birth of Elaine's father was proof that she might have a chance at motherhood.

She climbed the brick steps and pushed the doorbell. After several seconds, when she did not hear footsteps inside the house, she reached for the door knocker.

What kind of a fool got in a car and drove three hours without calling ahead to tell someone that she was coming? Libby rapped hard with the door knocker.

As the silence stretched, she realized this maybe was not a good idea. Irritated that her big speech and grand entrance had failed, she descended the stairs. As she walked along the sidewalk back to her car, she heard, "Libby."

She turned to find Elaine approaching from the side yard. She wore shorts, a T-shirt, and gardening gloves. "What are you doing here?"

"I came to talk to you. I know you said you would be back soon, but it could not wait. I'll lose my nerve if I wait."

Elaine knotted her brows and carefully tugged off her gloves. "Why don't you come inside? Which should I pour, lemonade or bourbon?"

"Maybe both."

Elaine opened the front door, and they walked together across the black-and-white-tiled floor to a large kitchen that reminded her of the remodeled one at the Woodmont Estate.

Elaine opened the refrigerator and pulled out two bottled lemon-ade-flavored waters. "Sorry, no fresh lemonade made."

Libby accepted the bottle and twisted off the top.

Elaine sat at the center white-marble island on a barstool and extended her hand toward Libby. "What can I help you with?"

Libby took a sip, wondering why her mouth suddenly felt as if she had eaten a handful of cotton. "Who is my birth father?"

Elaine did not answer right away as she fidgeted with the top of her drink.

"We're in the honeymoon phase of our relationship. Everyone is on their best behavior, trying to do the right thing."

"You think this won't work?" Elaine asked.

"It always happens to my relationships. Somewhere along the way it all sours, and I'm left on the outs. I thought my dad was the one guy who hadn't ever let me down. But he dodged telling me about you."

"He loved you very much, Libby."

"I appreciate the love, but I need honesty too. Believe me, if my dad were still alive, he and I would be having a very frank discussion right now."

"I don't want you to think less of your father. He was very dedicated to you and your mother."

"I know that. But that doesn't mean I wouldn't have had strong words for him. He should have told me about Olivia's letter."

"I gave it to him that day we met in Roanoke for lunch."

"Why then?"

"I knew he was sick, and I wanted to take what might be our last chance to talk about the truth. I thought over the years he might have had an honest talk about me. I understood why he did not when your mother was alive. He was protecting her as well as you. But after she died, I thought he would say something. I waited, knowing I had made my choice, and it wasn't fair to break the promise I made to your parents."

"What promise?"

"That I wouldn't contact you under any circumstances. And they also promised that they would not tell my grandfather about you. As

I've said, he had very unbending views about women who gave birth out of wedlock."

"That sounds so draconian."

"It was still like that thirty-plus years ago in the rural South."

"I have already decided I don't like Edward Carter."

"Don't be too hard on him. He was a man of his time. Not perfect. But he tried his best."

"His *best* meant that you didn't feel free to raise me."

"I wasn't ready to raise you or any baby. I had been accepted to law school, and I knew the next ten years would mean long hours of work. Olivia saw that. And as I look back on those busy years after you were born, I know I wouldn't have had time to be a good mother."

A cyclone of emotions swirled around her, and if she weren't careful, they could very well sweep her off her feet. "Who was my birth father? Did he know about me?"

"Yes, he knew about you. And believe it or not, he was very kind to me when he found out I was pregnant. He sent me money and all the help he could."

"But he didn't want to raise me. Was he young like you?" Anger turned her tone brittle.

Elaine folded her hands in her lap and pulled back her shoulders. "He was much older. And married."

"Married?"

"I'm not proud of the decisions I've made. I could get into the whys, but none of that really matters anymore. But I had to forgive myself a long time ago."

This was all old ground for Elaine, but Libby was trudging over fresh territory. "Who was he?"

Elaine drew in a slow, steadying breath. "Your biological father was Dr. Allen McKenzie."

Hearing her father's name slammed into her like a fist upside the head. "Say that again?"

"Your biological father was your dad."

She sat back, her spine pressing into the chair's back. "I don't understand."

"I was a senior in college and home for the holidays. I was working in my grandfather's medical office over the break, and your dad had set up his pediatric practice down the hallway. My grandfather wanted me to be a doctor, so he arranged for me to shadow your dad at his practice. Your father was good humored and terrific with the kids."

"Everyone always talks about how kind my dad was."

"He was kind. Please don't ever lose sight of that."

"He stepped out on my mother?"

"Once," she said. "Your mother was on a new round of medications, and she was keeping your father at arm's distance, and he was upset and frustrated. I had broken up with my boyfriend from college, and we both had a moment where we let our guards down."

Tears clogged her throat. "Where did it happen?"

"At Woodmont. I had forgotten my wallet, and he brought it back to me. My grandparents were gone, and I had the house to myself. I offered him a beer. One thing led to another pretty quickly. I quit that job the next morning, and we didn't see each other again for six months."

"You got pregnant on the first try."

"Yes. I've never had any problem getting pregnant."

Libby drew in a breath. "Too bad I didn't inherit that."

"I'm sorry. Your dad told me about your miscarriages when we had lunch last fall. For the record, Ted knew about that lunch."

Libby pressed her fingertips to her temples. "When did you tell Dad you were pregnant?"

"I was six months along. Olivia insisted I tell the baby's father. So I called him."

"And after you told him about me?"

"He came up to New Jersey immediately. He never once questioned that I might be lying. He asked my intentions, and when I told him I was considering adoption, he said he wanted to adopt you."

"I didn't agree right away, but as I got closer to delivery, it made sense. I would always know where you were, and I knew your father would love you."

"Did my mother know?"

"Your father said he never told her. He didn't want to hurt her. And he thought by giving her a child, he could make up for our indiscretion."

"Wow."

"Don't think less of him. He did the best he could."

Her body was numb, as if she had swallowed a gallon of Novocain. "I don't think you're right about Mom. She knew."

Elaine's brow knotted. "Your father swore to me she didn't."

"She was a smart woman." Libby shook her head. "All the times she took me to Woodmont. She often said the estate was an important part of history."

"She could have been speaking in general terms."

"Nope, I don't think so. She wouldn't have dressed me up and made such a fuss if she didn't know something. I think she hoped your grandmother saw us. I think she wanted her to know that someone like Mom could do a good job raising a child."

Elaine was silent for a moment. "I don't think your father ever suspected she knew."

"She was clever. She proved that at the end."

"Maybe."

Libby took a sip of the lemon water, grateful for the tartness that cut through the dryness in her mouth. "Thank you for the talk, Elaine."

"It was a long time coming, Libby."

"I guess better late than never." Bitterness soured the taste in her mouth. She hoisted her purse on her shoulder and turned to leave. "I can find my way out."

"I think we should talk more."

"Maybe some other time. Not now."

"Are you all right?"

"Don't have much choice."

"Where are you going?" Elaine rushed to ask.

The motherly concern was oddly touching yet annoying at the same time. "No idea."

"Libby, I'm giving you Woodmont."

"Funny you should say that. Lofton drunk dialed me last night and said you were going to do that. I told her to sober up."

"I'll speak to Lofton about that call. But the bottom line is that I want you to have it. It belongs to you."

"Your other daughter will not be so thrilled."

"She's never shown an interest in Woodmont. Besides, Lofton would either subdivide it for residential zoning or sell it whole in a few years."

"She might surprise you."

"I love Lofton and know all her strengths and faults."

"What if I don't want it?" Libby challenged.

"Do you want it?"

Libby shrugged. "I have no idea. Maybe."

"Think about it. You're perfectly suited for the property. You already have ideas for the place and know how to make it work financially. I want it to stay in the family."

"We'll see." She had always loved that property. "For the record, if I accept it, I would not subdivide it."

"Good."

"You aren't planning on going anywhere soon?" Libby asked.

Elaine raised an amused brow. "I'm staying on this side of the rainbow if I have any say in it. My doctor told me my cancer is in remission."

"I'm really glad to hear that."

To say that all the fences were mended between them would be disingenuous. Libby was nowhere near close to processing what she had learned today. "By the way, who do I look like?"

"Your great-grandmother Olivia. You're the spitting image of her."

The drive back to Bluestone felt daunting, especially considering Libby was going to have to fight her way through rush hour traffic. The wedding she was photographing did not kick off until tomorrow. She was essentially in no man's land.

She drove to Springfield Town Center outside of DC and walked around, buying coffee and a cinnamon bun that was not nearly as good as what Sierra might make. When she wandered into a clothing store and found herself in the baby section, she bought a large soft blue blanket and had it gift wrapped.

To just show up at Jeremy's house with a baby gift redefined weird. And still she drove to Dale City and parked across from the duplex that the two of them had shared just two years ago.

He had changed the white exterior to a deep blue, and someone had painted the front door a bright yellow. It had to be Monica's bold choice. Jeremy's color palette did not extend beyond antique white.

She was not so lost in herself as to actually walk up to the front door and ring the bell. That was the thing crazy ex-wives did. But she wanted to talk to Jeremy. Despite all the crap that had happened, he was still a friend. So she did what any self-respecting ex-wife would do. Texted him.

Hey. I'm in town. Can I drop off a gift for the baby?

The rolling bubbles appeared, stopped, and then reappeared. He was second-guessing whatever he wanted to say. And then finally, Sure. When?

Now. Parked out front of your house. She added an emoji with a chagrined expression.

The curtains in the front windows fluttered, and Libby waved, hoping she did not look like a stalker.

The front door opened; he appeared dressed in jeans and a stained T-shirt, his hair tousled.

Jeremy closed the door and crossed the yard but stopped at the curb. As he got closer, she saw the dark circles under his eyes. He was not sleeping. Which, if she was honest with herself, made her just a little happy.

She got out of the car, bringing the box wrapped in blue with her. Wariness radiated from his gaze, as it had when she had been pregnant and super hormonal. Was she going to unload on him?

"I'm not going to lose it," she said. "I was in the area and wanted to bring this for you."

He accepted the box, studying the big bow that had cost her an extra five dollars. "You didn't have to do this, Libby."

"I know. Open it."

One tug and the ribbon gave way, allowing him to lift the top. Inside was the blanket. "I didn't have time to get it personalized. But I figure the kid can't read, so it doesn't matter."

"He was born two days ago. We just brought him home."

Sadness and happiness twisted in her belly. "Wow. Congratulations."

"Thanks." He smoothed his hand over the fabric. "Soft."

"The clerk in the baby store said new parents can always use big blankets."

He replaced the top. "Good to know."

"Honestly, the gift was an excuse."

Thick brows knotted. "For what?"

"To see a familiar face. To talk with someone who knew my dad."

His brow knotted. "What's going on?"

She wanted to smile, but the tears choking her throat would not allow it. Unable to look at him, she sat on the curb.

He sat beside her, setting the present on his lap. "What's up?"

"I found out Elaine Grant is my birth mother."

"Who's she?"

"Remember Woodmont, that estate where the wedding was a couple of weeks ago?"

"Yeah."

"She owns it. Been in her family since the eighteenth century."

"You sure it's her? I thought your birth mother was a superspy or an international fashion model?" he teased.

Jeremy's deadpan question coaxed a smile.

Whenever they had drunk wine together, she would theorize about her birth mother. The common denominator had always been that circumstances had prevented her mother from raising Libby.

"She had the money and the means to raise me," Libby said. "But she was young and headed to law school."

"Do you fault her for that?" Jeremy asked.

"I want to, but I don't. I'm a little miffed that it's taken thirty-one years to find out the truth."

"Why the big secret? Did her family disapprove?"

"That's part of it." She tugged at the frayed edges of her jeans. "The big shoe to drop is my birth father."

He drew in a breath. "Who was he?"

"My dad."

"Your dad, as in Allen McKenzie?"

"The very one."

He whistled, running a hand through his hair. "Shit."

His shocked gaze was reaffirming. She could have told all this to Colton, but she was not sure he would have understood the depth of the news like Jeremy would. And Sierra would have been deeply disappointed in her father, and right now Libby could not handle that.

"Wow. And he knew?" Jeremy asked.

"Oh yes."

"And your mother. I mean, your adoptive mother—I mean, Mrs. McKenzie."

"I know what you're saying. I don't know. Possibly. Likely."

They sat for a moment, each staring at the cracked pavement in front of his house. Weeds had grown up through them, stretching toward the sun.

"So what are you going to do?" Jeremy asked.

"Get on with my life. Photograph a wedding this weekend. Go home. Keep working. One foot in front of the other. What's the alternative?"

His brows drew together, but he did not reach out and take her hand or hug her. "I don't know what to say."

Honesty hummed under the words, and she appreciated that he wanted to be there for her. Maybe if all this had come out sooner, and they were still together, the news would have bonded them closer. Libby would have found a way to deal with her losses better.

"How can I help?" he asked.

"You can't. This is all on me," she said, tapping her finger on the blue box. "You've got your own new life."

He ran his finger over the soft blue ribbon. "When my son was born, my first thought was that I was sorry he wasn't ours." He cleared his throat. "We tried so hard, and I know how much you wanted a child."

She sighed, pushing back grief that would always be there in some form. "I did. I still do. But you know what, I still might. Our time is up, but I'm not dead yet. As it turns out, I had a great-grandmother who had a very similar medical history to mine, but she ended up eventually having a son."

"That's great."

"Yeah. That's one of the silver linings in all this. I feel like I might still have a shot at it."

"Hey, do you want to come in and meet the baby? He's taking a nap, which means he's at his best right now. I can't promise how long it will last. He's a terrible sleeper."

"Like you?"

"Yeah. My mother used to say she hoped I had a baby that didn't sleep. Something about payback."

"Thanks for the invite, but maybe another time. I really do need to get on the road. I just wanted to stop and get a little moral support from a friend who knows me best."

This time he wrapped his arm around her, and she rested her head against his shoulder. "I'll always have your back."

Rising, she dusted the gravel and dirt from her bottom. "Thanks."

"Take care of yourself, Libby."

"You too. You're going to make a good father. That's one of the many reasons I picked you."

His brow knotted, and his Adam's apple bobbed as he swallowed. "You really think so? I feel like I'm messing up. Maybe I should be more patient when he doesn't sleep or needs a diaper change."

"Once he starts sleeping through the night, it will all get better. You'll figure out the dad thing pretty quickly."

"You really think so?"

"I know so."

She got in her car, waved goodbye, and drove off. At the first stoplight she removed Jeremy's profiles from all her social media accounts.

CHAPTER
TWENTY-EIGHT
LIBBY

Saturday, August 1, 2020
Virginia

Libby spent the better part of the summer working out of town. She took jobs as a second shooter, assisting other photographers because she wanted to stay busy and away from Bluestone. She made excuses to Colton about work and life and why she was too busy to see him or return home. However, as her excuses started to run together, the frequency of his communications waned. Colton was trying to keep up with her, but she was the one doing the running.

After several weeks, he stopped texting. Sierra called her daily, calling it her proof-of-life call, and each time Libby promised to be back in town soon. But when the work ran out, she took a week vacation to Paris and indulged in lavish foods and historical walks.

But running took stamina, and as the summer progressed, hers started to wane. By the time she landed in Dulles International Airport, she was not feeling well. She had been sprinting through her days, and her body was simply bone tired.

It was not until she was standing in the crowded customs line waiting for her turn that it dawned on her what really might be happening.

Another hour later, she was in her car and headed south, back to Bluestone. She made a quick stop at the grocery store, buying crackers, sodas, and chocolates—and three pregnancy tests.

She pushed through the front door and dropped her purse on the couch as she kicked off her shoes. She put away her groceries and carried the pregnancy tests to the bathroom. They worked best in the morning, so to try now would likely render a false read.

When she stepped under the shower's hot spray, she allowed the warm water to pulse on her face and willed it to chase the tension away. *It's the flu. A bug I picked up in Paris.*

When she had drained all the hot water from the tank, she reluctantly stepped out, toweled off, and slid on an oversize T-shirt, then opened each kit. She lined them up neatly on the bathroom counter and went downstairs and lay on the couch. The clock on the wall ticked as she turned off her phone and willed her body to relax.

Sometime during the night, she did drift off to sleep, and when she woke with a start, the sun was shining in the room. She jumped up off the couch, hesitated as a wave of nausea washed over her, and bolted up the stairs.

Libby should have saved one of the pregnancy tests and retested tomorrow, but it was too late now. If she needed more, she decided she would make another trip to the pharmacy. She followed their instructions to the letter. Once done, she lined them back up on the bathroom counter, and she went downstairs to the kitchen. She dug out a packet of saltines and a cold can of ginger ale from the refrigerator. It wasn't lost on her that her one-night stand with Colton had theoretically produced a pregnancy.

The last three times she had been pregnant, she had felt terrific. There had been no morning sickness. She had had energy and a strong appetite.

I have the flu. That's all.

She had not spoken to Elaine in the last five weeks, but Elaine had begun to email her pictures of Olivia and Woodmont. Libby supposed that was Elaine's idea of a soft sell.

Sipping the ginger ale, she climbed the steps to the bathroom and stood at the threshold, staring at the three white tests lined up on the counter. "It's the flu."

But a glance into the little windows said otherwise. Three bright-pink plus signs stared back at her. She picked each up and held them to the light.

"This is wrong," she muttered. "They are false positives. I can't get pregnant," she said to each stick. "The doctors said it was such a low chance that it was unlikely."

Immediately, Libby listed off diseases that might mimic pregnancy. Hormonal imbalances. Massive tumors. Or maybe it was cancer like Elaine's. Her worst-case list was more comforting than the idea of another lost pregnancy.

A hard pounding on her front door wrestled Libby's attention back to the moment. The pounding grew louder.

She tossed the sticks in the trash can and went downstairs. Sipping her ginger ale, she glanced toward the front door and saw the outline of a man. She crossed to the door and opened it. Colton was standing on her front steps. Talk about timing.

"Colton." Apologies rushed to the tip of her tongue, but all sounded lame, so she did not bother. "What are you doing here?"

He studied her a long beat, but it was impossible to decide if he looked mad, upset, or relieved. "Elaine tried to call you, but you didn't answer your phone."

"Elaine?" She glanced at her phone and saw two missed calls from Elaine. "Why? Is she all right?"

"Lofton has been arrested."

"Lofton. Why should that have anything to do with me?"

"That's what I asked Elaine, and she said you would know."

"How did you even know I was back in town?"

"I saw Sierra at her jobsite this morning. She said your car was back."

There was no sneaking back into Bluestone. "Does Elaine want me to bail her out?"

"No, Lofton is in the hospital, but she's headed to jail once the doctors release her. She wrapped her car around a tree. She's lucky to be alive."

"And where is Elaine?"

"New York. She's trying to get a flight back."

Libby gathered her purse, keys, ginger ale, and a sleeve of saltine crackers from the kitchen. "Great. Can't pick your family, right?"

"What's that mean?"

"It's a long story. I'll go now."

"I'll drive you."

"You don't have to. Seriously. I've been MIA all summer, and I'm honestly amazed you're even here now."

"So am I. And while I drive, you're going to tell me about your vanishing act over the last five weeks."

She would have argued if she did not feel like she was going to throw up on his shoes. "Fine. Drive."

He followed her down the front steps and to his truck. She slid into the passenger seat and hooked her seat belt.

After starting the truck, he pulled onto the quiet street and wasted no time getting to the heart of his irritation. "Where have you been?"

"Working. Vacation."

"You said you'd explain it all when you returned. You have returned."

"Obviously, I have had some stuff to deal with," she said. "And if you know me for more than five minutes, you'll realize I don't handle loss well."

"What did you lose?"

"My identity, the life I thought I knew," she said.

He was quiet for a moment, but his jaw was tight and pulsing at the joint. "Does all this have to do with Elaine?"

"Oh yeah."

"Want to talk about it?"

She rested her head against the seat. "Turns out she's my birth mother."

He shot a glance at her, his expression shocked and a little relieved. "What?"

"Yeah, it's a shocker, isn't it? Could have knocked me over with a feather." Her stomach tumbled, and she nibbled on a cracker.

"Are you sure?"

"Oh yes. When I go AWOL, it's usually for a good reason. I found a letter from my great-grandmother, Olivia Carter, to me in my father's study."

"Dr. McKenzie knew about Elaine?"

Laughter bubbled in her throat. "Oh, he sure did."

"I'm not sure I follow."

It still felt like she was telling someone else's story. "Allen McKenzie is not only my adoptive father but my birth father."

Colton did not speak as he processed the information.

"Dad had a one-night stand with Elaine. And here I am."

"That explains why Elaine said you'd know what to do for Lofton," Colton said.

"And for the record, Lofton is not taking the whole older-sister thing well. I guess getting knocked down a peg in birth order doesn't sit well with the landed gentry."

"I caught her throwing rocks at the greenhouse. I didn't realize it was her until she took off in her car. I was right behind her and saw her hit the tree. I pulled her out of the wreck and called the cops."

"Boy, you've had some night. We Carters are quite the handful."

"Why go after the greenhouse?"

She watched as the small streets of Bluestone gave way to the ramp that fed onto the interstate. "I suppose because it's the project that Elaine created to get to know me better."

"Is that what she said?"

"Yes." She pressed the cool ginger ale can to the side of her head. "She also wants to leave me Woodmont."

"Why?"

Her head fell back against the headrest. "Elaine knows Lofton won't hesitate to either sell it or chop it up into housing tracts."

"That explains a lot with Lofton." He released a breath, letting go of weeks' worth of tension. "I called Ginger and told her that Lofton was at the hospital."

"Good."

"You don't look well."

She sipped her ginger ale. "I've been running myself kind of ragged. I'm coming down with the flu."

"How did you find the letter from Olivia?" he said.

She eased back in the seat. "My dad had cleaned out his desk and left only the important papers. It was in an unmarked file. All I had to do was open the desk. But remember, I don't deal with loss well, so I spent the spring avoiding Dad's office."

"Okay."

She rolled her head toward him. "This hasn't been about you. It's all me and my crazy family."

A half smile tipped the edge of his lips. "I can deal with crazy families."

"Be careful what you say. There's no telling who else is going to fall out of my family tree."

He took the exit ramp into Charlottesville and followed the hospital signs to the medical center. He parked, and the two got out.

She downed the last of her ginger ale, staring at the hospital entrance. Now would be the time to get a blood test to confirm the drugstore pregnancy test that boasted a 98 percent accuracy rate was wrong. "There might be another shoe to drop."

A fresh tension rippled through him, as if he was bracing himself for round two.

She paused on the curb near the emergency entrance. Wasting diseases aside, she had to be honest with herself and him. "Remember when I said the chances of me getting pregnant were really slim? Well, even long shots are possible. I just put up a pink plus sign on not one, not two, but three home pregnancy tests."

He took her arm in his. "Say that again."

"I'm five weeks knocked up. Before you freak out, I'll remind you I've had three miscarriages." She felt tension ripple through Colton, prompting her to continue babbling. "The last three times I was pregnant, I felt amazing. But this go-round, I feel like roadkill."

"We were in the greenhouse five weeks ago."

"Like I said, don't freak out." She closed her eyes, fighting back tears. The odds were against this kid making it into the world, and that realization bound and twisted around her heart like barbwire. "With my pregnancy track record, I won't be able to go the distance."

"That doesn't mean you're going to lose this one."

"Seriously, don't bond with this kid. Don't." Tears welled in her eyes. "She'll leave, and she'll break your heart."

"She?"

"Or he."

He took her hands in his, unfurling her fists. "Once we deal with Lofton, we're finding Ginger. She'll run a test."

"It's still so early, Colton. I'll give it a few weeks and then track her down."

"We'll see her tonight. Do you have any signs you're in distress?"

"No."

"Then for now, it's all hands on deck to help you keep it."

She studied his face, searching for any sign that he was upset or angry. She did not see any traces. Hell, she thought she saw a glimmer of excitement in his eyes. "Don't get excited, Colton."

He shrugged. "Too late. I care about you and have spent most of the last few weeks wondering what I did wrong."

"You didn't do anything wrong."

He released a breath. "And I'm not about to start. I'm sticking with you and the baby."

Libby and Colton found Lofton on the fourth floor. The nurse directed them to her room. When Libby pushed past the curtain, she found Lofton lying in the hospital bed, clutching a plastic basin. Her face was pale and drawn.

"Lofton," she said softly.

As Colton remained by the door, Libby moved toward the bed. Lofton looked up and studied her a long moment before she closed her eyes. There was a bruise on the side of her face and scrapes along her jawline, likely left by the deployed airbag. "You sound just like Mom."

"Do I?"

"Yeah."

"Elaine asked me to check in on you. She'll be down in a few hours. Apparently, she's in New York."

She pressed fingertips to her brow. "Great."

Libby pulled up a chair and sat down. "Like it or not, we're stuck with each other. Can't pick your family, right?"

Lofton raised the small basin to her lips. She heaved a couple of times, causing Libby to stand up and turn away.

"I'm pretty sure Elaine wants us to be friends, and this is her idea of a bonding moment," Libby said.

"Until *you*, I was enough. She loved just me, and we were best friends. She used to call us the Two Amigos."

"And now you're one of the Three Musketeers."

"Exactly. It sucks."

Libby moved closer to the bed but remained standing. "I've no desire to get between you two. I had a great mother." She drew in a breath. "And a great father."

Lofton sat forward and threw up again. Libby pressed her hand to her stomach and hurried away from the bed.

"I'll get a nurse," Colton said.

Libby sat in a chair across the room and put her head in her hands. Her own stomach tumbled several times. "What the hell were you drinking?"

She wiped her mouth with the back of her hand. "Scotch. Dad's going to be pissed when he realizes I went through his bottle of Johnnie Walker Blue."

"At least you have good taste." Libby counted slowly, drawing in a breath until her stomach settled.

"What's wrong with you?" Lofton asked.

"A little pregnant."

"What?"

The nurse appeared, checked Lofton's vitals, and replaced the plastic basin. When the nurse left, Libby noticed more bruises on Lofton's arms. "You're lucky you aren't dead."

"You don't get to lecture me," Lofton said. "That's for Dad and Mom."

How could she go from no family to petulant little sister and a bun in the oven in five weeks? "No, but Elaine will. You scared her to death," Libby said. "You're smarter than that. And you told me yourself she is fragile."

"I get that. Believe me. I'm about to get arrested, and that's going to fly with the new boss like a lead balloon."

Libby had no words of comfort to add. "What were you doing at Woodmont anyway?"

"I was getting ready for Mom and Dad's renewal of vows ceremony. It's in two weeks."

"Why throw rocks at the greenhouse?"

"I started thinking about the party and how one day I wouldn't have access to the land, because it would be yours. I certainly wasn't going to burn down Woodmont."

"Smart decision."

Lofton closed her eyes. "I always thought Woodmont would be mine."

"Then take it. I don't need it."

"Mom says you get it. I think she's trying to assuage her guilt."

In Elaine's rush to make things right, she had hurt Lofton deeply. "Then I'll give it to you."

"I don't want it from *you*." She sat up and looked at Libby with bloodshot eyes smudged with mascara. "I want it from Mom."

"Since when do we get everything we want in this world? Do you want the house or not?"

"She won't go for it. She wants you to have it."

"I'll talk to her."

Lofton groaned and shoved back a tangle of blonde hair. "Don't talk to her. I don't need you pleading my case."

"What if we go halves on it? Both of Elaine's daughters will own Woodmont."

"I don't even know you. And now you're going to give Mom her first grandchild."

Libby rose, drawing a deep breath, hoping it would calm her stomach. "Stop whining, Lofton. You sound like you're five."

"I do not."

"Do too" rattled in her head but was silenced by the sound of footsteps approaching the door. The curtain whisked back, and Elaine and Ted stood there looking frazzled and terrified.

Elaine held up her phone. "You didn't answer."

"Sorry," Libby said.

"Always answer your calls. You have no idea how many worst-case scenarios have run through my mind." Elaine sounded like an anxious mother doing her best not to scold her adult child.

"I totally understand. Won't happen again." Libby stepped toward the door, grateful to turn her baby sister back over to their worried mother.

Elaine smoothed back Lofton's hair and kissed her on the forehead. "God, I'm so grateful you're alive."

"I'm sorry, Mom." Lofton's voice sounded small and a little contrite.

Elaine turned to Libby. "Thank you."

"Sure thing."

"I'll talk to you soon?"

"Absolutely."

Libby and Colton stepped out into the hallway, closing the door behind them. "Got to love family."

"Elaine will be in there awhile. I've texted Ginger, and she's waiting to see you."

Tightness banded around her chest. "I say we wait five or six months. Don't want to get the hopes up."

He guided her toward the elevator and pressed the down button. They stepped off on the first floor, where Ginger was waiting. She took the pair into an examination room.

"Libby," she said. "How are you doing?"

"I might be a little pregnant, but it likely won't last."

Ginger looked past her to Colton, her expression questioning. "That's not what Colton said."

"I've already lost three pregnancies." As much as she wanted to hope for this baby, she did not dare.

"Well, why don't we run a few quick tests and see what's going on," Ginger said. "Every pregnancy is different, and there's no predicting what will happen. One step at a time."

"I want to hear what Ginger has to say," Colton said.

Ginger regarded her brother a long moment as an amused smile lightened her expression. "Do you mind if Colton stays?"

"Sure. Why not?"

The examination took only a few minutes, with Libby lying on a gurney while Colton sat in a chair next to her. Afterward, Ginger wrote up some notes on her tablet and then turned her attention back to Libby. "Libby, you're indeed pregnant."

Tears filled her eyes and rolled down her cheeks. She stared at the tiled ceiling, trying to push back the feeling of happiness and hope.

"We have a great doctor on staff who handles high-risk pregnancies," Ginger said.

Colton rose and stood beside her. He had a determined "we will get through this" look that she thought was sweet but naive.

"Don't do that," she said.

"What?"

"Think we're going to get through this."

"I'm not."

"You are."

"Libby, it's a long road ahead," Ginger interjected. "You're not alone in this."

Libby would do whatever was necessary for this pregnancy except hope. She would not make lists of the things a newborn needed nor look at any blue, pink, or yellow paint swatches.

Colton's phone pinged with a text. "Elaine is just outside and wants to see you."

"Sure. Send her in."

The curtains pushed back, and Elaine crossed to her bed. She did not smooth back her hair or kiss her on the forehead like she had with Lofton. But she was here. And she looked worried.

"What's going on with you?" Elaine asked.

"Pregnant," Libby said.

"Really?" Elaine's face lit up with excitement.

"Don't do that around me," Libby said. "It's way too soon; trust me."

Elaine gently took her hand in hers. "Can I get a little excited if I promise not to show it?"

"Okay, but that goes for Colton and Ginger too. No victory dances." She cleared her throat and sat up, doing her best to ignore their terribly hidden goofy expressions. "How is Lofton?"

"Going to have one hell of a hangover," Elaine said. "Which serves her right."

"She's worried that you don't love her," Libby said. "She thinks I've replaced her."

"You don't replace one child with another," Elaine said. "You already know that."

Elaine was right. Even if this baby made it to term, she would never forget the three other children she had carried, loved, and lost. "You can't give me Woodmont. She's always wanted it."

"She doesn't know what she wants," Elaine countered. "If I gave her the property, she would lose interest because it's not in her blood. She doesn't see Woodmont the way we do. I love Lofton, but she has some growing up to do before she's ready for that kind of responsibility."

"Give her a break. It's hard to see the world one way and then find out it's not what you thought. She'll grow up, and like me, she'll realize Woodmont is home. Give her half ownership."

Elaine regarded her. "I'll give you fifty-one percent. And if you want to give her the one percent when she turns, say, fifty, then that'll be your choice. Like it or not, you two are sisters, and you'll have to work this out."

CHAPTER TWENTY-NINE

SADIE

Monday, March 15, 1943
Bluestone, Virginia

Sadie had given birth to her baby girl on Christmas Eve. The labor had lasted for hours, and there had been times she had thought the child would rip her in two. Her mother had wanted to send a neighbor for the doctor, but Sadie had begged her to stay. The last person she had wanted to help her was Dr. Carter.

When the six-pounder finally ripped from her body, she tumbled out in a wash of blood onto the mattress. She was scrawny and wrinkled, and her lips had a bluish tinge. Sadie's mother wiped the baby's face and body clean and swaddled her in a tiny blanket. She had moved to lay the baby in her daughter's arms, but Sadie had not been able to bear to look at the child.

It was going on twelve weeks now since her birth, and Sadie was struggling to care for the child. Miss Olivia had come by weekly with cans of milk and beans, but they had not seen her for the last two weeks.

Sadie's mother had taken to feeding the baby, and despite Sadie's distress, the little girl was growing like a weed.

Sadie sat in the truck outside the mercantile store with three jars of moonshine left from her stash, hoping Mr. Sullivan would be willing to trade for canned milk and Karo syrup. Come summer, like it or not, she would have to fire up the still and start making deliveries again. The sheriff would be watching, but it did not matter. She needed the money.

She climbed out of the truck, wrapping her frayed coat tight around her body, which had filled out a good bit since the baby. She crossed the street with a cold breeze snapping at her as she entered the shop. It had been six months since she'd last frequented the store, and she hoped today's visit would raise her spirits.

She started moving toward the front counter but held back as Mr. Sullivan finished an order for the preacher's wife. Sadie ducked her head and pretended to study a can of beans as the woman chatted about the Sunday service and the songs the choir was going to sing.

When she passed by, she paused. "Sadie Thompson, is that you I see lurking around?"

Sadie set the can of beans down. "Yes, Mrs. Morgan."

"We haven't seen you in services since before Thanksgiving. Your mother said you were ailing."

"I'm on the mend now."

The woman eyed a figure that surely was fuller and rounder than it had been. "Good. Hope to see you in church this week."

"Yes, ma'am." Hiding at home was no longer an option, and soon folks would figure out there was a baby in her mother's house.

As the woman left, Sadie approached the front counter. "Morning, Mr. Sullivan."

"Sadie, where have you been these days?"

"Like I told Mrs. Morgan, I was ailing."

"Sorry to hear that."

"Thank you." She reached in her pockets and pulled out a jar of moonshine. "I was hoping to make a trade. Canned milk and syrup for a couple of these."

"What do you need the milk for?"

"Seems to be the only thing that settles my stomach these days."

His frown deepened. "Have you seen Dr. Carter?"

"No need for that; the worst of it is over." Which was a big fat lie.

"I might be able to sell a few jars," he said.

"Sheriff Boyd don't know about this, so I'd be careful."

"I can find my way around Sheriff Boyd."

Smiling, Sadie set the jars on the counter. "I figure that'll do me for seven or eight cans of milk and syrup."

Mr. Sullivan set the jars behind the counter but did not regard her with his usual frown. Instead his expression softened just a bit. "Have you heard from your brothers?"

"Johnny writes often. Danny did send a letter saying he was in Italy. But not much more than that."

"War's bad," he said, more to himself.

"Yes, sir."

It did not take long before the order was boxed. She offered her thanks and left the store. As she crossed the street, the sunlight caught the shiny metal of a black roadster. Her belly tightened, and for a moment she did not move as she stared at the car. Memories from last spring flooded through her mind, and she thought for a moment she might get sick.

The front door opened, and Malcolm stepped out. Still looking innocent and fresh faced like Mickey Rooney, he settled his hat on his head and turned her way. The instant their gazes tangled, he paused. His eyes narrowed, and then he grinned.

"I didn't recognize you right off," Malcolm said.

Sadie tightened her grip on the box of canned goods. "I recognized your car right off."

He looked back, a grin tugging at the edge of his mouth. "It does hold fond memories, doesn't it?"

Sidestepping the comment, she asked, "What are you doing in town?"

"My cousin and his wife invited me. Olivia has been after me for months to visit, but frankly there was always something more appealing to do."

"That so?"

He leaned closer. "Now that I see you, I think this weekend might not be as boring as I thought. If you still have that green dress, we could find something fun to do."

"I burned that dress."

He stilled. "That's a crazy thing to do."

"Seeing as what you did to me while I was wearing it, it wasn't crazy at all."

The smile in his gaze dimmed. "I didn't do anything to you."

She spit on the ground by his feet. "That's a damn lie. You hurt me good."

"Lower your voice."

"Or what?"

"I'll have the sheriff pay a visit to your home. I won't stand for slander."

The idea of the sheriff arriving at her house and seeing the baby girl was enough to cool her rising temper. She couldn't hide the child forever, but she figured if she had a little more time, she would hatch a solution.

"Yeah, I thought that would shut you up. Girls like you don't need the trouble." He touched the brim of his hat. "Have a nice day, Sadie."

He walked past her like she wasn't even there and vanished into the shop.

She returned to her truck, set her bundle on the seat, and slid behind the wheel. If she were smart, she would just drive home and forget there ever was a Malcolm Carter. There was no changing her life now, and she would have more peace if she simply made the best of it. She slammed the truck door.

She watched through the store window as Mr. Sullivan pulled out one of her jars of moonshine, and Malcolm handed him several dollar bills.

She sat up, leaning over the steering wheel, watching as Malcolm exited. "Go on and drive, Sadie," she muttered to herself. "Best to get back to the farm and forget you ever saw him."

Malcolm scanned the street, and when his gaze landed on her, he touched the brim of his hat and winked.

Her temper roiled up through her with such heat she could feel her cheeks flush. As if he felt her gaze on him, Malcolm squinted as he studied her a bit longer. His head tilted, reminding her of a dog that had heard a whistle. After looking both ways, he crossed the street and held up the jar of her moonshine, as if he was offering a peace token.

There was even a lightness in his step, as if he had already decided that a little moonshine would get him exactly what he wanted from her. It sure had the first time.

Something in Sadie snapped. All God's good reason took one look at her and then took off running, leaving her alone with the devil sitting on her shoulder.

Sadie never could say why she lost her mind, but it abandoned her and made her forget about her mother, her baby, her brothers, the kindness of Miss Olivia, and even the memory of her daddy. All that was left in her was nothing but hate.

Malcolm was in the center of the street when she started the rumbling engine and put the truck in gear. Before she knew it, the wheels were rolling, and she was pressing hard on the accelerator. The engine revved. The next thing she knew, she was screaming as his body came at her fast. The grille caught him in the midsection and carried him over the hood of her truck. His body rolled off to the side and hit the dirt road hard.

Her heart racing, the surge of satisfaction quickly burned up under the glare of reality. In one blink, she had ruined her life and her child's.

Her belly tightened, and her breathing quickened as she stopped the truck and looked back. Malcolm was lying in the street. His hat had landed on the sidewalk, and he was missing a shoe. His body was still. Mr. Sullivan knelt over him and then looked toward Sadie, as if he did not know her at all. Which, she supposed, he did not, because she sure did not recognize herself.

"Sadie, what have you done?" Mr. Sullivan shouted.

She turned and gently pressed on the gas. The truck sputtered down the street like it did not have a care in the world.

CHAPTER THIRTY

LIBBY

Tuesday, August 4, 2020
Bluestone, Virginia

Libby turned to the first page in Olivia's journal and studied the face of the woman who was her great-grandmother. She traced her bright smile and tried to imagine her as an older woman sitting down and writing the letter to her. She could see now that the handwriting of the journal and letter matched. Clear, precise, it was a kind of old-world penmanship that had lost favor with the modern world.

After grabbing another handful of crackers, she ate several, wondering if she would feel this way for the remainder of her pregnancy. "If it means you make it into the world, spud, then I'll do it."

Libby stared at the young girl standing beside Olivia. Sadie Thompson. Elaine had said she hoped reading this journal would help Libby understand Olivia better. *"The woman obviously loved plants but could also draw incredibly well. The journal mentioned the hire of a local girl to assist."*

Libby kept staring at young Sadie's face. If the woman were still alive, she would be in her nineties. She closed the journal, and, after grabbing her car keys and a handful of crackers, she drove to Woodmont.

Margaret was well into her seventies, and if there was someone who might have heard about the Thompson family, she would have.

She nibbled as she drove. Opening the car window, she breathed in the warm, humid air, willing it to chase away the nausea. As tempted as she was to ask Ginger for something to help with it, she did not want to risk anything that might impact the spud.

When she pulled into Woodmont's long driveway, she was glad that Colton's car was not there. Now was not the time to get into a discussion about her pregnancy or how she was feeling. Anything scraping the surface of emotion or commitment would have to wait.

She parked around back and was glad to see Margaret's car. After grabbing the journal, she climbed the steps and knocked on the back door.

"Come on in!" Margaret shouted.

She pushed into the kitchen and found Margaret serving peanut-butter-and-jelly sandwiches to Jeff and Sam. For a moment she hesitated, not wanting to intrude.

"Hey, guys," she said, smiling.

"Libby!" Jeff shouted.

"We're eating lunch." Sam sported a milk mustache.

"I can see that." She set her purse and the journal on the table and eyed the sandwiches. For whatever reason, the idea of a PB&J sounded really good.

"I got plenty," Margaret said. "Take one or two."

"You would be a lifesaver." Libby wondered if Colton had told his mother about the pregnancy.

Margaret set a sandwich before her. "What brings you out here? Elaine has taken Lofton back to Washington, and Colton is not here."

"I came to see you, as a matter of fact." She bit into the white bread, which meshed with the smooth peanut butter and grape jelly in a soft gooey mess that was the best thing this side of heaven. To her surprise, her stomach did not protest as she took another bite and then another.

"What can I do for you?" Margaret asked.

Libby set down the few remaining pieces of crust and wiped her fingers before she opened the journal. "Elaine loaned me Olivia's journal."

Margaret rested her hands on her hips. "Okay."

The older woman did not look surprised, but then Margaret always played her cards close to her vest. She had been working at Woodmont when Elaine was pregnant, and she had guarded the secret closely.

Libby glanced at the boys, who were still preoccupied with their sandwiches. "You already know about Elaine and me?"

Margaret arched a brow and then nodded slowly. "I've known about your connection for a long time."

"How long?" Libby asked.

"About as far back as it goes," she said carefully.

"And my father." Libby was now aware that the boys were quiet and staring.

"That too," Margaret said.

"I like Elaine," Sam said.

"I do too. She's a nice lady," Libby said.

Jeff grinned as he reached for a glass of milk. "She bought us Power Ranger costumes for Halloween. I'm the Black Ranger."

"I'm the Red Ranger," Sam said, sitting up straighter and grinning.

"You're both going to be awesome Power Rangers," Libby said.

"Boys, if you two have eaten, why don't you have a Popsicle outside?"

"Can I have an orange one?" Sam asked.

Margaret moved to the freezer, pulled out two large Popsicles, and pointed to the door. "Outside."

The boys scurried off their seats and, after grabbing their treats, ran out the side door toward the big oak tree. Margaret stood at the screen door, and when she was sure they were settled for at least the next few minutes, she turned toward Libby.

Libby removed the picture of Olivia and Sadie. "Did you ever hear of Sadie Thompson?"

Margaret took the photo from Libby and stared at it a long time. "I haven't seen too many pictures of her from around this time. I heard she was a little wild, and I guess looking at this picture, I can see why folks might think that."

"You knew her?"

"Her father and brothers were farmers. The father passed in the late thirties. The boys got work at the same machine shop, but neither lasted that long. The oldest, Danny, went into the army in '38 and was shipped to North Africa and Italy. Johnny was army and landed in Europe."

"Did they survive the war?"

"They did. Of course, no one came back the same." Margaret was silent but finally said, "Sadie stayed behind with her mother. She always dreamed of leaving Bluestone, and there was a time when she had a job working for the Carter family. Miss Olivia told me Sadie drove her around, teaching her how to drive and helping her plant in the greenhouse."

"What happened to Sadie?"

"Why do you want to know about Sadie so badly?"

"I think whatever happened to her influenced Olivia. And that dictated what happened with Elaine and ultimately me."

Margaret continued to gaze at the picture of Sadie. "That poor girl didn't have a chance."

CHAPTER THIRTY-ONE

SADIE

Monday, March 15, 1943
Bluestone, Virginia

The truck's radiator was spewing steam by the time Sadie pulled up to her mother's house. Her heart hammered against her ribs, doing its best to rip right out of her body. She grabbed the supplies and hurried into the house.

"Mama!" She dumped the box of milk and syrup on the table. "Mama!"

Her mother hurried out of the side bedroom, holding her hands up. "Shh. I just got the baby to sleep. If she wakes up now, we'll hear about it for the rest of the day."

"Mama, I'm in trouble." Sadie pressed her hand to her side, trying to calm the pain knotting her belly.

Her mother moved toward her as her face turned ashen. "What have you done, child?"

"I saw him in town. I saw him. And he treated me like I was nothing but dirt under his feet."

"What do you mean by *him*?"

Sadie pointed to the bedroom where the child slept. "I mean the man that gave me that."

"That is a child," her mother said sternly.

Sadie turned back to her mother, unable to dig up any maternal feelings. "Well, it's his child."

"Please tell me you didn't tell him about the baby."

"No. I didn't tell him. Fat lot it would have done. He'd have denied her and called me a whore for having her."

"What did you do?" Her mother's voice dropped to a bare whisper, as if the sheriff were standing right outside their doorstep.

When she looked back at what had happened, it felt like a terrible dream. The devil himself had gotten in her brain and taken control for a split second. "I hit him with the truck."

"What do you mean you hit him?" her mother demanded.

Sadie ran her hands through her hair, knowing they would lock her away for years whether he lived or died. "I hit him with the truck. I ran him down."

"Is he dead?"

Images of the twisted body in the street rushed her, and even now she was not sorry for what she had done. She sure feared the consequences, but she was not sorry, even if it meant eternal hell for her soul. "He was in bad shape at best."

"Who is he? Do you know his name?"

She swallowed the tightness banding her throat. "Malcolm Carter."

Her mother's face contorted with fear. "A Carter. Good Lord, you tangled with a Carter."

"I should never have trusted him," she rushed to say. "But he had been polite and acted like a complete gentleman when I met him at Woodmont. And I ran into him at the dance, where he was so nice at first. But when we were alone, he changed, Mama. He didn't listen when I told him to stop."

"I heard you sneak out that night, and I should have run after you. But I thought, what harm would it be for you to have a little fun?" Her mother's mouth hardened into a grim line. "Did you kill him?"

Tears welled in her eyes and spilled down her cheeks. "I didn't get out of the car and check on him. I kept on driving."

"And folks saw this?"

"Mr. Sullivan for sure."

Her mother curled her fingers into fists. She stared at her child as if she did not recognize her. "Get a bag packed."

"What am I going to do? If Johnny or Danny were here, they would know what to do."

"There's nothing they could do for you now. You hurt, maybe killed, a Carter, and in this county there's no coming back. They'll see to it that you spend the rest of your life in jail."

Her mother hurried into the kitchen, opened a cabinet, and fished around the back until she found a red, white, and blue tobacco tin. She pried off the top and pulled out several one-dollar bills. "You're going to take this and get in that truck and drive, and you aren't going to stop until you get to Charlottesville."

"I'm not taking your money."

Her mother pressed it into her hand and curled her fingers into a tight fist over the bills. "Yes, you will."

"What about the baby?"

"She'll stay with me. Maybe there'll be a time when you can send for her. But for now, you can't run with a screaming baby."

Outside the distant roar of a car engine had her mother running to the window. "Whoever it is, is coming up the mountain. Go now! Don't worry about clothes."

"Mama, I'm scared."

Her mother hugged her close. "Run!"

All her life she had dreamed of leaving Bluestone. But she had never figured she would be chased off like a rabid dog. "The sheriff will find me."

Her mother pulled her out of the house, toward the truck. "Not if you go now and get on a train and go as far as this money will take you."

"I can't take that money. That's all you got saved from the piecework."

"You can. And you will." Her mother hugged her close. "I love you, baby girl."

Sadie drove as fast as the truck would manage, and it felt at times like she took some of the curves on two wheels. The truck was old and temperamental, especially now with the radiator leaking after slamming into Malcolm. But she could not afford to let up with the law so close behind.

The truck made it as far as the county line before the engine overheated and seized up. Sadie sat for a moment. "Please, just get me a little farther. *Please.*"

Out of the truck, she hurried to the engine and, after covering her hand with the edge of her coat, she opened the hot hood. Steam rose up, and there was a strong burning smell.

Given some water for the radiator, she might have been able to coax the truck to life, but she had no time for that. All that was left to do was walk. Her feet leaden and her mind still churning, she huddled under the folds of her coat and started walking. She recognized the rumble of an engine and knew it was Sheriff Boyd's Dodge.

OLIVIA

Olivia tugged off her gloves and tossed them, along with her hat, onto the table in the foyer. She had planned this day to go so differently, knowing Malcolm was in town. He needed to be taught a lesson about responsibility.

Excitement rumbled in Olivia's body as she thought about the news she had to share with him. She rushed into Edward's study, finding him at his desk. He settled the phone's receiver into the cradle and reached for the half glass of bourbon beside it.

Though her first instinct had been to tell him about the baby, their baby, his furrowed brow whispered caution. Had he somehow found out what Malcolm had done to Sadie? Surely Malcolm would not confess his sins, and if he did share the details, he would no doubt twist them to his advantage.

"Darling," he said, looking up. His smile was tense. "I was beginning to worry."

"Why would you worry? It's still daylight outside."

"Barely."

She kissed him. "I'm fine. Has Malcolm arrived yet?"

"So you haven't heard what happened in town?" he asked.

His ominous tone pushed her good news right out of her mind. "No."

"Sadie Thompson purposely ran Malcolm down right in the center of Bluestone like a dog. I just got off the phone with the hospital. He's in bad shape."

Her heart sank as she thought about the impetuous girl, who had no doubt acted before she had thought. "Is he going to die?"

"The doctors aren't sure. And if he does live, there's no telling if he'll lose his right leg or not." Edward crossed to the bar and refilled his bourbon. "I just got off the phone with the sheriff, who just left the Thompson house. The girl's mother swears she has not seen Sadie."

"Did he believe her?"

"Of course not. The Thompsons have been lying and cheating the law for years. It's a wonder they all didn't end up in jail together. I'm just grateful that girl didn't do more harm to you than she did."

"She never hurt me."

"Given more time, she might have! She tried to kill Malcolm!"

"Malcolm raped that girl." Her voice was measured with a resolve that Dr. Carter was unaccustomed to hearing.

"What?"

"You heard me. The last time he was in town and left us for the dance. He found Sadie there, plied her with booze, and he raped her in the back of his car."

Edward shook his head as he held up a hand. "Rape is a strong word."

"It is, and it is very appropriate."

"What proof do you have of this? Certainly not the girl's word. I've not even seen her in town the last several months."

"She's not been to town," Olivia said tightly.

Edward hesitated, and then a kind of realization hardened his features. "Was the girl pregnant?"

"She had a baby girl on Christmas Eve. Malcolm, at the very least, owes her financial compensation."

"He owes her no such thing."

"How can you say that? It's his daughter!"

"There's no proof. This all could be a story the girl made up because she knows she'll need money."

She could argue with him about the paternity of the baby, but no judge in this county would take Sadie Thompson's word over a Carter's.

"The girl is wild; she clearly has seen her share of men, and now she's violent," Edward said. "The best place for her is prison, where she can't hurt anyone else. At the very least, she should never be allowed to have another child."

"Sadie doesn't deserve to be locked away. She deserves our help."

"Are you insane? She tried to kill Malcolm!" He downed the bourbon. "And don't you dare blame this on their little peccadillo." He fisted his fingers. "I warned you to not embarrass me in public. Stay away from Sadie Thompson, or I will punish you."

"Don't threaten me, Edward."

"What will you do?"

She raised her chin. "I will leave you."

"And go where?" he challenged.

Rage roiled inside Olivia, but now was not the time for her to indulge her emotions. Her aim now was to help Sadie. She would deal with Edward later.

Olivia took the glass from Edward. "You're upset."

"Damn right, I'm upset. I don't know why you aren't."

She crossed the room and, in the hallway, removed the small bottle of laudanum she still carried with her. The vial gripped in her fist, she returned to the room and, with her back to Edward, refilled his glass with a healthy dose of bourbon and laudanum. Swirling the glass, she faced her husband, smiling. "I liked the girl. I thought I could help her."

"Some people refuse to recognize the opportunities before them. Sadie is such a person," Dr. Carter spat.

"Maybe you're right, dear."

"I don't want to hear any more about Sadie Thompson."

She handed him the glass. "I can see you're upset."

"I'm only looking out for you."

"I understand. Come sit with me by the fire."

She moved to the seat and patted the empty place beside her. He sat and wrapped one arm around her while holding his drink in the other.

"I thought the world of her brother Johnny, but now that he's overseas, there's no keeping her in check."

"He's fighting for us." She snuggled close to him, feeling him relax.

"Damn right." His breathing slowed, and his speech became more deliberate. "I'm not sure why I'm so tired," he said.

"You work hard, darling." Which of course was true. Edward could use a long, deep sleep.

When his head tipped forward, she took his glass and waited several more minutes. Certain he was out for the remainder of the night, she carefully eased him back on the couch.

Olivia covered him with a blanket and then kissed him on the cheek. "I love you, but you're wrong about Sadie."

After rushing to the foyer, she grabbed her hat, gloves, and the keys to the car.

SADIE

Sadie's hands trembled as she thought about Sheriff Boyd doubling back. It would be like him to do something like that. He was good at tracking, but not much else.

She lingered in the woods, drawing back into the shadows as the car came to a halt. The longer she stayed in the woods, the brighter the sun would become and the more time Sheriff Boyd would have to get word out to the law in the surrounding area.

Sadie backed farther into the darkness and tried to figure out where she could hide while not freezing to death.

"Sadie!"

Olivia's familiar voice had her halting. She hesitated, not sure if it was a trap. She stayed silent, not moving a muscle.

"I've been looking for you for hours. Edward told me the sheriff was looking for you."

Sadie gripped the branch of a tree, searching for any signs of Edward or the sheriff.

"You need to come with me now," she said. "I'll take you to the train station."

Sadie stepped out from the trees, pushing the branches aside as she moved slowly toward the road. Olivia got out of the car, and the headlights lit up her face, tight with tension.

"How did you know where to find me?"

"I know your truck broke down on the road to Charlottesville. You couldn't have gotten but so far on foot. I also saw the sheriff's car coming the other way, and you weren't in it."

Sadie hurried around the front of the car and got into the front seat. "Is my mama okay? She has my baby."

"I haven't had a chance to check in on them. My first priority is to get you to Charlottesville and put you on a train."

"He didn't arrest Mama?"

"Not that I know of." Olivia pushed in the clutch and ground the gears as she eased the car into first.

"I think I killed Malcolm."

"He's not dead, but you've done him serious harm."

Sadie hugged her arms around her chest. "He did his share of harm to me."

"He might not walk again."

She stared out the window at the dark trees rushing past. "He called me a whore. He said I deserved what I got."

"He'll have the rest of his life to regret those words along with his limp."

Tears spilled down her cheeks. "I'm not a whore."

"No, you're not." Olivia leaned forward into the steering wheel.

"You shouldn't be driving this early," Sadie said.

A smile tugged the edges of her lips. "I think that is the least of my sins right now."

Sadie smoothed her damp palms over the rough fabric of her overalls. "Where is Dr. Carter?"

"He's sleeping."

"Sleeping? Through all this?"

"I might have slipped him some of my sleep medicine. It won't hurt him. The poor man was exhausted anyway. I'll be home when he wakes up."

"He'll be mad as hell."

"Then I'll attempt to tell him again that I'm pregnant, and all will be forgotten."

"You have a baby in your belly? You shouldn't be driving like this!"

The car rumbled over a rut in the road. "This little guy will just have to hold on tight."

"You shouldn't be doing this for me."

"I couldn't have lived with myself if I didn't."

Sadie gathered the folds of her coat together, too tense to ease back in the seat. She did not want to leave home. "What about Johnny and Danny? When they come home, they won't know how to find me if I'm on the run."

"When you get to wherever you're going, write them, and let them know where you are."

"What about Mama and the baby?"

"I'll look after them."

"I don't deserve this kindness."

"You deserve much more."

Tears rolled down Sadie's cheeks, but she did not have the energy to sob or cry. It took almost an hour before Olivia pulled into the Charlottesville train station. She parked out front and set the brake. "The train will be here shortly. All you have to do is wait."

"Where am I going?"

"To Washington." Olivia took a handful of bills from her pocket. "This will buy your ticket. There are plenty of jobs now in the factories. With your skill with machines, you'll find work."

"I never figured it would be like this."

"Life rarely goes the way we'd like it," she said as she pressed the money into Sadie's hand.

Sadie dug her hand into her pocket and reached for the money her mother had given her. "Give this back to Mama. She's going to need it. I can't take her money."

"If she gave it to you, she wanted you to have it."

"No. I ain't taking her money. I took too much already."

Olivia accepted the money. "All right. I'll see that she gets it."

"And I'll pay you back." She had always wanted to leave Bluestone but had never pictured herself running for her life.

Sadie leaned forward and hugged Olivia. "You take care of that baby of yours. And if you ever need anything from me, all you have to do is ask."

A train whistle blew in the distance. "I'll surely call on you."

CHAPTER
THIRTY-TWO
LIBBY

Tuesday, August 4, 2020
The Woodmont Estate

"How do you know so much about Sadie Thompson?" Libby asked.

"She was my mother," Margaret said.

"Which means Malcolm Carter was your father."

"Yes."

"What happened to him?" Libby's mind scrambled up her newly discovered family tree, trying to figure out where her family intersected with Colton's. Thankfully, it went back three generations.

"Malcolm always walked with a limp after what Sadie did to him. But when he got out of the hospital, he never went after my grandmother or me. I didn't know until years later that it was Miss Olivia who kept him away. She threatened to leave Edward if there were repercussions against my grandmother or me."

"Is he still alive?"

"No, Malcolm Carter died in 2000. He married several times, had children by all his wives, but in the end died alone and broke in a nursing home."

"Did you ever see Sadie again?" Libby asked.

"When I was thirteen. The sheriff had died, and Sadie Thompson had become a bit of a folk legend, so Miss Olivia must have decided it was safe to take me to New York. You see, Miss Olivia hired my grandmother as her baby's nurse, and I spent many of my early years in the nursery with their son, Stuart. Then as we reached school age, Stuart went off to boarding school, and I went to public school and then later to work in the Carters' kitchen."

"You've been here ever since you were a baby?"

"Miss Olivia saved my mother, my grandmother, and me. And when it came time for my Ginger to go to school, Miss Olivia saw to it there was scholarship money that got her all the way through medical school. She did the same for Colton."

"After all that, why didn't she help Elaine?"

Margaret sighed. "Miss Olivia wanted Malcolm arrested for what he'd done to Sadie, but Dr. Carter covered for his cousin, so of course charges were never brought. After that she didn't trust her husband. He made her life here difficult even after she helped Sadie. Publicly he was always attentive to her, but behind closed doors he was distant and cold."

"They stayed married."

"Because of Stuart. She was free to leave, as her husband often said, but Stuart would always remain with him. She couldn't leave her son, so she stayed. From what I could see, they always lived separate lives. Miss Olivia focused on her son and her gardens, and Dr. Carter kept working at the hospital in Lynchburg until it closed in the seventies. To the day he died, he believed he was doing those women a service."

"Miss Olivia protected Sadie but not Elaine."

"She knew Dr. Carter would have shunned his Elaine and you. And she feared he would have made your lives as miserable as her own."

"So where did Elaine go when she was pregnant? I know she was in New Jersey when I was born."

"Elaine went to live with Sadie on the Jersey Shore."

"Sadie?"

"Sadie rode the train to New Jersey when she left Virginia and found work in a wartime factory. In those days, they were hiring women because there was such a shortage of men. After the war, she went back to school, and though it took her nearly a decade, she earned her college degree. She became a teacher."

"A teacher. Wow, that's amazing. So Olivia must have kept up with Sadie?"

"Miss Olivia took the train to New York every summer and stayed for a week. I didn't learn until later that Miss Olivia always saw Sadie on those visits. As I said, she took me on my first trip to New York when I was thirteen and introduced us."

Libby wondered how the meeting between mother and daughter had gone, but Margaret did not offer, and she did not press. "Did Sadie ever marry?"

"She did. A real nice fellow named Arthur. They never had children, but they were dedicated to each other until his heart gave out a few years before she died."

"Did she ever have any regrets about leaving you?"

Margaret stared out at the long driveway. "It was the best for both of us. I knew that as soon as I saw her, and she saw me. I know when she looked at me, she saw Malcolm. And my grandmother was the best mother I could have asked for."

Libby released a breath. "When did Sadie die?"

"When you were about five. Miss Olivia and I were with her when she passed." Margaret laid her hand on Libby's arm. "Sometimes there's no choosing between right and wrong. Sometimes you have to pick the best of the worst solutions and hope for the best. Miss Olivia did that, and she's the reason we're all standing here today."

An engine rumbled in the distance, and she looked up to see Colton's truck. The boys jumped up and down and started waving as their father approached. And for the first time in a long time, Libby was happy.

CHAPTER THIRTY-THREE

SADIE

Tuesday, April 5, 1994
Trenton, New Jersey

The worried expression on Miss Olivia's face proved she too knew a secret held too long grew toxic and could poison any life. Sadie's younger self would have pressed the matter, but now that she was dying, she did not want her last words to Miss Olivia to be harsh. "You do what you think is best, Miss Olivia."

"After all these years, why don't you simply call me Olivia?"

Sadie moistened her lips and allowed a slight grin. "It never felt right on my tongue."

Miss Olivia squeezed her hand in a strong grip. "Sadie. It's good to see you again. I want you to know how much I've always appreciated you. I wish we could go to lunch as we used to do."

"I'm sorry that I'm feeling so poorly." She tried to sit up but was hooked to so many tubes, and her body was so tired.

"Don't you worry about moving an inch," Miss Olivia said. "You just relax."

"I was having a dream," Sadie said. "I was remembering that time in the greenhouse when we were planting those shrubs."

"That was a fun afternoon. You were really clever about how best to arrange the plants in their beds."

"How is that greenhouse?"

"It's closed up. Too much for me."

"Never thought I would hear the day, Miss Olivia."

"Me either. But your name is still carved in the glass. It's important to me that someone knows you were there when I needed a friend the most. Coming from London and the war, being a newlywed to Edward, and losing two pregnancies was almost too much."

Miss Olivia reached for a cup and straw and held it up to Sadie's lips. She took a small sip, and though she craved more, she knew her stomach would not tolerate it.

"You shouldn't have come all this way."

"Like I told you earlier, I would not miss this for the world."

"Could I see Margaret?"

"Of course." Miss Olivia pushed open the curtain and spoke to someone. Seconds later a woman appeared. She was in her early fifties now, and gray streaked her hair, but Olivia still saw the child who had played with her Stuart in the nursery. "She's been here the entire time. She just woke up."

"I wouldn't have minded seeing her sleep. Reminds me of when she was a tiny little baby." In those quiet moments, she had thought maybe she could forget about how she had come to be a mother and let loose the love the child needed. She had always believed in time she would have been a good mother to her girl. But time was the one thing they had never had.

Margaret approached the bed. She smiled down at her birth mother, taking her hand.

"Margaret," Sadie said. "It's good to see you."

"And you too, Mama."

"How have you been doing?" Sadie searched the face of the woman, seeing neither signs of herself nor him in her face. She saw only Margaret.

She smoothed her hand over Sadie's tissue-thin skin. "Just fine."

"And Ginger and Colton?"

"Ginger has been accepted to the honors high school. She says she's going to be a doctor."

"Is she?" Pride swelled in her as she thought about the grandchildren whose pictures covered the inside of her tiny apartment.

"Miss Olivia saw to it she got the Carter Foundation Grant."

"My goodness." The world turned in directions she never would have imagined. "And Colton?"

"Still a wild guy."

"He's the spitting image of your brother Johnny. Wild and looking for adventure." Johnny had returned from the war and visited her once. It had been good to spend time with him, and she had mourned when he died fifteen years ago of a heart attack. He had been gone for so long now she couldn't remember the sound of his voice.

She turned to Miss Olivia. "How's Elaine and her girl?"

"Both are doing well. I see the girl in town from time to time. She reminds me of myself at that age. And Elaine had another girl. She wanted to be here, but the baby has a bad cold."

"Best she not be around me now. Better she just look ahead." Sadie closed her eyes, feeling the weight of life on her shoulders. "I suppose it's all worked out for the best."

"Not the best," Miss Olivia said. "But the best we could manage."

EPILOGUE

Libby went into ten hours of labor at thirty-six weeks into her pregnancy. As soon as she arrived at the hospital and the nurse examined her and declared the baby breech, the doctor was called and told to prep for surgery.

In all the birthing scenarios, she had never considered that her child would be upside down and backward. Okay, that was not true. She had come up with dozens of ways this pregnancy could have gone wrong, but for some reason *Baby stuck inside me* hadn't been one of them.

Colton was at her side as the doctor pulled her baby from her womb and handed her off to the nurse.

Sadie McKenzie Reese, a.k.a. "The Spud," weighed in at seven pounds, one ounce, and when she opened her mouth to cry, it was the loudest, most earth-shattering shrill Libby could have expected from such a small thing. It was also the sweetest.

Colton accepted the baby's swaddled form and carried her over to Libby. She turned her face toward the child's, wishing she could hold her. "Does she have all her fingers and toes?"

"She does." The child looked so small in Colton's arms. "And she blew the doors off the Apgar score."

Tears welled in Libby's eyes. "She'll need to be tough to keep up with her older brothers."

"Won't be long before she's running circles around those two."

Libby and Colton had married at Woodmont the day after Christmas last year, in the greenhouse with their family surrounding them. There had been Jeff, Sam, Ginger, Cameron, and Margaret. On Libby's side had stood Elaine, Ted, and, to her surprise, Lofton, who had arrived minutes before the ceremony. Sierra had been Libby's maid of honor, and Mrs. Mancuso had given her away.

Colton had been asking her to marry him for months, but she had refused to bind him to her for fear she would lose the baby. She had been twenty-eight weeks pregnant the day she had said her "I do," and though she had not told anyone, she had started to make the very smallest to-do list for the baby.

"Jeff and Sam were hoping for a brother," she said. She studied the little girl's pink face, pug nose, and rounded lips.

"They'll get over it and figure out there are advantages to having a sister."

She was excited for the boys—her boys—to see their new sister. She would never forget the babies she had carried and lost and would see to it that all the bottled-up love she had had for them would be lavished on Sadie, Jeff, and Sam.

"Elaine and Mom are outside," Colton said. "Elaine was pacing the hallway when I went into the waiting room an hour ago. Mom was quiet, which is how she gets when she's worried."

Libby adjusted the baby's blanket, tucking it close to her chin. "Send them in so they can meet their little Sadie."

QUESTIONS FOR THE READERS

1. What is the time limit on grief? Is there one?
2. Did Dr. Edward Carter have the right to make the medical choices he did for his patients?
3. Do you agree or disagree with Miss Olivia sending Elaine away to have her baby?
4. Libby was disappointed and angry after she discovered her father was her biological father. In the end, she was able to forgive him. Do you think on some level she knew the truth?
5. What do you think about Malcolm Carter's fate? Was Sadie justified in her actions toward him?
6. Do you see the greenhouse as a metaphor? If so, for what?

RECIPES

Buttermilk Pie

- 3 eggs
- ⅔ cup sugar
- ½ cup honey
- 1 cup buttermilk
- 1 teaspoon vanilla
- ½ teaspoon salt
- 1 prepared piecrust

Lay piecrust in a greased pan. Mix together the remaining ingredients and pour into the shell. Bake at 350°F for 35–40 minutes. Serve with fresh fruit or ice cream.

Chess Pie

- ½ cup butter, softened
- 2 cups white sugar
- 1 teaspoon vanilla extract
- 4 eggs
- 1 tablespoon cornmeal or bread crumbs
- ¼ cup evaporated milk

- 1 tablespoon distilled white vinegar
- 1 9-inch pie shell

Preheat oven to 425°F.

Cream together butter, sugar, and vanilla. Mix in eggs one at a time. Next, blend in cornmeal or bread crumbs, evaporated milk, and vinegar. When the mixture is smooth, pour into prepared pie shell. Bake for 10 minutes, reduce heat to 300°F, and continue baking for another 40 minutes.

Honeysuckle Syrup

- 1 cup sugar
- 1 cup honeysuckle blossoms
- 2 cups water

Place all ingredients into a saucepan. Bring to a boil, and as soon as the mixture bubbles, reduce heat, and simmer until water is reduced by half. Strain out the blossoms and let cool.

Lemon Cake

- 3 lemons
- 2⅔ cups all-purpose flour
- ½ teaspoon baking soda
- ½ teaspoon salt
- 1 cup oil
- 2 cups granulated sugar
- 3 eggs
- 1 cup buttermilk

Zest each of the lemons and reserve. Juice the lemons. Sift together the dry ingredients, including the flour, baking soda, and salt. In another bowl mix the oil and sugar. Mix in 1 egg at a time. Add ⅓ of the sifted dry ingredients, and when incorporated, add 1 cup of buttermilk. Alternate until all is blended. Mix in lemon juice and rind. Spoon batter into two round cake pans and place in a preheated 350°F oven. Bake for 1 hour and 20 minutes.

Glaze

- 4 tablespoons butter, melted
- 2 cups powdered sugar
- 2–4 tablespoons water
- 1 tablespoon lemon juice

Mix together melted butter, powdered sugar, lemon juice, and 2 tablespoons of water. Continue to add water until the desired consistency is achieved. Drizzle over a warm turned-out cake.

ABOUT THE AUTHOR

Photo © 2017 by Studio FBJ

A southerner by birth, Amazon Charts bestselling author Mary Ellen Taylor displays a love of her home state of Virginia that is evident in her contemporary women's fiction. When Mary Ellen's not writing, she spends time baking, hiking, and spoiling her miniature dachshunds, Buddy, Bella, and Tiki.